P9-DVZ-023

Praise for

Bold Sons of Erin

and OWEN PARRY's previous novels
featuring Maj. Abel Jones

"Parry offers a rich, lush portrait of a forgotten era,
whose excesses are filtered through the eyes
of his very moral protagonist."
Denver Post

"[An] entertaining book ... I admire Parry's work ... The
historicity, the mastery of period detail, the author's knack
for simulating nineteenth-century idiom ... He can hold
his own in evoking his era and crafting a plot ... If you're
one of those readers who experienced Patrick O'Brian's
death as a form of literary cold-turkey, Owen Parry's Abel
Jones books might well be the fix you need."
Washington Post Book World

"[Parry] conveys the era of the Civil War with great
mastery, capturing the pain, bitterness, and heroism
of the period. Moving forward at a stately pace, he finds
time to draw complex portraits of his characters
while never losing track of his narrative."
Chicago Tribune

"Suspenseful adventure ... sure to please
his devoted following."
Publishers Weekly

"Owen Parry's novels retell history from a rare and vivid angle ... [He has] a telling eye for period detail ... In both the richness of his speech and the earnestness of his outlook, Abel Jones is almost the antithesis of everything in America's currently cynical popular culture."
Bergen Record

"The plot is deliciously complicated ... But Parry goes beyond plot to offer a keen insight into a life in a hard place at a hard time ... A total original ... Jones has the power to grow on you."
St. Louis Post-Dispatch

"Jones is a memorable, magnificent character."
Denver Post

"A spiritual journey through America's tragic epic."
Portland Oregonian

"Parry goes beyond the boundaries of a straightforward mystery by exploring larger cultural issues of the times."
Civil War Book Review

"Parry's talent in character development will leave the reader asking for more."
Library Journal

"Owen Parry [creates] fascinating tales of war, conspiracy, and murder ... [that] will delight anyone who enjoys a richly detailed historical adventure."
Monterey County Post

"Superb period fiction [that] will appeal to both Civil War buffs and fans of historical mysteries ... Realistically detailed, bristling with intelligent suspense, and featuring a stoically introspective hero ... In addition to capturing the elegant cadence of Civil War-era dialogue, Parry has also authentically evoked the horror, confusion, and chaos that characterized the conflict between the states."
Booklist

"Because of the richness of Parry's prose, expert storytelling skills, and deft touch with detail, the ... time and place come alive."
Tulsa World

"Vivid, complex, and convincing ... the series is likely to win an enthusiastic following."
Kirkus Reviews

"Owen Parry deserves to be ranked with the best of contemporary Civil War novelists."
Flint Journal

Also by Owen Parry

HONOR'S KINGDOM
CALL EACH RIVER JORDAN
SHADOWS OF GLORY
FADED COAT OF BLUE

And in hardcover

OUR SIMPLE GIFTS

ATTENTION: ORGANIZATIONS AND CORPORATIONS
Most HarperTorch paperbacks are available at special quantity discounts for bulk purchases for sales promotions, premiums, or fund-raising. For information, please call or write:

Special Markets Department, HarperCollins Publishers, Inc., 10 East 53rd Street, New York, N.Y. 10022–5299. Telephone: (212) 207–7528. Fax: (212) 207-7222.

OWEN PARRY

BOLD SONS OF ERIN

HarperTorch
An Imprint of HarperCollinsPublishers

This is a work of fiction. Names, characters, places, and incidents are products of the author's imagination or are used fictitiously and are not to be construed as real. Any resemblance to actual events, locales, organizations, or persons, living or dead, is entirely coincidental.

❦

HARPERTORCH
An Imprint of HarperCollins*Publishers*
10 East 53rd Street
New York, New York 10022-5299

Copyright © 2003 by Owen Parry
Cover photograph © by Corbis
ISBN: 0-06-051391-8

All rights reserved. No part of this book may be used or reproduced in any manner whatsoever without written permission, except in the case of brief quotations embodied in critical articles and reviews. For information address HarperTorch, an Imprint of HarperCollins Publishers.

First HarperTorch paperback printing: August 2004
First William Morrow hardcover printing: September 2003

HarperCollins®, HarperTorch™, and ❦ ™ are trademarks of Harper-Collins Publishers Inc.

Printed in the United States of America

Visit HarperTorch on the World Wide Web at www.harpercollins.com

10 9 8 7 6 5 4 3 2

If you purchased this book without a cover, you should be aware that this book is stolen property. It was reported as "unsold and destroyed" to the publisher, and neither the author nor the publisher has received any payment for this "stripped book."

To the people of Schuylkill County

... a lie which is all a lie may be met and fought with outright, But a lie which is part a truth is a harder matter to fight.

—TENNYSON

BOLD SONS
OF ERIN

*T*HE MOON WORE A BANDIT'S MASK of cloud to rob the sky of stars. Cold it was in the boneyard, for October had shown her teeth. When the wind scraped down the hillside, dead leaves rose, riding a sudden gust to climb my back. They crackled and scratched and crumpled. My lantern glowed, faint as the hopes of Judas. Even that much light was a mortal risk.

That night was murder black and stank of death. I wished me far away, that I will tell you. But I needed the body.

If body there was in the coffin.

The boys dug glumly, dutiful but slow. For no one likes to retrieve a new-laid corpse. The soldiers I had brought along were Dutchmen, thick and quiet, as solemn as death themselves. Still, I hushed them every time they coughed. Vital it was that the Irish should not learn of us. For the sons and daughters of Erin adore their dead, and graves enchant them. They will kill for a corpse as soon as for the living.

Now, a Dutchman has his own odd superstitions, carried from the darkness of the Germanies. But the soldiers at their labor had other fears, far more real than demons or even the Irish. They believed what they had heard, that contagion lay in that grave. As for my Christian self, I kept me quiet.

I did not believe it was cholera, see.

The wind slashed through our uniforms, like bayonets

through Pandy. When I held the lantern high, it swayed and sputtered. If I lowered it down, the leaves attacked the glass, swarming like wild Afghanees at the kill. We were at work in the hills of home, in Pennsylvania, where miners dismayed by the war had turned to violence. But India was with me, too, its ghosts the sort that linger in the mind to whisper of life's swiftness and fragility. I believed the Irish had lied about the cholera and thought the coffin likely to be empty. Yet, death's transforming power touches all. Rare is the fool who smiles in a graveyard.

And I knew death.

I do not speak of Our Savior's death, not when I speak of that night, but of lesser fates that I myself had witnessed. First as a child in Wales, then as a soldier, when the heat of love come to scald me in Lahore. But let that bide. For now I was a married man and a major got up proper, and I had begun a new life in America.

I did not believe it was cholera. I declined to think it.

The soldiers grumbled over their shovels, glancing at me like children put to punishment. I did not mean to be hard with them, for they were of the invalid corps, and each had suffered in body, if not in soul. But healthy enough they were to serve the provost, to shepherd draft lists or guard a shipment of coal. And the four could dig the earth of the grave between them.

I did not believe it was cholera. My fears were of the Irish down below, in the patch houses, where the mine families spilled from crowded beds, all coughing and complaint. I feared their pastor, as well, at rest in the shanty above us, by his church. For well I knew the duplicity of priests, and the fierceness of their loyalties, which were not always simply to their faith. I had been told that this one lived with books, that he was clean and well spoken, with high manners. It did not tally up. Why would a gentleman deign to labor among those souls cast out of Donegal, from Mayo and Roscommon, or from Clare? I meant to make his acquaintance in good time, to see how much of the darkness of Rome was upon him and to test his tales of cholera out of season. For he had put his name to the cause of death, with the honor of his office as his bond. If we found no body in the grave, the priest would have to answer.

All that was to come. First, we had to dig.

I had been warned of violence, of the laborers' rage at Mr. Lincoln's draft and their taste for murder. But I had served beside such men in India. The Irish, I mean. Those famine lads cut loose to find their keep, in a world that did not want them or their kind. Lately I had seen them at their finest, climbing the slopes above a Maryland creek, marching into a torrent of death, falling only to close ranks again, and fighting as grandly as any men could do. I knew the Irish could fight, see. But I did not want their fight to be with me. I had come to admire certain of their qualities, their boldness in battle, and their reverence for song—although I could not praise them as a race. Nor do they count as true and proper Christians. Still, I thought I knew them well enough to keep me safe and sound while at my work.

How little I knew, in my vanity and pride.

I had forbidden my Dutchmen to speak a word, warning them not to clang their shovel heads. Such noises carry like whistles on the wind. And gales play tricks. Had the night been still we would have heard the steam engines down by the colliery, ceaselessly pumping water from the mines. Men slept, but the pumps could not. I knew their throb, that giant iron heartbeat, from Mr. Evans's pits just north of Pottsville, where I had kept the books before the war, and from the countless shafts that pocked our county. It is a constant stuggle, see. The earth tries to drown the men who steal her coal.

We should have heard the drumming of those machines. But the wind come down from the ridge to carry the sound off. That same blow would carry our noises down to the company patch, where the Irish miners slept in their exhaustion. Even nature seemed hostile on that hillside. I had cautioned my lads to be quiet, again and again.

Then one sound, abrupt as death, shut my fingers choke-tight over my cane. It almost made me reach beneath my cloak, just to feel the certainty of my Colt.

Twas the sound of a shovel meeting the wood of a coffin.

I did not think it was cholera. And yet I stepped me back. For I have reason to fear that cruel disease: The memory of my mother dead on the planking, with the locked door trapping me in with her staring eyes. And the loss in Lahore, much later, that haunts me still.

Cholera is too ready a companion. It follows a man over continents and oceans. Even in the fairest summer cantonment, it killed more soldiers than bullets ever did. The rivers of India swelled with bloated niggers, their shorelines ripe with corpses torn by dogs. It made no least distinction between ranks, and showed a hunger for both fair and foul. At night, the burning pyres stank of Hell. The comrade who shared your morning porridge shat himself to death and died in vomit before the bugler sounded you to your tent. Cholera is the bane of modern times.

The soldiers drew back from the rim of the grave, leaving only the fellow taking his turn in the hole. A sergeant he was, but one not shy of work. He looked up at me, face broad and Dutch in the lantern's cast. His whiskers were blond, but the light turned them bloody red.

"*Sollen wir doch weiter, Herr Major?*" Sergeant Dietrich asked me. "Now we must open the box, *ja?*"

"Go on," I told him in a lowered voice. Just loud enough

to be heard above the wind. "Clean off the box, and we will look inside."

He shook his head. Not to refuse my order, but in fear. "And if it is the cholera, *Herr Major? Ich will nit krank werden. Bitte, nun. Hab' Kinder, eine junge Frau . . .*"

"It is not the cholera. That I can tell you." I almost added something more, but had the sense to check my own emotions. "Clean off the coffin and open it."

He wished to obey me, for that is the German's nature. Your Dutchman is tame as the Irishman is wild. But fear of infection had frozen the fellow's limbs. He was a great ox of a farmer, as big as I am small. Although I do show well in the chest and shoulders. But the size of the heart is a greater matter than the length of a fellow's bones.

The others looked to the sergeant, not to me. For they were farmers from the south of the county, where the seams of coal gave way to stubbled fields and painted barns replaced the blackened collieries. The men were long acquainted, then melded close by war.

To give a command is a wonderful thing, but obedience will be earned. The soldiers did not know me, you understand. I was merely another bothersome officer, with a limp and a nasty scar upon his cheek, but otherwise no different from the others. When you serve in the ranks, all officers seem a menace. You only hope they will leave you in peace and not see you killed to curry a colonel's favor.

Those men owed me the loyalty laid down in regulations. But words on paper never conquered fear. Had an Irish mob rushed up from the patch, the Dutchmen would have fled to save their lives. Brave though they had been on distant battlefields.

"Get out of the grave," I told the sergeant quietly. "*Raus. Verstehe?*"

"Jawohl, Herr Major!" He scrambled up the sifting earth to stand beside his comrades.

I handed the sergeant the lantern, nearly losing our light to a blast of wind.

"Echtes Hexenwetter," one of the privates muttered.

Weather for witches. That is what he said. I knew it, for I had applied myself to the mighty German tongue and had some Dutch by now. We must ever seek to improve our lives, with study as well as devotion.

I almost dressed them down for their superstition, which I refuse to allow into my life. And I would have singed their ears, that I can tell you. For I was not so calm as I pretended to be. When our nerves are short we speak to blister gunmetal. But I let it go.

I do not believe in witches or such like. A modern man lends no ear to such nonsense. And darkness has no power over Christians. But we were in agreement on the weather, which pierced. A soldier who has served on the Northwest Frontier knows well the weather's power over the heart.

I laid down my cane and climbed into the grave, landing on the coffin's lid with a thump. My bad leg cropped a bother, but no matter. I took up the shovel and began to scrape the remaining dirt from the wood.

I did not think it was cholera. But I was not prepared for the foulness that awaited me.

THE MOON HID DEEP BEHIND THE CLOUDS, until its light was naught but a stingy glow. The lantern sputtered, held too high by the sergeant. It lit his face, dulled by animal fear, but hardly helped me see what I was doing. Twas not enough to clean off the coffin's lid, for I needed room to perch as I opened the box. Navvy's work it was and not fit for a major. Not when other ranks were standing about. But we must not be proud or succumb to vanity. I put off my cloak and went to it.

Despite the cold, I worked me into a sweat. Even though the soil was still loose from the burying, the task wanted all my back and shoulders could give. An awkward business it was. Since I am not tall, I had a devilish time lifting the dirt free of the hole. The wind was a wicked tease, as well, spraying the boneyard earth back into my face.

The soldiers above me mumbled, staring down at my doings in mounting fear.

Leaves rushed into the grave like rats, pestering me at my labor.

"Give me the bar," I said at last, handing up the shovel.

A fellow with a limp to rival mine own did as I asked. The metal streaked my hand with cold when I gripped it. And then I went to work again, trying not to make an infernal noise. The wood was cheap and it splintered.

I smelled the body at the first cracking. A great stink it made. Then the others smelled it and edged back.

"Hold out the lantern!" I ordered, not without temper. Smelling was not enough, I had to see.

Startled I was, though. For I had thought to find the coffin empty and all of it a ruse. Far too neat things were, with the Irish fellow who bragged of a general's murder dying all sudden of cholera, then plugged in the ground before the county coroner could make his way up from Pottsville to poke at the corpse. The swift interment was meant to prevent infection, according to the priest. Of course, I believed the Irish were shielding the murderer with a mock burial. While the killer ran from the law.

That was why I was doing my digging by night, one of the first acts in my investigation of the murder of General Stone, a poor fellow whose only sin had been an effort to recruit the sons of Erin for our army. Mr. Lincoln himself

wished to find out the guilty, although we had generals
dying by the hundredweight on battlefields from Maryland to Mississippi. Of course, a murder is a different
matter.

Now I smelled death. And that is a smell I know. Yet, there
was something queer about it, as if I sensed more than I
could properly tell.

"I can't *see*, man," I snapped, in a sweaty grump. "Hold
the lantern lower."

I smelled their fear as clearly as I smelled that rotting
corpse. But the sergeant bent over the grave. For sergeants
must bear the dangers others flee.

"*Herrgott erbarme*," the Dutchman prayed. But the fellow
did his duty.

"Lower!" I commanded. With the fear upon me, too.

I cracked the lid open broadly and a pulse of stench near
sent me scrambling myself. The lantern retreated, then returned again.

I gagged. I could not help it. And I heard a man retch.
Twas then I knew what it was that had struck me odd. The
smell was of death, indeed. But death has a great bouquet
of smells, and this one was not right. The man said to
have been buried would have been dead less than a week.
Now, that is time enough to stink profoundly. But the reek
I met in that hole was the one you encounter upon your
return to last month's battlefield. The fragrance of death
gone stale.

The lantern quit me again. I heard the big fellow free
his stomach of its contents. But I pushed on. By feel, I got
the lid all off and propped it against stray roots and crum-
bling dirt.

I straightened my back, yearning for one good draught of
fresh, clean air. I am not tall and could hardly see above the
rim of the grave.

"Hand the lamp to me, Sergeant Dietrich. Here. Give it over, man."

My God, the stink come high.

The sergeant did as bidden, though he did not want to approach the grave, nor to surrender the light. The world had gone dark as the blackest heathen's soul. And that light had grown precious to him. Still, he followed orders, passing the flickering lamp to my outstretched hand.

I lowered the lantern into the grave.

And found not a man but a woman, many weeks dead.

LOOK YOU. I was prepared for an empty box, or for a buried man. But the unexpected disarms us. The sight of a young woman's body—for young she was, despite her rictus grin and leathered flesh—well, the sight of such a one as that confused me.

She had a great shining luxury of cinnamon-colored hair and the good teeth of youth exposed by lips curled back. "O, thou still unravished bride of time . . ." I quoted Mr. Keats, who died young himself. But that was nonsense. For ravaged to a horror the poor thing was, though not by time. The vermin had gone at her, making a feast. The pennies set on her eyes had fallen away, but mercy was abroad, for the lids had locked themselves shut for all eternity. Although a worm squeezed out to have a look at me.

Glad I was that I did not see her eyes. For eyes accuse. And gladder still I was much later on, when I learned who she was and why she was buried thus. Intimacy enough there was between us.

Perhaps it was my quiet that drew him. Sergeant Dietrich edged back to the rim of the grave.

" 'Ne Frau ist es, doch? Was soll dass heissen, Herr Major?"

"Speak English!" I told him impatiently, for my manners

had gone frayed. "Yes, it's a woman. Hardly more than a girl, I think. And I don't know what it means."

"*Ich dachte mir es war ja ein Mann?* I think we are looking for a man's body, *nicht wahr?*"

I smiled grimly. "Yes, Sergeant Dietrich. We were looking for a man's body. Now we shall have to look for a living man."

"*Aber das Maedchen* . . . the girl? Even the Irisher *Katholiken* do not bury a girl in the grave of the other man. In the holy ground. *Herr-gott erbarme.*"

Now, I know little enough of the cult of Rome, but the sergeant called up what knowledge I possessed. We were, in fact, in their consecrated ground, within the low wall of piled stones that fenced the Irish cemetery. And that assured me the girl in the grave was Catholic. For even the lowest drunkard priest would not bury one of another faith within the sacred boundaries. No matter that the priest had lied about the cholera, the girl in the coffin was Catholic. And likely Irish herself, with that cinnamon hair.

But what priest would put a girl in a grave and rob her of her name? Even to help a murderer escape?

Nor had the priest done all of this alone.

I TOOK A CLOSER LOOK at the rotting girl, drawing the lantern along her ruination. Small creatures fled the light. Searching for a sign of her identity I was, perhaps a Psalm book placed into her hands, which might include the maiden's name inside it. For that is how we Methodists do our burying. But I found nothing. Good it was that I took that look, though, holding my nose like a child. For I saw two things that kept me from shutting the lid.

The girl was barefoot, see. Now, even the poor are not sent off without shoes. More striking to me still, her skirt was in shreds. And badly stained. Not only by the mildew and putrefaction.

"Who has a knife?" I called, just loud enough to be heard against the wind. *"Ein Messer?"*

"Jawohl, Herr Major!" A private handed a clasp knife to the sergeant, who passed it on to me. What little I saw of their faces was not happy, although they responded avidly to commands. Germans, see. Clear orders spoken sharply always please them.

I gave the lantern back to the sergeant and bid him hold it steady as I worked. For I had a most unpleasant task before me.

No man should enter a woman's chamber unbidden. And what room could be more intimate than a grave? Still, I did not see another choice. I had to shame her. Perhaps, to do her good.

I tell you, I did not relish the task at hand.

Now, I am an old bayonet and a veteran of John Company's fusses. Nor was I born with violets stuffed up my nose. But I had to steel myself to touch that girl. And to steady my hands as living things deserted her flesh for mine. The meat of her was dry in spots, but putrid and wet in others. I tried not to touch her skin with the knife, but in many a place the cloth of the dress clung to her, glued by death, and I could not be gentle. I prayed for her and begged her pardon as I worked, although I fear my thoughts were an awful muddle.

Now, you will say: "What right did Jones have to disturb the unfortunate creature?" But I will tell you: I was the only law in a lawless place. I sensed at once that this was no natural death. Twas murder, upon a murder yet unexplained.

She had not been wealthy. Or if she had been well-to-do, she was not buried so. Her undergarments were scanty as they were foul, if you will forgive my indelicacy. And though the light was bad and her skin browned off, I found what I was looking for easily enough. Whoever had killed her had not been content with a single, well-placed blow. Nor with a dozen. She had been stabbed until her belly was pulped.

And yet I found no mark upon her face.

I tried to turn her over. The flesh broke away in my fingers. Twas then I decided that I had seen enough.

Now, I am a clean and fastidious fellow. It comes from my sergeanting days in a scarlet coat, as well as from the sobriety of my nature and our Welsh disposition to tidiness. The mess left on my hands would have sickened Lucifer. I wished me down the hill and back through the patch, to where I could rinse my hands in the cold water of the creek. Dirtied though it was by the colliery waste. I wanted to be clean of death, at least. And to breathe good air.

I feared to take me home in such a state, to my darling, my Mary Myfanwy, to our son John, and to Miss Fanny Raeburn, who had become a delight to me since I brought her back from Glasgow to our hearth. I did not wish to enter my door with the stench of the grave upon me. For the scent of death clings. My uniform would want more than one washing, and with lye soap, too.

I picked the blown leaves off the girl and covered her up with her rags as best I could. Then I set the lid back on the box again, though lacking hammer and nails to make it fast. Anyway, I could not have risked the noise of hammering. I climbed out and told the fellows to shovel the dirt back in. And I set to rubbing my hands clean with leaves and weeds, for the little good it did.

I had come home to look for a general's murderer, only to find the corpse of a murdered girl. But I found no sign of the fellow whose name had been scratched on the wooden cross set on that grave: Daniel Patrick Boland, the man who had rushed to brag of General Stone's murder up on the high road.

Had Boland killed twice? Or was it all a ruse within a ruse, to mask the killer's true name from the law? Look you. The Irish may confess to their priests, but they will not confess to the law of their own volition. Yet, that was exactly what Daniel Boland had tried to do. He had rushed in upon one Mr. Oliver—not a fellow Irishman, but the superintendent of the Heckschersville mine and colliery—raving about the murder he had done and his wish to bind himself over to the authorities. And in less than a day, the local priest marked Boland dead of the cholera. I did not trust any of it. And time would prove me right, then prove me wrong.

Oh, I have much to tell you, and I will, but twas then I heard the sound that did not fit.

A TWIG SNAPPED. Just up the hill to the left, back in the trees. A friend to none, the wind had lulled. Betraying the spy. And India's wars had trained me to survive. I know the sound of a misplaced foot, in the rocky Khyber or by a homely graveyard.

"Put the lantern down," I whispered fiercely. "Down in the grave, man. Do as I say!"

The lantern sank below the earth. The world grew dark as Mr. Milton's Hell.

"Keep you low," I added. "And wait for me here. *Hier warten. Und schweige!*"

I have learned to pay attention to small things, for details keep us alive. I knew just where I had set down my cane. I grasped and found it, then took myself off for the treeline, scuttling along. A shadow among shadows, I wove between the crosses and crude headstones, then slipped across the wall and into the trees. I am good in the darkness, as an old foot soldier must be, and I did not think our watcher had seen much of me, once the lantern was suppressed. I was downhill, in the dark, not silhouetted where the occasional wash of moonlight might give me away.

My soldiers kept their silence, doubtless fearful. But my own dread was gone. Fear leaves me when there is action. Only to return when the battle is done.

The wind sprang up, attacking me with leaves blown on great gusts. Gales of them stormed between the blackened trees. Smelling of rot, leaves scraped my face and hands, hurling themselves at my body as if the devil himself had raised them to stop me. I used the noise to gain ground on the spy.

Now when a fellow is watching you—unless he knows his business like a scout—he will be most predictable. He will stand but a tree or two back from the edge of the grove. Easy enough it is to put yourself behind him. And the spy had something working on his nerves, for he had begun to shift about like a restless horse in his stall. He cracked another branch beneath his brogans.

That is how he told me where he stood.

Proud I was of my old skills, although I should be ashamed of how I got them. There has been too much killing in my past. For years I gloried in the soldier's life, though now it burdens me. But let that bide. I come up behind the fellow, who was small in stature, as I am myself. He was only a moving shadow amid the solid darkness of the tree trunks. I held my cane ready to use it as a weapon, although I did not draw the hidden blade.

I pounced.

I took the fellow down to the ground with ease, for I know my business. I had my cane across the back of his neck, where I could snap his spine if he made a fuss, and I spread my weight atop him.

Then I stopped.

It did not take the sudden tease of moonlight to dazzle my senses. I already knew, by the feel and the musky smell, that I had captured a woman, not a man.

SHE WAS YOUNG. A man can always tell. And the odd thing was that she did not protest, or struggle, or even ask that I free her of my weight. Her hair was raven, blacker than the night, and long and tangled. Leaves adorned it, like flowers worn at a ball. When I turned her over—rude in my astonishment—her face showed a wild loveliness in the moonlight. She had those Mayo cheekbones, cut by sea winds, and a forehead high and clear. Her dark eyes glowed, as if lit from within. Her stare held me, almost as if I were her captive. Warm she was. And though she did not writhe or fight, she had a feral quality about her, something pulsing and immediate. As if the hills and forests were her home. As if she were an animal caught in a trap.

She smelled of life. To an excess.

I had her by the wrists and I put my face close down to hers, although I did not intend any impropriety. I did not wish more noise than we would need.

"Now hear me, missy," I whispered. "I will let you up, if you will promise not to make yourself a fool. You will not call out, or try to run off, or I will make you sorry." The truth was that I did not know what I might do, for I am gentle with women, as all men should be. "You and I must share some words between us."

She laughed. Twas discordant, and wrong to my ear. "And what mought I have to say to the buggering likes o' ye?" she asked, deep-voiced and saucy as a girl from down the laundries. Although her scent did not speak much of soap. Oh,

Irish she was, and no mistaking it. And that made another mystery.

Why had she failed to cry out, with her own kind so near in their slumbers? Why had she failed to give warning to her tribe as we dug up the dead girl? When it seemed the ambition of all concerned to convince the world a man lay in that grave?

She moved herself brazenly under me and laughed when she felt my alarm. I could not like that laugh. Or her behavior.

I got myself up with a push of my cane and let the woman rise. I tried to help her. But she pushed off my hand. With a pallid, moonswept look, she tossed the end of her shawl back over her shoulder and stood defiantly. As tall as me she was, perhaps the taller.

I took her by the wrist again, firmly, but not hard enough to hurt. She struggled briefly, then let me have my way.

I thought I saw into the thing. And I took a chance.

"I believe we may have a great deal to say to one another . . . Mrs. Boland."

I had hit the target in the very center. I felt it in the way she tightened when I spoke her name. Twas but a guess, but not a guess unfounded. For who but a suspicious wife, unsure of her husband's fate, would have been watching over that doubtful grave?

"Ye'll take those hands off me this instant, ye black little Taffy," she told me, not once denying her name. She sought to sound imperious, but her voice was all a-quiver. "Let me go, or I'll scream and they'll all come over ye." She tugged at my grip again, but I would not release her. "I'll say the old words over ye," she warned, fair spitting now. "I'll say the old words and call down the strange folk upon ye."

I am not one to pause for superstitions, but I let go of her arm. I kept me close to her, though, for I was not about to let her run off before I had my answers.

"No, Mrs. Boland, you will not scream. And say what words you will, be they old or new. For now we have a secret, you and I. And those who are sleeping down below would not be fond to hear that you had let us open that grave. As you stood watching and silent. Oh, there is plenty for us to talk over, milady."

"I'll not be threatened by your likes," she said. A queerness there was in her voice, even when she was common-spoken and plain. Twas as if she only imitated the normalcy of our speech. I cannot explain the thing, but there it was: A strangeness to fit the night. "I'll not be threatened," she rambled on, "or I'll say the words none can call back upon ye, I will."

"Threatened you will not be. Nor do I wish to see you come to harm. But you will tell me who is in that grave."

"My husband it is. My Danny."

"You know that is not true."

"Tis my husband's grave, an't it?"

"That is not the same thing. Who is the dead girl?"

She did not flinch at the question, and so I knew that she knew at least some part of it. She merely said, "What girl, then?"

"The girl who was murdered elsewhere, dressed in another's rags, then put in a coffin and buried as your husband."

"Sure, you're talking mad enough for the friar's asylum." She threw back her shawl, then tossed her midnight hair.

"Well," I told her, "better an asylum than a prison. Or the gallows. Who is the girl? Who killed her?"

The moon come back to light her eyes, and she did a thing that no man could expect. She took up my hand, the right one. Lifting it to her mouth, she smiled, then began to lick my fingers. With all the death on them.

I froze. And she grinned at me. Her tongue swept over her lips.

"I know her now, the dirty slut," she said. "You've had your fingers in her."

Then she put my fingers in her mouth.

I lurched away from her. Almost stumbling over a fallen branch. I hid my hand behind my back, all reflexes and confusion. As if she might come after me and seize my hand again.

I felt an urge to slap her. And to vomit.

"The little man's afraid," she laughed. Fair cackling, a sound that pierced. "The little man's afraid . . ."

Twas then she began to scream. I did not expect that, either. She should have screamed long before, if she had a mind to do so. Why had she waited for me to find her? Why did she bring suspicion on herself? Then, only when compromised, cry for her Irish brethren?

I could not seek answers that evening, for she howled off like a banshee, racing for the mine patch down below. Screaming to wake the next county.

There are times when a man must take a stand. But that night was not one of them. With the grave but a portion filled in, I gathered up my Dutchmen and their tools, snuffed out the lantern, and trotted the lads away from the clustered houses. I kept them under strict command, for I knew they wished to run faster than I could follow. But I did not want one to lose his way and stray into the colliery patch. Bad enough would come, I knew, when the Irish learned of our business. And I did not wish to see one of my poor lads mobbed to death. Or thrown into a mineshaft and left to die broken-boned. They had already murdered a Union general. I did not think they would pause over killing a private. Or a major.

I will not pretend our retreat was made in good order. We fled. And a good thing it was that my leg had shown improvement. For we had not made a quarter mile's progress before I heard a medley of Irish curses and saw the bobbing of miner's lamps in the valley.

We were fortunate. The Irish were all too poor to feed them a dog.

two

"ON WHOSE AUTHORITY did you dig up that grave?"

Young Mr. Gowen was angry. He had risen from his desk in a flush of temper, near hot enough to melt the wax on his mustache ends. Had I believed him a foolish man, I would have paid attention to his fists.

"Damn me, Jones," he continued, with unnecessary profanity, "we've only just gotten the Irish quieted down. And here you go disturbing their dead in the middle of the night. Do you want another riot, man? Or worse? You know what happened in Tremont with that train." He drew his watch from his waistcoat pocket, but did not open its lid or bother to look at it. He merely weighed it in his palm, as if he liked to feel time in his grip. Gold it was, although the fellow had debts. "As the district attorney for the county of Schuylkill, I demand an explanation. I de*mand* it, Jones!"

"Now, now, Mr. Gowen," I told him. "There is no need for commotion. An explanation you will have, see. If only you will—"

"Don't play the little Welsh fool with me, Jones. I can see right through you." He shook his head with unnecessary bitterness. "You won't fool *me* twice."

He folded his arms. They settled atop a stomach that hinted prosperity. Yet, despite his rising prospects, prosperity was a quality young Mr. Gowen did not yet possess. If he knew me, I knew him, too, our fresh-made district attorney. Hardly a week in office he was, and as full of himself as young men are apt to be. But failed coal ventures had bankrupted him, and he lived at the mercy of creditors. Secrets will not be hid in our dear Pottsville. Young Gowen was full of dreams, but out of funds. Of course, his political victory would extend his credit handsomely, for power is as good as ready money.

"Oh, I know who you work for," he insisted, although it would emerge that he did not. "Don't think I don't. I know what goes on in Harrisburg. In Washington, too. You Republicans aren't the only people with a party organization."

He wore his collar too tight, as stout men will. The pink of his neck climbed into his face, like mercury in a thermometer, and his heavy mustaches quivered. "Boss McClure should know better. If he has Seward's ear, he damned well should know enough to tell him we don't need any more federal interference. Too much harm done already. Schuylkill County can manage its own affairs."

He calmed a bit and settled against the windowsill of his office, spreading his generous bottom along the ledge. Behind him I saw an earthen yard and the necessary closet. "Just let me handle things, Jones. I know these people, the Irish. Let me handle things and there won't be any repetition of that business with the trainload of recruits. No need for that sort of thing at all. Trouble for everybody." He weighed his watch again, without reading the dial. "As for murdered young women, no such thing, man! There hasn't been so much as a girl reported missing these last months." He ventured his first smile since I broached my business. "Had there been, I suspect it would have made a lively campaign issue. The Irish are very protective of their ladies."

I considered the great, big bulk of him, in his vigor and

his pride. His dark suit fit him to a fancy, yet somehow seemed too small to contain his fullness. There was nothing still about him and, despite his business reverses, we all sensed that Franklin Benjamin Gowen was a fellow with a future. I will give him that. He was but twenty-six or twenty-seven then, handsome and already a good doer at table. Rumored to have great plans he was, although few of us were sure of his direction. An Orangeman by ancestry, he attended the Episcopal Church that stood near his office. Twas the proper church for those with high ambitions, and the best address in town, although I am content to go to chapel.

And yet, for all his high-church ways, Mr. Gowen had chosen to represent the Copperhead Democrats, and the Breckinridge faction, at that. He drew his ballots from Irish Catholic miners, from German farmers unhappy with the war. He had that Irish gift of talk, when he did not speak in anger, but hard it was to pin down what he said. Later, of course, he would make a great career, as all the nation knows, building the Reading Railroad to a spectacular bankruptcy. He was the man who hanged the Mollie Maguires, the guilty and the innocent alike, and I would play a role in that sad travesty.

We could not have foreseen his future during the war, since young Gowen seemed committed to the Irish. But *he* would be the one to lay them low, for loyalty was not among his virtues. The poor devils were but his stepping stones to power. He fought for them when he needed them, and against them when he did not.

He loved books and literary evenings. But he did not much like men.

"Nothing but damned trouble," Mr. Gowen said sharply, without specifying the object of his scorn. This time, he shut his fist around his watch.

I shall always remember young Mr. Gowen the way he

appeared that day. So strong and brisk and confident. As if he had been born to rule the world. I knew the fellow thought little of me, for I had been but a clerk in a coal company countinghouse before the war took all of us in thrall. I was a small man, though an honest one. I wanted only a quiet life, with my darling wife and our son—and now young Fanny, my ward—with chapel on Sunday, morning and evening both. But war will have its way with every man.

Mr. Gowen, as we all knew, had bought himself out of danger from the draft, although his brother served with our 48th. Mr. Gowen had explained that he could not serve the colors, although it was his fervent wish to do so, because of family and business obligations.

He had ambitions that the war annoyed.

I sat and let him speak his anger out, for I was weary and did not want a scrap. After my return to Pottsville from the boneyard, I had gone home in the dray-cart hours of morning to set my uniform to soak in the tub in the yard. Fanny woke and wanted to help—she always sensed me near—but I did not want her to touch the leavings of death. Orphaned, she had seen enough at fourteen years.

And I thought, again, in the almost light, of the odd woman in the trees. Of the vileness of her doings with my fingers. If Mrs. Boland was not mad, her actions were all the worse for her wicked sanity. Twas not a matter I meant to share with anyone.

Fanny had a smile for me, as Fanny always did. She stayed out in the cold to keep me company. All quiet like. I had a soft spot for her that, curiously, my Mary did not share. But I will speak of that at the proper time.

Fanny slept in the kitchen then and always rose with the larks. The lass had been a lark of sorts in Glasgow. She perched and watched me in the morning gray, wrapped in a shawl my Mary had cast off, with her mass of ginger hair awaiting the dawn. She did not pester me with queries, but always was content to see me near, no matter my doings. At last, I sent her into the house to get up the morning fire. I had to wash before my dear wife rose.

I did not want my Mary or young John to smell the death on me. It carries a contagion, see. I do not mean the contagion of disease, but a contagion of the heart. I did not wish to bring death into my house. I tolerate no hint of superstition, but my Mary Myfanwy was in the family way, thanks to our blessed visit late in the spring, and even the soundest Methodist fears ill luck. I wished to keep the hard world from our threshold, to banish death through prayer and will and love.

And my son was already frightened of me, his rarity of a father, and of the new scar set upon my cheek during my recent sojourn in Her Majesty's kingdom. Our John was not yet two, but old enough he was to fear a stranger. And cruel war makes strangers of us all.

After a proper breakfast, with my Mary not quite content with my explanations, young John antic, and Fanny quiet and watchful, I enjoyed my daily interlude with the Bible, then took myself along to the county offices, to seek both Mr. Gowen and the sheriff. I wished a local writ to return and dig up that grave proper by light of day, for there was murder and mischief in those doings. But the sheriff had been detained at home, enchanted by his blankets, and the ancient clerk in the courthouse explained that Mr. Gowen might be found at his private offices, pursuing the business of law. A district attorney's list of clients swells.

I marched back down along Centre Street, which was still a black muck from a rainfall days before. Hats aplenty tipped to me as I tapped my way along, for I have a good report among my fellows. As I chanced by, Mrs. Wesendonck applied for assistance in locating her cat, implying it had been carried off by the Rebels, and she was not pleased when I explained that the federal government don't pursue stray animals. But then she is a German, and they are a stubborn folk. Mr. Yuengling's brewery wagons churned the length of the street, hauling sin in barrels, and the clang of unseen railyards sang of profits. The smoke from the Palo Alto mills and from our brace of ironworks invaded the sky, which was hard and blue and cold. A ragamuffin boy cried to his comrades, "Aw, ga wan wit cha! Youz don' know nuttin', yuz don't," warming me with the melodious speech of the native-born Pottsvillean.

Mr. Gowen was in his office, indeed, which had a fine location at the hub of things, just along from the Pennsylvania Hall Hotel, our city's finest, and across the street from the offices of Mr. Bannon's *Miners' Journal,* the newspaper of Mr. Lincoln's party and the one we took at home.

I had barely uttered my business to Mr. Gowen's clerk, who looked as though he suffered from obstinate bowels, when the door to Mr. Gowen's office opened and two fellows come galloping out. I recognized Mr. Heckscher, the great colliery owner. He was companioned by a foreigner. And when I put it thus, it tells you something, for we have all the nations of the world, or thereabouts, in Schuylkill County. At least all those which are civilized. When a fellow looks foreign in Pottsville, he strikes you queer.

This one had a narrow face, like an axe-head viewed straight on, and dainty little mustaches, flat as if painted. His waistcoat and tie flashed silken hues from east of the English Channel. He looked a grand sort, though not an especially good one.

"Ah, *Monsieur,*" he said to Mr. Heckscher, who did not note my greeting, "the method . . . it is not important, you understand. Only that the thing has been done at last. *C'est vrai?*"

Now, you will say: "That fellow was a Frenchman." But I will tell you: The devil spoke French, and English, too, but neither had been the first tongue that come to his cradle. His English pronunciation was too fine, and his French intonation was insufficiently rude. I could not begin to make the stranger out.

I let the matter go past me, for I had more important things on my mind than dandified Europeans and their commerce. I thought instead of Heckschersville, where I had spent a muchness of the night. And where a dead and nameless girl lay buried. Where a general had been killed. The mining patch had Mr. Heckscher's name, but he was too wise and rich to live in it. Rich men lived in Pottsville. Or in Reading, or Philadelphia. The patches were home to the poor, and to foremen and superintendents who slept with loaded pistols by their beds. Heckschersville was known as the worst and most commotive settlement in wild Cass Township, where even the mice were Irish and Union blue found less of a welcome than famine. But it sat atop one of the richest veins of anthracite in the county. The Irish may have hated the man, but they made Mr. Heckscher a fortune.

Of course, I did not connect the presence of Mr. Heckscher and his odd companion to my own doings, for coal bosses are uncommonly fond of barristers. They spend more time in chambers than in collieries, and what they cannot take with a pickaxe, they take with a judge's writ. I do not speak of Mr. Evans, my dear wife's uncle and my employer before the war, who ran a model establishment near equal in its qualities to the works of Mr. Johns of Saint Clair town. Mr. Evans it was who invited my bride and myself to come to America, when we were newly married but unlucky, with my Indian disgrace hanging over my head.

I always thought Mr. Evans a good man, and a just one. He paid fair wages and measured with honest scales. He let no drunkards into his mines. He used the stoutest timbers in his gangways, nor did he rob old pillars to the danger-point. His deepest breasts and galleries had proper ventilation, and but a few workmen were killed or maimed each year. His coal was clean, and known in Philadelphia. Like Mr. Johns, his fellow Welshman, he stood a very model of Christian probity. Although he had become a Congregationalist, for reasons of his own, I always believed his heart remained with Methodism.

Yet, there was more to come of Mr. Evans. That was the autumn when my heart was crushed.

As the street door slammed behind Mr. Heckscher and his fancy companion, I introduced myself anew to Mr. Gowen, who was ruffled and found my visit unwelcome from the first. He bid me sit down, politely though impatiently, but when I had barely begun to describe my petition, the fellow exploded in anger.

He called me names, which is a childish thing.

And yet, I like to remember him the way he was that day, a confident young man. With his future all before him and our little city enlivened by modern war's appetite for coal. He seemed a man for our times, did Mr. Gowen. Our Navy's ships fed the highest grade of Schuylkill White Ash Lump Steamboat into their boilers, at four-dollars-and-ninety-cents the ton, wholesale and government rate. We had been in a frightful slump before Fort Sumter was attacked, but the foundries and forges, the ships and locomotives, and all the great steam engines that increase the devastation of modern war demanded the one thing our county had to offer. We had entered the Age of Coal, which I predict will last a hundred years. Fortunes were being made between lunch and dinner, although intemperate men might still go bust.

I like to remember Mr. Gowen the way he was that morn-

ing, despite his sour demeanor toward myself. He seemed fit
to conquer the world. And, in his time, he nearly did. It took
all of J.P. Morgan's might to bring him and his Reading
Railroad down. But that was far in the future, the stuff of
high finance and not of war. It is better to recall Mr. Gowen
hopeful and hale, in 1862, than as I would find him in the
Year of Our Lord 1889, dead by his own hand in a
Washington hotel room.

But let that bide.

"DAMN IT, Jones, are you even listening to me?" I thought he
would pound the desk with his fist, but Mr. Gowen did not.
Instead, he took out his watch, then put it back.

"Yes, Mr. Gowen. It is listening I am."

And listening I was. But I had decided to let him blow his
steam. Although I am Welsh born and talk is our cakes and
ale, I have learned that there is often a great deal to be said
for not saying a great deal.

"Well, I want to know just what you thought you were
doing by sneaking up there in the dead of night to dig up the
grave of one of our citizens?"

"Was he a citizen, Mr. Gowen? This Daniel Patrick
Boland who was not in his grave?"

"What do you mean by that?"

"Well, then, I will tell you. It seems young Mr. Boland
voted, as a proper citizen should, for his name is listed on
the county rolls. I have examined them, see. And I suspect
he voted the Democratic ticket. But when the commissioner
attempted to register the men of Cass Township for the draft,
it appears young Mr. Boland remembered that he was not a
citizen, after all, and thereby was not liable for the draft."

"What are you implying?"

"I am not 'implying,' Mr. Gowen. I have only asked you a
question."

"No. No, I don't believe that quite. I think you're suggesting electoral fraud. Well, I'll have you know that I won this position by one-thousand, six-hundred and thirty votes, the largest majority of any candidate in this county."

"I did not suggest misconduct. Look you. I have only asked after Mr. Boland's citizenship. Since you are so concerned with the lot of citizens."

I know I should have shunned all confrontation. I needed to gather allies, not to make enemies. The truth is that I was peeved, and worn, and even good John Wesley had his pride. If Mr. Gowen believed that he must condescend to me, he still might have shown regard for our country's uniform. His own brother would die in Union blue before the war's end.

As to our recent elections, well, I fear that fraud is the stepchild of democracy. Oh, the counting of ballots is no common arithmetic. Yet, to be fair, Mr. Gowen had won his place beyond a drunkard's challenge. Although he had not won a majority in Pottsville, where the people are sensible.

"What's your point, Jones?" Mr. Gowen asked. "You still owe me an explanation. By whose authority did you open that grave?"

I sighed and sat me back. Twas then I reached deep into my uniform—a fresh frock coat, mind, not the one I had dirtied. I had transferred one bit of paper to my clean get-up, a letter carefully preserved in a wallet of oilskin. Its signature was my armor.

I handed the letter across the piled desk.

He swept the document from my hand and glanced over it as he stood. Then he sat down hard and read it through. He did not raise his eyes a single time. But his lips moved, as if he must taste the words to judge their power.

At last, he looked up. He stared at me. Pale he was, although by nature florid.

"This is infamous," he said.

"By the power invested in me by the President of these United States," I told him, "I forbid you to speak of the contents of that letter with any man."

He let the letter drop to his desk, then shook his head in anguish. When he spoke his voice was chastened, wounded and low.

"And he calls that democracy, does he?" He gave a little puff, but could not work up his old steam. "What, are we living in a new age of *lettres de cachet*? When an innocent man might find himself hurled into prison? At the whim of his political enemies?" He looked at me then, with that coldness I would come to know too well, that self-regard that would drive men to the gallows. "He's thrown away *habeus corpus*. Now it appears the man's trampling the rest of the Constitution."

"Mr. Lincoln," I began, in a voice too much the schoolmaster's, "is doing what he must to save our Union. Like you, he has read the law and knows his doings. And I will tell you, Mr. Gowen: I will not hear a word spoken against him."

"He's becoming a damnable tyrant, if you ask me. Why, look how little appreciation he shows to George McClellan. The ape's as jealous as a caesar."

"That is enough, now. As for your *habeus corpus,* I may not have my Latin or my Greek, but I know what it means. If you are so intent upon producing bodies, how is it you object to my inspection of that grave?"

He sighed. "Don't you see, Jones? I simply want to keep order. Cripes. That's what I was elected to do. These people of ours . . . these Irish miners and laborers . . . they've come here looking for honest wages, not for a war. Certainly not to squander their meager lives to free the nigger. Oh, I'm all for preserving the Union, you understand. I'm as patriotic as the next man. I wish circumstances had permitted me to serve under the colors. It doesn't take a prophet to see that we're all better off with one continental market, rather than with a country split in two. Let us hope for a negotiated settlement among reasonable men. But the Southrons do have a point, as far as I'm concerned, when it comes to the rights of the states. *And,* I might add, the rights of the individual citizen."

He got a little air back into his lungs. "Look here. The Union needs the coal that these men dig. The government can find soldiers elsewhere, but not skilled miners. Why stir up trouble with this draft nonsense when they're already doing their part for the Union by digging our coal? You know well enough what this county's been through this year. Work stoppages. Pumps laid idle, productive mines flooded. Good men driven to bankruptcy, when every other business is booming. All because of Washington's interference. Federal intransigence, the heavy hand of Washington, has nearly driven this county into open rebellion."

He rose, heavily, to his feet again. After all, he was a politician. Such men declaim when other men but speak. The vigor was drained out of him, though, the spunk gone. "If cooler heads had not prevailed, we might have had our own civil war right here in Schuylkill County, this very autumn. When hundreds of—nay, a thousand—miners stop work at their collieries to march to intercept a troop train and riot to set the recruits free, then I'd say we had come to the very brink of insurrection."

"And," I put in, as he paused for breath, "I believe the cooler head that prevailed was Mr. Lincoln's."

Mr. Gowen dismissed the thought, measuring the weight of his pocket watch yet again. "It was McClure. McClure and Andy Curtin. Pennsylvania men. They may be Republicans, but they know their constituencies. McClure knew what he was facing. I'm quite certain he gave Lincoln his marching orders."

It did not happen that way, for I was there for much of the desperate doings. Forgive me the sin of pride. Mr. McClure, who is a great political fellow of ours, explained the situation to Mr. Lincoln, how the miners had chased off the draft registrars and destroyed the records, and how all Cass Township was up in arms and refused to go to the war. Hotheads had put it into their ears that, after they were packed off to die, freed slaves would be sent down the mines at starvation wages. Twas a great lie, but lies abound in wartime. They satisfy the ear displeased by truth.

Mr. Lincoln hinted to Boss McClure and Governor Curtin that, if the law could not *be* satisfied, it might be enough should it *appear* that the law had been satisfied. And that had been sufficient for Mr. McClure, who called on the wisdom of Mr. Benjamin Bannon, Pottsville's own newspaper editor and speculator, who had been made our commisioner of the draft in reward for his party services. Between Mr. Bannon and Mr. McClure, our county enlistment rolls were tallied in such a remarkable way that it proved our draft quota had been met and exceeded, collapsing the need to complete the registration in Cass Township, that bloody-minded, errant outpost of Ireland. Mr. Lincoln was determined to fight our war to the finish, but he never fought unnecessary battles.

"What ever was he thinking?" Mr. Gowen grumbled on, "this rail-splitting hero of yours? Calling for a draft, then announcing that he intends to emancipate the nigger? What does he ex*pect* the Irish to think, for God's sake? As it is, they can't support their families, boom year or not. *And,* I might add, all because of the incompetence and mismanagement of colliery owners too blind to see the economies consolidation would bring them." He shook his head in wonder at such foolishness. "Millions to be made. *Mil*lions, Jones. Yet, the skilled miner can't be paid a living wage, and the colliery laborer lives a life of wretchedness. Then you tell him the nigger's to be freed to come north and do his work for half a loaf."

"Mr. Lincoln did not tell that to anyone. I believe the telling was by the Democratic Party, in these last elections of ours."

"Let's not make this a political discussion, Jones."

Now, I had gathered my temper back in and wanted no further fuss. "On that we are in accord, Mr. Gowen. Look you. Disagree we may about certain matters, but we both wish to have peace here in our homes. It is best that we appear united, at least where the law is concerned. And I have told you what I found last evening. There is a murdered girl set in that coffin. And not Daniel Patrick Boland, who likely is in Canada by now."

"There's no record of the murder of a young woman—or of any other woman—these last several months. Nor even of a disappearance. I've told you that." He steeled himself to look me in the eyes. His own were brown, but cold as the coldest blue. "I don't see the point in stirring up any more trouble. And we don't want to frighten people with tales of murdered young women, I don't think. What would you prove? For God's sake, man, even if there *is* a woman in the box, if no one's reported her missing, she can hardly be of consequence. Perhaps she's a beggar-girl, or a gypsy they found dead by the side of the road."

"Or perhaps she is not from our county," I said. "Or it may be that her death was kept concealed. I cannot say. But this much I will tell you, Mr. Gowen: A girl is dead, and murdered as ugly as the sins of ancient Rome. Before her, a brigadier general of the United States Volunteers was assassinated. That is two murders. And you are the district attorney, I believe. Now, I would think that you might take an interest."

"Some things take time. I've hardly taken office."

"Time will not help us solve these murders, see."

"If murders they are."

"General Stone was stabbed in the heart, I am told. Where he had stopped along the high road to Minersville. And the girl was stabbed until her body was pulped like a rotten apple. I think we may conclude that such is murder."

"And you suggest they're related? These murders? I don't necessarily see it."

"The man reported to have killed the general was said by every soul in Heckschersville and Thomaston to have died of cholera. But this is not the cholera season, and no other case was reported. And in the fellow's supposed grave I found a murdered girl. Now, Mr. Gowen, I cannot say *how* these matters are related, but a reasonable man might think them tied together."

"In the pursuit of justice, nothing may be assumed."

"In the pursuit of justice," I responded, "much must be assumed. And I assume that I will have the cooperation of the authorities of this county." I had my letter back in my hand and I gave it the slightest of waves.

He stared at me hard for a moment. Hard as coal deep in the earth. "You realize, Jones, that I'm the man who passed your name on last year, when a good fellow was wanted. I saw to it that your name went all the way to George McClellan. I got you started in this business. Now you're a major. We're members of the same social class now, you know. We have shared interests."

"I am not certain that I owe you thanks, Mr. Gowen. For happier I was working at my sums in the War Department. And I believe you would be happier if I were still there, too. That is what I think, begging your pardon. But we have both come some distance over the months. And now we have a task we must face together. To keep the peace while our country is at war."

Yes, he had passed along my name. As a fellow who knew his place and would do as ordered. Young Mr. Gowen had known a part of me, see, from our slight Pottsville acquaintance. But he was a man who drew conclusions quickly. In the end twas that would tumble him from his throne.

"And . . . you want me to provide you with political backing while you dig up that grave?"

"No, Mr. Gowen. I want you simply to enforce the law. You know as well as I do myself that, if soldiers are sent to dig her up now, there will be riot and bloodshed. It must be done by the hands of the local authorities. By men the miners may trust to some degree. By the power of civil law and hands they know. With mine the only uniform in evidence."

He snorted. "They might decide to hang you, anyway. As the district attorney, I could not guarantee your safety." He smiled at a small, private amusement. "And I don't think our noble sheriff would be much help."

"Then I will take my chances. But the grave must be opened proper. Perhaps you could approach the Catholics to have the local priest see that order is kept. The Irish will listen to such."

"I'm not sure they even listened to Bishop Wood when he was here."

"Well, I leave that much to you, the matter of writs and priests. But we must open the grave and take her out."

"And when do you expect to do this, pray tell?"

"This afternoon would be best. If that cannot be managed, then tomorrow. In the morning."

"Can't be done today. Or tomorrow."

"It will be done tomorrow, if not today. For the people by the graveyard must not be given time to think too much of matters. Certain I am that they are already unhappy."

"Doubtless. Once they found one of their graves disturbed."

Now, there is a thing I did not tell our district attorney. I did not tell him about the woman I caught in the wood, who I judged to be Mrs. Boland. She had astonished me, and repelled me. But the wretched creature would not leave my thoughts. I had thought of her as I washed myself clean at the pump in our backyard. I thought of her as I walked, as a man remembers a serpent found in his cellar. And I thought of her now. I planned to seek her out, to find a way to press her for answers. I was not yet convinced that she was mad. I had met things in India the wantonness of which refuses words. Suffice to say that demons lurk in some men. And in certain women, though you disbelieve me. I feared that woman, and smelled her in my nostrils.

"Well, then . . ." Mr. Gowen rustled about his desk, as if we had agreed our talk was ended, ". . . I suppose we'll have to see what can be done by tomorrow." He raised an eyebrow inquiringly. "Of course, the federal government will pay all costs."

"All costs within reason, Mr. Gowen."

He nodded. Then he threw a lever inside himself, the way a switchman throws one along the railway. He primped himself back to a confidence and straightened up his shoulders.

"You know, Jones . . . you and I do have a great deal in common, if only we let ourselves see it. Politically, we may not see eye to eye, of course. But politics are hardly permanent. Quicksilver, rather. Let me be frank: I'm well aware of those railroad investments of yours. You've been buying up shares with every penny in your pocket." He smacked his lips, as if approving of a tasty stew. "Well done, that's what I say! Good for you! There's money to be made, and if anything will win this war, it's going to be capital. Making money is the most patriotic thing a man can do."

I looked at him reproachfully, giving the floor a slight tap with my cane.

"*One* of the most patriotic things a man can do," he corrected himself. "But I also know you've been relying on Matt Cawber, following his money with your own. Well, Cawber's yesterday's man. Over the hill. Don't say I haven't warned you. Ever since his wife died, he's become the laughing stock of Philadelphia. Tearing down a mansion he'd only just built." Mr. Gowen tutted. "They say he doesn't even wash himself anymore."

"Mr. Cawber grieves for his late wife, I believe. She was a great, high beauty, and he loved her."

"Oh, grief. Yes. Well and good. But that sort of thing can be carried too far, don't you think? Anyway, take my advice. Pull your money out of those western railroads and put it right here, in the Reading. I tell you, Jones, the good years have only begun here in the anthracite fields. This war's a blessing, whatever little problems it may create. And the Reading's going to be the queen of all the railways in this land. She's going to become an empire, an empire of capital. Harrisburg is bound to amend the laws, to clear the way for the big investor, for the combination of resources. One power has to own the land, the mines, the collieries, the railroads, the waterways . . . even the docks in Philadelphia and New York. The ships that carry the coal. All in one great empire."

His eyes looked into the future he described, and I sat largely forgotten. "That's what this is: the Age of Empire. An Empire of Capital. And it's going to belong to men of vision, modern men. Even old man Heckscher doesn't understand. He thinks small. And that goes for Johns, too. And for Evans, your wife's uncle. It's all about consolidation, about concentrations now. The age of the small operator, of the family shop, is over. They've got the right idea up in Luzerne County, but we're going to overtake them. Wait and see. Give me ten years, and you'll see a changed landscape for business. Economies of scale, the efficiency of the monopoly." His expression grew rich as a cream sauce. "We have great years ahead of us. Great *decades*. If anything's holding this county back, it's nothing but damned obstinacy." He fingered his watch a final time—and now he paused to mark the fleeing time. "This war's destroying the old ways of doing business, that's the one good thing I'll say of it. Whatever else may happen, American industry can never turn back now . . ."

He looked at me again, as if he had just remembered my existence. "As an upstanding citizen of this county, you should want to be part of it. All that money your wife's minting with her dressmaking business—I hear she's taken on a third seamstress—at least put that much in the Reading. We can all grow rich together." He stared at me intently. "If we're not afraid to do what must be done."

I nodded, but only to pass the time and not in true agreement. "I did not know you were associated with the Reading Railroad," I told Mr. Gowen.

He smiled. "I will be."

three

As I left Mr. Gowen's office and crossed Church Alley, I spotted Mr. Heckscher once again, entering the Pennsylvania Hall Hotel with his foreign companion. Doubtless, they had their midday meal in mind, for bells across the town pealed twelve o'clock, and mine own thoughts had turned from death to sustenance.

I would have liked to take my meal at home, but there is sorry. The stove would be cold, with nothing in the pot. For my Mary Myfanwy was at her dressmaking establishment, hard at work as if she were a man.

Now, I believe a woman must have her freedoms—we are not the Musselman captors of our brides—and proud I was of my darling's commercial success. It kept her busy while I served our Cause. But a wife belongs at home when her husband needs her.

I will not deceive you. The first tensions of our married life had arisen between us. Sometimes I think the world has gone topsy-turvy. Our modern age runs like a wild horse, and war whips the beast to a fury. The days grow disordered, men mock the good, and liberties are taken without asking. At times, I fear the deepest bonds will break.

A brazier-boy sold chestnuts on the corner where I would have turned my steps, had my wife been at home. I bought a portion of the fruits, wrapped in a paper cone. They warmed

my hand against the bite of the day. With age, I have grown
to like the meat of the chestnut, pungent and bittersweet. It
confounds the tongue pleasantly, and the texture reminds me
of certain foods of India, where I left my youth behind and
more besides.

I had a muchness to ponder as I walked amid the horse
smells and the rush of delivery boys. And my thoughts
were not only of the insubordination of our modern
ladies. I wondered at Mr. Gowen's ill-matched concerns.
He sought to shield the Irish from outsiders, yet argued
that all virtues lay with capital. Twas clear enough he
wanted no part of digging up the grave with the murdered
girl. But he would play his part, indeed, or I would go directly to Judge Parry, who was a man impatient of all
nonsense.

I peeled a chestnut, laid it warm on my tongue, and wondered if young Mr. Gowen knew his own mind.

Nor could I forget that murdered girl, whose fate seemed
to concern no one but me. The sudden recollection of her
rottenness was near enough to put me off my chestnuts. She
had not seemed a gypsy or a beggar, as Mr. Gowen suggested she might have been. Of course, I cannot claim a thorough inspection. But something was rotten in
Heckschersville, if not in the state of Denmark.

Have you ever noticed Mr. Shakespeare's affinity for
graves? He ponders death, as all good Christians should. I
sucked the sweetness from another chestnut. And I
thought of the living woman, Mrs. Boland, who was so
queer, then of Macbeth's witches and Cleopatra. I do think
Mr. Shakespeare had Welsh blood. He had an eye for the
oddities in mankind that would elude the sharpest eye in
England.

It had come as a great surprise to me when Mr. Lincoln
told me I was to go home to Pottsville to look into the

murder of a general. Of course, I was the obvious choice, since I knew the place and the people. But our president had been cryptic, which was unlike him. Even Mr. Nicolay, his private secretary and, I thought, an honest friend to me, had been a very miser with his facts. I was told only that Brigadier General Carl Stone had been jaunting about the coal fields in an attempt to raise a regiment of volunteers. He had nothing to do with the draft or its enforcement. Yet, they found him dead south of Heckschersville, atop a hill along the Thomaston Turnpike. Stabbed in the chest, but otherwise unmarked. He last had been seen alive in Ryan's Hotel, a ramshackle house in Heckschersville itself.

Deep I was in my ruminations and chestnuts, when a tableau of the streets asked my attention.

A woman in a ragged shawl dragged a boy through the mud, crying, "Get-tup, or Oi'll take the belt to ye, oncet we're ta home. Oh, ye'll be gettin' the belt but good, Oi'm tellin' ye truly."

The child was willful, strong and unafraid.

"Oh, sir," the woman called to me, a perfect stranger, "did ye ever see the likes o' this one here?"

Now, children are fond of me, for I do not worry them, and I paused to see if I might lend assistence.

"Obey your mother, and you will have a chestnut," I bid the lad.

He wiped a blot of mud from his brow and said, "Shove your dirty chestnut up your ass, Shorty." But change his behavior he did. Of a sudden, he clutched his mother and begged, "You won't go off with that one, will you, Ma?"

I thought it best to make my way along.

MR. LINCOLN AND MR. NICOLAY HAD made it clear they wanted no reports sent over the telegraph. Nor was I to discuss the least thing I found with anyone else, but only with one of those two. It seemed a fuss to me. Generals had been promoted in plenty—Washington fair stank with them, from the saloon bars to the lowest harlot's alley—but there was a special matter to do with this fellow. They told me less than I would have told a bootblack.

I admit I was affronted by their secrecy, though self-regard is always out of place. I do believe that was the sin of vanity in me, about which Mr. Wesley warned us, as surely as do the Testaments, Old and New. Yet, I had served my masters well and loyally. And now I was not trusted with full knowledge of a matter I was expected to explain.

I had set aside another business I was pursuing for Mr. Lincoln, an affair of folly, if not of treachery, at Harper's Ferry earlier in the autumn. It took me up to Pottsville on the railways, only to find my old friend Hughes the Trains overseeing the loading of the general's coffin—sealed with leads—onto a freight wagon in the yards. The box was to go to Washington, without the least delay, and a trio of armed soldiers would travel with it. Next, I had learned from the provost that the murderer had been found out, a miner named Daniel Boland, only to die of cholera the very same day. The authorities seemed relieved and disinclined to question the coincidence. But that was all too neat for Abel Jones. And so it was I went to digging up corpses. And found a girl who should have been a man.

Troubling none, I was on my way to Market Street, where my darling keeps her shop. If I could not eat her cooking at home, I might at least feast my eyes upon my beloved. For she is fair as Heaven on a Sunday. Strolling and tipping my hat I went, amid the noontide hubbub, wishing I had bought a double portion of chestnuts.

Foosteps rushed up behind me.

A hand dropped onto my shoulder.

A voice roared into my ear.

"Jones, *Jones!* Major Jones! I saw you going in and coming out! I saw you! Had to catch you, had to come out after you! Gowen can't be trusted in the least! Don't trust that man!"

A very storm of spittle and breath swept over me, nor was the breath as sweet as one might wish. Twas Mr. Bannon, the editor of our newspaper and commissioner of the draft, a man in the prime of life and well respected. The Republican Party looked to him for sagacity and the anthracite industry looked to his paper for figures, and he and his brothers owned at least half the town.

Mr. Bannon's hands were smudged with ink, as was his cheek, and his shoulders jumped as he spoke. He had abandoned his office without his hat and his gray hair streamed down to his mighty beard. A drop of wet hung from his nose, and I was not certain its predecessors had not found rest in his whiskers.

"Waste of talent, waste of talent!" Mr. Bannon warned me. "Can't believe he went over to the Irish. Can't be trusted, in little things or big. Traitor to his class. I thought that you should know, you—"

I backed me up most delicately. I did not wish to offend his august personage, for even Mr. Lincoln paid him heed on political matters, while Governor Curtin viewed him as an equal. But a conversation should not resemble a rainstorm. And I fear his breath recalled the dead girl's smell.

"—can't believe a single thing he says. Democrat, you know. Traitor to his kind. You can't believe a single thing Gowen says."

Suddenly, he changed his tack and his tone. "What *did* he say, Jones? What did Gowen tell you? Anything for the pages of the *Miners' Journal*? What did he say to you?"

"He said that I should buy railroad shares," I told him. For newspapermen must be answered with a caution, no matter their political allegiances.

"But . . . but you've been buying railroad shares for the past year! Everyone knows that, everyone knows! Evans at the Miners' Bank told me that you . . . I mean to say, why would Gowen tell *you* to buy railroad shares?"

"He told me to buy *more* railroad shares," I responded. And I would need to speak to Evans the Bags at the bank, who was no relation to my Mary's uncle, Mr. Evan Evans, and who should not have been telling the town my secrets.

"But what did he say about General Stone's murder? What did he say?"

"We barely spoke of it."

His eyes narrowed at that, and his shoulders jumped again, as if they were unhappy in his coat. "I know why you're here," he informed me. "I know everything, know it all. I know you've been sent here straight from Washington. And I know why."

He leaned in closer and shared his breath, while his latest nasal effusion found a pillow in his beard. Now, Mr. Bannon was a great, high fellow, with a house of some magnificence on a hill across the valley and brothers with houses still finer, including Cloud House, a wonder of our age. I did not wish to give the man offense. As a stout adherent of Methodism, I would not even slight a beggar's feelings, for that matter. But Mr. Bannon's breath stank like an open latrine on a summer day when the commissary has run out of quicklime. I do not mean that unkindly, you understand.

"So . . . what can you tell me about the general's murder?" he asked. "What about it?"

Now, that is how these journalist folk are, see. First, they tell you they know all there is to know, then they beg for scraps of information. And though I think our free press is a glory, a journalist is a spy without a cause.

"He is certainly dead," I answered. "I believe that has been confirmed."

"But do you believe that nonsense about the Irishman, Brogan or whatever his name was? Don't tell me you believe that Irishman murdered Stone, then dropped over dead with the cholera, just like that! Do you believe Brogan killed him and keeled over dead?"

"Cholera is a terrible disease," I said.

"But do you believe *any* of it, Major Jones? Do you believe a single thing we're hearing? Can we hope for any justice, now that the Democrats have taken over the county?" He stepped closer, to allow me to communicate any intimate confidence I intended. The gusts from his lungs recalled the dead piled high at the Siege of Delhi. After they had been sitting a number of days. "What do *you* believe, honest man to honest man?"

"I believe everything that has been proven, Mr. Bannon. The rest will be proved or disproved in good time."

He drew out a pad and a stub of pencil that had been chewed upon like a schoolboy's. His shoulders leapt and glistening beads of wet fell on the paper.

"So . . ."

"Look you, Mr. Bannon. I must go along, if you will excuse me. For things there are to do, and things aplenty."

"But . . . but . . . I want to *help* you, to send out a clarion call for information . . . mobilize our readers . . . report the things they see . . . Irish terror . . . Mollie Maguires . . . White Boys . . . readers writing to me all the time, Jones . . . terrified, utterly terrified . . . the things they see, things they see . . . all over the county . . ."

I wonder if he saw me flinch at his mention of "White Boys." I had encountered such words in cold New York, where a matter ended badly. But I had not yet heard of "Mollie Maguires," although I would hear much in times to come.

Even more than the reminder of old evils, twas his remarks about his readers writing in with reports from all over the county that seized my attention. Instead of running off, I paused a moment, leaning on my cane and steeling my senses.

"Now, Mr. Bannon, fair is fair, and you have asked a muchness of questions of me. Now I have one for you. Important it is not, but I must ask you a little thing: Have any of your readers—has anyone at all—mentioned a missing girl these past few months? A young woman, I mean. Let us say, between fifteen and twenty-five? Very like toward the lesser of those ages?"

I saw suspicion in his eyes, and, perhaps, something else. But that soon passed, replaced by a quizzicality. His shoulders leapt and he ran the flat of his hand back through his hair. Defying Mr. Newton's laws, the current drop clung massively to Mr. Bannon's nose.

A passerby greeted us both, and the great drop fell as Mr. Bannon responded.

"No, no. Nothing of the kind," he said, turning back to me. "Last July . . . July, I believe it was . . . serving girl ran off with a silver tea service . . . Irish, of course . . . Irish . . . caught her in Port Clinton, sorry business . . . seems the heir had gambling debts and put the poor thing up to it, promising marriage . . . promising marriage, Jones . . . embarrassing . . . I believe she's still in the county jail, and let that be an example . . ."

"And the lad? This heir who corrupted her?"

"Oh, he was punished severely. His father forced the boy to go to Harvard . . . afraid he might run off to join the army, afraid he might join up . . ."

"Because he despaired of the girl?"

"Nothing of the kind," Mr. Bannon insisted, "nothing of the kind, Jones. Plain, black-Irish baggage with bad teeth. Saw her at the magistrate's. No, the boy had just run through his credit with his gambling friends. He was terribly embarrassed."

I bid Mr. Bannon adoo, with neither of us the wiser for our encounter. He mumbled about deadlines, presses and presidents, striding off with his shoulders all a-twitch. I made my way around the back of Market Street, to the lane behind my Mary Myfanwy's establishment. For a gentleman must not be seen going in at a dressmaker's shop.

THE ALLEY WAS rich with wastes discarded by storekeeps more concerned with convenience than cleanliness, and I fear it had been used frequently by souls more impatient than modest. Twas all guarded by cats and a drunkard who snored to frighten the rats away. Our Pottsville lacked some civic discipline, and the dust put me in mind of the Lahore slums. Of course, our town was not so dirty as London. To say nothing of poor Washington, where the measles was raging again.

I found the back door to my darling's establishment and let myself in with the key she had presented me.

All unsuspecting I was.

That was when my troubles really started.

I stepped in to find not my Mary, but a woman in a profound state of undress. She wore the richest smells of femininity, and precious little else, I must report. She had thick, golden hair. Upon her head, I mean. And a profound abundance of pinkness about her person. Her face was painted to set off jolly blue eyes.

She let out what I took for modesty's cry and chastity's complaint. But no sooner had I covered my eyes, than I realized that the brazen creature was laughing. As freely as toughs at a coon show. I stumbled backward, grasping for the doorknob and apologizing with Christian desperation.

She laughed to beat the band, while I beat my retreat.

Not only had I seen too much, I had seen far more than I realized in my confusion. Twas only when I was back in the alley, with my eyes full open again, that I put a name and person to the lady's face.

The drunkard had wakened to sing of County Antrim.

A lady she was *not*.

Nor had she any business to do in my dear Mary's shop, annoying dresses meant for proper customers. I wondered if she had sneaked in by the back door, intent upon making off with stolen goods—although I must be fair: Theft was not among the vices assigned to her reputation. But I nearly felt it my duty to burst in through that door again to demand an explanation. I hesitated only because I feared my gesture might be misunderstood.

Dolly Walker it was in that room, a woman of disorderly vocation. Mrs. Walker kept a crib along Minersville Street, which was not Pottsville's most esteemed address. I had not been able to avoid the report that her house was the very best such establishment in our little city, but I hardly considered that a mark of quality.

I will admit my own youth was imperfect. But now I am a Methodist and married.

I rushed around to the front of the building, violating every social convention. I had to alert my darling to her intruder.

The good citizens along Market Street must have thought I had joined a fire brigade, such was my haste as I hurried along the planks. My dear wife's shop was a narrow affair, with a narrow door between two narrow windows, and lettered glass that read:

Fine Apparel for Ladies
Made to Order
Finishings and Alterations
Accouterments and Sundries
Mrs. A. Jones, Proprietress

I rushed through the door as if storming the Kashmir Gate a second time.

"Mary," I cried, "a dreadful thing has happened!"

My darling looked up from hemming a skirt and the pins in her mouth fell away. Rising, she grew pale as fresh, blue milk.

Looking back, I believe she feared an accident to our son, who spent his days in a neighbor's charge until Fanny returned from her lessons.

"Abel?" She raised the white flame of a hand to cover her mouth.

The shop assistants clustered nigh, as women are given to do, faces bright with the expectation of tragedy. I wondered if one were a party to the monstrous crime underway in that back room. Two of them were Irish, see, and thus disposed to schemes and misbehaviors.

"Mary, you won't believe what—"

I caught myself. I dared not blurt out a thing that might bring scandal upon us. I grasped my angel by her arm—I fear a touch too roughly—and hastened her toward the hallway whose brevity led to that scene of wanton intrusion.

"Mary, Mrs. *Wal*ker's in your back room. Mrs. *Dol*ly Walker." I fear I blushed, for husbands do not discuss such

persons with their wives. "The one who has an establishment on—"

My dearest darling laughed.

Out loud she laughed, as plainly as Mrs. Walker had
done herself. Then, as swiftly as she could subdue her levity, my darling disciplined her expression to one more prim
and fitting.

"Abel . . . there are certain matters that need not be discussed between the two of us. And certainly not here. I must
ask you to let me run my business without any of your fussing. Mrs. Walker is a very good customer, and she—"

"Good Lord, Mary! You don't mean you *know* she's
here?"

Just then the creature herself come feathering out of the
back room. She was dressed to the nines and pleased with
herself, like a cat in a rich man's dust-bin. When she spotted
me, she could not restrain her mirth.

"Oh, now, Mrs. Jones!" the scarlet woman said, as if
she and my wife were most familiar. "I gave your 'usband
a nasty fright, I did. I didn't know as the gentleman was
expected."

I was nonplussed.

"I just wanted to settle me bill before I went off," Mrs.
Walker continued. "I couldn't be no 'appier with the gown."

Returned to her proper decorum, my wife told her, "Settle
next time we will, Mrs. Walker. Your credit is good and there
is no need of hurry."

Mrs. Walker looked at my wife, and then at me, and then
at my darling again. With a smile as learned as a professor's
lecture. "And those little costumes you're making up for the
girls?" Mrs. Walker said. "Not too dear, for they ain't to last
forever."

My Mary nodded.

Mrs. Walker's smile cut even more deeply into her painted cheeks. She directed her merry blue gaze toward me again.

"I'd keep me eyes on that one, I was you," she told my darling. "Come in upon me like a raging beast, the gentleman did. 'E's a wild one, ducks, and you've got your two 'ands full."

She disappeared back into the depths of the building. In the fresh silence, I heard a gathering up of parcels. The back door clacked shut. And still I saw her unseemly and insolent smile.

"Come along, you," my Mary Myfanwy told me, leading me toward that same back room.

"Mary, I—"

"Now you will hush until you have heard me, Abel. For I will have none of your moralizing where honest business is concerned."

She closed the door behind us. To me, that little room full of cloth and half-sewn dresses seemed unbearably squalid of a sudden. It still smelled of the scent of Mrs. Walker.

"Mary, I cannot believe you—"

She set a finger firmly to my lips. "Hush you. And listen. I live in this town and you do not. You have gone off to your war, and that is fine. But you do not know the half about your dear Pottsville, and do not think you do. So keep your sermons to yourself this once." She did not put her hands upon her hips, but she might as well have done so. "Mrs. Walker is the very soul of discretion. She comes and goes by that back door, and by that door alone." Mary pointed. "And she pays her bills most promptly and don't complain. Which is a thing I cannot say of the high and mighty ladies of Mahantango Street." She closed upon me as if we were condemned to fight with knives. I believe I feared her in that instant. "And would you have even that sort of woman go naked through the streets, Abel Jones? Would you have her go about uncovered, for all the world to see?"

"I would not have her in the streets at all. Her shame should be hid—"

"Oh, wouldn't you now?" She made a spitting face, which I fear was unladylike. "Men! It's fine and good to have her there, when the likes of her are wanted, but hide her away you will for your guilty pleasures . . ."

"Mary . . . darling . . . it's only . . . I mean, don't you see, Mary dear?"

"Don't you 'Mary dear' me until we have each spoken through our business and you have agreed that you should mind your own."

Now,. this was most unlike my tender sweetheart. Becoming a woman of business had addled her nature.

"But it's only that I don't feel my wife should be associated in any manner with—"

"Oh, don't you now? Aren't you the king of the castle, gone for months then coming home to give commands to all your humble servants?"

"You mustn't compromise yourself, my dearest. Don't you understand—"

"I understand that many's the husband from high up the hill who does not think himself above visiting Mrs. Walker's boarding house. Many a man to whom you bow and scrape."

" 'Bow and scrape' I do not, Mary. And is it a 'boarding house' now, that sink of evil Mrs. Walker runs?"

"Call it what you will. She pays her bills."

"But Mary . . . were the ladies of this town to learn that she patronized your—"

"Oh, the lot you know, Abel. As long as they can have credit, they'd have their dresses made by Satan himself and give him a kiss for the asking. Nasty little sneaks they are, nine out of ten, and they make me ashamed of the female race itself. Stealing from their husband's pockets to pay for their scrap of lace! They're worse tarts, the half of them, than any girl who works for Dolly Walker."

"Mary!"

I must have looked a fright to freeze the esquimaux, for she softened in an instant. Then she reached out and took me by the hand. Women with child are changeable, and husbands must be forbearing.

"Oh, Abel, I'm sorry. It's just that . . . sometimes you live in a fairyland in the clouds, where everyone tells the truth and reads the Bible. Life isn't *like* that."

She almost called a tear into my eye. I know life is not like that, see. I know it all too well. It is only that I yearn to believe in goodness. After all that I have seen of the world. I long to believe in rectitude and kindness. Even if it means I play pretend. Perhaps it comes from growing up an orphan—although my Mary's father, the Reverend Mr. Griffiths, took me in and fed me for a time. A hard man he was, with the sternness of St. John the Baptist, but none of the gentle love of Jesus Christ. Thereafter, I learned much of life in India.

I did not weep, but my wife did, all unexpected. She took me in her arms, almost as if I were her child as well as her husband.

"Oh, my dear," she whispered. "I've never known a man so strong and so fragile."

"I did not know you had known so many men."

"You know what I am saying. Do not pretend with me."

"Well, I am not made of glass, that I will tell you."

"Nor am I," my Mary said. "Look you, Abel. We have made a start in life, although we started late. And life with you is all I ask of Heaven. But we have a son, and another child coming"—she placed my hand upon her swelling person—"and they must be provided for. If . . . if anything should happen to you . . ." Another jewel escaped my darling's eye. "You wouldn't want me to be one of those poor women lining up outside Mr. Potts's office in the mornings, would you? Begging for him to help them apply for a pension? With their husbands dead and buried far from home, and the widows left bare of a penny for a loaf?"

Twas I who did the holding now. She was frail as a crystal glass on a ledge.

"Do not worry," I told her. "For I am a bad penny and will always turn up."

She wept.

"I will always come back to you, my darling," I assured her.

"That's what every one of them tells his wife. Don't you know that?"

"But we are different, see. And you will not be rid of me so easily. A war is not enough to keep me from you."

"Don't laugh at me."

"Laughing I am not." Oh, I loved the smell of her. Wherever she might be would be my home.

"I'm so afraid, Abel. Afraid you'll be gone forever. That you'll leave John and the baby and me alone. I don't know what I'd do, after waiting so long."

"And there is Fanny. She is our daughter now."

Mary stiffened, putting an inch between us. "She is welcome to stay in the kitchen, for your sake. But she is not my daughter."

"Well, a daughter never harmed a house."

"That is a lie," Mary said. "And she is not my daughter."

"Well, we will see."

She looked into my eyes. With those Welsh-green eyes of hers from up the valleys. So serious she was, and lovely as Heaven's Grace.

"Wickedness," she said. "Most men come to ruin through their wickedness. But not you. The greatest danger in your life is your goodness. Don't you see that?"

I tutted her and held her, and stroked her back, which pained my Mary at times.

"Goodness is never a danger," I told her.

"Yes, it is," she muttered into my coat.

four

"No, IT'S NOT," Father Wilde insisted. "It isn't that simple at all."

He turned his back on his bookcases and stepped toward me again. His elegance of manner was as out of place in a mining patch as a holy Hindoo monkey would have been. A lock of white hair—of utterly white hair—fell onto the youthful skin of his forehead. I hardly thought him a man of thirty years. Even his black cassock could not age him. And the curiosity of his hair only made him more striking.

"You cannot simply impose the law on these people," he continued. "They must be made to understand its purpose. We must all of us educate them, Major Jones. It is our obligation."

As he passed a table, he brushed a tobacco-keeper with the back of his hand, then passed his fingertips over a fancy decanter, the contents of which did not pretend to innocence. His fingers were long and delicate, almost a woman's, and I judged him the sort of fellow who likes to touch the world, who yearns to feel the character of things, but whose intelligence warns him off. The sort of man whose strictness is particular, not uniform. Whose duty is a refuge, not a vocation. I have known such in the army, see, and recognize the signs. I will even allow that, to some measure, I am speaking of myself.

"You must endeavor to understand them," he went on. "The Irish have experienced the law only as an instrument of oppression, not of protection." He paused in his lecture, settling his fingertips upon the spine of a book spread pages down. "Indeed, can we claim it to be otherwise, even here? In America? Really, you know, these people must be won for the law. First, they must see evidence of its benefits."

"First," I said, "they must learn not to murder."

His eyes flashed for a moment, as if confronted with a servant's insolence. But his tone remained almost blithe, more Sussex than Sligo. If Irish, Father Wilde's family was of the very best. If English, they were not the worst in the county.

"I shall agree with you that they must learn, although I do not share your confidence that they have murdered." The smile he gave me was a practiced thing. Perhaps it was a smile they teach to priests. "I don't suppose you've heard of St. Kiaran, Major Jones? Or St. Kyran? Or Ciaran, with a C? Who watches over our fine, new church? He rose from the working classes of his day to found the monastery of Clonmacnoise, where learning was valued and preserved among the Irish. I should like to imbue that spirit into my parishioners. For learn they must. If ever they are to advance."

He smoothed the cloth of a chairback. "But these are hardly matters of concern to you. No more than the Irish themselves would concern you, had you no interest in criminal affairs. So I shall confine myself to your interests and lay mine aside: If you persist in opening that grave, I cannot answer for any disturbances. The villagers are frightfully upset over the grave-robbing two nights ago. And, of course, there is concern for infection."

"Father Wilde, if you look out your front window, I believe you will see my men about their work. The grave will be opened. As I have told you. You have seen the papers yourself."

"Then I must forbid you to open Daniel Boland's grave. As the priest of this parish. It's a sacrilege, you know."

Twas the strangest business. He spoke as if reading the lines of a play without much care for their meaning. Twas almost like a schoolboy's recitation, a matter of necessity, not passion. His accent suited manors, not the mines. He might have been talking hunters with a squire. We spoke of murder gruesomely done, but the fellow never relinquished the tone of the class that breakfasts late. I would have thought a priest would be more earnest, for that is a quality of the first importance in a religious fellow. We Methodists are splendid in our gravity.

"Forbid me you cannot," I told him, holding my own voice in check. "And is it not a sacrilege to bury a body in another's grave, to dissemble identities and even the cause of death? Would it not be more than merely a crime, but a terrible sin for a priest?"

He did not flinch. "Whatever are you talking about, my dear man?"

"I believe you know full well."

"I fear that I do not."

"Daniel Boland is not in that grave. He never was."

"And how on earth might you know such a thing, Major Jones?" He eased back toward his bookcases, as if they exercised a magnetic force upon him. Strange it was. His parish house was little more than a shanty, but filled with handsome books and painted china. He even had a pair of pictures hung, the themes of which did not adhere to religion. Not even of the misfortunate Roman variety.

"I know because I was the one who opened the grave," I admitted. "There was no robbing. Only the corpse of a lass where a lad was to be. And no least hint of cholera. Only of a second murder, and a wicked one."

The priest remained as calm as a cold Welsh Sunday. "But you're speaking fantastically! I buried Daniel Boland myself. There are numerous witnesses."

"Who were not shy of the cholera?"

"Manly sorts, you know. Elders. The Irish aren't afraid of death, not really. I rather think it's life that unnerves them."

"Father Wilde, I do not see your purpose. Even priests must obey the laws of the land. There have been two murders. And you are playing with me. I am not such a fool that I cannot see it. You seem not the least concerned, but I think you are."

For the first time, a shade of annoyance colored his voice. "My concerns," he said, gesturing at the gray sky past the window and the valley below that sky, "lie with those entrusted into my care. With their immortal souls, certainly. But also with the injustice that is done to them. Of course, I am aware of the report that this general of yours was killed nearby. Upon the road to Minersville, I believe. And, yes, I am aware that Boland, perhaps in his cups, claimed he had done the crime. He was an unsettled young man, unhappy, I think. But I cannot believe him a murderer." He sighed, a schoolmaster despairing of his pupil. "Be that as it may, I will not have the Irish blamed *en masse,* sir. That would be no law, and certainly no justice. Furthermore, I have a serious concern about the incidence of cholera in this village. Unearthing an infected corpse may have deadly consequences."

"Consequences there may be, but I do not think they will arise from cholera, Father Wilde. And I do not believe that you believe it, either."

"That, sir, is rude."

"A girl is dead. Murdered. Weeks, perhaps months ago. Do you not find that rude?"

"Such a loss would, of course, be unfortunate. Especially

if the poor thing died without receiving the sacraments. But I have no intelligence of a murdered girl."

"But that you do, Father Wilde. From me. *She* was in that coffin, not Daniel Boland. Who likely is in Canada by now."

"Daniel Boland is dead of cholera morbus. I know nothing of this girl of whom you speak." The ghost of a smile crossed his lips. Thin lips they were, in a handsome face whose bones looked made of glass. Waiting for life to shatter them. "But do I see it now, Major Jones? By your own admission, you have yourself interfered with the sanctity of the grave. Might I not suspect that the government, wishing a pretext to send troops among the Irish, removed Boland's body and placed a young girl's corpse in his coffin? To sow confusion and alarm?" That white hair might have been the emblem of the coldness in his soul. "After all, *you* were the last one to have knowledge of the contents of the coffin. By your own admission, I must repeat. You may have a writ today, but did you have a writ to violate that grave two nights ago?"

"I had the authority. And you will not—"

"But *what* authority? *Whose* authority? I will not see these people abused, Major Jones. I simply will not have it. I shall protest the matter to the diocese and, if necessary, to Bishop Wood himself. Know-nothingism abounds in the county seat, and in the state capital, as well. Let us not pretend otherwise. I find your commercial interests fond of damning the Irish, even as they exploit their labor. And the government in Washington may welcome them for its war, but will not put fair value on their work. It hardly seems a model of Christian fellowship—isn't that what Protestants proclaim? Fellowship and brotherly love?"

Smug he was, and a great surprise to me with his debating-club twists and turns, a smooth fellow in a place that was all roughness. I had known priests in India, where the Irish died in droves from drink and the heat. The most seemed decent fellows, if benighted. They might dissemble sobriety, but they did not lie about murder. And harder they were on a wastrel than was our colonel. I encountered a fierce, brute fellow up in the wilds of New York, whose faith burned in him. He, too, championed his Irish, but in the rough accents of Mayo, not in the fancy-dress speech of the university.

"Father Wilde, you are an educated man and—"

"Shall that be held against me? Are you one of those who would prefer that Catholic priests be ignorant and rough, Major Jones? To keep the Irish downtrodden and illiterate?"

"That is not what I meant to say."

"But it is what I think, you see."

"Then you would be wrong," I told him bluntly, although I am most respectful even of Musselman and Hindoo holy fellows. "You are quick of wit, while I am not. But I will see this matter through to the end. And if you will oppose the law, Father Wilde, you will find that the law will oppose you in return. Even your holy office will not shield you."

"Ah, a threat! That is unbecoming of you."

"No. It is not a threat. Two are dead. And if the deed was done by Patrick Boland, he will be found out. If by another, then I will find him. And nothing will stop me, see."

"That does sound rather like the sin of pride. One of the major sins, you know. Even for Protestants."

I was deep in frustration and trying to keep my temper, which has not always been the best of friends to me. So bedeviled I was that I had to look away from the fellow. My eyes were not focused, but they happened to point in the direction of a portrait hanging from a bookcase.

He mistook my gaze.

"My sister. Lady Caroline Wilde-Dudley. Not much of a resemblance, I'm afraid. Do you smoke?"

"Smoke I do not. And I will not change the subject."

"And you *will* dig up that grave. I know, I know. All that famous Welsh tenacity . . ." He set to preparing himself a pipe. Then he stopped, the instant he realized his hands were shaking. He looked up at once, eyes asking if I had noticed.

I looked away, as if I had seen naught.

He shifted to put his back to me, then returned to filling his pipe. "You must try to understand my position," he said to the bookcases and, secondarily, to me. "I petitioned to come to a parish of this sort, you know. Irish miners. Their families. I have made it my personal care to assist them, as they accustom themselves to their new homeland." Of a sudden, he turned back to face me. "Oh, nothing romantic about it. No longing for martyrdom in the cookpot. Not that sort of thing at all. But aren't *they* the poor, who are beloved of God? The poor for whom Jesus Christ had infinite mercy? The poor whom we are called to love as our brothers?" He shook his head. "Dig up their graves? Worst thing you could do."

He sat down across from me and made to light his pipe with a wooden match. For a moment, he remained quiet, concentrating on steadying his hands. I smelled the instant sweetness of fired tobacco.

"They are devout in their faith," he resumed. "But I'm afraid their faith is impure. Oh, they believe in the Church, certainly. But half of them still believe in fairies, as well. They cling to the past, to spells instead of medicines. These people need education, not threats. Honest wages, not maltreatment. They must be led into the modern world."

He puffed, looking down at the bowl of his pipe, then lifted his eyes to me. "It would be all too convenient to accept their devotions, while ignoring the heathen practices that persist among them. But I, for one, believe that we who have given our lives to the service of Our Lord Jesus Christ must not abandon them to their ignorance. Modern faith is not about bogeymen and pitchforks, after all, but about the challenge of living a life that is pleasing in the eyes of God. And I should not think Him pleased by charms and incantations."

Father Wilde feinted a smile. "Many of my fellow seminarians would disagree, Major Jones, but I am not convinced that the faith of the fool is a worthy faith. Nor am I convinced that ceremony without understanding is a valid form of devotion. You will find I differ with Cardinal Newman's approach to the times as much as I do with your Dr. Pusey's. Why, I've always felt rather sorry for the hounding that sort gave poor, old Colenso. I do believe the fellow meant well. Although I would not defend his mathematics. But you see, I'm hardly the Ultramontane sort your people prefer in a Catholic priest. Don't you agree, after all, that Protestants rather enjoy a close-minded priest to whom they may condescend, but won't quite like a fellow who believes God gave us brains so that we might exercise them? I prefer a thoughtful devotion, if you will."

At last he managed a smile of some authenticity. "These are challenging days for us Catholics, but days of great spiritual renewal, as well. Especially, in the English-speaking lands. Newman has done us well, in that respect. He simply feels the diffidence before God of the newly converted. Rigor answers his doubts."

Like you, I knew the name of Cardinal Newman. A fellow who left the Church of England, where the incense was not thick enough for his nostrils. He led young men astray who were confounded by the pain of modern times. But let that bide.

"You will do your flock no good by hiding a murder," I told the priest. "Or two murders."

"And do *you* mean to do them good, Major Jones?"

A colliery whistle blew, shrill enough to pierce the

deepest grave. Twas not the hour for such a blowing. But I knew what it meant. Our period of uninterrupted digging was done. We had been noticed by someone in the valley.

I rose to my feet. For I was not confident the shabby fellows we had hired for the digging, or even the deputies placed over them, would stand up well against an Irish mob. They would need spine.

I looked down at the priest, who puffed his pipe and did not think to rise.

"Where will I find Mrs. Boland?" I asked him. "When the fuss is done, I want to talk to her."

"I'm afraid you shan't be able to do that."

"Why not?"

"She's disappeared. Hasn't been seen since her husband died." He gestured, lightly, toward the woods with his pipe. "We're all very concerned about her. An unusual person, you know. Odd habits. One of those of whom I spoke, the sort who cling to the old, rural beliefs opposed by the Church."

"You mean she's mad?"

"I shouldn't think so. Upset, of course. Show me the wife who wouldn't be. No, my concern is that the poor woman's run off in her grief and might come to harm. Personally, I rather fear she took the cholera from her husband. She may be lying dead out in the forest."

"She is not dead. I saw her."

For the first time, his composure failed him utterly. He reconquered himself with the swiftness of an Alexander, but not before a blush had spoiled his cheek.

"Oh? Where was that?" His voice had an unmistakable quiver in it. He stabbed his pipe back into his mouth, lips thinned to disappearing.

"Not a hundred yards from this house. In the night."

He had to remove the pipe from his lips again, if only to stop it from shaking.

EVERY MINER was sullen as a Herod. A hundred of them there were, both men skilled in the ways of the pit and laborers whose tools were picks and shovels. Black-faced and black-handed, with all the color stolen from their clothes, they stood beneath a washwater sky and muttered. They reminded me of Afghanees from the hills, gathered to resist a foreign intruder. Such men never think outsiders good.

Their wives and children, gray the lot of them, stood by. When the colliery whistle blew, the miners had come up from their gangways and galleries to join the lesser men who worked the yards, marching all together through the patch of company shanties, collecting their families, and trudging on up to the graveyard. Quiet as death they come, and hard-faced. Some were black as minstrels in a show, with white eyes, while others—the men who tended the mules or machinery—were but smudged in comparison. Breaker boys with hands cut raw stood in little bands, defiant of all authority in that hour, and yearning for the excitement of disaster. The great pack of them gathered just beyond the piled-stone wall that separated their dead from the rest of the world.

We were encircled.

My hired navvies dug and did not talk. They would not even glance up at the mob. The deputies, unwilling to a man, looked at their boots or made excuses to move closer to the horses. Only our teamster, perched upon his wagon, looked as though the world was as it should be, no better and no worse. He watched us all, with an expression more of apathy than alarm.

As for my Christian self, I would not be daunted. A murmured threat is a cowardly thing, and a grim-set face is often

an empty dare. A few of the Irish carried pick handles or
sticks, but they looked more troubled than confident to me.
And duty must be done, no matter the cost. I met the eyes
that searched me out from the tattered ranks of the crowd,
returning every gaze until it weakened.

I knew those faces. I am not so hard as that white-haired
priest would have me, and I know the Irish are human, if
truculent and wanting a proper scrub. I do not mean to suggest the least indulgence. I am no friend to tumult and disorder. I know full well the Irish tend to vice, nor would I
wish such neighbors for my family. But I wished the Irish
no harm.

Their leanness and their rags make me uneasy, see.
Speaking as a Christian, who has read his Bible through, and
more than once. Simple enough it is to condemn, when a fellow knows his belly will be filled. We overlook our brother's
plight, so long as we may banish him from view. The priest
was right about that much. Those miners and their families,
pale to a wasting and coughing in the cold, might have liked
to hang me from a tree. Yet, I could not hate them any more
than fear them. The Irish are a burden we must shoulder, although you will agree they must behave.

I think my true emotion was "embarrassment" that day.
Although I cannot explain the reason why. My thoughts
were as confused as when I make an effort to read in Mr.
Emerson, whose genius lies beyond my comprehension.

Oh, the Irish.

I thought of the green flag of their volunteers, climbing
the slope across Antietam Creek. Those men fought for our
Union like maddened tigers, peerless in the extravagance of
their courage. Yet, they did not shout for Lincoln and liberty. They rushed forward with cries of "Fontenoy!" and "*Erin
go brach!*" As if the Rebels wore coats of red, not gray. As
if the Irish cared naught for the names of countries or the

passage of centuries, but only for wreaking vengeance for old wrongs.

Whatever their flaws, those men were brave to a folly.

The Irish at home stood hard against the war, unlike their brethren under General Meagher. Quick with their hatreds, those miners knew only that everyone wished them ill who did not share the sorrows of the Gael. I might have been a Chinaman, for all the human brotherhood they saw in me.

Twas in Black '47 and thereafter that England let them starve to death on the roads and watched their children die at the poor-house gates, while grain ships left the Liffey and the Shannon, brimming full to enrich Britannia's merchants. Parliament denied there was a problem, for many of its members were absentee landlords who found the Irish tenant an inconvenience. Millions died of neglect and blackened potatoes.

Some claim that half the population died. Of course, the Irish are given to exaggeration. But the landlords stayed in London, or idled in the country homes of their kind, far from the typhus, hunger and foreclosures. They let the Irish die and called it virtue, arguing that the poor must not be indulged. The blight upon their praties struck the Irish like the plagues of Egypt. It set the living to wander the great, wide world. And bitter they went.

I met them first in India. They came to fight and drink their soldiers' pay, sweating in scarlet coats that smelled of voyages. They were savage with the Hindoo and the Seekh, as if those brown men had been Cromwell's own. No soldiers were as careless of their lives as were the Irish, and their battle cries cut deep as bayonets. The niggers feared them worse than grape and canister. Yet, in the barracks the Irish were shiftless and docile, and had to be forced to their tasks by corporals and sergeants. Lions in their cups, they were meek in the morning, and most of their ailments were

cured by a stint in the lock-house. They would have swallowed gin in the heathen sun, at noon, if we had let them.
They sang, and cursed, and wept like little children. Laugh
they would at a comrade's grisly death, only to bawl and cry
as they reminisced. In garrison, they were troublesome and
untidy, but no man stood more stalwart in a fight. They
feared their priests, held grudges, and told lies.

I had an Irish soldier whom I liked, young Jimmy Molloy,
with whom you have made acquaintance. But he went
wrong and spoiled his life for a trifle. Twas only his luck and
a passage to America that gave him a second chance and set
him up proper.

Well, all of that was far away in India, where different
rules apply and character fails us. Now I stood in the stub-
ble of a graveyard, above the elms and below the silver
birches, in the autumn chill that pricks.

I marked a well-hewn Irishman who stood out from the
rest, as some men do. Black as polished coal he seemed, although his flesh was white as mine or yours. He did not have
the smeared face of a miner—not that day—but wore a
beard like a pirate's in a book. Handsome in a stern and
manly fashion, he looked as if his mouth had never smiled.
At first, I thought him in the prime of life, perhaps of mine
own age of thirty-four, but beards deceive. At a second
glance I judged him ten years younger. What he possessed
was that special thing for which we lack a word, but which
sets a man apart as born to lead, despite his age or family an-
tecedents. He did not give commands or say one word. Yet,
I sensed that men would follow him into peril.

I would not have chosen that fellow for mine enemy.

My navvies dug slowly and should have been finished
long since, given that the grave had been turned time and
again. Part of their slowness was fear and sloth, but part
come of their payment by the hour. Hired from the waster

class of Pottsville, they were men of the streets, whose appetites killed pride. We had brought them in a wagon, under guard. For many's the man will accept a task, only to change his mind as the work approaches.

The guards themselves, a dull confusion of deputies, fingered ill-kept Colts and looked all nerves. They thinned ranks without permission, until only a sturdy pair were left beside me, while the others stood ready to flee, over by the horses. I meant to do all I could to avoid a fight, because I knew a fight would bring no good, but also because I did not trust my men. A coward with a pistol is no match for a man of courage with his fists. And I did not believe the Irish were afraid of us.

They let us dig, the Irish did. Watching all the while. Somber as Pushtoons lurking in the Khyber. Even the children kept their peace, but their eyes were avid and anxious, for they had caught the spirit from their parents. The wind pulled hair from shawls, blew shawls from shoulders. And a great, swollen miner's paw would catch the fabric, replacing it on a slump-shouldered wife with a delicacy that would have shamed a lacemaker. Great ones for the family they are, the Irish. Although not half so responsible as the Welsh. For the Irish love and squander, as if they think tomorrow is a myth, while the Welshman saves, and mends, and minds his business.

The wind keened. Its force drove copper leaves across the hillside. Overhead, the clouds were dark and slack-bellied, and the air moistened our faces. All smelled of earth and rot and approaching rain.

Father Wilde come down at last, with his skirts blowing black behind him and a little cap clutched to his head. The Irish marked his appearance and kept their distance. Yet, somehow, they paid him less deference than I expected. As if he were a player unsuited to the day's match. He took his stance apart from the pack and folded his arms over his chest, reaching up now and then to secure his cap. He wore that expression which priests and such are taught for times when the world is not to rights. Impassive to a blankness he was.

I could not see his eyes from where I stood.

One more fellow joined us for the finale. A gentleman in a long, brown coat come stumbling up the hill, his anxiety too urgent for his legs. As he rushed up I saw the look of a man who was frightened every day of his life, the face of a man born to be blamed for the heedlessness of others. He wore a Derby hat that tempted the wind, and when he reached to snatch it back he showed the world the bald crown of his head.

I decided the fellow must be Mr. Oliver, the superintendent of the works, to whom young Boland had confessed his crime. I had not had time to visit him before we began our digging, since calling on the priest seemed more important, given the power such folk hold over the Irish. But I had meant to call on him when we finished.

His aspect matched the report that I possessed of him. When Daniel Boland approached him, wild with the need to confess his crime, Mr. Oliver had done his best to avoid the business, putting young Boland off as best he could. As the superintendent of the mines and the colliery, Mr. Oliver bore the responsibility for good order and obedience to the law. But he had gone down to Minersville to see the magistrate only under protest, after the Irish had pressed him to it and given their promise that he would not be slain for his troubles.

Curious, how the killer had been so anxious to confess, and how his countrymen had so urged Oliver to report the confession—if the tale I had been told was correct in its facts. Of course, a general's murder was a dreadful deed

and it might have been that the Irish feared the draft would
be imposed with bayonets in retaliation. Perhaps young
Boland truly was the murderer and the actions of the Irish
common sense. But the entire affair smacked of a scheme
to me, with Boland the sacrificial lamb who was not quite
sacrificed in the end. Perhaps he had done the crime and the
Irish had pressed him to confess as the price for helping
him escape thereafter. But why had the priest abetted them,
pledging his word that Boland had been "taken by the
cholera," before the law could make itself felt from
Pottsville—which was not ten miles away? Was Father
Wilde such a champion of the Irish? Or was there more to
his doings than he suggested?

And why were so many educated men in Pottsville willing to credit the story just as presented? Who was the girl in
the coffin? Who put her in the grave while Boland ran?
Again, the role of the priest suggested collusion. And why
had the general been murdered in the first place, when all
that he had sought were volunteers? Had the Irish thought it
a ruse and believed him a spy, come to collect information
for the draft? Why had Mr. Lincoln and Mr. Nicolay been so
reticent?

And where was Mrs. Boland this fine day? The woman
who had run away, only to appear to me by the graveside in
the night? The woman the priest said clung to the old, pagan
ways of Erin's past? The woman of whom he seemed to be
afraid?

I did not know where the trails would lead, but I did not
think our journey would end nicely.

Puffing from his haste, the bald man in the long, brown
coat approached me, drawn, no doubt, by my uniform,
which was the only Union blue in evidence. He did not
speak until he stood spit-close. And then he kept on glancing at the Irish. As they watched the two of us.

"Good God, what are you doing? Good Lord, what's going on?"

"I am Major Abel Jones," I said, by way of introduction, holding out my hand, which he ignored. "And what is being done is plain to see."

"You can't dig up that grave."

"Not that one, but another, then?"

"You can't dig up *any* grave." He cast another fearful look at the Irish. His voice was that of a native-born American, but he had the ill-nourished look of a Manchester man.

"I have a writ from the district attorney, and papers from a judge," I told him.

"That's not what I mean. I don't care about your legal papers." The wind snatched at his hat and he barely caught it. Despite the cold, his scalp shone bright with sweat. "Look what you've done here, man! Everybody knows how these people are about their dead. You've gone and shut down the mine and the colliery both. They didn't even leave a man on the pumps. The shaft's going to flood. There's going to be Hell to pay."

"And you would be Mr. Oliver, the superintendent of these works, I take it?"

"My name's Oliver, all right. But that doesn't matter one bit." His eyes were as unsteady as his nerves, and his skin was colorless. Convinced I was that his line come out of Manchester, for such have a pinched and nasty and nervous look. "What matters is that you've shut everything down. We're losing money by the minute, hand over fist. Mr. Heckscher's just going to have himself a fit."

I sneaked a look up at the priest. His interests lay elsewhere, confirming my judgement that Mr. Oliver was not viewed as a serious fellow. He might have approved their pay slips, but he did not rule the Irish or their lives.

"Well, I am sorry for the loss to your business," I told him. "But the law must have its way, and there is true."

He drew himself up, as if he meant to threaten. Perhaps he thought I might be made to fear him, since, slight though he was, he stood the taller of us.

Ah, if size were all that mattered to mortal strength, elephants would rule over the world.

"Well, you're on company property," he declared, most rude and abrupt.

"Company property is it? The boneyard? And the church, too?"

"It all belongs to the company."

"And the bodies?"

"This parcel of land has been lent to their church in sufferance." He fired off the last word like a cannon. "As a matter of Mr. Heckscher's generosity."

I sighed. "Mr. Oliver, there have been two murders here. I do not think your company stands above the law where such crimes are concerned."

"*Two?* Hold on there. Nobody's said anything about two murders. Who said any such thing?"

"Wait, then, and you will see."

He chewed his lip and tried me a final time. "You're trespassing on private property. You've interfered with the pursuit of honest business. You—"

"I do not think I have interrupted your work, Mr. Oliver. It seems to me your miners did that themselves."

"And they'll pay for it. It'll all come out of their wages, don't think it won't. And don't think they won't hear about this in Pottsville."

Twas then I heard a too-familiar sound. Of an iron shovel striking wood gone damp.

The digging stopped. The whispers of the crowd swelled to a warning.

I excused myself from Mr. Oliver and strode to where the navvies had paused in their labors. They stared up at me in that special terror of drunkards deprived of liquor. When Temperance comes by law, as it surely will, such fellows will be spared their lives of misery.

"Keep to your work, like honest men," I told them. Although not one looked an honest man to me. A black-toothed, black-hearted lot they were, and ashamed I am to say one fellow was Welsh. But even we are not a perfect race.

The deputies looked more fearful than the navvies. As if the Irish had the law and the pistols, and we were in the wrong and weak besides.

Well, weak we were. But at such times a fellow must not flinch. For men smell fear as wild animals do.

"Take yerselves off, ye darty English bastards," a first voice called.

"The little one there in the soldier suit's a Taffy. That little sod in nigger-lover blue."

"Lord Kiss-me-arse, that's what I'd call the likes o' that one there."

"'Tis na wonder they're calling their terry-bull draft down upon us," a whisky-ravaged grampus declaimed, "for if their Lincoln's brought down to recruitin' crippled dwarves, the Rebels will all go marching high into Canadee."

Laugh they did, as nasty children will. And then that black-bearded fellow stepped to the fore, the young one who drew the eye. Trouble now, I thought to myself. But he only glared about him, with lips still frozen hard and eyes of fire. He hardly made a gesture beyond the turning of his head.

The crowd quieted. And the black-bearded man faded into it again.

I looked to the priest and saw that he had been watching the business, too. With a face that said Old Rome was on its guard, and not only against Welshmen.

I realized the priest had decided to let me learn my lesson. But I was not yet certain what the lesson would be.

I had the navvies heave up the coffin and slide it onto a bed of leaves and grass. Twas a struggle for them, for their bodies had been poisoned by liquor and were not worth their wages. But I wanted the coffin up above ground. I did not want the poor fellows trapped in the hole, if the Irish took a mind to interfere. And I thought I would let the miners see my purpose. Let them feel the shame of a young girl's murder. Let them explain such doings, if they could.

I felt a surge of anger toward the priest. No man of the cloth should have had his hand in such matters. He should have taken his stand on the side of the law.

The coffin come up in tatters, with the lid barely fixed to the sides. But I marked that it had been nailed shut, a thing my invalid soldiers and I had not been able to do. Of course, we had been forced by Mrs. Boland's cries to leave without filling in the grave, and the Irish had been confronted with our doings. They were the ones who closed the box again, the men who knew full well of the murdered girl. I wondered how many of those in the crowd had blood and guilt on their hands.

To be honest, the box looked a ruin. Many's the woman who gasped at the battered sight of it.

Something was wrong. I realized that much in a moment. And a brace of seconds later I knew what it was.

With the coffin split and splintered, the navvies should have been gasping at the stench. But there had been no change in their postures of defeat, not even a grimace beyond those already settled over their faces.

I forgot all else and rushed toward the coffin, grasping a pick from a workman on my way. I went at the lid with something near to a rage, for I already understood what they had done.

Although I did not understand it precisely. Not yet.

Lord, I was a fool, though. I should have seen it clearly. Otherwise, they would not have let the digging proceed.

The top of the box come off with a creak and a crack.

All I found inside was a strangled cat.

The lot of them, the wicked heathen lot of them, exploded into mirth, as if Christmas had come early. Oh, they laughed. And snickered. And called me names, not least "the King of the Pussies," as well as things that I dare not repeat. Someone even lurched up with a squeezebox, and the sorry lot of them began to jig.

They swarmed in over the wall, onto the holy ground. Dancing on the graves, they were. One bow-legged paddy, with a face as round as the moon, took up the cat and swung it over his head. He kicked up his legs and howled and grinned, with teeth as black as fresh-dug anthracite.

A brazen girl come skipping past me, dancing by herself, with her hands on her hips and an insolent grin on her face. Of a sudden, she hiked up her skirts to her knees, then dropped them again. "And that's as close as ever ye'll get to it," she told me. Other girls, less bold, laughed at me, too.

They laughed and laughed.

Their revelry did not last. The priest come down the slope and put a stop to it. He strode in among them, his cassock a magical armor, calling, "*Stop it*, stop it this minute. Stop it, all of you."

His voice was not all fineness now, but fired by earnest anger. He saw that things had gone too far, and knew their mockeries only spread their guilt.

Now, I know where to look, even when a battle has grown desperate. It is a gift. And I looked for that young, black-bearded man who ruled them with a grimace. But he had sneaked off, leaving the mob to the priest.

"Go home! All of you go home. *Now!*" Father Wilde commanded them. He raised one hand, in a gesture of anathema.

And the Irish obeyed, for his tone was of the pulpit. "Get along with you. Go on . . ."

Go they did, slumped things, as we imagine lepers in the Bible. A few of the men paused defiantly, but their wives tugged them along. And the children seemed shrunken and crushed by their disappointment, for they had expected more violence and revelry, although I doubted a single one could say why.

The only remaining laughter come from the deputies and drunkards in my service, and from the superintendent, Mr. Oliver. All laughing at me they were.

Well, let them laugh, I thought. For I had been the butt of jokes before, and still come right in the end. I would see this through, and there would be more than strangled cats at the end of it.

Oh, I was sore. There is the truth of it.

I started in to barking, like the sergeant I had been in my India days, and got them in the wagon and onto their horses. Ready enough they were to go, and Oliver hurried off. But I was scorched with rue.

I could not leave until I had a last, bitter look at the coffin. Twas but a thing of splinters and raw boards. Emptied, stripped of death. And scrubbed clean of the dead girl's waste and ruin. A nasty job that must have been.

I do not like to be shamed. I have my pride. The priest was right about that. I could not think clearly for the heat behind my forehead. I know a good soldier does not abandon the field to the enemy at the battle's first crisis, but I did not see what step I might take next.

I sensed him and turned. The priest, I mean. He had taken off his little hat and the wind lofted his white hair.

"You knew," I said. "You knew the box was empty."

At first I thought he would not answer me. Then he said, "Graves are best left alone. I told you that."

"No matter what is in them? Should there be no justice, then, but only . . . only . . ."

"True justice may be a separate thing from the law," he said.

I looked at him. Angry as a disappointed child, I was. But the chill of the day and the wind stole the heat from my voice. "In Heaven, perhaps. But here on earth there is the law of men. And the law must be satisfied."

"Even if the law is unjust?"

"The law is not unjust."

"Isn't it? And what about the men who impose it? Are they just and impartial?"

I saw that he would argue on forever, reducing evil to a lightness of language. I lacked the cleverness men such as he acquire from books and classrooms. For all my lamplit reading, I could not match his speech. But I could not let the matter go, despite myself.

"And the girl?" I asked him. "The dead girl? Whose body is taken off to the Good Lord knows where? Has she had justice, then?"

"I told you I know nothing about a girl."

"And Boland? Where's his body, then? The body you swore was rotten with the cholera?"

"I did not swear. Priests don't, you know. As for Boland's body, did you take it? The other night? You really should return it, you know. If only out of common decency."

I did not think the fellow much of a churchman, with his smugness and dissembling. I thought he belonged in the common room of a club, with younger sons gone bad, not in a Christian church. Not even a Catholic one.

I had no inkling of it that day, but I faced a desperate man. Whose shame was so great even God must have turned away from him. That day he was my master, the father confessor too proud to confess. He was no murderer, that I do not mean. But I am not certain his crime was not the worse.

I must not go too quickly.

That day the priest nearly brought me to tears of rage. I fear I might have struck him, had he stood closer.

"And you do not care who is guilty, then?" I asked him, my voice a weakened thing.

"I care for repentence. If even a murderer repents, he may be forgiven. Through God's Grace."

"Any crime may be forgiven, then? Any sin?"

"Even Protestants believe that. Don't they?"

I chuckled to myself, the peculiar way we do when we are broken in a fray. It is a form of laughter next to heartbreak. I had come to the end of my words.

Father Wilde looked at me with eyes as fierce as the sky, which had grown darker still, with running clouds.

"What do you know about guilt?" he said. He said it low, almost to himself.

Queer it was. I could not answer the fellow. Although I know as much of guilt as any man ever should.

He had no more spite to offer me. Yet, we could not take our leaves of one another. Something held us fixed to the boneyard earth. As if we both already saw that our fates had grown together like wild vines. I think we hated each other in that moment.

Down the slope, my companions of the day pronounced their restlessness, passing their impatience along to their horses. A blown leaf scratched the scar on my cheek, pursued by a scouting raindrop.

Abruptly, Father Wilde turned to go. And in that instant I found my voice again. I called to him, as his flapping cassock caught on a wooden cross.

He freed himself and swept round to me again. With mad rage on his face. As if he had let go of himself the moment he turned away.

"The young man who concerned you?" I called. "The one

with the black beard? The one they all looked to? What was his name?"

He opened his mouth and I sensed what he would say. He was about to tell me he did not know the person of whom I spoke. But then he stopped, thought hard, and changed his mind. Although I could not say why.

"Doubtless, you mean Kehoe. John Kehoe. A Wicklow man. Not of this parish."

"You know him, though?"

Face as cold as the day, he shook his head. "They call him 'Black Jack,' for what that may be worth to you." He looked at me with a strange light in his eyes. "As for knowing him . . . I'm not certain the fellow knows himself. Something of a rabble-rouser, I don't doubt."

"And where might I find Mr. Kehoe from County Wicklow? If I wished to set a question or two before him?"

This time, a pair of raindrops struck my face.

"He's not of St. Kiaran's," the priest said. "I believe he makes his home somewhere east of Pottsville. To the extent Kehoe has a home. He's something of a rover. Always calling around on Irish business. That's all I can tell you."

He turned toward his parish house again.

I rushed up behind him, unwilling to let him go, now that he had told me at least one thing. The slope and the change in the weather gave my leg a nasty time. Strange it was, for my leg had grown much stronger. Twas as if my body sought to warn me, to tell me I should leave well enough alone.

The priest strode up the hill, determined to leave me behind him, and good riddance.

I stopped at a stab of pain and shouted after him. "And Mrs. Boland? What about her, Father Wilde?"

When he turned that final time, he had mastered his features, becoming again a priest and not a man.

"I pray for her each day," he said. The wind was such I had to strain to hear him. "As I will pray for you, my son."

And he showed me his back with a firmness beyond dispute. Stalking up the hill he went, toward his church and the ramshackle house full of books that sat beside it.

He left me alone on the hillside. The rain come up, and I turned me down toward the fidgeting deputies. On my way, I nearly stepped on the dead cat. Twas orange, as I recall.

five

"*N*EVER SEEN NOTHING LIKE IT. Nope, I ain't. Way they cut that feller's heart clean out."

The speaker was one Mr. Lennie Downs, a teamster who drew on the county payroll and whose fingers had an affinity for his nose. The rain fell in veils and curtains as the afternoon yearned toward evening. I shared the driver's bench at the front of the wagon, while the navvies huddled, wet to the bone, in the open bed behind us. Protected by India-rubber capes, the deputies slumped on their horses. Mr. Downs had been speaking without pause, even as his fingers conducted their meaty investigations of his nasal passages. It is a nasty habit. He was undeterred by the downpour that come over us and delighted by the doings back in Heckschersville. For Mr. Downs was a man who liked to talk, and now he had a fine, new tale to tell.

I feared I would be mocked back home in Pottsville.

Tucked into my cape, but sodden little the less, I had lent the teamster only half an ear. Most of what Mr. Downs recited was gossip or common complaints about the Irish miners. But when he spoke of a heart cut out, I leaned over toward him, struggling to hear clearly through the rain.

"What did you say, Mr. Downs? About a cutting up?"

He used his free hand to jick the reins and urge the mules along, for they were not enamored of our climb. We had taken the high road known as the Thomaston Turnpike, a muddy, rutted track no longer used for haulage. The coming of the railway spur had robbed the pike of its purpose, and now it was only a short way down to Minersville for those who could afford to risk an axle. We passed between the remaining trees and gashes where the coal had been stripped from outcroppings in the hillside. Our climb was slow and miserable, and the closer we got to the summit, the less inclined the mules were to cooperate. They shied, as animals do when they grow wary.

"Just saying as how I ain't seen nothing like it. No, sir. They didn't just kill that there general feller. Chopped him up between the teats like he was beef for a stew. Yes, sir. Just like beef for a stew. Wasn't that feller just a sight to see! They cut him up like he swallied a goldpiece and they went to looking for it smack in the middle of his chest. Yes, sir. They hollowed him out like a bowl."

"Who told you this, Mr. Downs?" A trickle of water had found the nape of my neck, which did not improve my spirits.

"Tole me? Nobody tole me, Major. I *seen* it. Yes, sir. Seen it myself. Who do you think come out to pick that feller up off the ground? Wouldn't no Irish touch him, not likely. Constable puked every time he looked under the blanket. No, sir. Me and my mules and my wagon. That's who come out to pick him up off the ground. Lying just up there, atop the hill. Mr. Gowen's orders."

"Mr. Gowen?"

"Yes, sir. You know Mr. Gowen, don't you? New district attorney. Fat, handsome young feller. Say he's going places. Tole me to go out and bring the general in."

"And where do you mean by 'just up there,' Mr. Downs?

"Straight on ahead there. Can't see yet, for the rain. That's where they found him. Yes, sir. Raccoons or what have you got at him first. Made a terrible mess in my wagon. He was just atop the hill, there at the crossroads."

Of a sudden, I shivered, although my thoughts were a nonsense. Perhaps it was the rain upon my neck. Or the gloom of the dying day. But I will tell you a thing, and hope you will not laugh at Welsh beliefs—not that I hold to any superstition. I merely report, as is the chronicler's duty. Look you. If you go to Wales, in all her awful beauty, you will not find a crossroads atop a hill. At least not often. Not if the roads were laid in Christian times. For when two roads meet and cross atop a hill or on a mountain, that makes a devil's cross, where witches gather to call upon Old Night. Not that I credit the existence of witches and such like. And not that I believe un-Christian things.

Perhaps it was but the haunts of childhood returned to me. The Reverend Mr. Griffiths, my guardian for a time, found it a joy to lock me in the cellar, and I was afraid of the dark as a little boy. He made noises at me and spoke through the door of ghosts. A vicar of the Established Church, he taught me of the Martyrs with his strap. But I must not be too hard, for he was a troubled man, and disappointed. He was the father of my darling wife, to whom his demeanor was ever generous and kind. A very model of a parent he was to Mary. But I was the son of the woman he wished to love, see, the one who would not have him, who chose a chapel preacher in his stead. In the years before the cholera come among us.

The Reverend Mr. Griffiths never liked me, but he took me in, and that is something worthy of a Christian. But I recall my terrors in that cellar. The Merthyr rats were real, but it was the unseen things that made me cry. I begged Mr. Griffiths to let me out of that place, as I have never begged another man.

The old fears linger in our adult hearts.

"There. See? Just up there." Mr. Downs separated his hand from its intimate endeavors to point beyond a deputy's rain-slicked horse. "Just atop the hill, where it's all bare. That's where they massacred the poor feller. Dead as Julius Caesar, that boy was. Yes, sir! Dead as John the Baptist, rest his soul. Had to scoop the half of him up with a shovel. With his face all still, like he was just sleeping one off. And do you know just how damnation stupid them Irish are? Cut him all up for plain meanness, then forgot to take the feller's money out of his pockets. Now what's the sense in that? No, sir. Hang a dozen Irishmen, and the rest'll straighten up quick enough, I'll tell you. That's what Lennie Downs has got to say. Get on, now, mules. Get on."

The crest was a swamp of mud, yet I was relieved. For all my childish fears had been but foolishness. There was no crossroads atop that hill, but only a fork in the way, which has no meaning in the old tales. A rough track led into rain-swept trees. We passed it by, remaining on the turnpike.

I chastised myself for my silliness. But that was just the start of my realizations. I saw at once that I had shown no fortitude, but had let myself be quashed by the corpse of a cat. The miners would likely be having the laugh of their lives, enjoying their beer and their whisky. They had made a fool of me and my authority. But worse, I had let them do it.

I like to think that I do not lack courage. But I had run away like a little boy.

"Stop the wagon, if you please. Let me down now, and thank you."

"Yes, sir. Yes, indeed-ee. I need to empty some water myself about now."

"That is not what I meant, see. I am going back to Heckschersville. For there is a business I have left unfinished."

"You're going back there? Alone? Christ awmighty!"

"No harm will come to me, Mr. Downs. But call for me in your wagon in the morning, or send another. I believe there is a hotel or such in the town. Apply for me there."

"There's two of them Irish flea-pits. But you don't want to stay up there in Heckschersville, Major. They don't like Welshies, and they don't like soldiers, neither. To tell the truth, they didn't seem to like you much at all."

"Being liked is not my purpose, Mr. Downs."

I got me down from the perch, which was a trick. For though I am most capable, I must be wary of my bothered leg.

A deputy's horse loped up beside the wagon, almost nudging me. I do not like horses, you understand. I have ridden upon their backs, when such was a necessity, but a donkey was sufficient for Our Savior, and a good pair of boots is quite enough for me.

"Major says he's going back to Heckschersville," Mr. Downs called to the moderately curious deputy. "Tole him that weren't smart."

Streaked with rain and anxious for his hearth, the deputy leaned down toward me. "I wouldn't do that, now," he told me frankly. "That's one bad idea, if you don't mind me saying so." He looked at Mr. Downs, then back at me—doubtless wondering if he would be held responsible for my straying from the fold. "Don't mind me asking, why would a body do a thing like that?"

It was a reasonable question, I suppose. But I was not inclined to explain my decision.

Perhaps I knew how foolish it was myself.

"Go on with you now," I told them. "For it is no good standing in the rain. And tell Mrs. Jones that I am well and will return tomorrow."

"Want my horse, Major? She'll go, if she has to."

"I will walk, thank you."

The deputy looked down at my leg and cane.

"I will walk," I repeated. "Now get you home." I turned to Mr. Downs. "Do not forget to send a wagon or such in the morning."

And they obeyed me. But as they left, I heard the teamster muttering. Perhaps he spoke intending I should hear.

"I tole the damn fool, Ab, and you heard me when I tole him. Welsh don't have a lick of sense, if it ain't to do with money or singing hymns. Get on, mules. After I come out for that general feller, I had to sweep my wagon down with quicklime. Get on, now."

GLAD I WAS that I wore good boots, not shoes. For the mud had such a great suck to it that I think it would have liked to steal my legs. I recall hoping that my other uniform had come properly clean, because the one I wore would look a sight. The mud leapt onto my rubber cape and crept beneath its folds. As if the muck were a living thing that hoped to drag me down. The weight of the wet and the slop fair bent me over, and I will admit my leg gave me discomfort.

Twas not yet late enough to call it night, but dark rain hid the world. I curled my hands beneath my cape, for the cold had a sting impatient for the snows. Glum I was, but determined. I would have answers before I next left Heckschersville. Nor would I subscribe to Irish threats or succumb to the pranks of drunkards. I could defend myself as well as any man. And better than most, that I will tell you plain.

Not that I intended violence, mind you. But I wished to have my questions answered proper.

The rain pressed down the evergreen boughs and bent the birches where miners had ripped the earth. The sky grumbled. A wind made every drop of wet a lash. My going was slow and miserable, and when the gale blew through the gashes the miners had left on the hillside, it seemed to draw a howl of pain from the stone. Twas a broken, bitter place, all ruination, each dig abandoned once the coal was gone. It is a queer thing, but I find a certain eeriness where the earth has been torn apart, as if some desecration has been done. It is only good business, I know, and I myself had my small profit from it when I worked in a colliery countinghouse. But I wondered if, one day, our lovely county would look like that entirely, bare and wounded.

The hard rain did not help my failing mood. Determined I was, but dreary and losing spunk. As if my act of resolve to return to Heckschersville had drained all of the manly vigor from me. I did not even find the strength to sing myself a hymn as I went along.

I slogged.

I would have jumped at the woman's voice, but the mud would not allow it. It seemed to hold me fast the moment she spoke.

"Bist Du der Freund? Der lange verborgene Freund? Bist Du endlich gekommen, um meiner zu hilfen?"

She was but a moving lump at first, a grayness in the gray, all bent and crouched and wrapped in a hundred rags. Her voice was decrepit and pained, yet she sounded queerly hopeful as she approached.

Now, my Dutch is not sufficient to make out mumbles. But I thought I heard the German word for "friend," followed by a question about help.

"Nix verstehe," I told the emerging form. *"Kenne Sie nix, gute Frau."* Thus Germans say they do not understand or know a person.

She worked her way through the clinging mud toward me. I thought she must fall, but she only laughed at her troubles. If the scraping that left her throat might be called a laugh.

The oddest thing was that I began to smell her. Despite the rain, with her ten feet away.

"Ja, ja. Der lange verborgene Freund ist zu uns gekommen! Endlich is er gekommen!"

I began to suspect the woman was deranged, for clear enough it seemed she had mistaken me. Perhaps she was thinking of someone loved and lost, as elders will.

Her stench was awful. The beating rain could not wash it away. As she neared, it enfolded me like a blanket.

Now, I have been a soldier and do not imagine the world perfumed with lavender water. But the reek of her caught in my throat as she leaned toward me. I do not think I have ever smelled a living thing so rancid, or so foul. She smelled as if she had been dead a week.

"Madam," I tried, "I am not this friend of yours. *Nix Freund, verstehe?* Do you speak English? Are you in need of help?"

I do not know why, but my voice began to fail me.

A hand stretched out from her rags as she staggered closer. Near to a claw it looked. *"Ja, ja. Englisch, Deutsch. Alles egal. Die alte Sprache ist die gute Sprache."* And then she began to chant in words that were utterly foreign to my ear, despite my travels and all my years in India. Twas strange as anything ever heard by man, and might have been the very speech of madness.

Her hand nearly touched me, then faltered. I thought she had slipped. I steeled myself and reached out to keep her from falling. For she was old and troubled, such was clear.

Of a sudden, lightning flashed and the crone recoiled. The shawl or hood that had clung to her head fell away.

Oh, light enough there was to see that face. I never shall forget it. Beneath a wild thatch of hair, the woman was leprous. Either with that horrid disease itself, or with some mold that chews upon the skin. Rotten as a corpse she looked, as if she were dying from the outside in. I may have gagged, I cannot say for certain. Yet, I could not move or look away.

The worst part of the creature was her eyes, not the ravaged flesh. One eye was a lump of pus, overgrown to sicken the strongest stomach, while the other glowed and bulged in mortal terror.

She was afraid. Of me. She reeled back through the slop, snarling out her dread through broken teeth. Waving her hands to fend me off, as if I meant to attack her.

God knows why the woman took fright of me. Twas not a thing a fellow might explain. The scar upon my cheek is not so terrible. And though I am no handsome man, I think that I will do for common intercourse.

"Falsch, falsch, falsch!" she screamed. *"Ist 'ne Luege, 'ne Luege. Er ist nicht der Freund . . ."*

She stumbled backward through the mud, drawing her cowl to conceal her hair and face again. Her attention turned to spirits concealed from my view. She no longer seemed to see me at all, but waved at some apparition imposed between us.

"Er ist der Tod, und nicht der gute Freund! Lass mich in Ruhe, du braune Heidenshure! Lass . . . mich . . . in . . . Ruhe!"

I understood the repeated word "false," the words for "lies" and "death," and that I was not the friend she had expected. Oddly enough, she spoke of a "brown whore" of some description. Then she howled in her nonsense language fit to raise the devil.

She tripped, but did not fall, as she retreated. She seemed afraid to turn her back upon me, although I meant her no harm of any kind. With hands outstretched, she sought to hold off demons. Lost in a maze of delusions, she was. Howling at Heaven and Hell.

Of a sudden, she crouched down, swinging her claws at

the rain itself and lunging at the air. As if invisible birds had come to plague her.

I stood fixed to the spot. Or transfixed, I should say. For though she fled as swiftly as she could, the image of that face remained before me.

When she judged the distance between us sufficient for safety, she twisted about and scuttled into the trees, disappearing into the early darkness.

Now, I do not have a superstitious bone in my body. It is simply that some things are reluctant of explanation. You leave such matters alone, and that is that. As I continued down that hill, shuddering with the cold, I recited Bible verses to myself. For Scripture spoken aloud is a soothing thing. And I will admit to looking around behind myself, but only now and then, at peculiar sounds.

Soon enough, I heard the pump-house engines, throbbing like native drums. The other colliery noises, the bangings and scrapes, were down for the close of the working day, and buildings deserted until the morrow loomed out of the downpour. I passed the yards and the rain was so thick I could not spy the high wheel of the colliery, though I saw a black-windowed office. Mr. Oliver and his clerks would have taken themselves home before night fell, and wise they were. Then I smelled mules, but could not see their barn. Slick to break a leg, sets of rails traced over the earth, the narrower pairs for the pit cars and the broad-gauge for the locomotives come up from the depot to take off the coal. A wooden bridge over the creek led toward the patch, dividing the worlds of labor and of rest. Up a gentle grade lay a scatter of dwellings, little more than outlines in the gloom. The patch was not laid out in rows, as were most company settlements, but had grown up haphazard on a hillside. As if those shanties themselves refused all discipline.

Lamps shone in the windows, though few and turned

down low. Kerosene costs money at the company store, as do candles, and collieries watch their inventories closely to insure that no supplies are taken home. Yet, I looked upon those weak lights with longing, wondering why I had been such a fool to come back in the rain. By now, I might have been nearly home, where the stove would be warm and glowing in the parlor. I could have spent my night with those I loved.

I am a headstrong man, and sometimes foolish. Although I like to think that I mean well.

After it lulled me with a moment's slackening, the rain struck back with little nails of ice. Twas full dark come. The night had dropped a blanket over the mining patch, hiding all its secrets from the world, and the only sounds were of pumps and pounding rain.

Wet through, despite my cape, I wandered about in the deluge until I heard a piano and the unsteady hum of men gathered in the warm. That one place was well lit, with a poorly painted board nailed to the porch, declaring I had arrived at the T. RYAN HOTEL, which offered ROOMS, MEALS, LIBATIONS.

I did not even get through the door before the music broke off and the world fell silent.

A PLOT OF RAGS had been laid just past the threshold and I stood there letting the worst of the water run off me. Covered with muck I was, and wet as a river. I fear that my appearance was undignified.

Two dozen men crowded in that place, and their eyes were fixed upon me. I sensed a mood well short of Christian charity.

The air was thick with the smells of wet wool, sweat and beer, of ashes acrid in a tub and coal burning in the stove. Above their half-drained glasses, the younger men held pipes of modern fashion, but their elders smoked the long clay pipes of Ireland. The walls were bare, except for a bit of green bunting, faded now, and some fraternal order's paraphernalia. There was no motion but dawdling smoke and the publican's rag as it swept along the bar.

I saw him, sitting back-to-the-wall. John Kehoe. The black-bearded fellow who wielded such authority.

"A good evening to you, gentlemen," I said to all the room. Giving my feet a last swipe on the cloths, I hooked my rubber cape on the rack by the door. I kept my cap in hand, though, for the brass upon it costs a pretty penny.

No one replied to my greeting, so I took me up to the fellow behind the bar. The tip of my cane skittered over the grit ground into the floor by the boots of countless miners. Twas not a place to please the high and mighty.

I gave a glance toward Kehoe as I went. Of all the faces in that room—some hard and set, while others smiled wickedly—only his seemed empty of expression.

Except for his eyes. They burned hotter than the coal behind the grate.

The barkeep was twice broader at the hips than at the shoulders. If ever he had gone down the mines, it had been years before. Red ghosts of hair clung to a freckled scalp, and his pug nose was as Irish as the shamrock.

At my approach, he dropped his rag and crossed his arms over his apron.

"Good evening, sir," I said. "I would like to take a room for the night, if you please."

"No rooms," he said. "We're full up, bucky-boy."

"Well, then, I would gladly share a room with another."

"They're all shared up already. Every one."

"I believe there is another hotel in town, then?"

"Mrs. Egan's full up, too. Go ask her."

"Then I will have my dinner and take my leave."

"You can take your leave, but you'll leave without your dinner. For the cupboard's bare and the pot's as empty as promises."

That was a lie. I smelled a proper stew. And kitchen noises chinked and chimed through a curtain.

"Then I will have a glass of water, thank you."

"The well's dried up. And the tap's run out on the beer." He glanced at the litter of bottles lined up behind him. "And all of those are only for decoration."

I heard the first titter of laughter behind my back. But I would not be vanquished quite so easily.

"Glad I am," I told him, "to find you have such a prospering business, sir. I have a bit of business in mind myself. Then I will bid you farewell."

I did not give him time to reply, but turned and marched me over to John Kehoe. He sat between two younger men, at a table cut as rough as the local manners. Nor did I wait for a proper invitation, but drew up a chair and sat me down to the three of them.

"Good evening, Mr. Kehoe," I said. "I am Major Abel Jones. Pleased I am to find you here tonight."

His eyes were as black as his beard. Black fires, if you will credit such a phenomenon. He did not reach to take the hand I offered.

The two young men attending him stood up and left the table. The silence gained another layer of quiet.

"My," I continued, "it is a terrible night. There is good, to come in out of the rain. I do not remember such a cold October." And I will tell you: That much was true. For my boots and stockings were wet and cold as Lord Franklin's. The stove sat well across the room, where the old men gathered round it, but that tavern's warmth seemed a lovely thing to me. Although I have taken the Pledge myself and could not approve of the establishment's purpose or patrons.

I watched Kehoe, and he watched me, and I kept a firm grip on my cane. I was prepared to fight my way out of that room, if need be. Although I must admit the odds was bad.

I wondered if they could trace the outline of my Colt beneath my frock coat. It is a heavy thing and hard to conceal. The truth is that I was sorry to have it by, for I suspected it would do more to provoke them than to protect me.

"You're either a madman," Kehoe said of a sudden, in a voice that did not lack some education, "or the greatest fool ever to crawl his way out of Wales."

At that he got up, but not to start a fight. He was a hard man to sense, yet I could tell that much. He left me there and strode across the room. I sat and pondered the ghosts in his voice, the plaint of the Irish tongue and worlds abandoned.

The other faces in the room turned from him to me, then back again. I wondered if they were disappointed that he had not yet seen fit to turn me out. Ready enough for a fuss, the lot of them were.

Kehoe marched up to a fellow who might have stepped from a *Punch* cartoon of an Irishman. Not of the lowly bogtrotter sort, but the old man of the cottage, white-haired, pink-faced, and nimble with his wits. The old man was one of the smilers in that room, as if the world amused him in countless ways. The pipe he smoked was long as a grenadier's forearm.

Kehoe bent down over him, with undisguised respect, and I saw I had been wrong on the matter of authority. "Black Jack" Kehoe might have been the leader up in the boneyard, where all was tactics and doings fit for the young. But the man to whom he spoke was the man without whom nothing could be done in Heckschersville.

The old fellow looked at me with a glint in his eyes that passed for Irish charm. He nodded to Kehoe, lips shaping quiet words. He met my stare and smiled, friendly as a neighbor on good terms. Then Kehoe straightened his shouders—broad they were—and come back toward me.

The old man's companions got up, but for one, leaving their cards laid out upon the table.

"Do you play a fair hand, man?" Kehoe asked me. His voice sought to be jovial, but it did not come easily to him. "Mr. Donnelly's asking the joy of your company."

I ignored the bit about playing cards, an endeavor we Methodists shun, but got me up to follow my new go-between. With my trousers dripping and clinging like Pandy's puttees.

The men in the room had wanted a fight and their disappointment was thick as the smell of dinner. But surly as they were, they minded their business. They lifted their beers again and re-lit their tobacco.

Mr. Donnelly, the fine pink fellow, stood up. Tall he was not, though of a higher stature than myself. He stuck out his hand as if we were ancient friends. I leaned my cane on the back of a chair, then shut my palm against his own. At once, I sensed I had taken a very deep plunge.

His grip was not that of an old man. We made a proper contest of our strength. With neither gaining the advantage, I give him that.

"Ah, Major Jones," he began, with our hands clasped over the table, "here I am wishing and hoping to make your acquaintance, for all that I've heard tell of your great curiosities, and what happens, by the Grace of Our Lady? In you come, prompt as the landlord after his rents!" He made a face of theatrical consternation. "But you're drowned and dreary, man, and in want of a friendly bit of hospitality!"

He let go of my hand at last, and I resumed my grip on my cane, which hides a blade within. For I was not yet certain what to expect.

Mr. Donnelly raised his voice, calling to the barkeep.

Again, he seemed an actor on a stage. I believe the word for such a voice is "stentorian." And I will tell you: All his audience heard him.

"Michael, me boy, I don't believe the cousin's coming, after all. Sure, and a rain like this would keep the devil away. So I'll give you back the room you've been holding this while, and you can bestow a berth upon the dear major. Who's been serving our fine, new country in his lovely blue coat. And see if that old woman of yours can't borrow up a bit of the warm for his dinner. No man nor beast should go hungry on such a night."

He did not pause to hear a reply, but cast his authority wider. "What's the matter with the great lot of you, then?" he asked the sullen assembly. "You'd think it was the first hour of a wake, with all the gloom come upon you." He turned his smiling face toward the piano, which was as battered as the fellow who played it. "Casey, give us some noise, lad. I can't hear meself think for the quiet."

The piano started up, though out-of-tune. It struggled against the drumbeat of the rain.

"Sit down, Major Jones, sit down. If you don't object to gracing the humble likes of us with your company. But I haven't yet introduced meself all proper. Thomas Donnelly, yard boss of the colliery, they give me that distinction. And master of the scales, under Mr. Oliver. Lucky I am to have such pleasant work."

I saw at once who made the decisions for the Heckschersville shaft and colliery. It was not Mr. Oliver.

"You've already made the acquaintance of Mr. Kehoe," he went on. "This gentleman here is Mr. Swankie Cooley. Mr. Cooley's been good enough to come up to us from Primrose, to discuss our efforts for the poor relief. But could it be you aren't familiar with our association, Major Jones? The Ancient Order of Hibernians? We're pledged to make good

Americans of the Irish. And a terrible labor it is." He grinned. "Isn't that right, Mr. Cooley?"

Now, Mr. Cooley was another small man, with a look as unkind as Mr. Donnelly's was merry. His face was pitted, like dust struck by the first raindrops. He was of middle years, with a workman's hands, but a paymaster's eyes. While Mr. Donnelly was shaven, but for his whiskers, Cooley wore a narrow beard the color of barley broth.

Cooley was a blade of a man, set up for cutting others.

"That's right you are, Mr. Donnelly," was all the fellow said. He sounded as Irish as tinkers in the wood. He did not offer his hand.

"Now, Major Jones, I'd be pleased to stand you a drink to start off our friendship," Mr. Donnelly said. "But it's whispered to me that you're strong against that temptation." He shook his head. "Ah, isn't the jar the very bane of the Irish! A curse and a comfort at once, the old poteen! Yet, here I am honored to sit with a famous hero of the war, the pride of all the county, and I find myself at a loss for a proper welcome." His smile diminished. "But what could it be brings you back to us, on such a night as this? After such a bothersome day? And you as wet as a silkie!"

Now, I am Welsh, not Irish, and not one to be fooled by all their blarney.

"I am looking for Daniel Boland," I told him, "who confessed to the murder of Brigadier General Carl Stone."

Kehoe and Cooley took on aspects even stonier than before, but old Donnelly made a great show of his surprise.

"But Danny Boland's dead of the cholera this long week! Didn't you hear the black news, Major?"

"Boland is no more dead than you or I am. He is in hiding. And I will find out where."

Mr. Donnelly threw up his hands to the Heavens. "Sure, and I'm glad to hear it! For Danny was ever a lovely boy, though headstrong." He put on a quizzical mask. "But Father Wilde claims he died of the cholera. And I've never known a priest to tell a lie." He smiled again. "Why, haven't you met Father Wilde yourself, this very afternoon?" The slightest twist come up at the side of his mouth. "Then you know what a splendid gentleman he is, in addition to the blessed vocation he's called to. Ah, he's out to give the lot of us our letters, you know, in the cause of our advancement! It's a fine, fine fellow he is, our Father Wilde." Donnelly leaned toward me. "But where is it you've run into our Danny? Surely you've seen him, to be so certain the poor lad's still among us?"

"You know I have not seen him, Mr. Donnelly. For he is hidden away. After succumbing to guilt at his deed and confessing to Mr. Oliver. He either ran out of fear . . . or was persuaded to run."

Mr. Donnelly chewed that over and found the flavor wanting. "Now, wouldn't that have been a foolish thing? To confess to a murder? And to our Mr. Oliver, of all people, who was bound to report the matter to the magistrate? I've never heard the likes in all me life."

He held up a finger. "Now, I will tell you a thing, if you will listen, Major Jones. For I find I've taken a most unusual liking to you." His eyes glowed like fires of peat set into his skull. "Danny Boland no more killed your general than Napper Tandy was tsar of all the Rooshians." He held me with his eyes, as strong men will. "And mark what I say, if there's any bit of sense in you: No man among us killed your General Stone. And if we'd had a mind for killing generals, twould not have been that one we would have chosen for the doing of it, that I can tell you." He tamped down the fire of his stare—hotter than the red-bellied stove it had been—and sat back. "Now, is there anything else you're after knowing, to satisfy your official curiosity?"

"I would like to speak to Mrs. Boland."

His eyes narrowed. "And why would you want to do a thing like that?"

"Because she knows her husband isn't dead, see. Because she's looking for him as hard as I am."

Oh, that got a reaction from the lot of them. Each man stiffened, in his different way. Kehoe grew yet stiller, while Cooley tensed like a terrier sniffing a rat. Mr. Donnelly drew into himself and his skin stretched tighter over the bones of his face.

"And how would you know what Mrs. Boland's doing?" the old man asked me. "Have you been after seeing our Mary, then?"

"Yes. I have seen her."

"And where might that have been, pray tell?"

"It does not signify."

"Oh, doesn't it now?" he asked. "When no man in this town has seen her this week? Not since her Danny was taken by the cholera?"

The publican approached with a plate of food for me, but Donnelly waved it away. "Keep it warm, now, Michael. We still have a bit of business to conduct." And as the barkeep faded away, he said to me, "Perhaps you had something to do with her disappearance yourself, Major Jones?"

I ignored that last remark, for it meant to provoke. "I saw her on the hillside. Two nights ago." I almost added: "Below the priest's house." But a sudden light blazed upon my thoughts. I wonder they did not mark the change upon my face.

Clear enough it was that the priest warned no one I had claimed to see Mrs. Boland. But something far more interesting come to me: She had been lurking in the trees between the boneyard and the priest's house. Given mine own preoccupation that night, I had assumed her interest lay in our doings with the coffin. But what if she had been keeping watch on the priest, more interested in the living than the dead? That would explain why she did not scream when we first disturbed the grave. She did not want to be found any more than we did. And if her interest had been in the priest and not the coffin, that also explained the alarm he betrayed when I told him I had seen her near his dwelling.

Did Mary Boland mean the priest some harm?

I saw at once that Father Wilde's role in the affair was even greater than I had suspected. Although I could not yet begin to say how or why. I could not even say if he had been blackmailed into certifying the false cholera death, or if that had come about of his own volition. Curious I was about the trace of mockery in the tone Donnelly had used when speaking of the priest. Was there a contest of wills in the village? A conflict over murder, confessions and fugitives?

My thoughts were all a rush and a muddle, but I will tell you this: When there is trouble between the Irish and their priest, there is trouble, indeed.

Donnelly canted his head, slow of reply. Even he had needed time to regain his composure after the revelation of my encounter with Mary Boland. And I had not even told them we had conversed. To say nothing of the grim thing she had done.

"Ah, and would that be the terrible night when the grave-robbers took Danny's body?" Mr. Donnelly said at last. "And left a cat in his place?"

"No one left a cat. They left a young woman."

"Not Mrs. Boland? Surely? And I do believe I heard tell of a cat found in the poor boy's grave this afternoon. A terrible scene it was, or so they tell me. We'll have all the grandmothers talking of curses and spells."

"Who was the young woman in the grave?"

"Is it Mrs. Boland you're referring to, Major? Was *she*

down in the grave? I'd be sorry to hear it." He leaned in close again, skin tight as a drum. And with all the smile quit of his round, pink face. "Do you know what the womenfolk say about Mary Boland and where she's gone off to? They say she's been taken by fairies, that she's gone over to the Good People, once and for all." He shook his head. "She always was the queer one, Mary Boland." He smiled again, a hard, small, wicked smile. "Of course, no man among us believes in fairies. Or in banshees and little people under the hill. Not here in America."

I thought of that old woman on the high road.

"No, Major Jones," he continued, "on that I would agree with Father Wilde. The old ways and the odd ways only shame us. They mark us as backward and foolish to all the world. Such carryings-on are a gift to Ireland's enemies. Whoever they may be." The cottage-master's twinkle returned to his eye. "But how can you get that into a woman's head, I ask you? Ah, the things a woman will get herself on to believing! They're a different race, Major, a different race from the likes of you and me."

"Well, I saw one of a different race this evening," I told him. "Coming down the hill on the Thomaston Turnpike. As old as the hills she looked. And Bedlam mad." Twas my turn to shake my head. "She put me in mind of lepers I saw in India."

All the noise of the room caved in to a silence. At times, my voice is louder than I wish. It comes of the report of many a musket and the blast of guns rolled too close to my ear.

Mr. Donnelly struggled to call up a smile. But even his lifetime of practice was insufficient.

"I take it she wasn't a fairy queen, then, Major? Beauteous to dazzle and lead good men astray? Why, now that I think of it, I'll wager you met the madwoman talked of by the Dutchmen over the mountain. They say she lives in the crags on Gammon Hill, but wanders about." He forced that mechanical smile wider still. "The digging Dutchmen—the farmers—claim she's a witch. Oh, they're worse than the whole pack of us, those poor, superstitious Germans. Grown men talking of witches and hexes and spells." He reached across the table to tap me, three sharp times, upon the wrist. "We don't have witches in Ireland, not a one, did you know?" He laughed. "Oh, fairies and leprechauns. Spirits and ghosts galore. But not witches, Major. Not a one. Maybe Saint Patrick drove them out with the serpents?"

His transplanted countrymen did their best to laugh with him. But Irish gaiety is a fragile thing.

When next Mr. Donnelly spoke, his voice was steely.

"We'll have no witches, nor any other such nonsense. No fairies, or changelings, or any such carryings-on. Danny Boland's dead, and his wife is gone from us. No one knows where. And if some other girl is dead, no man among us had a hand in the business. And no man among us harmed your General Stone. That I will swear to you."

He leaned across the table, so fierce of visage I thought he would grasp my coat.

"Now, hear me well, Major Jones, and mark what I tell you: We want no part of your war to free the nigger." He nodded, slightly, to himself, as a judge will passing sentence. "We want no part of any war at all." He held up his hands. Bruised and gnarled by decades of labor they were. "We want honest work. And honest wages. And you'll find that we will settle for no less."

He stared at me, ablaze with a thousand hatreds. "Leave us alone, and we'll dig your filthy coal. So you can fuel your country and your war. But we'll not be conscripted to feed your guns, while the high and mighty go prancing about like lords. And we'll not be blamed for crimes that are not our doing. The sons of Erin will work for their wages, so long as there is no cheating in the tallies. But we're done with bowing our heads to any man."

Donnelly sat back. Ever so slowly, he smiled again. "But you'll be wanting your dinner and a rest."

six

*M*Y SLEEP WAS MARRED. I dreamed, at first, of India, and of
the torrents of war that bloodied my youth. Yet, India was
here, and now, and cruelly so. Men in blue and gray fought
in its fields. I saw them go forward, toward fate, and ached
to warn them. The Irish Brigade it was, surging up that hillside at Antietam, blithe as if set off for the county races.
Eager for the scrap and the slaughter they were, a wild tribe
all valor and no sense, shouting, teeth bared, eyes bulging
with the terrible fever of battle. Meagher led them on.
"Meagher of the Sword," the Irish called him.

Thomas Francis Meagher. Handsome and no older than
myself, his life was a legend told over cups of whisky. I saw
him advance in my dream as I did that day. Careless he was
of the danger hissing past him. He stayed upon his horse as
his lines moved up, although the other officers had dis-
mounted. Waving his saber and having a holiday lark, he
chided their green flag forward with a grin. He barked commands I could not hear from my spot down in the hollow,
where I had thought to find General McClellan and met only
the waste of battle. The wounded men around me writhed
like snakes.

Meagher's horse was shot in the snout. It splashed blood
for ten yards on every side, coating men still whole with
equine gore.

When a wall of Rebel musketry stopped them cold, the Irish refused to give an inch they had taken, but stood exchanging fire, firm as the Guards. Falling with sudden contortions, the wounded and dead made way for those ranked behind. Some men looked heated almost to a madness, while others fired off-handedly, as if a battle were no more than a sheep-shearing. I never had seen braver men in a fight.

How real it was, precise as the painted miniatures we stole from the ranee's palace and sold to a chaplain. Yet twas not the Rebels on that ridge, after all, but brown-skinned sepoys, mutineers to a man. They, too, were as real as a doorknob in the hand, as true as noon.

Then General Meagher come telescoping toward me, his progress impossibly swift, and he was cackling. His face was that of the hag met on the hill, a monstrous sight. Racing toward me with unearthly smoothness. Carried by winds. Until I smelled the sulfur of the pit.

Twas not the face of that leprous old woman that woke me. Not that at all. A thing far worse followed after, though worse in a different way. India will not leave me alone, see. Although the mortal distance could be no greater between us. Memory chews upon me like a maggot. Then, sometimes, it perfumes my sleep with loss. I thought of the woman. Not of my wife, I do not mean, may God forgive me. But of the woman in India. The one I loved unreasonably. Ameera. A pagan she was, and of another race. I will not lie, I loved her so much that when the cholera took her I could have put my fist into God's face. That is a blasphemy. I know it. And it shames me. But how else can I tell you what I felt?

She comes to me in dreams, although I love my dear wife without stinting. Nor do I wish my present happiness elsewise. But in the corners of night, Ameera comes to

me. So queer it is. She is never unhappy with me, the
sweet child, but ever intent on stroking my hair, the way
she used to do, and telling me in nigger talk how she loved
me. I feel that touch. That, too, is real as death. More real
than much of the waking life I know. She comforts me, as
if she were the elder. As if I needed succor and protection.
She was a dainty thing, the child who had my child. She
laughed and claimed her family were all conjurors, although she had been sold to a procuress, then to me. She
said she cast a spell to keep me safe, that I was favored of
her god, her Allah. I let her prattle, just to hear her voice.
Her laughter was all music, see, her slightest smile a
dance. And her heart was true. She died unscarred by time,
while I was marching. They burned her in a pile of heathen corpses.

I woke up in a rush of tears, my hands outstretched to
grasp her in the dark. Oh, do not think me faithless to my
wife. Fidelity has never been in question. Our marriage is
a fortress against the world, and our four years together
have been blessed. We have a son, our John. I lack for
nothing. It is only when dreams play tricks on me that I
stray.

I *am* a happy man. And still that brown child comes to
stroke my hair.

Why are we made so? Why are we cursed forever, if once
we open our hearts? I would not wish to think the Lord
spiteful or jealous. Not of our meager, mortal loves, not of
the rags of happiness that never cover our loneliness entirely. It must be Satan's work, this torment of memory. Surely,
Jesus wills us to forget, to look forward to our great reward,
not backward to our losses.

I longed to read the Gospels, for reassurance. This world
is more than I can understand.

When I woke my back hurt like a wound. For I had

made my bed upon the floor. My room, though cleaner than I had expected, was barren of curtains and, frankly, I feared an assassin's shot through the window's glass. I had blocked the door as best I could, with a dresser and a chair, but could not cover the window. So I shaped a bit of a dolly in the bed to give them a target, then laid me down in a corner with the blanket, ready to fight the devil who attacked me.

But the only intruders arrived in dreams, and my flesh is not as young as it once was. My old bones hurt.

Confounded, I sat against the wall, in the space between sleep and waking. I huddled in the dark, listening to the buckshot of the rain. While ghosts of my own making filled the room.

Now, you will laugh, but I wanted to cry out. A dream is nothing, I know. But I wanted to shout my pain for the world to hear. And if pain is too dignified a word, then let us say I wished to shout my confusion.

And you will laugh again, but I will tell you: I think that there are cubbyholes in time, little nooks behind the ticking clock. That is where we find ourselves when we are not yet free of our dreams and not yet returned to the world.

I thought of a swirling stew of matters as I sat there on those planks, wrapped in a blanket as thin as an old excuse. Pondering the truculent ways of the Irish I was, only to wander into the Gospel of Luke. I thought next of business matters and of railroads, then made myself remember the war for a bit, to banish the impropriety of my dreams. For there was more to my dreaming than I dare tell you. I thought of the war, and of Mick Tyrone, my friend, whose letters apprised me of events out in the West, where matters were undetermined. Names like Corinth and Iuka pretended to mark the progress of our armies, but betrayed a lack of resolve to any veteran. The important thing was that my surgeon friend was hale and hearty, which I could tell by the bitter complaints in his letters.

He is a great Socialist, Mick Tyrone, and so expects the perfections of Heaven on earth. His is a creed designed for disappointment. I mean no disrespect to Mick, who is a good man, but find such folk a bit silly, with their notions of a Godless Garden of Eden. The Christian's strength is that he knows that Man began with a Fall and the lot of us have been tumbling ever since. The most resolute man is a leaf upon the wind. But the Socialist expects better of his neighbor than of himself, believing mankind born to generosity and that he alone thinks hard and selfish thoughts. Myself, I think on Joseph and his brothers.

I pondered the war in the East, as well, where things were a wicked muddle. While I had been in London and Glasgow, McClellan had made a mess down on the Peninsula. I do not wish to be unfair, but I have come to a great dislike of the fellow. Not because of our skirmishes over young Fowler and such like, but because McClellan killed men to no purpose. He lacked the stomach to make an end of a battle, to dare all. He kept reserves long after they were needed, withdrew whenever he feared for his reputation, and lacked the strength of heart that makes a leader. All bluster he was, and pomp, and organization. He built the Union's armies, to be sure, but lacked the fire to win the Union's war. I had my fill, and more, of Little Mac.

Then, in the green and gold of the waning summer, General Pope failed our soldiers at Bull Run, on fields where we had been bested the year before. By the end of August 1862, the problem was not our troops, for they were game. Ill-led they were, and such men deserved better. When General Lee moved north and McClellan resumed command, the poor lads cheered him, for they did not understand that a lion in the camp is not the same as a lion in the field. Little Mac fed men and clothed them and trained them. For that much he deserved the nation's thanks. But I damn him for the bloodbath of Antietam.

I saw much of the campaign, for I had been sent by Mr. Nicolay to keep an eye on a fellow on Little Mac's staff who was suspected of the gravest disloyalties, all tangled with the disgrace at Harper's Ferry, as it proved. I must confess I entered the business reluctantly, for I do not like the mantle of the spy. And I had been most content in my work, for upon my return from Britain, with a new scar on my cheek and my new ward, Fanny, sent home to my Mary Myfanwy, Mr. Seward and Mr. Lincoln had let me go back to my work in the War Department, inspecting the books and the quality of supplies.

Lovely work it was, all numbers and ledgers and ink and correspondence. Better-suited I was for that than for the young man's spectacle of war. I will not claim I was happy in Washington that summer, for I lived still separate from my wife and son—and bonnie Fanny, on whom I fear I dote—but I was content, and even pleased, to do my part in the supply offices. The wonderful thing about the keeping of books is that a fellow knows what he has done at the end of the day. And numbers do not lie, except when liars tally up the sums. Oh, there are few things finer than honest ledgers.

Washington stank like a pig dead a week, for summer in our capital is monstrous. But I had old friends and got my newspaper every evening from Fine Jim, who worried me with his talk of becoming a drummer boy. I had *Frau* Schutzengel's cooking for my supper, and I fear I was a terror to the clerks whose work I was given to oversee. But every man must do his duty proper, and a Welshman will not tolerate things otherwise.

But contentment is not to be our mortal lot. When Mr. Nicolay called at the summer's end, out I went to join our hastening armies, with all the world believing I had been sent to investigate irregularities in matters of beeves and bedding, when the irregularities lay in a traitor's heart. Perhaps I will tell you of that affair one day. That is how I found myself in high Maryland, visiting with the boys from Schuylkill County itself, the fellows of the good, old 96th, as they marched through the dust west of Frederick. Twas grisly hot as they neared the pass on South Mountain, only to find the Rebels primed for a fight. Our boys did the Union proud, as Colonel Cake barked, "Now, Pennsylvania! Do your duty!" He added something else, I fear, but the newspapers did not report it, so I will keep it mum.

I tried to keep up with their handsome attack, despite my resolutions to mind my business, but the lads soon left me behind, a-sweat and limping, for my leg does not like slopes and the way was steep. Where others had faltered, the 96th went over the stone fence the Rebels had embraced, then stormed their way to the very top of the pass. I heard our 48th did equally well. And yet, good men were lost, Major Martin and young Lieutenant Dougherty, felled by Confederate ball. The action is forgotten now, but desperate enough it was that September day.

The cursed thing—begging your pardon—is that General McClellan could have smashed Lee's army after that, had he possessed the courage of even a dog. He should have bit at the Rebels' heels, snapping behind them all the way, instead of letting them flee us unmolested. As Lee drew up his lines on the Sharpsburg heights, Little Mac dawdled and quoted de Saxe and Napoleon. And when he finally sent our boys in, the Confederates were coiled and waiting. First Little Mac sent in his right, and when it threatened to carry the

day, he failed to support it, preferring a fresh attack head-
long in the middle. That is where I saw the Irish Brigade,
performing better than such a plan deserved. And dying for
it. At last, as the brute day waned, he sent in his left, too late
to decide the issue of the war, but still in time to shatter an
enemy corps or two.

And Little Mac paused again. He claimed that he had carried the day, but barely carried a creek. I had not even seen
such gore at Delhi. And all for naught. But McClellan
praised himself to the very skies, asking the assembled lot of
us had we ever seen a battle better executed. I said nothing,
of course, for I am but a jumped-up clerk and need to mind
my temper. But I will tell you: The execution was of those
thousands of boys, in blue or butternut brown or ragged
gray, the common soldiers of both sides, who deserved a
proper answer of the war, not just another savage, blood-
soaked maybe.

Mr. Lincoln understood his politics. He, too, claimed the
battle was a victory, though he saw through it. McClellan
had been given a second chance, had failed, and would have
to go. But I must not get ahead of my own story. Suffice to
say I was glad to leave the stink of death behind me, when
Mr. Nicolay startled me with a counter-order to return to
my own dear Pottsville. When I heard I was to go home and
the reason for it, I am not sure I regretted General Stone's
murder. That is but a jest, I must point out. But happy
enough I was to return to the arms of my dear, if newly
querulous, wife.

And now I sat in a mining patch, afraid of my dreams
and the darkness. The rain dwindled, then stopped. Long
before the gray light come up, the colliery whistle blew to
wake the miners. Tired I was, and lulled with bitter reveri-
es. When the whistle called again, bidding the miners
leave their homes behind, the window had just begun to

frame a grayness, and the furniture—sparse—in my room emerged again. Twas then I laid me down on the bed at last, just to rest my bones for a pair of moments, and fell asleep to the tramp of boots as the miners trudged down blackened lanes to bury themselves.

I THOUGHT THE POUNDING on the door was cannon. For I had fallen back into dreams of war. Then I heard the voice of Sergeant Dietrich, calling my name as if I was murdered twice.

He was in a proper Dutchman's fit, the poor fellow. When they are riled, there is no talking to them. A Dutchman is a steady, reliable fellow, if lacking in zest and outward signs of joy, but when confronted with the unfamiliar, he goes to pieces like a frightened child. That is what would happen, half a year hence, at Chancellorsville, and that is how Sergeant Dietrich behaved that morning.

Hammering on the door with the butt of a Colt he was, wailing, *"Gott im Himmel, der Herr Major ist ermordet in seinem Schlaf!* He is killt all dead by the Irish!"

Twas all a nonsense. And more than a little ruckus ensued, I will tell you. There was howling throughout the house, with doors slamming and Irish voices raised in alarm and wonder. A woman keened as if the roof were burning and a deep voice swore, "Sure, and I ate the very same supper meself as the little bugger . . . we didn't pizen him even a little, your honor." You would have thought the whole world was at sixes and sevens.

When I shifted the dresser and let him into my room, the sergeant's expression collapsed into disappointment at the sight of me safe and sound. Not that he meant me ill, see. But even Dutchmen like a bit of scandal.

The Irish publican who was master of the house was honestly relieved to see me. For no such fellow likes a corpse upstairs. And clear it was that Mr. Donnelly, the leader of the whole pack of Hibernians, had not decided I was worth the killing. At least not yet. I do not approve of alcohol and have taken the Pledge myself, but I give you that a barkeep likes things quiet.

I had a sip of coffee for my troubles, though it was thin, and toasted bread from the stove-top, dripped with lard. My dinner and accommodations cost two dollars, which was dear, but I paid the fellow and tried not to be surly.

"Nun, ja, Herr Major," Sergeant Dietrich told me, "half the night we are driving in the wagon to come to you. *Sie haben so eine Angst in uns alle gejagt. Der Herr* Gowen is waking the provost marshal who is *tief im Schlaf, und* then everyone is excited . . ."

Now why, I wondered, should young Mr. Gowen be worried about me? I will tell you what I thought that morning, and I was not far from the mark: I did not think he wanted more attention from Washington or even Harrisburg. Whatever pie he had put his fingers in, it had not been baked for the benefit of outsiders. He wanted quiet, as surely as did that publican.

"Ja, ja, und the *Frau* Jones, she is so worrying in her *Nachtkleid,* I tell her *alles ist in Ordnung, ja, aber* she says to me that I must go now *und, Gott im Himmel,* she is like the wild animal with *Angst* for you, she believes she is the general who makes everyone listen to her . . . *aber* I am explaining—"

That is my darling Mary, see. A lioness protecting those she loves. I thought, though, I had heard something about a night-dress, which did not please me, for I am a friend to propriety. Queer it is, the way the Good Lord made us. My dearest had seen me off to war with the best heart she could muster, but now that I was come home, my absence for one night filled her with terror.

I hope she did not fear some misbehavior. I cannot control my dreams, but I am fully master of the rest of me.

The morning was gray, but thinly so, and a soldier learns to read the many weathers. I do not wager, but if I did, I would have bet the day would turn a fair one.

We made our way out through the muck to the wagon, where Mr. Downs was scouring his nose.

"There he is!" the teamster cried when he saw me. "Riz' up like Jesus Christ awmighty Himself!"

I did not think that was an apt comparison.

Now, those who are unfamiliar with our ways in the realm of coal think only of the reek of winter chimneys or of the hiss of a sack emptied into a cellar bin. But the miner's world is particular in its noises and its scents. Coal has an odd perfume, sharp, but not unpleasant, although the dust plays havoc with clothes on the line. A colliery grumbles steadily through the day, a great, insatiable, living, working thing, and there are hoots and whistles and constant shouts. You smell mules and men and earth. Metal clangs abruptly, wheels squeak along gangways, and the weigh-master's chalk strikes a tally on his board. Taken together, you have the sound of our age, of modern times, relentless and productive. I believe it is the sound of America's future.

That was the song we heard, played on iron, wood and rock, as Sergeant Dietrich mounted his horse and I climbed up on the wagon beside Mr. Downs, whose forefinger had wandered into his mouth.

"*Nun*, we go back to Pottsville, I think," the good sergeant declared.

"Not quite yet, Sergeant Dietrich. For I have calls to pay before we go."

Twas not a popular idea. The teamster, the sergeant and the three weary guards all wished to leave Heckschersville and the Irish far behind them. But I held a rank that gave me license to command them, and I did.

First, I turned us up the hill past the graveyard, for I wished another interview with the priest. The coal dust thinned as we climbed away from the colliery and the day's first shaft of sunlight struck a cross. Twas strange, when I thought of it, how the boneyard separated the houses in the valley from the church and priest above. The fellow lived like the missionaries in India, separate from the sheep he was called to tend—although I will tell you this: Our mission folk in India lived ten times better than that Catholic fellow, no matter the books and gewgaws in his parlor. The Romans fill their churches with all the gaudy ornaments of popery, but ask a quiet hardship of their holy men. At least, it is that way among the poor parishes I know. I hear that their high churchmen live like princes.

My knock received no answer, so I took me around back of the shanty that served as a parish house. I found the priest in his garden, scrubbing his clothes in a tub in the morning chill.

Twas strange, that. These Catholic sorts are not allowed to marry, but they always seem to have an old woman by to clean and cook and see to their looking after. And I believe the parish ladies compete to do little things for a priest who is young and handsome. But this fellow stood so far apart from his flock that he washed his shirts himself.

He looked up from his labors at my approach. His first expression was one of surprise and not a pleasant one. But he straightened his back and ordered his features, shaking the wet from his hands.

"Oh," he said. "You again."

"Good morning, Father Wilde," I told him. The sun was cracking through the haze, and the rain had left the whole world ripe and glistening.

He drew a canvas cover over the wash tub. "Well, what is it? I'm busy." He gestured toward the tub.

"Yes. I see."

"I've given Mrs. Brady leave of her work," he said, which was more than I had asked. "A sick relative. In Tamaqua, as I recall."

"Well, that is very good of you," I said. Then I paused. To see what else he might feel compelled to tell me. I had my questions, but I have learned to wait.

In a moment, he said, "I hear you risked a night among us. Rather bold, I should say. And I believe you made the acquaintance of Mr. Kehoe and our Mr. Donnelly."

"And of a Mr. Swankie Cooley, too. Please, Father Wilde. Go on with your work, if you will. I am content to talk with a man at his labors."

"I don't mind a rest," he said, moving himself a step farther off from the tub. I don't know Cooley. One of the Hibernians, I should suspect."

"Yes, I believe that was his business. Something about the poor relief. Does this 'Ancient Order of Hibernians' work in harness with your church, then?"

"No."

"I see."

We both waited. And, again, twas the priest who broke the silence.

"The Church frowns upon the order, but does not forbid it."

"I was told they hope to make good Americans of the Irish."

The priest could not help but smile, although he soon

enough turned his lips to a grimace. "Look, Major Jones. The Catholic Church has no use for secret societies. Not that the Hibernian Order *is* a secret society, precisely. But the danger is always there. The Church is organization enough for all Catholics. Oh, if the Hibernians content themselves with their pipes and beer and mourning for all they left behind in Ireland, that's one thing. But oaths . . . any oaths or pledges taken outside of the Church are condemned by the Church."

"And they take secret oaths?"

"Not to my knowledge. But the danger is always there."

"It seems that a great deal of danger lies here and there."

"Don't be coy, Jones. I've told you the Church's position. The Church stands for public order and social advancement through law-abiding behavior and honest work. The Church is ever willing to defend its flock, even in temporal matters, should that prove necessary. But I simply wanted to make it clear to you that the Church bears no taint of any such nonsense or tomfoolery."

"Then you do not see eye to eye with Mr. Donnelly."

"It isn't the obligation of the Church to see 'eye to eye' with anyone."

"But you yourself, Father Wilde? Do you and Mr. Donnelly get along, then?"

"Donnelly's something of a village elder. And the miners' spokesman with the coal company. I believe he has the best interests of his people at heart. Our personal relations are irrelevant."

"You told him I had visited you yesterday."

"I was asked."

"But you did not tell him about Mrs. Boland. That I reported seeing her to you."

"I didn't think of it," he said. He was a stoical fellow in many regards, but the morning chill was as hard as ice, despite the thickening sunlight. He turned, slightly, to reach for a black coat that hung over a sawhorse.

And I saw a stain on the back of his shirt. But a few inches long it was, below the shoulder.

"Father Wilde?" I said. "Your back is bleeding."

He wheeled his body to face me, front to front, with a look I have seen on men in the middle of battle, when they are killing with relish.

"That's absurd." He drew on his coat, one sleeve then the other, and settled it over his shoulders and chest.

"Perhaps I was mistaken," I said.

"I should rather think so." He tried, unsuccessfully, to bring it off with a smile. "I'm afraid I'm not much of a success at laundering my own clothing. Perhaps I stained my shirt."

"Most likely that," I agreed. Then I took a turn at smiling. "Look you. I have been a soldier far too many years for sense," I told him, "and not only in our Federal blue. I served in the ranks and learned to wash things proper." I stepped toward his washtub. "Would you like me to show you how it's done, then?"

He leapt forward to meet me. Blocking my approach to the covered tub. "I'm nearly finished. Really, there's not so much to it, is there?"

"But the stain on your shirt?"

"Mrs. Brady will see to it when she returns. Although I fear she'll chastise me for my carelessness."

"Well, then, I will leave you to your laundries." I turned as if I were about to leave, but the truth is that I was playing with the fellow. For something about him angered me to a degree at once unreasonable and unfair. Determined I was to have a few answers before I went back down the hill.

"Well, I wish you luck with your investigations," he said, with frank relief. "And I really shall pray for—"

"Ah, that reminds me," I told him, turning back again. "I'm terribly forgetful, Father Wilde. I did have a few questions, see."

He stood there, miffed to the mashers, and folded his arms across his chest, with his hands tucked into his armpits.

"The queerest thing happened to me yesterday," I began. "I was walking back along the turnpike in the rain—wasn't that a rain of all rains, Father Wilde?—and the strangest old woman come out of the trees to meet me. A sorry creature she was. Disfigured like a leper from the Gospels. And mad, I do believe. She seemed all fears and spells and incantations."

The subject seemed a relief to him. "Ah, that would be the old German widow, no doubt. Quite an unpleasant creature, I'm told. Mad, indeed. One of God's poor, whatever the specific nature of her affliction. It's shameful that the Lutherans don't look after her, I must say. She's said to be something of a hermit. I believe she lives in a shanty on Gammon Hill."

He seemed nearly affable of a sudden. "I believe I may have spotted her once myself, you know. From a distance. In the summer. I was picking blackberries. We have lovely blackberries on the hillsides."

"I would have thought there was danger of contagion," I said. "She appeared severely diseased." And that she had done. As bad as the worst beggar in India.

He shrugged. "I can't say, of course. But she hasn't bothered anyone here. On the contrary, I believe she flees when spotted." He shrugged. "But she has nothing to do with us. She belongs to the German farmers in the next valley, if she belongs to anyone. I've heard they go to her for spells, when their cows take ill. Odd, that she should be down as far as this."

"And speaking of spells," I said, "Mr. Donnelly said that the women of your parish believe Mary Boland to be a changeling, that her soul was robbed by fairies."

His face darkened. The morning might have been bright as gold, but his mood turned black as tar. For all that, the young priest was a handsome man, and the more so because of that white hair, not despite it. He commanded the eye, and might have been a great lion among the ladies, had his vocation been otherwise.

"No matter what Donnelly may have told you, the women of this parish believe in Jesus Christ, Our Savior. And in God, the Father. They believe in the Holy Trinity. In Mary, the Blessed Mother of God. And in the Christian saints and martyrs. All this drivel about fairies and hauntings belongs, if anywhere, to folk tales told by the fireside. You simply cannot take it seriously."

His expression turned to business, as surely as a merchant's might have done were trade the subject. "Of course, there are pagan vestiges among them, little practices and ridiculous superstitions. The Church condemns all of it. But it takes time to eliminate the traces. Time and education. But I won't allow you to believe for a moment that anyone in this parish puts faith in that sort of thing." He took a deep, determined breath. "They put their faith and trust in Jesus Christ."

"And in you, Father Wilde?"

"I think you're being insolent."

"But you will not deny there are certain superstitions among—"

"Jones, be fair." He looked away, disgusted with me and the world. "The correct word for all this is 'folklore.' Yes, it has pagan roots. And yes, the Church properly forbids all such practices and the naïve credulity associated with them. But why, I ask you, are the Irish chosen to be mocked when they repeat their old legends? At a time when the English are writing works of literature about their own countryside beliefs, their ghosts and fairies? Why, the Germans have made something of an industry of collecting such tales and publishing them with the full approbation of their finest universities. Why is it, then, that the Irish alone are considered backward, if ever they make the least mention of rural traditions?"

"Did Mary Boland believe in 'rural traditions,' Father Wilde?" It was something of a blind attempt and forward, but I wanted to know more about Mrs. Boland. And of one thing I was convinced: The priest knew a great deal more than he was telling.

"Mary Boland . . ." he said, with an almost pained reluctance, ". . . was an unusual woman."

"Was she, then? How so?"

"Jones, must we? Really?"

"Father Wilde, there is a matter of murder. Of two—"

"Oh, yes. I know. And you suspect me of telling lies about death certificates. I know all that."

"I saw her, you know."

"You told me that."

"I saw her clearly. And close. Closer than you are to me. I had her in my grip."

His pale looks grew far paler with each word. And his voice abandoned him.

"She is a beautiful woman, if moonlight did not deceive me," I continued. "With a wild beauty . . . all that long, black hair . . . and a saucy mouth on her . . . her language . . ."

He had closed his eyes. I let him think for a moment. At war with himself, he was. Twas plain to see. But I had no inkling how deep his battles went.

"Mary Boland's beauty is a curse," he said.

"A curse, is it? That is an odd word to use, Father Wilde. For a priest, I mean. A 'curse.' "

"An affliction, then. I regret my intemperate language."

"An affliction to whom? To her husband, Daniel Boland?" I had a sudden intuition, see, and thought I might solve at least one murder on the spot.

"To him, certainly. And to herself, I think."

"You heard their confessions, of course."

He reared up. Becoming fully the priest again. "I'm sure you know we cannot discuss such matters."

I ignored that point, for my interest lay elsewhere.

"But Daniel Boland did not come to you with his hasty confession of murder, Father Wilde. He went to Mr. Oliver, at the colliery office. Why was that, do you think? The Irish do not love mine superintendents."

"Had Daniel Boland come to me to confess, I couldn't have told anyone. And he wanted his guilt to be known. Evidently, he felt remorse."

"Perhaps I am wrong, but I believe that the rule among you is such: Had he made his confession to you in that closet you have in your church, you could not have reported his doings to anyone. But if he had come to you outside the church, simply as a figure of some authority, then—"

"He didn't."

"But why? Why Oliver? Whom I believe the people here despise? *Why* didn't he come to you? It seems to me you were the natural choice. For advice and comfort. For help."

"Only Daniel Boland knows the answer. And he's dead."

"Yes. Of cholera, I'm told. But might Mrs. Boland not know, as well? And your Mr. Donnelly? And half the village? Or all of it?"

"You would need to ask them."

Twas then I took my plunge. Into the wrong pool. I thought I had the business figured out, see.

"Did Daniel Boland commit murder out of jealousy, because General Stone made advances to Boland's beautiful wife? During the general's stay here, did he meet Mary Boland and try to—"

I did not even finish. Nor did I need an answer in words. I saw by the smirk on the priest's face that I had gotten it thoroughly wrong.

"Perhaps you should pursue that line of reasoning," the priest told me. He nodded his head, a dishonest man, hiding crimes when he should have been saving souls.

Of a sudden, I sensed an untoward bitterness in me.

"Really," he went on, "that does sound like a plausible explanation, Major Jones. Although I had not heard it. Quite plausible, I think. Jealousy, the green-eyed monster and all that."

"No," I said. "You don't believe it. Do you? You know better."

"Now, really, Jones!"

"You know the truth. But you will not say. For reasons of your own."

"That's unpardonable!"

"I hope that all your reasons for silence are good ones, Father Wilde. And that God will judge them so."

"I don't think I need you to tell me about God."

Angry I was, and spiteful. "And why is Mary Boland watching your house at night? Why are you afraid of a mere woman?"

"You're mad yourself." The priest turned to go, stalking off.

Mad I was, though not in the sense he meant. I have a temper. And sometimes it gets the best of me. Especially when my own foolishness trips me up.

That morning, my mood was positively wicked.

"Father Wilde," I called after him. "The blood's soaking through your coat.

It was a lie. But he turned. In alarm.

The moment he saw the set of my face, he knew that I had tricked him.

"You're a bastard," he said. Which was not priestly speech.

I was a fool, but Father Wilde was a greater one. For he trudged inside and slammed his rickety door behind him, disappearing into the bowels of his shanty.

I stepped up to the tub and lifted the canvas.

The linens within were browned with streaks of blood.

seven

*I*T IS FAR TOO EASY to misjudge the man you do not like, to think him vicious because he tilts his cap to the left, not to the right, as you do. I should have known better, as a man and as a Christian. But I was snared, as easily as a youth in the flush of temper. I did not like the priest, who was arrogant. I saw his fear, but failed to weigh it wisely, and all my calculations went amiss. As we rattled down the hill toward the village and its black castle of a colliery, I blamed the priest for a range of indefinite crimes, upon the evidence of his bloody shirt and linens. Events would prove me wrong and shame me for my errors, although his shame was greater than mine own. A sinner does not have to be a criminal.

But let that bide.

I was not finished with the people of Heckschersville. My darling wife was worried for my safety, as Sergeant Dietrich reminded me again. But duty must come first. I had another call to pay before we returned to Pottsville.

As we descended toward the pall of the colliery, with its fumes and fires and noise, I savored what I could of the lovely morning. Despite the dust thrown up by the works below us, the sunlight seemed a foretaste of salvation, and the wind come fresh off the hills, ripe with the memory of rain and chilled to bracing. Even the barren trees shone bright and hopeful, and a wife at her washing seemed as splendid a fig-

ure as the statues of Michael Angelo, who is famous. Twas
as if this earth held naught but beauty.

I lifted up mine eyes. How can men fail to believe in God
on such an autumn day?

We entered the black vale of coal. Drawn by mules, full-
laden cars come out of a tunnel's mouth. Weighed, then
hauled up the tipple track by cables, they emptied with a roar
high overhead, feeding the maw of the great machine. Rock
spewed from a breaker chute, worthless. On the other side of
the blackened building, wet coal shimmered out of metal fun-
nels and into the rail cars, bound for Pottsville, then for distant markets. Whenever a mule boy emerged from below, he
masked his eyes from the glare of the day, which set even the
dust clouds to shimmering. The mules shied their heads
slightly and trudged along the track laid into the ground. The
noise was near as ferocious as that of a battle.

I marked Mr. Donnelly by the scales, as he marked me.
He was the cleanest man upon the grounds, which is not
high praise.

Licked by the switch beyond the level of custom, a
wronged mule brayed. Metal struck metal, while engines
chugged and steam combined with dust. A gray miasma en-
veloped the breaker itself, near as thick as a dust storm in the
Punjab. It is no wonder that miners die of their coughs.

I got me down from the wagon in front of the glorified
shanty that served as an office. Inside, amid the most
unashamed human smells, a pair of clerks bent over their
ledgers, with Mr. Oliver correcting the fellow nearest me.
The room looked orderly enough for so rough a place, yet
something there was that hinted at indulgence.

For all the din of the colliery yards, Mr. Oliver had not
heard our wagon approach. When he noticed me, he
straightened his back and frowned in blunt dismay.

"Jones," he said, otherwise bankrupt of speech.

"Good morning, Mr. Oliver. A word, if you please."

He glanced, almost fearfully, from one clerk to the other. One of those fellows bore a family resemblance to Mr. Cooley, Mr. Donnelly's companion from the tavern. No doubt, the clerks spied upon poor Oliver, who seemed almost a creature kept for sport.

"In here," Mr. Oliver said. "Come on in the office. Let's talk in there. Though I don't know what on earth you could want to talk to me about."

Nervous he was as a corporal caught shirking his duties.

His office was a collection of papers, maps and blueprints, many long untouched, their surfaces gray with coal dust. It smelled of cheap cigars and unchanged stockings. Mr. Oliver was so unsettled he seemed at first to want me to take his chair behind the desk. Then he gathered himself, sat down, half rose again, bid me sit, and finally lowered his leanness where it belonged. His chair, one of those newfangled sorts on a swivel, creaked and tilted him backward.

Behind his crumpled shoulders, the window was smeared to a fog. Yet, the day was so rich its light would not be kept out. The stove was dead, a needless economy in a mine office. The room seemed colder than the world without.

"What is it?" he asked, almost shouting, when I failed to begin my queries at once. His Adam's apple bobbed. "I can't tell you how busy I am. I couldn't even begin to tell you."

"Well, I am sorry to interrupt your labors," I responded. The shadow of a bird swept past the glass. "But there are questions I would have answered, Mr. Oliver."

"What sort of questions? I don't know anything. Nothing but what I told the magistrate. I mind my own business."

"And Mr. Heckscher's business, of course."

"It's my business to mind his business."

"Why did Daniel Boland come to you to confess to murder?"

He nearly jumped out of his chair. He was so nervous I decided he was not guilty of anything much himself, for it is the small misdeeds that leave men unsteady.

"How should I know? Why would I know why?" He shook his head so vehemently his chair turned with his body. "I didn't have a thing to do with Danny Boland and his troubles, not a thing. He should've gone to one of his own kind and kept me out of it."

"You serve as a figure of authority, Mr. Oliver."

"He should've gone to his priest."

"Now, I have thought that very thing myself. That I have. Why do you think he did not go to Father Wilde."

"How should I know?"

"Was there any matter of contention between Boland and the priest?"

He waved his entire torso in denial, with that chair unsteady beneath him. "I wouldn't know anything about that. Not my business. They keep to themselves, the Irish." He said it as though he were the only white man surrounded by all the heathen tribes of Africa.

"Was Daniel Boland a good worker? He was a skilled miner, I believe? Not simply a laborer."

"Boland was a miner, all right. With papers. Paid by the ton. Same as every other miner."

"But was he a good worker?"

Mr. Oliver shrugged, calming now that our talk had turned toward business matters. "Not bad. He wasn't a big man, you know. Worked hard to make up for it. Sober, most of the time. Handsome, the way they are sometimes. The men used to tease him about his wife."

"What did they say of Mrs. Boland? The men?"

He gave his head a slacker shake and the motion of his Adam's apple lessened. "Well, she was one fine-looking woman, I'll say that. Just a pearl. That's what she was. A pearl. A pearl among swine. Though I don't know how any man could stand the stink of her. Oh, I saw her myself enough times. She'd wait for Boland some days, just out past the yards. They used to tease him something awful about it." He lowered his eyes, thinking over some detail he might not wish to share. "Only times a miner's wife waits by the yards is on pay-day, before her fella can sneak over to Ryan's. Or when there's trouble down below. Somebody hurt or killed. It's no place for a woman, otherwise."

"It sounds as if they were very much in love."

He made a face that discounted the heart's importance. "Hadn't been married so long. Couple years maybe. He was no end of sweet on her, everybody knew that." He tried a feeble smirk. "You'd think it'd wear out sooner, that a fella'd just get sick of it."

"So they were happy, then, the two of them? As best you know?"

"That's not the kind of thing I bother about. I just care if they work, or if they don't." He dipped his chin toward his chest a pair of times. "They always said she was strange, though. I remember there were voices raised against Boland marrying her in the first place."

"Strange in what way?"

He wrinkled the corner of his mouth in distaste. "Oh, some Irish way. They get all sorts of things into their heads. I don't even try to figure them out." He looked about as if we might be spied upon, then leaned toward me—chair creaking—and lowered his voice. "The truth is they're god-damned savages. You'll never civilize a one of them. Not even that high and mighty priest of theirs. They're worse than animals, and I'm the fella who should know."

Mr. Oliver lowered his chest almost to his desk top, bringing his weary face as close to mine as he could. His tone dropped to a whisper. "Listen, Jones. I know there was some

trouble between the two of them a time back, between
Boland and his wife. Now, I don't know what it was about,
and I don't want to know. I don't care a damn. None of my
damned business. But Danny Boland went wild for a bit.
Didn't come to work regular. When he did show up, he was-
n't worth a peck of mule shit. I should've let him go, but Old
Man Donnelly wouldn't have it. If Mr. Heckscher'd found
out, it would've been me out in the cold."

"I take it you get on well with Mr. Donnelly?"

"Donnelly's all right. Keeps the Irish in line."

"Except when they march on troop trains and force the recruits out of the cars. Or when they threaten insurrection. Or
when generals are murdered on the roads."

"Now, you listen to me," he said, sitting back up and ter-
minating our brief intimacy. Still, his voice was not as force-
ful as he wished it. "That's all behind us. The draft's in
abeyance up here, and that's the best thing for everybody.
No need to make any more trouble."

"A general is dead. And a girl was murdered before him."

"Well, I don't know a thing about any dead girl," he
said. "I told you that." But something there was in his tone
of a sudden—something small—that made me disbelieve
him now. "As for your dead general, well, maybe he
should've minded *his* own business, instead of aggravat-
ing the Irish with his recruitment nonsense." He tried to
look me in the eyes, but failed to maintain the glare he had
intended. "Meddlers always get themselves into trouble,
don't think they don't."

He sat back in his creaking chair, with the daylight rich
behind him.

"And . . . I suppose I am a meddler here, Mr. Oliver?"

"I didn't say that. I didn't say anything. But you just tell
me why this general matters so much? Doesn't seem to be
no shortage of them, judging by the papers."

"Because he was murdered. And because the law is the law."

He sniffed, almost laughed out loud, but did not trust himself to do so. "Well, now, you know that's a no-good pot of beans. The law's only the law when the law has a mind to be the law. At least in this county. And you and I both know it."

"Was Daniel Boland a violent man?"

"Danny Boland? Not likely. Wasn't even a drinking man. I told you. Always mooning over his wife, that's what I always heard tell. Just a little fellow. Oh, not small like you are. But smaller than the typical fella. Liked to sing. But, then, they all do."

"And what exactly did Boland say when he made his confession of murder?"

Mr. Oliver grew excited again. "What did he say? What do you mean? He said he killed that general, up on the hill, and that he did it all by himself." His Adam's apple pulsed back to life and he ran a palm over his baldness, where sweat shone despite the room's chill. "And that's all he said. Over and over. Couldn't shut him up for the life of me. He just kept saying, '*I* killed him, *I* was the only one killed the general.' Over and over. Until they took him away."

"Who took him away?"

"Oh, Donnelly. And the boys. There's a young fellow comes around now and then, coal-black beard. Not employed by the works. He just seems to pass through. They took him off. Claimed the boy didn't know what he was saying, that he was raging with fever."

"So . . . they knew of the murder, then?"

"Well, that's neither here nor there. Boland was shouting it all down the street before he come busting in here. Just ran down the street hollering, 'I killed him, I killed him!' " Mr. Oliver shook his head in wonder at the memory. "I swear to God, I've never seen a man so desperate to convince the world he'd committed a crime. A murder, at that." He pondered the matter. "I suppose it's all that Catholic business, all their nonsense about confessions and things like that. Maybe that's what drove him to it."

"Well, I have only a few more questions, Mr. Oliver. Mary Boland, now. You said that she was a beautiful girl"—no sooner had I said it but I remembered it was the priest who had agreed with the word "beauty," while the overseer deemed her a "pearl"—"but the Irish thought there was something queer about her. Do you have any—"

The glass exploded inward an instant before I heard the shot. I threw myself to the floor, falling amid a thousand bits of glass. The ball had punched into the door behind me, splintering its panel.

"Jesus," Mr. Oliver cried, "what the hell?"

Then he saw me on the floor and joined me there. A moment later, I was up, with my back against a side wall and my Colt out from under my frock coat.

Fresh air rushed into the room. Most of the glass had shattered away, but all I could see were birch trees, dust and a mule-driver with a dumbfounded look on his face.

I heard shouts and clumsy commands given in German. Boots thumped over planks, rushing through the outer office.

"Herr Major! Herr Major! Sind Sie wieder ermordet?"

I opened the door, its upper portion a thing of splinters, and disappointed Sergeant Dietrich a second time with my good health and well-being.

Fortunate I was, for the glass had not even struck my face, although I cut my palms a bit when I threw myself down to the floor. Mr. Oliver was not quite so fortunate, for the back of his neck and head were bleeding. He looked astonished, as if awakened to the Day of Judgement on a Tuesday.

"Sergeant Dietrich," I said, in my terse voice of command, "tell your men to come back from wherever you have sent them. They will not find the man who fired the shot.

No need to make a fuss." When he failed to jump to his duty, still marveling at my good health, I said, "Do what I tell you, man!"

I turned me back to Mr. Oliver, tucking my pistol away. "Sit you down there, and let me look at the damage."

He took his chair obediently. I turned him so his wounds faced toward the light. Framed by the shattered window, I was unbothered. For there had been time enough to think things through, after my soldier's alert at the sound of gunfire. The shot had been but a warning. You do not shoot to kill a man you cannot see properly. The window glass itself had been the target. Twas meant to make a fuss, and that was all.

"Well, you may yet live to be a hundred," I told Mr. Oliver, with his blood on my paws, mingling with my own. I drew a bit of glass from the fringe of hair ringing his scalp. The poor fellow cowered at the discomfort. "The head always bleeds more than is sensible," I assured him. "There is no serious injury. Although you could do with a wash and a pair of plasters."

Twas then I realized that the fellow was weeping. He dropped his arms atop his desk, then buried his bloodied face in his gartered sleeves. Sobbing.

"I don't want any part of this," he cried.

NO SOONER HAD I STEPPED OUT onto the porch of the office than Mr. Donnelly himself appeared, dragging a boy by the ear and shaking an ancient musket.

"Get along with you," he told the boy, "you dirty, little bugger."

At the sight of me atop the steps, Donnelly smiled like all the sunshine in a Galway summer. He shoved the lad forward. Ragged and thatched with the reddest hair of Leitrim the boy was.

"And there you are, Major Jones!" Donnelly called as he approached, "And your fine, lovely morning all spoilt! But it's happy I am to see you've taken no great injuries from all the shooting and banging we've had amongst us." Fair grinning he was, between grimaces at his prisoner. "I've told them, haven't I told the great pack of them, a thousand times, if once, they're not to go after their hunting near the colliery. And to stay out of the yards. Ah, but the young are hard-headed, and do not listen."

He shoved the boy toward me. "Speak your piece now, Master O'Neill, or the major'll haul you off to the county clinker."

The boy was the very picture of repentence. He scraped and bowed as if to an English landlord.

"I'm sorry, sir," he told me, "for all your endangerments. I meant na harm, I didn't, sir."

"No," I told the lad, "I am certain you did not mean me harm." And that was true, for I marked no powder traces upon the boy's cheek, no stain of the sort left by muskets.

I went down the steps, relying upon my cane no more than was necessary. For I do not wish mankind to think me unable. I smiled at the boy. And as I smiled, I stretched out my hand and grasped him by the right shoulder, giving it a friendly squeeze.

He did not wince. Yet, a boy his size, had he fired the great antique cannon that Mr. Donnelly dandled, would have had his shoulder bruised to a misery.

That boy had no more fired the gun than I had.

"Ah, but that's princely good and understanding of you, Major," Donnelly told me. Smiling that little smile of his, the cat that ate the canary. "And won't he be in for a grand strappin' when Johnnie O'Neill comes off his shift, for that window's bound to come out of the father's pay. And him with six at home, and another one coming, God bless us." He glowered at the lad with that grand theatricality the Irish enjoy. "Oh, won't you be sorry then, young Napper, you'll get such a belt from your da. Now it's off to the house with you, and tell your mither of all the troubles you've made us."

Released, the lad ran off like a hound at the horn.

"May I see the musket, Mr. Donnelly?"

He put on his little smile again, for he knew what I was about. Twas all a game, see, and he loved the sport of it. He handed me the weapon.

It had not been fired, of course. The bullet had come from another gun, fired by another hand. Twas all a show fit for the stage.

I played my role in it and sniffed the barrel. It smelled of ancient powder, not of any newly burned off, and I cocked the hammer back to find only rust in the mechanism.

"Ah, Major Jones," Donnelly said to me, as if we were sharing a joke in an Irish saloon, "tis an age of miracles, is it not?"

"I'm certain his father will do the lad no great harm. When he comes off his shift," I said, handing back the gun.

"Oh, nothing from which a fine, young lad won't recover. He'll get what he deserves. Now, I'll be taking meself back to the work for which I draw me wages, by your gracious leave."

"Just a moment," I told him. "I *do* have a question for you, Mr. Donnelly."

He turned with that ready smile of his. "Sure, and I thought you had fired up your whole, great volley of questions yesterday evening."

"Did someone put Daniel Boland up to confessing to the murder of General Stone? The way someone put that boy up to claiming he fired the shot that broke Mr. Oliver's window?"

I saw at once, from the satisfied shape of his smile, that I was wrong again.

"No," he said. Just that. And then his smile dissolved into

a hard-boy look I had not yet seen on him, an aspect fiercer than the worst of the night before. "But you're after reminding me of a thing I wanted to tell to you meself. Tis only this: Danny Boland no more killed your general than Cromwell's in Heaven with all the German Georges. Now, I've told you that nicely. And I've told you no man among us killed your general. If you wish to call me a liar, do it now and do it to my face."

I thought he was done, for twas clear he was seething to a heat beyond all words. I expected him to turn and strut away. But he had a last message for me.

"And you're wasting your time with that coward of a priest," he said. "For he's bound to be judged by a higher sort than you."

PERHAPS YOU DO NOT KNOW the Irish well. But I will tell you: They do not speak ill of their priests. They may chafe under the yoke of the church, and feel it is unjust in its judgements and penalties, but they would no more slight a priest than spit at God. As we rode up the hill from Heckschersville, I pondered that. And time enough I had. For turnpike they may have called it, but the way was a mire and a swamp left by the rain. The mules struggled.

I found that only my left hand had cuts that asked minding, so I bound it in my handkerchief, an affectation upon which my dear wife insists. She seems to think the handkerchief the one and only test of true gentility. I keep one in my pocket, just to please her. That morning, I was glad to have it with me, for Mr. Downs, the teamster, attempted to supply me with his own rag, which had done veteran service.

Our going was slow. Twice I had to dismount to lighten the wagon for the mules. Twas a nasty muck to walk through, that I will tell you. Mr. Downs rattled on about Irish assassins and shots fired in broad daylight. He was not afraid, but delighted. He was the sort, I think, who rushes to see a man run over by a runaway team or a locomotive. He had a mighty appetite for disaster, no less than all those journalist fellows do.

And yet, I would not call our journey unpleasant. I had a muchness to think about, but my weary mind went wandering. Late birds sang, instead of continuing their journeys of desertion to the Confederacy. When we left the vale of anthracite behind for a stretch, the sky was as pure and blue as the pools of Heaven must be. Except for the muddy roadway, the whole world seemed washed clean.

I recalled Mr. Donnelly's voice as he spoke of the priest as a "coward," and his insistence that young Boland had neither killed the general nor been put up to his confession. Mr. Oliver claimed the lad had been eager to confess. So where, then, was the sense in any of it? They knew by then I no longer believed their nonsense about cholera, but they would not offer the least hint things were otherwise. Twas clear as the day that Boland's wife knew something worth the telling. She had not run off with the fairies, but what she knew worried the lot of them.

The priest took up a great deal of my thoughts, with his bloody shirts and lies. And then there was that girl dead in the coffin, butchered months before, then stolen away to be replaced by a cat. No one seemed to care a whit about her, and all of them denied the least knowledge of her existence. Except for Mary Boland, who had tasted the corruption of death on my fingers and said, "I know her now, the filthy slut." Perhaps grief over her husband's disappearance had driven Mrs. Boland into madness. But I believed she was telling the truth when she spoke. She, at least, knew the girl who had slept in the coffin. And I believed they all did. At least, all of the Irish.

They were as closed to me as the darkest secret cult of pagan India.

Deep in my thoughts, in the piercing blue of the day, I hardly noticed the fork in the road where the general had been murdered.

A horse shied under one of the soldiers riding ahead of us, and I realized where we were.

A sudden chill come over me. I feared that old hag would come spooking out of nowhere. But we met a different spirit entirely, if another dark one.

Black Jack Kehoe stepped out of the trees, with a hunting piece under his arm. He did not threaten or speak. He even tipped his cap as we rolled past. But his eyes were brazen and fixed upon mine own.

I understood his appearance as a message. But, for the life of me, I could not see what that message meant. Oh, yes, it announced that he had fired the shot that knocked out Mr. Oliver's window. But why identify himself with such a crime? It did not seem the way the Irish did things. They were all silence and secrets, tricks and sneaking. Why would Kehoe wish to draw my attention? It seemed to me that my interest was the last thing he should desire.

I could not answer the riddle that day, for I had more facts than I could fit together. And facts joined wrongly make a greater lie. We did have a pleasant noontime meal in a drummer's hotel in Minersville, where we interrupted our journey. The Dutchmen insisted on stopping, see. Though they are slow, they like their victuals regular. And truth be told, I had quite a hunger myself.

Mr. Downs did not join us for our luncheon. Given his habits, I counted that a blessing. He watered his mules, then rallied himself in a tavern along the street.

The hotel where we took our repast was run by a German woman, whom my Dutchmen seemed to know. Sometimes I think them more clannish than the Irish. But a proper *Frau* knows how to set a table, that I will tell you. Such folk are ever generous with their portions, though you will pay a fair price before you leave.

I enjoyed a helping of pea soup, thick with chunks of ham and served all steaming. I will admit I took a second bowl. With brown bread fresh from the oven, spread with fat. When the world goes awry, a good meal never hurts.

eight

*M*Y WIFE DID NOT EMBRACE me upon my return. Not even when we were alone in the back room of her shop, amid the piles of cloth and half-made garments, with the smell of ammonia rising from the pot the seamstresses used through the day. Now, my Mary Myfanwy is not one to fuss in front of others, but I did expect a squeeze behind the closed door.

Instead she stood in a chin-up pout, as if I had said cruel things of her cooking. Which I never have done.

"Worried I was," she told me, proud as a princess. "And you off with the Irish in your foolishness. When they have already killed themselves a high general."

"Now, now," I told my sulking beauty, "it was my duty, see. And nothing is come of it."

She glanced down at her waist, although our expectations were hardly evident. And my darling's eyes come back up hot and fierce.

"Duty? 'Duty,' he says! You listen to me, Abel Jones, and I will tell you what you shall hear. And do not make that face at me, for I am not a child who must be humored." She put her hands on her hips, a sergeant dressing down a hapless guard. " 'Duty,' is it? '*Du*ty?' With one child born, and another to come, God bless us!" She turned to an invisible audience, posing and declaiming. You might have thought she had Irish blood herself, although she does not. "And with an orphan taken in, no less, from the Lord knows where in the corners of Glasgow City!" She almost spit that last bit out, although her manners are those of a perfect lady. " *'Duty,'* the man says!"

"Mary, dearest, I—"

She plunged toward me as if wielding a bayonet. But a scolding finger was all the pride of her arsenal.

"You will listen to me, Abel Jones, and I will tell you where your duty lies. I will tell you what is—"

"Darling, the ladies in the shop, certain they are to—"

She made a great, popping *"pah"* sound with her mouth. The effect upon me was startling, for Mary is, by habit, most demure. She did lower her voice a tone, though. For even in anger, my wife respects propriety.

"Your duty is right here, Abel Jones! To your family! And I will not have any of your grand speeches." Red in the face she was, although complected pale, as the best Welsh are. She folded her arms across her bosom and lifted her chin again. "I think the Irish are right, that is what I think. I think this war is a wicked bit of nonsense, and no good to anyone. Taking you away and—"

Then she wept, and adjourned her temper, and fit herself to my arms.

"Now, now," I told her, petting her hair. Gathered back and shining it was, as black as a raven's feather, though far lovelier. "I am a bad penny and will always turn up."

"Oh, bad penny or good," she sobbed, "I want you here with *me.* And now I have you. If only for a time. I understand it, I do." Oh, how the lass wept. "I know that you will go away again. I know the hard ways of the world well enough. But I cannot bear you sleeping under a stranger's roof when your own bed is near and waiting."

She pulled away again, deciding between more tears or freshened anger. "Oh, why can't they let us alone?" she demanded of the four walls, of the piled dresses and stacks of cut brown paper. "Why can't they leave us to our lives and keep their war to themselves, if war they want?"

"Soon it will be over, soon enough," I told her, although I admit that bordered on a lie. How is it, then, that we are quick to dissemble to those we love, but not to strangers? "And then we will be happy, you will see."

She looked at me with a love-wrenched face that would have cracked a heart carved out of marble. "We *are* happy . . . when they leave us to ourselves." She balled a tiny fist, and her eyes flamed green. "I hate them, I do. I *hate* them for the taking of you."

"Mary . . ." I reached for her, but my darling eluded my grasp. "Now . . . you do not hate them. You know that. For hatred is not Christian, and—"

"Fiddlesticks!" she declared.

And then she wheeled her mood about as sharply as a crack regiment turns on parade. Her voice switched to her tone for daily things. "I made you a German pot pie for your supper yesterday. Now it will not be fresh. And that is what you deserve."

"It is always better on the second night."

"And you put an awful fright into your Fanny. The little thing believes you walk on water, with angels in attendance. But the lass has a mortal terror of the Irish."

The Lord knows what the child saw or heard in the slums of Glasgow, where I found her. For Scotland though it was, the Irish were there in masses, living in daunting squalor. Or perhaps she had heard our local fears repeated. For the people of Pottsville like to give themselves a fright, with tales of Irish massacres and such.

"She is a good girl, Mary. You will see."

My dearest picked at a bit of careless stitching that caught her eye. She pulled the threads right out, with a face gone sharp. One of the seamstresses was going to get a talking to, that much was clear. She will have no less than the finest work, my Mary.

Twas queer how she was with Fanny, who was thirteen or fourteen. We did not know the lass's age with certainty, see, for her childhood had been troubled and lacking in documents. Poor Fanny was so pleased to have a home and proper meals that I do not think she felt my Mary's coldness. At least not at first. She slept in the kitchen and did not think it a slight, for the stove was lovely warm. I had thought she might sleep in the front bedroom with our John, who was not two, but Mary would not hear of it. The room was for our son, and that was that.

I insisted that the child be sent to school, though, for every human being needs their letters. Fanny took it in good heart, sitting there with children half her size and repeating silly rhymes. Then, in the ripeness of the afternoon, she would go to our home to do the chores, where you might surprise her singing. When time was left her, she come down to my wife's shop to learn a trade. Good fingers she had, my Mary admitted as much, and she worked as if a lash hovered at her shoulders. The lass sang in our chapel choir, and I do believe the heavens stopped work so the Lord might hear when Fanny gave us a hymn. She looked a pretty thing, especially after some months of proper meals, with her fresh-cream skin scrubbed up and her rust-colored hair less a tumult. I did not see how Mary could resist her, for I could not.

"Oh," my Mary said, dropping the ill-sewn garment, "Mr. Bannon stopped by the evening last."

"Bannon the Inks?" I asked. For there were Brothers Bannon in the multiple.

"Himself. The newspaper man. Anxious he was for your company."

"Well, I will look in on him, then. And now you are the one with a face on you. What is it you want to say? For there is something, Mary."

Oh, didn't she soften her tone at that, coming close as a cat wrapped round the hem of your trousers.

"Now, I will have you keep your temper with me . . ." she began.

I might have pointed out that she had lost her temper with me but minutes before, but the observation was better left unreported. Tactics matter as much in a marriage as ever they did on a battlefield.

". . . but I wish a favor of you."

"Anything for you, Mary *fach,*" I told her. Which I expected her to understand meant anything that was reasonable.

She took a deep breath, almost as a man does before plunging into trouble. "I want you to pay a call upon Mrs. Walker, for there is a matter troubling her."

I must have gone white as fresh milk. "Surely, not *that* Mrs.—"

"Now, Abel, will you listen? I will tell you the why of it, if only—"

"Mary, the woman runs a house of shame, she isn't fit for—"

"Will you not *lis*ten to your wife for a moment, you hardheaded man? I know what Dolly Walker is and what she isn't."

I was flummoxed. What does a fellow do when his own dear wife—and a proper Methodist wife, at that—asks that he visit the lair of a common procuress? It is not done, and that is that. And I wished to hear no more of it.

"Mary," I said, in a voice I fear was colder and more imperious than intended, "I will not hear that woman's name mentioned between us. From this day forth, I forbid you to have any commerce with her. Why, she should no more be in this shop than . . . than . . ."

"Oh, for*bid* me, will he? And the great, growling lion of Merthyr has not even heard what I have to say to him!" I fear her gorge was rising. I will admit her anger disconcerts me.

I thought it best to take my leave and go see Mr. Bannon, before we had told the town of our disagreement. Or of my Mary's mutiny, to put the proper term to the matter between us.

Mary was aglow. And not with joy.

"I did not mean it as it sounded," I explained, hoping to calm her until we could speak at home, where the walls are thick and Widow Forester, next door, hard of hearing. "I would not be harsh with you, my darling . . ."

" 'For*bid*,' he says." Her eyes were narrow as a perturbed cat's. "He for*bids* me to run my business, that I have built up with no help from him and—"

"I will be home for dinner, my sweetheart," I assured her, as I slipped out the back door.

I heard her growling behind me, which was an alarming thing. For she really is a delicate creature at heart.

"And he did not even hear what I have to say, the proud, little, prancing peacock . . ."

THE WAR HAS MADE the whole world topsy-turvy. Next, we will have women going for soldiers, or claiming possession of public office, or arguing the law before the bench. I know we all must favor social progress, which is a common good, but we do not want Mr. Carlyle's French Revolution. A man needs order, if he is to thrive, and so does a country.

My Mary Myfanwy and I would speak, indeed. That we would do, and she would understand who was head of the household, once and for all. I would not have rebellion at my own hearth, nor could I show forbearance with tainted persons.

Now, you will say: "Abel Jones, you claim to be a Christian! Christ pitied Mary Magdalene, and even Mrs.

Walker might be saved!" But I will tell you: I am not Jesus Christ, and Dolly Walker was not Mary Magdalene, and that was long ago, anyway, and Mary Magdalene did not come to my Mary for her glad rags. Nor had the gay Mrs. Walker turned to penitence, as far as I knew.

Twas my duty to bring my darling to her senses.

I cannot say I looked forward to the interview.

She had waited for me all those bare years, with a true heart, though I had believed that she had long forgotten me. Now, we were wed and happy at last, with a very marvel of a son, another blessing on the way, and no debts beyond the paying of the rent. I had endured travails beyond description in my time, and I know the ways of the world and the dangers it poses. I only wished to protect my precious family. And my Mary was treating me like a recruit who could not tell his right foot from his left.

It is a thing of gross ignomiy, when a man is not the master of his household.

True it is that I must share the blame. For I had been indulgent with her. Now, she had grown stubborn and rebellious. That is what comes of letting a wife start a business. She begins to think she has become a man.

But let that bide.

If Bannon the Inks wished to see me, I wanted to see him, too. For I was not content with his answer that no girl had disappeared these past few months. I hoped that he might find me a better response, in one of his many pockets. For he liked to claim he knew all the county's doings.

Down Centre Street I went, with the day still blue and the dust down from the rains. The shop fronts shone bright and their windows promised wonders. Oh, ever a joy it is to stroll the prosperous streets of our dear Pottsville. As soon as the ways are paved, our city will be fit to rival any.

I took me upstairs from Mr. Bannon's bookstore and stationers to the offices of the *Miners' Journal*. The rooms smelled of tobacco smoke and worse, for journalists are never moral paragons. Scribbling the lot of them were. Now, I like a nice newspaper in the evening. But I would forbid my son to go a journalist. Their habits are irregular, and what virtue lies in a pen put up for purchase? There is no honest life without honest work.

Bannon himself come marching out, waving sheets of paper like signal flags.

"No, no, *no!*" he cried. "It's John Greenleaf Whittier, not Henry Ward Beecher. Beecher's no more a poet than I'm the Queen of the May." Then he spied me out. "Oh, Jones! Just the man!" He thrust the still-wet papers upon the sleeves of his subordinate, closing their discussion with, "And tell the type-setter I want to see him. When all this has been repaired."

He greeted me with an ink-sleek hand and fair pulled me into his office, which, to my dismay, held a certain accumulation of personal odors.

"Shut the door, shut the door!" he cried. "Lovely poem. Don't suppose you've seen it? Course not. How could you? Hasn't been printed. Lovely, lovely, lovely. All guns and sacrifice and martial glory!" He shook his head wistfully. "How I envy you young men your fields of battle! A war must be a glorious affair."

I sat me down, stretching out my bothered leg, and propped my cane beside me.

"What is it, what is it that I wanted, Jones?" Then he seemed to remember. "Oh, yes. Now I have it. You're Washington's man—do you know anything about this Russian fellow?"

"Russian fellow?" I asked.

"Yes, yes. The Russian fellow. One's been strolling

around town. Gone now, I'm told. Missed him, there's bad luck. Can't find out anything about him." He looked at me, expectant of an answer. "Now, what's some sort of Russian aristocrat doing here in Pottsville? You tell me that. What's some mysterious Russian doing here?"

I had been dealing with low-born Irish, and not with the aristocracy of any nation. Not since I left Glasgow, anyway. And certainly not with Russians.

"Can't think for the life of me," Mr. Bannon went on. "You really haven't heard anything? Not simply holding it back from the press? Wait a minute . . . I'll bet the fellow was here on behalf of the Tsar of all the Russias himself, to buy up coal leases and—"

Then I had him, I did. I remembered the high-smelling gent who come out of young Mr. Gowen's law office. The one with the narrow blade of a face and the accent that did not fit any place in my memory. Who mixed his French and English without shame.

"—it's all going to contribute to the growth of our native industry." Mr. Bannon sat back, as if a specter had popped up over my shoulder. "But that's no good. Is it, Jones? That's no good at all! What if the tsar *does* buy up all the leases? It'll be the end of the small operator, the independent businessman. And the small businessman is America's future! I'll have to write Washington, Harrisburg . . . put a stop to this right now. Russians coming here and thinking they have a right to just buy up everything our own honest work has earned us." He slapped his soft hand down upon his desk. "Why, I'll be damned if I'm going to let the Russians take over this county!"

I suspected that Mr. Bannon had got a bit ahead of himself. But I wanted to know more about this Russian myself. Why would such a fellow trouble to visit our district attorney? In the company of Mr. Heckscher, the great coal fellow?

I kept that slight encounter to myself.

"Now, Mr. Bannon," I said, "I must ask *you* a question. About that dead girl I spoke of."

I thought I saw a bit of the odd pass over his face, but it was not enough of a change to make me certain.

"What's that? What? What dead girl, Jones? Is there a dead girl? That would be news, you know."

"When we spoke in the street, Mr. Bannon, I asked if a girl had been killed or reported missing some months ago. You told me . . . that you did not seem to remember any such. But you are a busy man, with much upon your mind. So I thought that I should ask a second time, see. If a young woman has been reported as missing? Or anything of the like?"

He shook his head. "Haven't heard a word said. Not a word. And I expect I'd hear something, you know." He hooked his thumbs into his waistcoat pockets. "Of course, who knows what goes on up in those coal patches? Barbaric, the way they live. No desire to better themselves, the Irish." He picked up a pencil and a bit of paper. "But what about you? Have you discovered anything? Anything new about General Stone's murder? Anything you can share with the reading public?"

The truth is I had naught but questions myself. And no answers to fit to them. I seemed little closer to the truth of the general's murder than I had been on the day I arrived from Washington.

Mr. Bannon must have read my face, for he did not press the matter.

"Terrible business," he commiserated. "Irish are nothing but trouble. Every one of them a born assassin. Drunken. And Democrats to a man. Utterly lacking in ambition, want the world handed to them. All they do is breed and burden us all with children they can't feed or clothe. Why, they'd make the Pope king over all of us, if they could, and turn this place into another Ireland! Never should have let them into this country. We're going to rue the day. They don't appreciate a thing they're given, not one thing."

He stood up with a wheeze. His nose had dried since last I had seen him, although his beard was colored with ancient stains. "Well, work to do, work to do! Be sure to let me know, won't you, when you find the general's murderer? Come to me first, Jones. After all, this *is* the Republican paper."

"If I should come to any newspaperman, Mr. Bannon, I will come to you."

"There's the spirit, that's the thing!" He pressed me toward the door. And as I took my leave, he added, "Don't you go trusting Frank Gowen, either. He'll lead you down the garden path and laugh about it."

I WAS GLUM. I did not know where to turn me next. Even my home had become a dreaded thing to me. For the matter between my dear wife and myself was yet unfinished. And I was wary of the sort of finishing it might take. My wife is a gentle creature, all in all. But when she takes a notion, she is determined.

The confidence I had felt but an hour before had vanished from me. Leaving a sorrow and unexpected loneliness.

I think in that low moment I might have given in on Mrs. Walker. So long as she continued to use the back door of the shop. I did not want a breach in the wall of the fortress that was our family. I did not wish my Mary to think me a tyrant, after all. But I feared Mrs. Walker would bring shame down upon us. And I knew enough of shame to want no more.

We had built ourselves a lovely little life, and when the war was done we would have it back. We wanted nothing time might not provide. But a man does not wish to hear whispers behind his back, or to have the honor of his dear wife questioned. I feared a scandal, more than I feared war.

We had a home now. And I did not wish it spoiled.

I borrowed the rest of the afternoon from my duties and walked down to Tumbling Run, which is as lovely as any glen in Wales. The trees come down to the water and quiet reigns. I have always liked to walk a turn or two, as Mr. Shakespeare has that fellow Prospero put it. It calms the mind, indeed. My marching days are done, but that is different. My leg is fine, when I may set the pace.

I found myself alone in the mellowing light, and I whacked at the dunes of leaves with my cane as a child would. We must preserve our dignity with others, but it's pleasant to be jolly by ourselves. The leaves were brittle as crackers, with the color of copper upon them, stretching through the trees along the valley. Queer it is how so much death surrounds us. Autumn brings nature a death list in the millions. And yet it seems so beautiful to us.

The air was like cold water, fresh from the well.

I forced myself to think again of duty, of a murdered general and a nameless girl laid down in another's grave. Of an old madwoman and a young priest fraught with books. And of the Irish. I had the sense that all of the answers were there, lying upon the ground before me, obscured not by piled leaves but by the limitations of my faculties. I will admit I like to be of service, and to win the approbation of those placed above me. But I am, finally, a small man. And now I do not speak about my stature. I know there is no greatness in me, but do not find the lack to be a trouble. I only want my life to be undisturbed. But ever again I am sent to look at death, to prod it until it answers me by name. I wished that I were still a clerk in Mr. Evans's counting house, where profit and loss was measured in dollars, not souls.

If only men and women were clear as numbers.

With the light already beginning to flee, I turned about and made my way back to Pottsville, passing through the miasma of foundries and iron works, with their spilling fires and turbans of smoke and railcars shunting and clanging. Our age is harsh, with the quality of metal, and I wonder if there will be beauty left for our children.

As I followed the long thread of Centre Street again, with the lighting of the lamps in all the front windows, a sadness filled me, a grief beyond all reason. I had the sense that, even had I been able to run, as in the days when my leg was unimpaired, time would always outpace me. Twas as if the drapes were always drawn shut in the moment before I could see some truth inside, as if life refused to let me have a good look at it. My quarrel with my wife come to seem a petty thing, fruitless and ill judged. What did it matter what the great world thought of us, if we were happy together, with our son and the little one to come? With Fanny, young and beaming in the lamplight.

All at once, I wanted to rush home, and the few blocks remaining seemed a boundless desert. Darkness fell, and carts and carriages slowed, while men and women buttoned their coats higher, chastened by the cold end of October.

I turned up Norwegian Street and nearly collided with a Presbyterian, a Mr. Murdoch renowned for inventive parsimony. The Presbyterians have a hard creed, for they believe the world is made up in advance, as if God had lost interest and moved on. As if our paths are set and we are powerless to alter them. I could not bear to think our choices useless, or to think that some are damned, no matter their striving. What if my Mary and I were born to be sent apart upon the Day of Judgement? How could I bear to lose her for eternity?

Now, our house is not grand. And it is rented, for I had put our savings into railway shares and did not wish to buy property until I might do so confidently. Yet, it seemed to me, that autumn night, to be the finest haven in the world.

I had not even set my hand to the latch, before the door pulled open. Twas Fanny, who had been watching. John, though nearly two, was on her hip. Crying, as if in fear of all the world, which is unlike him.

A bit of a glow lit Fanny's cheeks and the color did not come from the lamp alone. The corners of her lips rose. But her smile lasted barely an instant.

"Oh, Major Jones!" she greeted me, for my wife insisted upon a certain formality between us, "a wicked, bad thing hae cam o'er us. Hoosh, na, Johnnie, there'a a braw laddie." She turned her great, warm eyes to me again. "The Missus is gone for to see him up the hoose, and weepin' her eyes out."

"What is it, Fan? What is it, girl?"

"Her uncle, your Mr. Evans, sir. The lass run doon to say he's collapsed and he's dyin'."

nine

HE WON'T LAST THE NIGHT," Dr. Carr told me. "Perhaps not the next hour." He shook his head, as medical fellows do when they are confounded. "It must have felt like an explosion in his chest. He's only drawing breath by willing it."

We stood in the receiving parlor of Mr. Evans's manse. A fine house it was, though not so grand as many that would come later to our town. Of three solid stories, plus the servants' attic and kitchen cellar, it was faced with brown stone in the midst of a prosperous row on Mahantango Street, where the quality live. And yet, twas the queerest thing. For all the respectability of the furnishings, there always seemed a sparseness about the place, as if each room wanted another bit to be properly finished. Twas a cold house, even when the hearth and all the stoves were going. Perhaps it suited Mr. Evans well that way, for there was a sparseness about him, too, and he did not let emotion disturb his purposes. He avoided false enthusiasms, went quietly to his church, and led a life that merited emulation.

Mr. Evans had never married, although he seemed fond of the company of children. My Mary had ever been his favorite, I knew that from my own boyhood, for I had been kept apart during his visits, allowing him to enjoy her unmolested. And when our John was born, Mr. Evans come as near to jubilation as ever I have seen him. Our presence was expected at Sunday dinner, which was served early, and then we would sit for hours as he coddled the child. After the war called me away, my wife and son still went up the hill each Sunday, and Thursday nights were added to their visits. Mr. Evans never failed to exclaim over John's robust health and vigor, and he praised the boy's intelligence until even a father wearied of the repetition. Our John is a splendid child, but I did not wish to see him grow spoiled or haughty.

I know Mr. Evans was a respected man, but am not certain he was fondly liked. For he was a careful, private fellow, and Pottsville expected largesse among the wealthy. Our high society wished to be treated and petted, and the poorer sorts desired their allotted joys of gossip, complaint and envy. He kept himself so much apart that he even declined to become an elder of his church, when the honor was offered, as it is to all the fellows who grow rich.

Fortunate in the matters of this earth, an unaccounted sadness walked beside him. Except when he was fussing over our John, his smiles were as fragile as his tastes were frugal. He did not touch a drop of alcohol and watered down his summer lemonade. Yet, any guests who found themselves invited to his house—much to their surprise, if not bewilderment—were treated generously. His table was simple, but never pinched or mean. He handled his miners and laborers well, accepting their respect, but fleeing their gratitude. Nor would he hear my own thanks when he helped us to America, gave me work and set us up in Pottsville during our struggles. He made do with old suits, as long as they might be brushed into a decency, and even new clothing seemed worn upon his shoulders. Lean he was, in all regards, and tighter with words than a Welshman is apt to be.

Now, he was dying. With a suddenness evocative of battle. I thought, again, of all those Sunday dinners, with roast beef on the platter in its blood. I remembered his Christian calm when I showed him how his former keeper of accounts had cheated him, although he helped the fellow to jail thereafter. He was a fair man, in an age that could not lay claim to that virtue. Mr. Evan Ezekial Evans had led a worthy life and would die unblemished. That is something, in these days of scandal.

"No hope, then?" I asked Dr. Carr, who had grown gray in watching others die.

"He's already more of a ghost than he is a man. And in great pain, Major Jones. Yet, he refused my offer of morphia. He insisted, with all his strength, that he must remain awake, until he had spoken to Mrs. Jones and to you . . ." The doctor frowned, testing words inside his mouth before speaking them. "And . . . there is someone else, I'm afraid. You must expect another visitor this evening." He drew his watch from his waistcoat. "I hope the gravity of the situation is clear to her."

I thought I heard a hint of disapproval in his voice, which is unlike a doctor. For they know secrets that are best kept hid, and they learn early that they must not judge. I wondered who on earth the fellow might mean by this female visitor? The truth is Mr. Evans had no friends.

Twas then I heard my Mary's footsteps, clipping down the stairs in a terrible hurry. A moment later, she looked into the parlor. Locks of hair had strayed from the bun at the back of her head, and she wore that pallid look the dying impose on the living.

"I heard the door," she told us, then bore down on me. "Abel, I so hoped it was you. He's so anxious to speak with you. I do not think I have ever seen him so determined about a thing. You must come up."

My darling held out her hand to me, and I took it. How trivial the afternoon's fuss had come to seem by evening.

We two went up the staircase, hand in hand, with my darling ever half a step ahead. My leg makes for a slight delay, but I think I would have walked those stairs without complaint had they led all the way to the moon, just to have the holding of her hand the while.

I did not know what Mr. Evans might want of me, except to have my promise I would look after his niece, who was his last remaining relative, but for our John. And that promise he should have, though there was no need to ask it. Otherwise, I could not think of a thing that mattered, for the truth is that all he had done for me had been done for my wife's benefit. He treated me well, but I do not think he warmed to me. Strict though he was, I believe he found me self-righteous, though that is a nonsense. He was reconciled to our marriage and cherished its fruits, but I fear he would have liked a grander husband for Mary. He always looked at me a bit askance, although he valued my work and paid me fairly.

Perhaps he wished me to look after his colliery, until it could be sold. His mining operation seemed as close to a child as anything he possessed, and he had taken great pride in building it up while other men went bankrupt right and left.

Well, we would see. I resolved as a matter of course to comfort the old fellow, and to promise all that I might fairly do. Of course, I had my duties as a soldier, and such must take precedent.

I never had been in Mr. Evans's private rooms. I never had been above the main floor of the house, where the dining room and parlor were my boundaries. Upstairs, the hallway light was but a flicker. The walls were bare of pictures and the carpet runner looked older than the ages. Things smelled of mildew not quite scrubbed away.

His bedroom was all shadows, with only a silk-draped lamp on the bedside table. Small he looked in his vastness of sheets, much smaller than ever I thought him. His arm sought to point me out as I walked in, but lacked the strength to lift itself more than an inch or two. His face was gray as paraffin and one eye had shut tightly, already free of this world's deceitful light. Ever a fastidious man, he was reduced to an embarrassment now. His mouth hung open and he drooled on the pillow. But the one eye that had not quit him blazed at the world.

He tried, again, to raise his forearm, but could not.

"Uncle," my wife said, "I have brought you Abel, as you asked. See? Here he is, Uncle Evan."

The faintest nod answered her. But when Mr. Evans spoke, his voice surprised me with its brusqueness and clarity.

"Leave us, Mary. Leave us now. Your husband will call for you, if you are needed."

At that, his arm come up a bit higher and a finger pointed back toward the door. That had been it, see. He had not been pointing at me in welcome, but telling my Mary to go, that we must be left alone.

I did not understand what he might want. In his dying hours, if not moments. What need for privacy now? Why seek an intimacy with me on his way to God?

As my darling made to leave, he called after her, voice still bell-clear. "Don't let her come up . . . until Abel and I have finished. I will send him down to you."

"Yes, Uncle."

When the door shut behind her, he told me, "Sit down. There."

I took the chair pressed up against the bed.

He grasped my wrist. Quick as a cobra strikes. And he held me fast with the strength of a strapping young miner. I saw him wince at the pain of his doings and wondered at the effort it must cost him, but he would not let me go. As if he feared I might run from the room.

"How are you feeling, Mr. Evans?" I asked him. Twas a foolish question, I know. But our words do not come near the grandeur of death.

"Listen to me," he insisted.

I leaned closer. I could smell death already upon him. His whiskers lay flaccid and his flesh had lost all suppleness. Yet, his grip was almost monstrous in its power.

"Listen to me," he repeated. "To my confession. I must confess. To you."

"Now, now, surely you have nothing—"

"Quiet, you," he snapped. Imperiously. As if death itself were speaking, all dark majesty. "Listen. I must tell you . . . I must tell . . ."

His good eye closed and I thought he might be leaving us. But his grip did not slacken and his breath wheezed on.

The eye popped open again and sought mine own.

"Your wife . . . Mary . . . our Mary . . . is no niece to me . . ."

"But—"

"She is my daughter."

As soon as he forced out the words, the poor fellow sighed. His grasp of my arm relaxed, though not by much. He still wished me his prisoner. As if to take me with him on his journey. Or perhaps to hold himself yet among the living.

How much seemed clear to me then! Although he had been a loving father to Mary, I always judged the Reverend Mr. Griffiths harshly. For he had not been loving to me. Now I saw the goodness of the man, and of his wife, taking in the child of the wife's wastrel brother and saving the little girl from the shame of bastardy. Loving my Mary as their own, as good Christians.

"Good it was, then, of your sister and her husband to take the child in. You may be grateful that—"

Something in the terrible look of him stopped me. He

turned his head from side to side on the pillow, with liquid escaping the corners of his mouth. Twas a grim denial.

"She was my sister's daughter."

I did not see at first what the old man meant.

"She is my daughter. My daughter with my sister." He began to growl like an animal in torment. Weeping as if the Day of Judgement were upon us. And perhaps it was. "God forgive me, I have sinned a terrible sin. The judgement was set upon the child, in all God's cruelty. The crooked back, the pain sent to the girl . . ."

Her back is not crooked. That is a lie. There is only the faintest of curves to my darling's spine, a nothing. No one notices. I swear to Heaven and earth that she is beautiful.

"God forgive me," Mr. Evans said. "God will never forgive me."

I said nothing. For I could not know God's mind.

"I'm sorry," he said, slackening his grip. "I'm so sorry."

Still weeping he was, but I wished to take my fists to him. To pound him until he was dead, then to beat him more. Not because of the great sin he had committed. But because he had told me of it.

"It's a blessing," he said. "A blessing that your son was born without her deformities. The boy's healthy. Strong. My grandson . . ."

I sat there raging. It took all of my power not to bellow at him, not to scream out the rage that had blown up in me. I wished to shut his mouth, no matter what deed the shutting would require.

He did not need to share his secret with anyone. And not with me. Oh, not with me. For the love of Jesus Christ. He should have taken his evil to the grave.

And yet, dear God, had he not done what he did . . . my Mary Myfanwy might not have graced this world. I saw that, too.

My heart was swollen, vivid with crimson hatred. And I wanted to weep like a child handled unjustly.

Right he was to hold my wrist. For I wanted to run from him. And from myself.

"You couldn't understand," he said, as if reading my thoughts. "No one could understand. No one but me . . . and her. My sister understood . . . my darling . . . she was so lovely, so lovely . . ."

He gasped for air, for life, as he remembered. Digging his fingernails into my flesh. Like the fangs of five cruel vipers.

I would not flinch. I would not be the weaker of us.

He turned his head away from me, away from the lamp, peering idly into the room's dark corners. He released my forearm, as absently as a child turning from a toy.

"She must never know," he told me. "But you must care for her."

There was no tone of command left in his voice. Only a plaint. I felt the strength drain out of him, the life going.

"She will not know," I told him. "She will never know." My voice must have sounded as wintry as all the snows. For the anger was all inside me and would not come out.

He nodded. Perhaps to me, perhaps to a ghost just glimpsed and newly welcome.

"Go now," he said. "Tell Mary not to come to me again. I could not bear it. Tell her I'm in too much pain." He groaned, but not to convince me. Twas a lesser misery, dying. The agony of his life must have been boundless.

"Yes," I said.

"Send Dolly up," he begged, a different soul now. "I want to see her last."

YES. THAT IS WHO the devil wished to see before death took him. Mrs. Walker, the keeper of a whorehouse.

Forgive me. But I had come up short of charity and forbearance. And yet, my rage deserted me before I reached the bottom of the staircase. I saw my Mary standing there, face desolate. I almost wept at the sight of her.

I took my darling in my arms and held her so tightly I fear I caused her pain. She misunderstand the violence of my emotion and asked, "Is he gone?"

"No, dearest," I spoke into her hair, into the wondrous, familiar scent of her. "Still with us he is."

"Does he want me to go up to him?"

"No, my darling. Not now." I did not want to release her. Yet, I softened my embrace a degree, for I did not wish to do my love an injury. Or to harm the child taking form within her.

Would that child, too, be healthy? And of sound mind? Like John? And as for John, were there weaknesses yet hidden in the boy, the fruit of elder seed too closely mingled? A thousand fears pierced me. Had Mr. Evans hated me, he could have done me no worse a turn than making that confession.

Might it all be untrue? Could his confession have been no more than the madness of a mind in terror of death? Had his body's distress confused his thoughts to a horror?

I longed to think it so.

I saw that other woman then, past the sheen of my beloved's hair. Standing in the archway to the parlor, veiled in black, she told her expectations by her posture.

"Mrs. Walker," I spoke across the hall, "he wishes you to go up to him."

Let him die with a whore beside him, I said to myself. Yet, that savagery passed in an instant, as soon as I saw her running toward the stairs. There was a truth about her grief that would not be denied. Not even by me.

Perhaps she even loved the wicked man. For love is a land without maps, akin to death.

I saw the doctor, too, back in the parlor, with a question unspoken, waiting on his lips. Perhaps he was impatient with Mr. Evans and wished to be home at his dinner. We none of us can know another's heart. And perhaps it is good so.

"You knew," I said to my wife, although my tone was soft and not accusatory. "You knew about your uncle and Mrs. Walker."

"Not now, Abel. Please."

I refreshed our embrace to assure her I meant no ill. But I could not refrain from whispering, "You knew," a last time.

She did not lift her face to me, but spoke with her cheek to my shoulder.

"Oh, my dearest, I would not have secrets from you. But hard it is to tell you of such matters." She clung to me, enfolded by my arms. "So hard you make it, for you are set in having the world the way you wish it to be. But the world goes where it will."

Yes. The world. Forgive my speech, but on my blackest days I fear that I find God a disappointment.

I dreaded what else my wife might say. Her words rang true, until I wished she had lied and comforted me.

She sighed. "Times there are when I feel I must protect you." Tears watered her voice. "I would have no secrets, but I do not like to see you disappointed. I know how good you want the world to be."

I am a fool. That much I understand. I have a terror of things out of place and fear the beast within me. I long to believe there is justice at the end of things. And goodness in the heart of every man. I know it is folly. But that is how I am made. Or to speak truly, it is the way I have made myself. I cannot bear the world as I have known it. I wish a better one.

Was I the weaker of the two, between me and my darling?

Did Mary bear the pains of the heart as stalwartly as the aches that touched her back? Was I a coward who bullied his wife to persuade himself the world was in good order?

Did she . . . pity me?

Pride comes before a fall, and I was fallen.

I did not love my wife the less for any of it. Not for that dying sinner's revelation, and not for my darling's keeping of secrets. No, in that hour I loved her all the more. Nor did I pity her. I only loved her, see, and feared I was too slight to be deserving.

Twas not long thereafter that Mrs. Walker appeared at the head of the stairs. Her veil and hat were gone. Tears streaked her face.

She looked down at my Mary and nodded.

THE BURYING TOOK PLACE in an autumn drizzle. A great crowd assembled. In addition to his fellow colliery owners and the sound men of his church, our chapel's congregation turned out in full, along with every one of Pottsville's notables. Even Mr. Gowen stood in the wet with us, and Mr. Bannon suspended his scribbling for the somber length of the doings. But most impressive to me were the ranks of miners at the graveside. For the funeral fell on a working day, and those men were paid by the ton. Attendance meant lost wages. Yet, there they stood, caps off, in their Sunday clothing, while the cold rain soaked them. I sensed fear in them, along with their respect, for they did not know what would become of Mr. Evans's lands and leases, of his mines and collieries. A miner's winter is long when the works go still.

I, too, had concerns, and I will speak of them honestly, as my penance. With such a death, there comes a question of legacies. I was the man who put order into the books at Mr. Evans's counting house and I knew the worth of his coal properties to be handsomely above one hundred thousand dollars. There was the house and, perhaps, there would be private accounts. I did not wish to dwell upon such matters, but I wondered what might pass down to my Mary Myfanwy. We should not think such thoughts when relatives leave us. But we do.

At times, my pride swelled up and I decided we would have no penny of inheritance from him, that we had no need of that vicious old man's money. We would refuse it, no matter the amount. And then I would think again, staring at my wife until she wondered at me, and I would decide that no legacy could be great enough to atone for what he had done to her. She deserved all he had, and more. And then there was our son, and the child to come. Money is the only true security for a family, even in our dear America.

Pride and greed, greed and pride. Such was the stuff of my thoughts. And when I caught myself thinking so, it shamed me and I turned to read the Gospels. But it never was long before those thoughts returned. Loaves and fishes could not content me. My thoughts strayed to dollars and shares.

I wondered what he might leave to Mrs. Walker. I was jealous of it, no matter the amount. Although I told myself his wealth was his to bestow. Even on a harlot.

These matters were new to me, see. You will think me a fool, but I had never pondered an inheritance. Mr. Evans had been but fifty-nine. That is a proper age for any man, and many leave us sooner, but he always seemed a fellow of health and vigor. I had not thought of his death. Nor of his sins.

I read the Bible aloud with my wife, while Fanny listened and kept our John becalmed. Fanny took the Book's admonitions seriously, as if the Lord had written them just for her, and she loved the stories. Together, we prayed for Mr.

Evans's soul. That is a Christian's duty, and I did it. It did not rankle. I only got my hackles up when my Mary said she had always felt a special closeness to her uncle. I cannot say why, but it made me wish to berate her.

I minded my tongue, and tried to order my thoughts.

I needed to turn to my duty, for time fled. Between Mr. Evans's death and his interment, I made a round of calls about the town, seeking information that might help me. But clear it was that no one wished me success. All parties, no matter their political persuasion, wished no more trouble on Pottsville. The general was dead, and that was that. No one gave a fig about that girl. They hardly seemed to believe me, although I had felt the pulp of her corpse in my hands. Had Sergeant Dietrich not backed my tale, I fear they might have made me out a liar.

I even returned, quietly and to my wife's dismay, to watch a night in the woods below the priest's house. But Mrs. Boland failed to appear, and all I got for my trouble was the sneezes.

I decided to return to Washington, to press Mr. Nicolay for more details about General Stone, to try to make some sense of the blasted matter, and to ask why a Russian might have come to Pottsville. I recalled, too well and too late, what that odd gentleman had said as he left Mr. Gowen's office: ". . . the method is not important . . . only that the thing has been done . . ." Might he have referred to the murder of the general? 'n speaking to Mr. Heckscher? Why on earth would a Russian have an interest in such a deed? Were these matters related, or was I seeing spooks?

I would not bother my Washington superiors with tales of fairies and changelings, that was certain. I would not want them to think me superstitious. But they would hear my report about the Irish, for what it was worth.

The fact is, I was stymied.

The rain fell on the graveyard, steady and cold, and the parson read the verses Mr. Evans had specified, each of which had forgiveness as its theme. He had planned his own burying, see. Dr. Carr must have warned him of the deficiencies of his heart, for Mr. Evans left instructions for his funeral, addressed to his church, the undertaker and me. Everything arranged itself, with hardly a decision required from any one of us.

The parson said that Mr. Evans would be remembered by all as a good man. He should have said, "By all but one."

I could not shake his sin from my thoughts. Twas almost as if he had passed it on to me. At home, I would take my wife into my arms at any stray moment, until she found me silly. A part of me feared she might be gone of a sudden, although that was unreasonable. I have seen a muchness of death in my days, and know it is part of God's plan. But I could not find my ease by day or night.

Even Fanny sensed a change in me. She sang my favorite hymns of an eve, and her voice was pure and true, but she saw she could not reach me, for all her trying. She sat by the stove and puzzled out her grammar, asking now and then for my help with a word. Perhaps she feared I had turned cold and would send her back to the streets. But it was not coldness in me, only confusion. And more fear than ever I felt on a battlefield.

Above all, I worried over the health of our John and the child to be. For great sins pass down through the generations.

One good thing there was, and that was Mrs. Walker's common sense. I give her that. I had worried that she might create a public scandal by appearing at the burying, but she did not. It was her gift to her dead lover's reputation. But I did not doubt that she would come in the darkness, in her veil.

The parson spoke too long and said too little. My Mary

was a fine little soldier, composed in her widow's weeds and unshaken by the cold and wet, although I worried for her health. She had cried much between the death and the ceremony, for Mr. Evans had been her last family tie. Now she was as bereft of relations as me. We had each other, two against the world, to defend our family.

Afterward, a cold meal had been arranged in Mr. Evans's house. Twas a small affair of ham and mumbled condolences. Mrs. Walker had not been invited, of course. But I had the queerest sense that she should have been there. As if she were his widow, legal and proper.

Mrs. Walker did not appear, but Mr. Hemmings did. His law offices handled Mr. Evans's public and private affairs. He come up to me directly.

"When would Mrs. Jones like to hear the will read?" he asked me. "We could do it this afternoon, if she'd like." He glanced about us, then leaned closer and whispered, "There is one other party who must be present, I'm afraid."

Yes. Of course.

I almost told him we would have the will read without delay. On the very verge of saying so, I was. Then I stopped myself.

I begged his pardon and stepped over to my darling, drawing her aside.

"Mr. Hemmings asks when you would have the will read out," I told her.

I almost saw the hint of a smile at my new deference, although she had the sense to banish it quickly. "Whenever you think it fit, Abel," she told me.

"Then, with your permission, I will have Mr. Hemmings wait until I return from Washington. It will only be a few days."

I was punishing myself, see. For my eagerness and greed. My darling acquiesced. Then a certain dowager approached us, a woman whose only joy was another's burial. She carried a plate eaten down to the slops, with her appetite for misery unabated.

I placed my lips next to my darling's ear and said, "Another party must be present, when the will is read, Mary."

My darling did not flinch, but whispered, "She loved him."

ten

*E*VER HEAR THE ONE about the cannibals cooking up the missionary feller?" Mr. Lincoln asked me. He was a lovely, sad man, fond of jokes.

"No, sir, I have not," I assured him.

Mr. Lincoln slapped his knee and sat back, putting on that mischievous smile he liked to wear in private. He placed his hands upon the arms of his chair, chewed the air for a moment, then leaned forward again. More lined each time I saw him, his face could seem a map of human sorrows. Yet, he laughed with the innocence of a child, displaying his brown teeth.

"Well, there's this cannibal family out there on one of those South Sea jungle islands." His eyes twinkled in anticipation, for he liked a well-told tale as much as a Welshman does, and he loved to affect the voices of the characters. "Catch them a big, fat missionary, size of a Dutch saloon-keeper. Conk him over the head, and put him in the pot." Mr. Lincoln gestured as he spoke, describing the action with huge, worn hands. "And he's cooking up just fine, all salted down and rendered . . ."

Now, something there was about Mr. Lincoln's story-telling that let you not only smell the poor fellow cooking, but made you want a slice. Although I do not mean that improperly.

". . . Mrs. Cannibal, she's stirring in a little of this and a
little of that, so that everything's going to be fixed and on the
table when the little 'uns get home from the cannibal school-
house." He sighed, savoring foreign and forbidden aromas.
"Smells so good that ole Mr. Cannibal's getting right fidgety
about now. Hungry as a bear in April. Twice that hungry. So
he wanders on over to that pot"—Mr. Lincoln stretched his
fingers toward an invisible cauldron—"and he's lookin' to
tear himself off a little piece of haunch or maybe some back-
meat, and ole Mrs. Cannibal gives him a smack with that big
stirring spoon of hers." Mr. Lincoln yanked back his hand,
shaking it and grimacing.

Leaning still closer, he smiled again. Casting just a brief
glance toward Mr. Nicolay, his confidential secretary, who
completed our party of three.

"Well, Mr. Cannibal needs to fix on something to take his
mind off all those cooking smells. So he starts in to rooting
through the chests and trunks that missionary fellow had carried on into the jungle with him." Mr. Lincoln paused, as a
tenor will to heighten the ear's demand. "And what does he
find in there? In the heaviest chest of them all? Well, he finds
him a big chest full of diary books. Everything about that
missionary fellow's written down in there, neat as a pin,
going all the way back to his childhood and his studying . . ."
Mr. Lincoln shook his head slowly, in mock wonder.

"Well, Mr. Cannibal runs out to Mrs. Cannibal, waving
him a passel of those little diary books, crying, 'Lookee
here, darlin' of mine, that fat feller was borned and bred in
Boston, Massachusetts!' And his wife just puts down her
spoon, gets up a look of high consternation, and settles her
hands way up on her hips. 'You just throw every one of them
books on the fire this minute,' she tells him, 'before the chil-
drens git home. I don't want 'em thinking about where meat
comes from and spoiling their appetites.' "

Mr. Lincoln laughed to bursting, slapping his baggy trouser-knees like a minstrel in a show. "Doesn't that just beat all?" he asked us.

Mr. Nicolay, who was of German extraction, did not understand the humor, but sought to please Mr. Lincoln with a smile. Then he watched us. Waiting.

Mr. Lincoln's laughter faded. And he put on an expression as serious as ever a look could be. With those lonely, prairie eyes that burn in the memory. He leaned toward me yet again, earnest as a casualty list.

"John here tells me you've been asking where the meat comes from, Major Jones."

"EVER BEEN TO MISSOURI?" Mr. Lincoln asked me.

Guns and caissons rattled by in the distance, accompanied by faint shouts and the crack of whips. The smoke of a city in autumn dimmed the horizon, but enough late sunlight struggled through the windows to varnish half of Mr. Lincoln's face.

"No, sir, I have not," I told him. "I hear it is disreputable."

Mr. Lincoln shrugged. "Parts. Out to the west. But St. Louis now, that's a fine city. Important city. Vital. Our German citizens saved it for the Union. Very patriotic folk, the Germans, when the bug catches 'em. Although I would be grateful if Mr. Schurz would be a little less angry and a bit more helpful. Spain didn't work out for him, but now I'm growing inclined to pack him off to China. Or to visit those cannibals. Anyway, plenty of our Missouri citizens had a mind to go out with the South. But the Germans wouldn't stand for it. Raised up their own militias, bought muskets for their singing circles. Kept St. Louis in, and that kept Missouri in." He nodded, gratefully. "I made a passel of colonels and generals out of them after that, figured they'd be best at leading their own kind. Truth be told, they've been little worse than those West Point boys."

I did not see what any of this had to do with my inquiry about the details of General Stone's background and the matter of Russian visitors to Pottsville. But Mr. Lincoln had a way of circling a problem, as I believe Red Indians like to do. Then he would leap upon the matter, when least a fellow expected it.

"I had their votes, as well. One thing you can say about the Germans, they don't have any patience with slavery." He made a cradle of thumb and forefinger for his beard. "Has to do with all those revolutions that didn't work out and drove them over here in the first place. Well, when I asked 'em who might be fit to lead troops who spoke Dutch, nearly all of them said, 'Carl Stone.' Well, that didn't sound much like a German name to me, but sometimes they change 'em. Hurrying up to be Americans. Or to leave some part of their past behind. So I gave General Frémont a hint—then a second one, 'cause that man never would take the first one—that this Carl Stone fellow should be made a colonel and put in command of a regiment of Germans. Well, Frémont got his back up, the way he liked to do—never met a man who could squeeze so much blood out of an imagined insult, excepting George McClellan—but, the third time I gave him a hint and a strong suggestion to go along with it, he put some eagles on *Herr* Stone's shoulders."

Mr. Lincoln made a slight rearrangement of his great collection of limbs. The window light climbed higher up his face. The President's House was quieter now than it had been in his first year, when office-seekers loitered on the stairs and Westerners spit tobacco juice on the carpets. There were new velvet draperies, and the halls were clean. Mr. Lincoln's office smelled of liniment, not cigars, although its simplicity had not changed.

"I understand Stone gave a fine account of himself, and more than once. Pea Ridge made him a general. Seemed he was born to lead men. Unlike General Frémont, who I believe was born to lead cotillions." He gave his cheek a scratch, then dropped his hand. "Come high summer this year, with the war's appetite for recruits outstripping the number of those willing to be et up by the army, General Stone asked to be relieved of his command. All of a sudden. Said he could do more good persuading working men to join the colors than he could do on the battlefield."

Mr. Lincoln's face grew weary. "Now, I never have found a shortage of officers willing to sacrifice themselves to the hardships of service in the rear, but this feller's lead didn't seem to pour into that particular mold. Stanton was all for letting him take a stab at rounding up folks willing to be fitted into a uniform, and that seemed to be that. Last I heard of him. Until the telegraph office got a message from McClure up in Harrisburg, telling me Stone's been murdered. In your Schuylkill County, too, which seems to be a place that has more trouble before breakfast than the rest of the country has in a week."

He turned to Mr. Nicolay. "John here suggested we have you take a look, so we did." Mr. Lincoln returned those great, sad eyes to me. "Seward didn't tell you anything about the Russians, because, frankly, we thought we ought to let that dog lie down. Didn't really seem to bear, given the circumstances of Stone's death. That was a mistake, not telling you, and I'm sorry for it."

"But what about the Russians, sir?"

A flurry of thoughts swept over his brow before he spoke again. Twas queer. Mr. Lincoln could speak with all the grand formality of Cicero, when the occasion asked it, and he kept his pockets filled with words, as if he had plucked a luxuriant row of books. But his favorite role was that of the country lawyer, the man of simple language masking great wiles. He had played that role so long it fit him like an old, favorite coat. I believe he hid behind it, although he was no coward. Ever underestimated by men who lived above their mental economy, he lived within the means of his thoughts and spoke for a wounded nation.

But let that bide.

I heard footsteps running up and down the hall, likely those of a child. If so, I was glad of any joy returned to the President's House, for Mr. Lincoln had suffered the tragic loss of a son earlier in the year. And it was said his wife made certain difficulties, although such gossip is not always sound.

Slowly, as if unfolding a delicate package, Mr. Lincoln resumed his explanation. "After Fort Sumter . . . do you know which of the European powers was the first one to recognize the enduring integrity of the Union? It was Russia." He smiled wistfully. "The greatest autocrat in the civilized world, the tsar, was the only one who insisted that the world's greatest democracy remained indivisible. Although I do hear he has some reforms in mind for his own folks, to be fair to the fellow. Tsar Alexander wouldn't even entertain *un*official ambassadors from Richmond. And Baron de Stoekl, his minister to our government, remains the one diplomat in this city I can trust not to cheer on the Rebels at every turn."

He waved his endless fingers. "Oh, not that I'm inclined to exaggerate Russia's affection for these United States. No, Major Jones, the Russians have their own interests, as all people do. They're still smarting from the licking they took in the Crimea. They want to spite the British and the French. And they know London and Paris have more than a peck of sympathy with Richmond. So the tsar's just balancing things out, warning them that the brawl ain't necessarily finished and that he's still spitting mad."

"Given how close we have come to war with Britain . . ." I said.

"Just so," Mr. Lincoln agreed. "This country needs friends, and it needs them badly. And we don't need friends who just send us polite little notes and ask us to tea. We need practical demonstrations of friendship. For all the world to see. Seward and Welles have some ideas on that, by the way. But the point is that the tsar did this country a very good turn, just when we needed a good turn done."

All this was of great interest, but I could not yet see the bearing on General Stone and his murder.

"Here's the fly in the molasses," Mr. Lincoln said. "A few months back, Baron de Stoekl put a curious request to Mr. Seward. Tsar Alexander himself asked that General Carl Stone be arrested and put on a ship for St. Petersburg, where he would be tried for treason, attempted assassination, and bad manners in general. Apparently, Russian agents had been looking the world over for him. The war news brought him to their attention, though I still don't quite see how. The baron was a little evasive on that point, as well as regarding the true identity of our General Stone."

He made one of his crackerbarrel-philosopher faces. "Now, I'm a politician, Major Jones. Though I don't know if any man should make that claim out loud. And I faced a dilemma, with our secretary of state all fit to jump off the roof, except he couldn't make up his mind which way." He put on a little smile that was no smile at all. "You remember some time back when I told you about that fellow balanced atop a fence, trying to decide which way to jump? Same thing. If I broke every law in the country that hadn't been broken already and wrapped up General Stone as a present for the tsar, I might have made the Russians happy. But our German voters wouldn't be quite so fond of me next time around. And our recent elections weren't exactly a shout of approval from a people united. As it is, our German citizens are complaining because they think I should have freed the slaves last year, won the war this year and prepared to invade Europe next year. While reducing the cost of beer. On the other hand, that request was the only thing the tsar ever asked of us."

This time, Mr. Lincoln smiled truly, for I had learned to tell the difference. "I'm surprised the tsar's forgiven me for sending him Simon Cameron as our minister—Old Simon's already out of there, by the way, and trailing a whiff of scandal you can smell from here to the Pennsylvania statehouse. Seems to have found St. Petersburg a bit on the chilly side and took to warming himself with the wrong friends. Napoleon III would have called it an act of war, had I sent that man to France."

He paused for a long moment, dark eyes piercing. Letting me make the connections, if I could.

"So," I began, "while I do not mean the slightest disrespect, sir, it must have seemed something of a blessing when this General Stone was murdered." I saw another thing, too. "And, once he was dead, it mattered little who should have the body. In the confusions of war, the loss of a corpse is easily excused. So it was sealed in a coffin and hurried along to Washington by the railroad. And now it is on a ship upon the waters, sailing for Russia, as a present to the tsar."

Mr. Lincoln's eyes narrowed, but his twist of a smile was friendly. "Major Jones, I'd fear for my old occupation, if you ever decided to take up as a circuit lawyer."

"I was sent to Pottsville . . . as something of a bloodhound, then. To see if an unfortunate scent might come up. To see . . . if anyone had a mind to trouble Washington about the matter, or to create an embarrassment." The words were almost painful now, for I had been used deceitfully. "To see if anyone might be inclined to pursue the matter. But not to find the murderer, unless such could not be avoided."

"I'm sorry, if that hurts your pride," Mr. Lincoln said.

"No harm was meant. But we had to know if all this was going to blow up somehow."

I will admit my sentiments were wounded. I believed that I had served Mr. Lincoln well and proper over the past year, yet I had not been trusted with the true purpose of my doings. I did not even have the dignity of a bloodhound, but had served as a canary in a coal mine.

"No harm was meant," Mr. Lincoln repeated, a degree more forcefully. For he read men as you or I would read a book. "Your services are valued greatly, Major Jones. And you *were* trusted. I relied upon your discretion, you see."

I nodded absently, thinking on things.

His face grew as dark as the war itself. Commanding my attention. "The truth is, I'd be content to leave well enough alone, to a certain point. Maybe that offends you, in the mood you're in just now, Major Jones. But I have to look at things through a different window. General Stone is dead. And so are tens of thousands of other soldiers who wore this country's uniform. I'd even let the Irish have the blame, since they don't seem to mind it and that's an explanation a Missouri Dutchman can understand. But while you were up there rasslin' Irishmen, I'm afraid the problem has gone and gotten nasty as a stall that hasn't been turned over in a month. The scandal may not be making much smoke in your Schuylkill County, but it's starting to flame up just about everywhere else."

"And how is that, sir?"

"It appears there was a great deal more to this General Stone than met the eye. And not just to do with Russian bears and shenanigans on the other side of the ocean." He turned, as ever, to Mr. Nicolay. "John's heard from some of those folks who share a common ancestry with him. In fact, he's heard from a passel of them, and not only from St. Louis. It appears that Carl Stone was something of a leader among our political radicals, folks bent on carrying revolution back to Europe. When our war is over, presumably."

He moved his great bones in his chair. "Socialists, Communists, Anarchists . . . Among some of our recent immigrants, revolution seems to be a substitute for checkers. Now I've got the Germans and other folks screaming bloody murder, demanding that I produce Stone's assassins. And they're convinced that's exactly what it was, Major—an assassination." He wrinkled his face in disgust at the thought of such doings. "The truth is we need those Germans, Major. The Union needs all of them, every one. Native-born Americans started this war, but it's going to take our new Americans by the hundreds of thousands to finish it."

He shook his head, slowly, as if the effort pained him. "And I'll tell you this: If the Russians *were* involved in some sort of political murder, it's going to be a cold day for this government. Seward might suggest overlooking it, I expect, and he'd have a good argument. I could make the argument every bit as well as he could, for that matter. But there are some things we just can't tolerate. We can't let this country turn into a rough-cut version of Europe, where folks try to solve their problems by bombings and assassinations, instead of through party caterwauling and ballots. *I* won't stand for it. I'd have to bid up the game with the tsar, and see if he chose to fold or call. Either way, we'd lose the one friend this country has at the moment."

He looked almost frightfully glum. And when Mr. Lincoln was blue, he liked a joke. He cranked up one corner of his mouth and said, "All those complicated European philosophies they're arguing about . . . and we're having a bushel and a peck of trouble just sorting out the bad apples of democracy. Those Germans now," he said, with a sly little smile for Mr. Nicolay, "the problem is they just think too much. Can't help themselves. And the last thing you want in politics is a fellow who thinks too much, who's got so many brains in his head they've squeezed out all the common sense. Politics takes a smart man, at least most of the time. And the lower a man's position, the smarter he has to be. But a genius seems to me a downright menace to the practical business of government."

He made a deep sound, laughter's ghost, at the back of his throat. "I can't say I've studied 'em properly, but, near as I can figure it, all those radical programs don't add up to much more than a full moon over the hen-house. Your Socialist expects the state to make folks good, the Communist expects folks to make the state good . . . and an Anarchist doesn't think the state's good for anything but target practice."

I must admit I know little of such doctrines, except that their adherents put faith in their own notions, not in God. It is no wonder such folk are unhappy. Poor Mick Tyrone, my friend, bedevils himself with the miseries of the world, and always sees the canker on the rose.

"And did these Socialist fellows and such like tell you any more about General Stone?" I asked Mr. Lincoln and Mr. Nicolay. "A hint of his crimes? Or another name, perhaps?"

Both men shook their heads, in physical harmony.

Twas Mr. Nicolay who spoke next. "That is the thing, Major Jones. They all wish to know what has happened to him, why he is murdered, who is to blame. They speak of conspiracies and revenge. But they will say nothing of the man himself. They are fond of secrets, these people, and do not part with them easily."

"Whether they have secrets or not, the Union needs their support," Mr. Lincoln stressed. "Even more than we need the tsar's, if it comes to that."

"Mr. Pinkerton has looked into things," Mr. Nicolay said, "but he has found nothing."

Mr. Lincoln grimaced at the mention of Pinkerton's

name. "I don't think we'll have much more use for Mr.
Pinkerton's services. Mr. Davis never created half as many
Confederate soldiers as Allan Pinkerton created in his own
head. He and George McClellan are two peas in a pod."

Both men looked at me.

"Major Jones . . ." Mr. Nicolay began, "we need you to
find out who has murdered General Stone. We need the information truly this time. And we need to know why he was
killed. We need to know more of the man himself, of his political affiliations, of the Russian interest in the matter . . ."
He looked as serious as ever a German fellow could look,
and that is saying something. "We must rely on you."

Mr. Lincoln leaned toward me one last time. The light had
left us and he sat in shadow, but his eyes were little fires.

"I don't suppose you have any of these bomb-throwing
radicals among your circle of personal acquaintances?" he
asked.

"OOOCH, MAJOR JONES!" *Frau* Schutzengel cried, rushing
down the hallway toward me. A mighty locomotive she was,
trailing clouds of kitchen steam behind her and signaling her
approach with the wave of a rag. "You are coming back to us
again! *Und* so soon! I make a big *Apfelkuchen* for the dinner!"

Now, I must confess that, charged by the remarkable bulk
of dear Mrs. Schutzengel, I always feel the impulse to step
backward. I have withstood the assaults of Johnny Seekh
and Jimmy Pushtoon without flinching. And I know that my
Washington landlady means me no harm. Still, the good
woman has a way of filling her hallway that puts me in mind
of a rush of irregular horse. A part of me fears a trampling.

I stood my ground and she pulled up short, firing her
oven-drawn sweat in all directions and sweeping a hand
across her generous brow. Queer it is. We always wished to
embrace, I think, for we had become great friends, but such

things are not done by polite society. And though Mrs. Schutzengel was a fervent Communist—which I believe is akin to a Unitarian—she did not mean to compromise her manners. Nor did I.

We shook hands.

"Dear Mrs. Schutzengel," I said, "there is good, to see you again."

"*Und Ihre Frau, Herr Major?* Your wife? She is good? *Und das Kind?* The little boy?" she asked. "*Und das Waisenkind, die Fanny?*"

Ah, there lay troubles yet unsettled. But a family's dismay must be kept private.

"All are healthy and wanting for naught," I assured her. "Although there was a certain loss. An uncle."

She knew the outward bits of my life, for we often talked in her parlor, with dinner behind us and my *Evening Star* in my hands. Mrs. Schutzengel would read her dauntingly thick German books and grunt—though nicely—when a paragraph displeased her. Bit by bit, we shared scraps of our pasts, although I fear that I told more of mine. I am a Welshman born, see, though I have become an American. And talk is our cakes and ale.

"*Der Onkel* Evans?" she asked. "The great capitalist?"

I nodded. "Not quite so grand as all that, Mrs. Schutzengel. Truly."

"Then I am sorry. Because he is your uncle. Although he is an exploiter of the workers *und Mitglied der Parasitenklasse.*" She wiped a bead of sweat from the tip of her nose with the corner of her kitchen rag. Fair soaking the good woman was, for she did not stint on effort at her stove.

Behind her back, the kitchen clanged untowardly of a sudden. Mrs. Schutzengel turned and barked, "*Gott im Himmel, was ist denn das für eine polnische Wirtschaft!* You spoil the dinner *und* I hold back your wages!"

"My *wife*'s uncle," I clarified. For I still thought of him as such, although the man himself had told me otherwise. As soon as I had spoken, a coldness filled me.

I roused myself, resolutely, from my moment of despond. For I had larger matters to attend to, and a man who neglects his duty has little worth. "Look you, Mrs. Schutzengel . . . I have need of your counsel, perhaps of your help. But it must remain a quiet matter, between ourselves, see. It may be terribly important. Perhaps we might speak after dinner?"

Her face turned purple. I do not exaggerate. And sweat come up afresh on her forehead, as if her boiler had been restoked, until the woman fair glistened.

"Nach dem Abendessen? Nein!" She looked about her in wounded fury, although we two remained alone in the hall. "After the dinner, he wants to talk to Hilda Schutzengel! To his friend, the Schutzengel? When he has the problem now?"

She slashed the air with her rag and I felt the spray on my cheek. It smelled of chicken broth.

"No!" She shook her massive head and stamped her foot. I do believe the china shook behind the parlor wall. "Her dear friend, who does the duty in the war against those Rebel *Aristokraten und gegen die Sklaverei, und* he thinks the Schutzengel makes him wait until after the dinner!" She brought down her imposing foot again. More shook than merely the china this time. "It is now that we are talking! *Gleich jetzt.*" She pointed to the parlor. "*Marsch, marsch.* I tell the girls not to ruin the dinner *und* I come to you *gerade!*"

I went docilely, for Mrs. Schutzengel's friendship was commanding. Lovely it was to have such a friend, when a fellow needed help. But I will confess I would have waited, willingly, until our meal was behind us. For I feared the girls she had taken on in Annie Fitzgerald's wake would not do justice to Mrs. Schutzengel's standards. And I like to find proper cooking on the table.

One of the new girls was a Lutheran, from Sweden, where the people think all flavor is a sin. She was large and pale, and prone to unsightly blemishes. The other creature, small and dark, claimed to come from a place called the Kasubai. At night, I heard her weeping in the attic. In the morning, she fetched our night pots and sang her country's songs off-pitch in the yard. Between the two of them, they could damage a dinner.

Mrs. Schutzengel swept into the parlor, muttering about the lack of pride and diligence among the members of her beloved working class. Still vivid with sweat she was, and she glowed in the day's first lamplight. Sitting herself down in her high-backed chair with a great exhalation of breath, she intertwined her fingers and asked, *"Oooch ja, was denn?"*

I sat down myself, closer to her than usual. Listening for the tread of other boarders upon the porch. My questions did not want a larger audience.

"Mrs. Schutzengel," I began, "have you ever heard of a German immigrant fellow named Carl Stone?"

Her expression did not change, but for a pruning of the chin that pled ignorance.

"He lived," I added, "in St. Louis before the war. He became a colonel, then a general, of volunteers."

Still nothing.

"Now, you must keep a secret, if you please," I continued, "but perhaps this will help you remember. This General Stone seems to have been a political radical of sorts. He was wanted by the Russians. By the tsar himself, I am told. For revolutionary doings."

Mrs. Schutzengel grunted. "In Russia, to cross the street without permission is to make a revolution, I think." She leaned toward me, to the degree her bulk would permit, puffing a little. "Maybe 'Stone' is 'Stein.' But this is a common name, *ganz gemein*. It tells nothing."

Abruptly, she looked down at my uniform. With suspicion. Twas the first time she ever had done so. "*Und* why are you, Major Jones, interested in a man who wishes to make a revolution against the tsar? This is America *und* we do not have the *Geheimpolizei* in the government, I think. *Es gibt hier kein Russentum und kein Preussentum.* Why is this man interesting to you, please?"

"Look you, Mrs. Schutzengel. The fellow's been murdered. And our government simply wants to know why." I considered my words, then lowered my voice near a whisper. "There is a . . . a suspicion of Russian involvement, see. Nothing definite, but—"

"*Die Russen!* Here? In Washington? *Was fuer eine verdammte Schweinerei!*" She stamped her foot so hard it nearly forced her to her feet. "No Russians!" She proclaimed. "*Keine Kosaken, hierher, nein!* No to the *Tataren-Barbarei!* No Russian *Czarismus-Schwindel* in America!

I fear that, had she been a locomotive, she would have burst her boiler on the spot. We had little discussed the Russians in the past, but she always made it clear she did not like them. Now I found her enthusiasm alarming. I do believe the temperature climbed higher in the room, although the stove would not be lit until dinnertime.

"No Russians!" she declared, bobbing up and down in her martyred chair. "*Freiheit fuer die Polen! 'Runter mit dem Czarismus!* Down with the Tsar!"

"Yes, Mrs. Schutzengel, yes," I tried to calm her. "But it may not be the Russians at all, you see. That is what we must find out. I didn't mean to excite—"

"*Scheisskerle sind die alle! Tausende haben die Schweine in Ungarn erschossen!*" She waved her kitchen rag as if lofting a banner above a defiant barricade. I understood but little of her German, which come too fast for my apprentice knowledge, yet I fear she was unkind to the Russian race.

"Please, Mrs. Schutzengel . . . will you help me . . . perhaps your friends could . . ."

"Carl Stone is his name? Who makes the revolution for the peoples? *Ein echter Revoluzzer, meinen Sie? Und* a general? Murdered? *Die Kosaken haben den armen General kaltblutig ermordet?*"

"Yes, I do believe that sums it up. Now, if you could—"

She leapt from her chair. Which was a sight to see. "*Die Russen-Schweine* will not kill generals here in America! *Schlechter als die Rebellen sind die!* Worse they are than the Rebels!"

Had mine own visage betrayed the slightest Russian quality, I fear the dear woman might have slain me on the spot.

"But perhaps it wasn't the Russians, see. That is what we must find—"

"*Jawohl!* It is the Russians. I know it."

"Well, there is the matter of proof, of course. We cannot—"

"*Komm doch!* Come! We go now to see *die Verrückte Maria!*"

"I beg your pardon?"

"We go to see Crazy Maria. She will know your Carl Stone, I think. Or she will know who will know him." Mrs. Schutzengel paused for a moment, gripping my forearm with a strength born of wielding skillets. "But I must trust you, *Herr Major*." Her face was as earnest as any I ever have seen, and the sweat seemed to freeze in its tracks. "You must not say where you have seen this Crazy Maria. You must not say to any persons that you have seen her at all. You must promise me this, because—"

"Yes, yes. I promise."

"—they are wishing to hang her."

That gave me pause, I will admit. Things did seem to be happening with despatch. Already half the way to the front door she was, nearly forgetting the need of a coat and scarf.

"But . . . who wishes to hang her?" I begged of my landlady's retreating, but hardly diminishing, form.

She turned to me with a face of such anger I lack the words to tell you of it.

"Everybody," she said.

eleven

MRS. SCHUTZENGEL'S BOARDING HOUSE stood on a quiet lane, so we had to turn down Seventh Street for a cab. Hardly a lamp still burned in the Patent Office, but the General Post Office glowed. The lanterns were lit on the corners and shops were closing, with each proprietor's son or daughter latching the shutters then giving the doorway a sweep. The street was dense with Germans, who are a conscientious folk, and they never forget a title. As we hastened along, we were honored by greetings of "Guten Abend, Herr Major," and "Guten Abend, Gnädige Frau," with a nod that was almost a bow to Mrs. Schutzengel. For Communist though she was, she owned a good deal of property in Washington, as I had come to learn across the months, and your German respects a deed as much as the Hindoo reveres his idols.

Nor did our passage excite a smile, except from the half-witted Negro who haunted the street and sang colored songs for pennies. Twas strange that no one laughed, I must admit, since I fear the two of us made a curious pair. I am not great of stature, although I do show strong in the chest and shoulders, and my bothered leg goes along as best it can. Mrs. Schutzengel topped my own height by seven or eight inches and, had she served along with me in India, I might have enjoyed a generous shade at her side. The good woman was

big. Yet, she moved with an alacrity that astonished.
Children and dogs got out of her way as she plunged along
the boards that fronted the shops. And I do believe draught
horses shied in the street, although it may have been but the
mud giving under their hooves.

Now, I will tell you the queerest thing: War is a sin and a
Christian must doubt its morality. But war produces wealth
in heaps and piles. Not only were the shops ever bigger and
brighter, but the dusky city was building itself higher and
broader and finer with every month. The year before, our
cannon had blocked the avenues. Now lumber carts and
wagonloads of brick encumbered movement. Much was
shoddy work and speculation, I will grant you. But all was
rewarded by War and its boundless appetites.

Strange it is that God allows such things. But his ways are
ineffable.

Nor was I guiltless myself, I will admit, for my railroad
shares had earned a tidy profit.

Yes, the railroad, that paragon of speed and modern
times. As we approached the vivacity of Pennsylvania
Avenue, where the decent women kept to the northern walk,
while those bereft of honor patrolled the southern side, I
heard a locomotive's shriek from the yards just by the
Capitol, a trumpet of progress that pierced the city's evening. I could not see the great vehicle, for blocks of buildings interposed between us, but I imagined it bringing new
troops, with their shining, young faces, or delivering the
fruits of our Northern industry to nurture the army across
the Potomac River.

Now, I will tell you a thing, though you call me untruthful:
I already had decided we could not lose the war, but for the
Lord's ill temper. I saw our triumph as certain, if only our
will did not fail us. Twas but a matter of how long our victory would take and how much misery our nation need endure.

My conclusion arose from all I saw, still more from what I felt. Our Northern states bloomed with commerce and great energies, with ever new additions to our mills, more miles of track laid down, and improved methods of molding iron or even forging steel. We had been in a bit of a bust before the war, but now it seemed that a dollar invested sprouted up gold pieces in no time at all. We were the future, see.

Only the April before, I had seen our Southland, all pomp and dust, carelessness and valor, as much a place of the past as sullen India. I did not know half a million more would die. But I knew that we would win. The South could swagger and fight, but we could work. And you and I know which the Lord rewards.

My journey from Pottsville back to Washington had taken me through a landscape of smoking chimneys and piled freight, past laden canals and railways overcrowded. The antique superstitions of Irish miners and rumors of fairies and witches seemed but a dream to me, as the cars raced past a world new-engineered. A journey through Southeastern Pennsylvania gave a man the sense that nothing was impossible for our America. God willing, of course.

I had paid such matters even more attention than was my habit, for I like to read on the railway, but had been disappointed by the book I brought along. I did give Mr. Chaucer a fair try, for I have been told he fathered our English language, but the fellow could not spell and I set him aside. Nor could my German grammar hold me an hour. Certainly, we must not indulge ourselves with excuses and must strive diligently for our personal improvement. But the German tongue is a feast I can only nibble.

Let all that bide.

MRS. SCHUTZENGEL PICKED OUT a cab from the line fronting Brown's Hotel, giving the driver instructions in a dialect that forbade my understanding. But in I got, after letting the good woman squeeze inside herself, which took not a little time. I fear the carriage's springs complained, and I know the rig sat lower.

"*Nun, ja,*" Mrs. Schutzengel said, once we were properly on our way. "Now you must make the promise again that you say nothing of the woman I take you to, the Crazy Maria. No word. Not even to your great friends."

"But *Frau* Schutzengel, I must use the information, see, or there is no purpose to—"

"Yes, to the informations. *Ja. Die Fakten muss man haben. Versteht's.* But you do not speak of the Crazy Maria to any person. This you must promise."

As serious as a wound to the heart she was.

"Yes," I told her. "I promise." I hoped that fate would allow me to honor my word.

We rattled past the great, unfinished outline of the Capitol, winding south of its littered grounds to rejoin Pennsylvania Avenue's proper course.

"*Na, gut,*" Mrs. Schutzengel said, as the horse strained up the slope. "Now you are listening. The Crazy Maria is not a Communist person. We are very few, because we are the most advanced, *wissen Sie doch.* The Communists will lead the . . . *oooch, wie sagt man?* The four fronts of the revolution, we will lead. The Crazy Maria is once the Fourierist, like your Irish friend, Dr. Tyrone. Then she becomes a Socialist, but the men are too weak and do nothing. They only make the talking always. So now she is a Bakuninite. *Ob was daraus wird, weiss Ich nicht.* Because she has been so many persons, she knows many peoples. I think she knows so much it is a great danger to many, if she is stolen back to Europe. That is why she hides, not because she is afraid of the hanging . . ."

Twas then I made a dreadful mistake. I asked, "And what, Mrs. Schutzengel, is a 'Bakuninite'?"

Twas dark in the cab, but I do believe her face glowed like a stove.

"*Ach, diese Verrückten! Laute, dumme Anarchisten sind die*, stupid anarchists. Crazy peoples. They do not understand that there must be organization for the world revolution! It does not happen from wishing and shooting the idiot policeman . . ."

Now, I am not a fellow who believes in harming policemen. I began to wonder if I had not opened a door that had best been left shut. And locked.

Thereafter, Mrs. Schutzengel endeavored to explain the complexities of the great political and economic thoughts of Europe to me, telling me tales of all sorts of nasty fellows, a suspicious number of whom had French names, which cannot bode well for any human endeavor. In little more than a minute, I was lost, although she spoke with a passion even our poor horse must have felt. I chastened myself for my lack of proper attention, then realized, as we passed the Marine barracks, that her fervor did not require me as an audience, but was a machine that went all of itself.

The cab rolled down past the Navy Yard, where forges sparked despite the hour and dark hulls bobbed as tethered elephants will. We turned along the shacks and slops facing the river. A sentry stopped us at the head of the Eastern Branch Bridge, witless, but obliged to show his authority. He held his lantern to reveal himself, not us. The hack driver made his explanations and showed his pass, after which the soldier barely cast a glance into the shadows of the cab. A deadly assassin might have made his escape across that bridge, suffering only a lazy pretense at vigilance.

Hooves and wheels clopped and clattered over the planks. A naval cutter rolled at anchor out in the stream, with lanterns hung fore and aft. I wondered where on earth we might be going, but did not wish to interrupt Mrs. Schutzengel with a question, since she was enjoying her own lecture immensely.

Look you. That is how it is with all these disciples of revolution, tumult and what-not. Speeches are their substitute for prayers.

Perhaps our America will make Christians out of the lot of them.

Full night it was as we stopped at the iron gates. Brick buildings loomed behind brick walls, ill lit and barely attended. The guard was not a military fellow, but an old gummer, and the only other souls I saw were a brace of Negro women taking down a line of wash in the courtyard. A lamp set on the ground lit lofting sheets.

"*Frau* Schutzengel," I said, in rising concern, "this is the city madhouse."

Mrs. Schutzengel grunted in affirmation. "Now you will be quiet," she told me. "I am making all the talking here."

TWAS NOT A PLACE where I wished to spend much time, nor did the company warm me. I suppose such unfortunates must be locked up, to spare the rest of society. Perhaps their surroundings matter little to them. It may be they are no longer truly human, but creatures half declined to an animal state. Yet, I cannot enter such an edifice without imagining myself thus confined. Perhaps it awakens old fears of cellars and locked doors. Or echoes a charge once leveled against myself, at the end of my Indian days.

A succession of queries produced a fellow in shirtsleeves, dinner napkin still clutched in his hand. Mrs. Schutzengel introduced him to me as "Dr. Pankow." They seemed to be on old, familiar terms. He excused himself for a moment, then reappeared in his coat. With a little, leather-wrapped truncheon in his hand.

We crossed the yard toward a long building of two stories, not unpleasant, but for the window bars. The noises began to reach us some way off.

Inside the brick fortress, Mr. Milton's Pandemonium awaited, a gas-lit Hell.

A guard, fat and dull, unlocked a gate within, opening a fetid corridor to us. We went along single file, with Day-of-Judgement screams and clashing manacles attending our progress. Horrid faces, half-devoured, pressed against barred gaps. One fellow tried to force his hand through the narrow opening of his cell, seeking to grasp Mrs. Schutzengel's skirts. He pushed so hard he stripped away the skin of his knuckles and fingers before our eyes. He noised at her like a beast.

"The criminally insane," Dr. Pankow called over his shoulder. Then he added, "Syphilitics," in a dismissive tone.

Another door awaited us. A gray-haired fellow sat before it, rising belatedly at the doctor's approach, still chewing the dinner he was eating from a pail. Our host did not bother to speak, but only made a gesture with his billy.

As the guard unlocked the door, the doctor turned a pleasant face to us and said, "We must keep the women separate, of course."

A voice but one cell back shrieked obscenities to scorch the soul, all directed at the feminine aspects of Mrs. Schutzengel. Now, I am an old bayonet and a veteran of John Company's fusses. Soldiers come to know the extremes of language. But the things the creature called to her drew beads of sweat from the innocent woman's forehead. I marked that her hands were shaking.

We passed into the women's ward, and the invitations

from the mad were tendered to the doctor and myself. The most defiled souls of heartless India did not exceed such moral desolation.

A woman, missing her nose and with lips chewed ragged, squeezed a skeletal arm from her cell to claw at me. I am ashamed to say I jumped like a young recruit spying his first cobra.

The words she hissed mocked every mortal love.

Dr. Pankow produced a key to the cell at the end of the hall and opened the door. I half expected some harpie to fly out and clutch him.

Behind my back, a crazed voice begged, "Two bits, just two bits, Mister. I do anything at all, for just two bits . . ."

I followed my companions into the cell, and found an old slump of a woman seated at a desk. Outlined by lamplight, she was not chained, but did not rise or make the least gesture, either of welcome or refusal. She merely paused over the document she was writing, as if she had heard the buzzing of a fly. Her face was crudely made, as if carved by an amateur's hand, but all of Mr. Faraday's currents shone in her eyes. And those eyes judged me.

Her look was so piercing I could not meet it long. I glanced about and found shelves of dark-browed books. But I was not so distracted I failed to see our host pass his key into Mrs. Schutzengel's hand.

"*Danke, Herr Doktor,*" she told him. But her tone was condescending, telling the fellow he might leave us without further ceremony.

And he went, shutting the cell door gently.

"*Du, Hilda,*" the old woman said at last. She laid down her pen and shifted slightly, to face us full on. Her clothing was clean, though worn past recommendation. Her aspect was as hard-used as her garments.

Out in the corridor, the doctor's withdrawal left a wake of shrieks.

"*Maria . . . wie geht's denn?*" my landlady asked.

The old woman shrugged with her eyebrows, too weary to lift her shoulders. "*Diese Armen sind nicht zu retten . . . auch nicht mit unseren Mitteln . . .* "

I understood that she felt sorry for her companions in that ward, but did not think they could be helped. Then she and Mrs. Schutzengel launched into a mighty German conversation, firing words as swiftly as bullets leave one of Mr. Colt's revolvers. I could not get but shreds of it, though I recognized the word for "trust" and had no doubt what the old woman's repeated glances in my direction meant. I heard my name spoken a few times, always with my rank attached, for even revolutionary Germans respect authority.

I began to expect a lengthy ordeal, with Mrs. Schutzengel translating between us. Thus, I was taken aback when the woman spoke to me directly for the first time. In English worthy of the strictest schoolmistress.

"Please, Major Jones," she said. "Do sit down." She gestured toward her cot, which was neatly made up. "I trust you will forgive the indignities of my situation?"

I sat me down on the little bed, while Mrs. Schutzengel possessed herself of a wooden chair kept for company. I believe the legs and spindles cracked at the strain.

Twas then I noticed the tear about to break from the corner of the old woman's eye.

"I beg your pardon," she said, looking away almost girlishly. She reached into her dress and produced a lace-trimmed handkerchief washed to transparency.

"*Es war mir eine Neuigkeit, dass Sie verwandt waren,*" Mrs. Schutzengel said in a comforting voice. "*Ich bitte . . .* "

The old woman straightened herself, as a soldier will in the wake of a moment's self-doubt.

"You must forgive my loss of decorum, Major Jones," she told me. "My dear friend has brought me unexpected—and sadly unwelcome—tidings. Which, I do believe, she first had of you."

She smiled and, had she not been of the milder gender, I would have thought her a lifelong devotee of tobacco. Perhaps it was medicine or such like that whittled at her teeth. But they did seem to be her own, which is ever admirable in those of a certain age.

She extended a hand toward me, letting the fingers trail down.

"But I have forgotten myself, my dear major! I am the Baroness von Zachen und Lann."

I rose as good manners required and gave the hand she offered a friendly shake.

"*Ah, les americaines* . . . " she said, with a cat's smile, to Mrs. Schutzengel.

"Pleased to meet you, mum," I told her, sitting myself back down.

"You see, Major Jones . . . I am not unacquainted with the late General Stone. In fact, we were cousins, although I was the elder." She smiled, all sadness. "I hear a great deal still. My friends are kind enough to bring me news. But word of . . . of Carl's loss had not yet reached me. Dear Hilda did not know of his altered name. We must all be discreet, you understand." She cocked one eyebrow. "But it's definite? He's gone from us?"

"Yes, mum. I'd afraid it is true. If we speak of the same person."

She reinforced herself with a deep breath. "And shall I understand that agents of the tsar have been the instruments of our loss?"

"That is not for me to say, mum. Not until I have finished my—"

"Yes, of course. That's why you're here, after all."

The woman seemed all composure to the inattentive eye. But the hands held in the folds of her lap clutched one another, as men and women do when deep in grief. No more tears escaped her eyes, but her fingers wrestled in sorrow.

"My comrade is convinced that you may be trusted, Major Jones," the woman continued. "And given that Carl has been murdered, it would seem not only that I should bring no harm upon him by telling you something of his life, but that I might help identify those responsible for his death."

"It likely would be a help, mum."

She had to pause again, to collect her manners from the debris of grief.

After looking from me to Mrs. Schutzengel, then back again, the baroness began to tell her tale.

"He was a child of unsettling beauty . . . a true *enfant d'or*. Born Carl von Steinbrock, eldest son of Count Friedrich von Steinbrock, in Estland. A subject of His Imperial Majesty, the Tsar of all the Russias, you see. Although Carl's blood was of the purest Baltic German lineage. The Steinbrocks had been ennobled at a time when the Prussians were rude pagans, living in huts. In the old chronicles, you may read of Otto von Steinbrouck, who extended his hand all the way into Karelia." She smiled, this time at herself. "But I must not bore you. Suffice to say that, although such families ultimately saw their lands conquered by the Russians, they soon were recognized as indispensable. Without his Germans, the tsar's administration would be even more grotesquely inadequate than it is, his courtiers even less civilized, his armies less adept.

Examine the annual list of honors and you shall find more
than a mere seasoning of German names." She canted her
head, amused at the quirks of history. "Borders may
change, Major Jones, and new allegiances may be demanded . . . but lineage endures. Why, breeding even has
value to the revolution."

Her head drifted from side to side, remembering. "I recall
him in vignettes, you see. As if memory begins with a wa-
tercolor sketch. Riding his first pony, waving a wooden
sword at all of us. And telling the poor peasants he intended
to slaughter them the moment he came of age. Later, he was
almost fatally striking in his Corps of Pages uniform. The
ladies of St. Petersburg adored him. A bit too much, I fear."

A grimace shadowed her face, then fled. "We assumed
Carl would elect the cavalry as his arm, since he rode with
such a passion. All of the Guards regiments competed for
him, and he gave us all a start when he joined a regiment
of foot. If quite a good one. Perhaps it was the lovely uniforms that drew him, who knows? Oh, but his family had
high hopes for him! Nor did he embarrass his father exces-
sively. I do not recall more than minor debts at cards and a
mesalliance or two. And we ladies of the court heard
everything, Major Jones. I was quite close to the tsarevna
in those days. An unpleasant character, and petty. But useful to my family, of course. I do believe she took some interest in Carl herself."

The alertness that had filled her eyes was gone, replaced
by the soft light of revery. Even the abrupt cries of a woman
down the corridor could not penetrate her remembrance. Of
course, she must have grown used to such dreadful sounds.

"His family . . . my own family . . . held only the highest
hopes for Carl. And those hopes might have been realized,
had it not been for the events of 1848. Of 1849, really, if
we speak of the incident that changed everything."

Astonishment reborn illumined her features. "We none of us perceived anything of the kind in Carl. Oh, there were stories told afterward, of course, a report of a Polish seamstress with whom he had fallen in love . . . we are to believe that she was the one who introduced him to notions of social justice." The baroness tutted over the past. "I may tell you now that the rumor of the seamstress was true. At the time, it was an annoyance to the ladies of the court, who had sought Carl's attentions for themselves. And I will tell you that a dozen of his fellow officers tracked down the young seamstress in question—after the incident, I mean—and raped her in turn. I am told they were drinking claret, but I suspect it was something more potent. They seem to have done other, still more brutal things to her person—most of the officers were, after all, of Russian families—before they shot her. They hung her body, disrobed, from a lantern on Nevsky Prospekt. I do believe that may be why Carl never married."

"But the 'incident,' mum?"

"Yes," she said, voice cooling as if filtered through ice and snow. "No one could have foreseen it. Not even Carl himself. When our armies marched into Hungary to put down the revolution on Vienna's behalf—the Habsburgs do seem to delight in military incompetence—I fear our Russian soldiery misbehaved. Rather badly. Beginning with the generals. If report is to be trusted, the incident began with the extermination of every living creature in a Hungarian village from which a shot had been fired. The killing was carried out by Carl's regiment, on the order of their colonel. We are told that Carl, though barely a lieutenant, argued that a Russian straggler had fired the shot, not one of the villagers. But colonels in the Russian army will not be contradicted by lieutenants. I do not suppose colonels are contradicted in any army, unless by a general. And this colonel was a relation of Prince Gortshakoff's. The Guards, you know."

She spoke with a wryness that mocked a world abandoned. "Ah, but the colonel was a true Russian. A jumped-up peasant, sly. I knew him, slightly, at the court. He had porcine eyes and a nose that would not do. I do not believe he ever liked Carl, though he made a false pet of him. He had that jealousy that lies at the heart of the Russian soul, especially of anyone with German blood in his veins. But he was devious, and patient—beware the Russian lifted into power. He didn't arrest Carl on the spot. Instead, he agreed to spare a single villager. He ordered Carl to find the prettiest girl and bring her to his, the colonel's, tent. In the morning, he would release her."

The screams down the hallway had broken into sobs. They echoed.

"Carl did precisely as ordered. He delivered a lovely girl to his colonel. The tale has been embellished to render her one of those amber blonds who so unsettle the gentlemen of Budapest. And that night, when his fellow officers were contentedly drunk and snoring, Carl disarmed the sentry before the colonel's tent—a word would have done it, of course—stepped under the flap, and shot his colonel through the forehead. We are told that the girl begged Carl to shoot her, too, but that he dragged her off wrapped in a greatcoat."

She curled her lips in the parody of a smile. "We are wise to suspect such romantic details. Had Carl and the girl been seen, how might they have escaped? We cannot know what the poor sentry reported, since he was executed the next morning. But the evident facts were that the colonel lay dead, and that Carl had shot him. An official version of the event was put about in St. Petersburg, claiming that a crazed Hungarian gypsy had crept into the colonel's tent and killed him. And I knew one officer who could never quite believe that Carl had shot his own colonel. He insisted that the girl herself must have done it, and that Carl, foolishly, had taken pity on her. That was all nonsense, of course. Carl fled. And, from that day on, every nobleman in the empire of His Imperial Majesty, the Tsar, has yearned for his death. The Russians out of a spirit of vengeance, the Baltic Germans because he played into the hands of the Russians, who are forever warning the Romanoffs of German disloyalty."

She paused for a moment, letting some bitter memory pass. "The family was ruined, of course. They could not show their faces at court. In fact, they were confined to their ancestral estate for . . . I believe it was five years. Lands were seized, the daughter was unmarriageable, doubt was cast on the younger son's inheritance of the title . . ."

Of a sudden, she laughed. Not as a baroness should, but like a fishwife. "Oh, it served them right, you know. Every one of them. They treated their peasants worse than cattle. They were impossibly arrogant, as only Germans lording it over Slavs can be. The Baltic nobility claimed the old count died of a broken heart, but the truth is he had been drinking himself to death and whoring himself sick for years." She leaned toward me, face set anew. "Oh, yes, I can remember the privileges, the beauty of my youth. But 'Good riddance,' I say. When the revolution comes, all of them, all of the aristocrats, must be exterminated. *Nam nuzhno chistit novoe obshestvo.* The coarseness of the Russian tongue expresses it rather well, I think. Such a massacre is the only way. Otherwise, they will come back. They always do, you see. The French were much too indecisive, when they had their chance. And the vultures came back to roost."

"But . . . Carl Stone did not come back."

She chuckled delightedly. "But that's just it, you see!

He *did* come back. He grew a beard, put blacking in his hair, and returned to St. Petersburg. And when he learned what his brother officers had done to that Polish girl, Carl bided his time until they suspected nothing. Then he and his revolutionary acquaintances set a bomb in the officers' mess of his old regiment. Five were killed, as I recall—not counting the servants and orderlies—and several more were crippled or had their precious faces marred." She smiled at me. "Flying glass and bits of wood do not make so straight and handsome a scar as you wear on your own cheek, Major Jones—a light saber, I presume? Ah, but the officers, even those from the minor families, were outraged. Or, when I consider the matter, perhaps those from the humbler families were the most demonstrably outraged."

She smirked, in grim satisfaction. "Even then, Carl didn't leave Pieter. Not until the arrests began and his comrades begged him to go, to show himself somewhere else, in Berlin or Paris or Rome, anywhere that might attract the attention of the secret police and draw them off the students and conspirators of St. Petersburg—Russians do prefer the conspiracy to its consummation, you understand." She sighed. "So Carl went to Paris, argued with Monsieur Lassalle, robbed a bank in Geneva, conspired in Italy, harbored members of Young Ireland who were in flight after their little cabbage-patch rebellion, even—"

"Please, mum. Forgive me. But you said something of 'Young Ireland' just now?"

That very instant I recalled old Donnelly's words in the tavern up in Heckschersville, to the effect that no man among the Irish had killed General Stone and, had they wished to kill them a general, he would not have been the one chosen. Had the fellow been known to them? Were there more conspiracies at work than anyone imagined?

From her vantage point in the madhouse, the baroness was dismissive. "Oh, I believe he helped several of the Young Ireland exiles. When they were badly in need of help. Out of money, with London onto their scent. That was in Aix or Toulouse, I'm uncertain now. And, later, in Milano. I remember that part. Of course, it was no more than an act of charity. The Irish are hopeless as revolutionaries, my dear major. There's always an informer in their midst."

"But how did he come to America?"

She smiled, warmly now. "Carl always was a romantic, you see. Europe had grown too dreary for him. After 1848, all the fight went out of the people. The best men left. For America. I saw Carl not long before he took ship. That was in Brussels. He came to say goodbye, at great risk to himself. We had grown quite close in only a few years as hunted creatures. Although we had not much liked one another at home—he thought me humorless and anxious for prestige." She smiled at that, too. "Carl was the happiest I ever had seen him, happier than he was as a child, on the back of his pony. He had quite talked himself into the idea of America, of building a new world then coming back to the old world again, to complete the revolution. It was all rather vague, of course. Carl was still more the dreamer than a theoretician. He was brave, but too impulsive. His thoughts lacked rigor. I believe he sailed from Cherbourg, but it may have been Oostende."

"And did you see him again, mum? In America?"

"Oh, yes. When it could be managed. I had to leave Europe myself, you see. After an event of which your friend"— she glanced at Mrs. Schutzengel—"could speak more informatively than I might do. I saw Carl twice in St. Louis, once in Chicago. Then he visited me here, hardly a month ago." Her smile broke down. "He told me about his plans to recruit workers and miners for the Union cause. He was convinced that the future of the entire world depends on the outcome of this war, Major Jones. Although, personally, I believe the world shall get on, in any case. The revolution is inevitable. It is only a matter of time."

"But . . . did he say anything about the Irish? Anything specific? About Irish miners?"

"Why, yes, I believe he did. Yes. He felt they misunderstood the war—I fear he had almost lost his passion for revolution and fallen blindly in love with his new homeland, you see." She laughed again. "What a lovely irony that he should have become a general, after all! As for the Irish, Carl was certain that, given his own history, he might be the one to convince them of the justice of the Northern cause, of the necessity of supporting the Union. I believe he went with a personal commission from General Meagher, a letter. To the Irish, explaining Carl's . . . credentials. Meagher was a Young Irelander, you know. Although he and Carl only met here, in this country, through mutual friends. I believe Meagher was exiled to Australia and mounted some sort of colorful escape. I do believe the Irish are better at escaping from prisons than they are at staying out of them."

"So . . . General Stone went to persuade the Irish to enlist? Backed by General Meagher?"

"Why, yes. I believe I've said that."

"Yes, mum. But I can't quite see . . ."

"You may be certain it was the Russians who killed him, Major Jones. They have been trying to do so for thirteen years. In fact, Carl mentioned that he feared a Russian agent was onto his scent—isn't that what one says in America? I do not doubt that the tsar's hand reached out to strike Carl down. The tsar's hand . . . or at least Prince Gortshakoff's claw."

I could see it all, of course. I could see it clearly. Yet, I cannot explain why, but I still was not entirely convinced that the man had been killed by Russians. I wished to pursue another round of investigations where the bloody deed had been done. Or perhaps it was only that I longed, selfishly, to go home again. To see my darling wife. And my son. And Fanny. But, above all, to hold my wife to my breast. For though I had run away from the horrors I learned at that old man's deathbed, I now yearned homeward, aching to clutch my loved ones in mine arms. And, I will admit to you, I wished to hear Mr. Evans's will read out. For though it shames me, I will tell you: Even in that madhouse, talking to a fugitive baroness whose own past courses were as yet unexplained, my mind strayed to the will. I wondered if my wife would have her share passed to her honestly— and no portion, no matter how great, could be too much for what that foul man owed her—or if the fellow would have made a great share, or even all, of his fortune over to his paramour.

We should not think about such things, or in such selfish terms. But we do.

"I have trusted you," the baroness said. Twas then, with a shock, that I realized she could not be as old as she appeared. Her story suggested that she could not be more than fifty, nor even so old. Life had, indeed, treated her harshly. For it was the wreckage of a woman that sat before me. Perhaps there even was a touch of madness. I could not say. For I was a-swirl with doubts within doubts behind doubts. I had not quite got all her tale in order, though I saw the logic in it.

"I have trusted you," she repeated, in a tone that suggested our interview had neared its close, "not only because my old *Kameradin* trusts you, but because I wish to see the Russians exposed for what they are. They cannot be trusted, not ever. They devour what they can, and destroy the rest. My own kind have been fools to serve them. German and

Russian blood is not compatible. Even the revolution will not change that. They must be mastered."

"Yes, mum," I said absently.

She sighed from the heart. "And this is my life. You see? A prisoner by choice, in an American asylum. I do not think the Russians or anyone else will find me here, don't you agree?"

"Yes, mum. I suppose that is true."

She turned to Mrs. Schutzengel with a smile that mixed true warmth with clever falsity. "I have not been as careful, nor as wise, as my old friend, Major Jones. After all, she was the one who threw the bomb. I only helped with the plan."

My face must have recorded my bewilderment. Mrs. Schutzengel got up an awkward grin.

"It was only a little bomb," my landlady said meekly.

"But it struck its target, did it not?" our hostess continued. "It only cost the Prussian minister an arm, but it did manage to kill his wife."

I fear I saw Mrs. Schutzengel in a new and confounding light.

"Am I to believe she hasn't told you of her moment of triumph?" the baroness asked me. "Ah, but dear Hilda always was the best of us at keeping secrets. Had it not been for her, I would have been arrested in Dresden, you know. Or in Mainz. But she hasn't told you that, either, Major Jones? Really, I do believe she'd be an even better addition to the Union cause than poor Carl. She's quite the most lethal of us all." A fresh thought paid her a visit. "I shall need to write to his sister. I believe she's in Venice just now."

And that was it, or nearly so. Mrs. Schutzengel rose, and I followed her example. But in the very process of leaving, I saw I could not be content with one question unasked.

"Begging your pardon, mum," I said to the baroness, who already had returned to her paper and ink, "but if you were a woman high up in the Russian court . . . how did you come to be a revolutionary yourself? If you will excuse the asking?"

She adorned her face with her bitterest smile of the evening. "Oh, I have Carl to thank for that. Although I suppose a certain wildness—a tendency to stray—runs in the blood. After . . . the incident . . . well, I was his cousin, after all. I prayed I might escape any serious penalty. I believed myself a favorite of the tsarevna, you understand. But she was a capricious woman, too stupid to be intelligently cruel, but with a savage's canny instincts for devising the perfect torment. She *was* sly enough to wait until the first grand ball of the season. Then, in the midst of all those glittering dignitaries and ambassadors, surrounded by all the princes of Russia, its ministers and all the jewel-smothered wives of St. Petersburg society, she turned to me and cried out, 'What is this *fil*thy Jacobin slut doing in my presence?' "

She closed her mouth firmly and stared at me.

"And . . . and that was all? An insult made you into a revolutionary?" I asked, incredulous.

"Not quite all," she said, in a lowered, luring voice. Her eyes gleamed with hatred. "The very next night, a fair-sized party of officers burst into my father's house off the Prospekt. We called it our palace, but everyone does that sort of thing. It was certainly nothing worthy of the Stroganoffs. Not nearly grand enough to be forbidding, once the daughter of the house had been called a 'filthy Jacobin slut' at a court ball, and by the tsarevna herself." She assumed a matter-of-fact expression. "I do not know how many there were, in truth, but they seemed an endless number to me. To this day, I cannot abide alcohol on a man's breath."

She looked down at the floor, but only briefly, before her searing eyes returned to mine. "Perhaps I belong here, with these women. It's a miracle I'm not like them, you see. They insulted me until the morning light came in the window, then stumbled off. They were singing as they walked along the canal, I remember that clearly, a song about soldierly comradeship. My father could not bear the disgrace and shot himself. He was a weak man." The ghost of a smile, of something horrid and deformed that pretended to be a smile, twisted her lips. "Did I mention that the captain to whom I was affianced was one of the party? He wanted them to shoot me when they had finished, but I wasn't a seamstress, after all. I was a baroness-in-waiting. And that counted for something."

MRS. SCHUTZENGEL HAD ORDERED the cabman to wait for us and I was relieved to spy the silhouette of his vehicle. When the asylum's gates clanged shut behind us, I felt as though I had escaped from a world of which I wished no part. What had we to do with Russians and revolutionaries, even if they took to settling old scores? We had worried about the Russian bear in India, of course, alert to his fussing about in the Afghan hills. But Russia was far away from our precious America. I wondered if their tsar—and all the nasty sorts he kept about him—were not better banished from our policies and thoughts.

I smelled the rancid stink of Europe's squabbles. Twas worse by far than the odors of a madhouse.

We rode in silence, except for the dull thump of hooves and the creaking of wheels. I wondered how much might be believed and which things truly bore on the matter at hand. I had heard that General Meagher of the Irish Brigade had, indeed, been a revolutionary in his time, as Carl Stone had been. Both seemed to have been converted to the American cause, although Meagher still preached of liberating Ireland, about which a fellow could read in most any newspaper.

Twas queer. I now knew far more about the murdered fellow, but somehow had even less sense of the man. Had he been the sort to make decisions coolly? It did not much sound like it, although men change with the years. Had he been the type who takes on a passion without the ability to reason through to the end? The kind who makes each pursuit into a love affair, all headiness and fire, with no sound grip? Had he gone to Pennsylvania after deliberating carefully and deciding that he best could serve our Union in that manner? Or had his flight from the battlefield to become a glorified recruiting sergeant been but another whim in a life of fancies? Had he . . . behaved untowardly toward women? Toward Mrs. Boland, perhaps? Or others among the Irish? Their men would kill for honor, that I knew.

I wished that I might have seen him alive, if only a single time.

And would that woman lie about the Russians, to have her revenge upon them? Was it her interest to make them out the villains, whether they were guilty of murder or not? I felt a deep-down weariness, to see how Europe's ghosts crept to America. Europe seemed the serpent in our Garden.

It was only after we recrossed the bridge into the city proper that Mrs. Schutzengel spoke to me.

"What gives me sadness, Major Jones, is that she sometimes *is* mad. Only sometimes, *wissen Sie?* She is speaking all the truth to you, I think. About the important things, *die wichtigen Sachen.* But there is a secret inside of her secret, if my English words can explain it. We have said to her how wise it is to hide in the asylum, where no one finds her. So she is believing everything is her plan and her choice, *die eigene Wahl.* But sometimes we think . . . sometimes we are glad she is there, for another reason. She is very sick, you see. Sick like those men and women, in the head and the body. But only sometimes in the head. But that is bad for the revolution, *verstehen Sie?* She wishes only to do the killing now. More and more killing. But America is not the place for the killing. And I think the killing becomes more important to her than the revolution. The revolution is not to kill, you see. It is to make the world the better place. No tsars, no kings, no emperors . . ."

Of a sudden, Mrs. Schutzengel began to sob. Her great bulk quivered in the shadows of the cab. "When they have killed my Josef, when they have shot him down like the dog in the street, I, too, have only a great anger. But anger is the enemy of the revolution, I see now. Ooo ch, a little anger, yes. But not the anger that blinds the peoples." She sought to master herself, but her sniffles would not quit. So she blew her great cabbage of a nose with a roar the Rebels must have heard in Richmond. "Some of the times, I am telling myself, 'Hilda Schutzengel, *lass es, lass es mal!* You are in America now, and you have the goodness of life given to you. *Europa ist weit weg, nichts mehr als ein Alptraum aus der Kindheit.* Leave the old things behind you. Leave them behind.' And then I think that is the sensible way to be . . ."

She leaned toward me in the shadows of the cab and her emotions filled the air like a powerful scent. "Then I think again, 'No! As long as there is no justice, you must fight!' I think of my Josef then, of my old happiness that was as big as the ocean, and I know that I must fight. Until all of the tsars and kings have gone away. America is not the end, Hilda Schutzengel! America is the beginning! The future must be freedom for all the peoples . . . ' " She sat back. "Ooo och, Major Jones. I think maybe I am only the silly old woman now, who can do nothing . . ."

That drew a question to the front of my mind.

"Mrs. Schutzengel . . . would you happen to know the age of that woman, the baroness? She looks as old as Methusaleh's wife, although I don't mean to be—"

"Thirty-seven years," she said. "I have seen the papers."

"Good Lord. She looks sixty! At least. Oh, I realize she could not be more than—"

"Thirty-seven years," Mrs. Schutzengel repeated. "She is very sick. In many ways. *Sie hat sehr gelitten.* There is much suffering."

"And you . . . you and your friends . . . you really won't allow her release. Will you?"

She made a sound that was near akin to a groan. "No. It is for the good of everyone this way."

I thought of the ghastly moment that must come when that woman, the fallen baroness, would learn that her place of refuge had been no more than her prison all along.

"She is dangerous to all," Mrs. Schutzengel explained. "To us. To herself. She is sick in a terrible way, *ganz ohne Hoffnung.*"

I understood that tone of voice, for I have used it myself. It is the timbre that seeks to convince itself.

"Last year," she continued, "in Baltimore, Maria has made an attack upon a little girl, a pretty, little girl. She has made bad scratches all over the face of *das Kindlein*, the deep ones that make the scars. Then she is choking her. *Und* all the time Maria is screaming to the people that the little girl is an aristocrat, that she must be killed, that all like her must be killed. But the little girl is the daughter of a dustman only. That is when we must convince her that the asylum is a hiding place. We do not wish her harm, *verstehen Sie?* But we are not safe with her upon the street, none of us."

"And you . . . you really have killed? With a bomb? For your revolution?"

"And you, Major Jones? When you are serving the Queen of England, *weit weg in Indien?* What are you killing for then? Not even for a revolution, I think."

This world is never quite as we would have it. Not as I would have it, certainly. My wife is right about that much. I long for a better world. Where everything is as clear as a ledger book.

As we passed below the outline of the Capitol again, I realized that Mrs. Schutzengel had withdrawn into the corner of the cab, to the extent her girth allowed her to withdraw. She whimpered, as a distraught child will do.

"No tsars," she sobbed to the night beyond, "no kings."

twelve

"GODDAMN IT, ABEL," Mr. Seward said, "you're harder to find than an honest Congressman. Where the devil have you been, man?" He stabbed his cigar back into his mouth, then tore it away again. "Well, get the hell in and let's have a talk."

I did as I was bidden by our secretary of state and climbed into his carriage, which was so thick with smoke you might have thought it a battlefield at the height of a cannonade. Fit to choke a Methodist it was.

Taking a seat opposite Mr. Seward, I arranged myself and my cane to leave a goodly space. Young Fred Seward, who had intercepted me upon Mrs. Schutzengel's porch, come climbing in behind me. He was a man more decorous than his father, but not half so alive.

"Damn me all the way to Hell and call me three-quarters sorry," Mr. Seward declared, examining me as he stoked his mighty cigar, "I thought we were friends, the two of us. And here you come creeping down to Washington from that Irish bog up there in Pennsylvania and don't even stop by to tip your hat and have a spit."

Now, when a great man tells a fellow like me he "thought we were friends," he wants a thing he fears you are loathe to give. And I did not "come creeping down to Washington," but took the train and did not hide from any man.

The carriage, perfumed with the burning flowers of Cuba, did not abandon its station along the street.

"Now, you just tell me what that little Dutch sneak Nicolay's been telling you," Mr. Seward said. "Sticking his damned whiffer into my business, is he? That what Nicolay's doing, Abel? Worried about our German voters, is he? As if those sausage-eaters had anyplace else to go!" He cleared his throat, with a sound approximating the Falls of the Niagara. "And getting all high and mighty about the Russians, is that what he's up to?"

I was dismayed by his queries, for I had grown quite fond of Mr. Seward, despite the moral violence of his vocabulary. I did not wish a breach between us, and certainly did not want him for my enemy, but could not break my trust with Mr. Nicolay. Or Mr. Lincoln. There appeared to be discord between men I admired. And I found myself between their lines of battle.

I began to stammer out an apology, although I was not certain one was in order. But Mr. Seward proved deaf to interruption.

"You just listen to me, Abel, and I'll tell you what's what. Goddamn it." He drew on his great cigar as if to swallow it. The tip flared up and sparked like a gunner's fuse. A moment later, our secretary of state belched smoke like a twenty-pounder. "Tsar's about the only friend we've got. And I wouldn't trust the man with a bag of rotten apples. But we need him, damned if we don't."

He straightened his back like a rooster primed for a match, although it made the good man little taller. Two "banty birds" we were, as he once put it. But small of body does not mean small of heart.

"Listen here," he said, yanking the cigar from his lips again, "if the Russians are up to some sort of trouble, you just leave it to me. You tell me first. Anything you find out up there. You don't need to go running to Lincoln's little lap-dog with everything. I'll handle de Stoekl." He grimaced. "Pompous sonofabitch. German blood himself, you know. Russian minister, or not. 'Baron' this, 'baron' that. Hell of a combination, Germans and Russians, when you put 'em to-gether. A body'd expect the combination to turn out smart and sturdy. Instead, you get the dreariest drunks on earth. And de Stoekl's dull even before he gets to his liquor. I'll take an Irishman, anyday." He snorted. "Though I can't say I'd want to take him very far—any chance we'll ever per-suade those micks to vote right, Abel? What do you think? Have the Copperheads got 'em so spooked they can't see past the next swig of liquor? My people are worried sick about New York City, and to Hell with some two-bit coal mines."

Again, he did not pause to let me answer. He hammered my knee, leaning in with that big-nosed, little face that put me in mind of a hawk. "I'll handle the Russians. Those beer-pot Germans, too. Anything you learn, come straight to me. Nicolay's got other things to worry about. Plenty of 'em, besides his sauerkraut and pig's knuckles. And the president's got enough on his mind. More than enough. No need to worry him with the minor dilemmas of foreign relations."

He drained the smoke from his shrunken cigar, gurgled, and puffed out a cloud. "I've got plans for the Russians, damn it all. When this war is over. When we've won. They've got something I want, and I'm going to get it from them, if I have to take a cane to Thad Stevens myself along the way."

"Father!" Fred Seward exclaimed. He always sought to tame his parent's speech, but I fear Mr. Seward relished the lad's discomfiture. They were not unlike the Adamses, *'pairy-fill,'* as those Frenchmen say. "You know that Congressman Stevens is one of the finest—"

"Oh, turn off the tap, Fred," our secretary told his son. "Abel and me, we're old friends, the two of us. We're pals." He offered me a "between us" sort of glance. "I trust him. And he trusts me. As for old Thad Stevens, Lucifer himself couldn't stand that self-righteous bastard."

The son gave the father a doleful glance, but kept himself quiet thereafter.

"Thing is, Jones," Mr. Seward started up again, "the Russians are broke. Flat busted. Haven't got a penny. Still haven't recovered from that mess in the Crimea. Trying to build up their army and navy. And they haven't got a pot to piss in." He grunted. "Oh, this war has our government plenty tight, too. I can count a damned sight better than Chase, when it comes to that. But the war won't last forever. And, by God, the world's going to see us come out the other end as the richest people on earth. Mark my words. And, before I die, I'm going to see these United States even bigger." He puffed what little was left of his stogie and threw himself back against the plush of the carriage. "They'll call me a fool. Let 'em. I'll have the last laugh."

He dropped his cigar on the floor, where other stubs had preceded it. Father and son evidently had waited much of the evening for my return. "Right now, I don't want trouble where trouble doesn't need to be. This General Stone of ours is dead. Stone, or Stein, or Bierstein, or whatever his name was. Can't bring him back by making a diplomatic row, can we? Just to please a pack of four-eyed Germans who couldn't fight their way out of a beer hall."

He punched my knee again. Twas my bothered leg, but no matter. "You find the Russians had a hand in this business, you let me know. And, by God, I'll tear into 'em! But I know how to do it, Abel. Without spoiling anything we don't need spoiled. Understand me?"

I cannot say in truth I understood. For I did not think Mr. Lincoln and Mr. Nicolay sought discord with the Tsar of all the Russias, either, although they faced political calculations. Of course, I knew enough of government to see that Mr. Seward was the fellow who bore the official responsibility for foreign matters. But there is more to government than official duties. It is, above all, a matter of personality, though not, unfortunately, of character. The man is more important than the office, and power ebbs and flows on personal credit.

I feared that Mr. Seward would seek a promise of me, which I would need to decline. But the secretary was clever enough to know each fellow's bounds. Behind his bluster, he judged men with a keenness. And he loved books, which speaks well of any man, although he did not reveal that taste to the public. He never read where his voters might see him enjoying it. Americans do not like learned leaders, see, but wish to think their politicans plain. Gruff to the world, Mr. Seward acted the common fellow. But he had a mind near rich as Mr. Lincoln's.

I was relieved when he drew out a fresh cigar, for his manner said our conversation was ended.

"Well, now we know where we stand, goddamn it. Fred, make room for the major to get down. Get out of his way, for God's sake! Go on in and get your supper, Abel, old friend. Sorry to sneak up on you so late in the evening. But, damn it, man, you should have come to see me, instead of making me hunt you down like a goddamned Indian." He smiled to show old teeth and wrinkled skin. "Between the two of us— you and me—we'll handle this. No need to worry Lincoln with trivialities."

I was dismissed and went gladly. With more to ponder than a fellow likes. I even wondered if Mr. Seward really had expected me to satisfy him, or had only made a display of his queries for another purpose entirely. That is how these diplomat fellows are, see. They say one thing, but really mean another, and calculate each passion they pretend. Worse, Mr. Seward's career had been in politics. Although I liked the man, who had been fair to me, I knew enough of the world to fear that the wedding of a political mind with a diplomatic position was as risky as mating Beelzebub with Lucifer.

I was out of sorts as I climbed the steps to my boarding house. Fortunately, Mrs. Schutzengel had set a lovely cutlet of pork in the pan for me, which lifted my spirits at once. She made fresh coffee, then she gave me pie.

"JAYSUS, I'M HAPPY," Jimmy Molloy declared. "I'm a horrible happy man, Sergeant Jones—beggin' your pardon, it's 'Major Jones' I'm meaning." He had been waiting for me after breakfast, when I come back in from my business down the yard. Now he stood before me in the hallway, waving a cup of Mrs. Schutzengel's coffee, as if he meant to splash the walls and the world. "She makes me so happy, that Annie does, that I've never been so miserable in me life."

He looked at me with the sorrowing face of a private soldier the morning after pay-day.

"Now, Jimmy, I meant it when I told you that you are to call me 'Abel.' For we are in America now and friends, after all, and you have become a respectable married man. As for being misera—"

He started up again, unable to listen for long. For he was Dublin Irish, see, and shed words as freely as storm clouds shed their raindrops.

"It's just that she'll never leave off her making me happy, morning, noon, and night, then morning again. And when she's not making me happy, she's doing this and that for me own blessed good. Oh, it's a wicked thing for a man to have to suffer! And her with them eyes that don't even close to sleep, I swear it on the grave o' me late, sainted mother, and on the graves of all o' me lovely fathers in their dozens, and an't it always done for me own good? She's got an eagle eye, that one. Oh, she ought to have been a peeler, not a woman. Turn her loose, and she'd find a snake in Ireland.

He canted his head to the side, like a fellow playing a comedy. " 'Annie Fitzgerald,' says I, 'I'll not be regulated constantly by a woman,' and 'Oh, won't you?' says she, 'It's only for your own good. And me name's Annie Molloy these days, as if ye haven't noticed the change.' Oh, she's the devil got up in a petticoat, the way she comes after a man to tell him which o' his buttons to button up first. And all for his own good." He shuddered at the intrusion of another intimate memory. "Jaysus, she's a nasty one for the washing up, as well, with her baths and her scrubbings and her 'Change your linens, or ye'll have no dinner this evening.' Sure, and it ought to be a crime to be made so happy as that woman wants to make me."

Molloy looked at me with eyes that aped the saints in those oiled-cloth portraits that Irish women buy of nuns come peddling. He might have been that fellow pierced by arrows, for all the agony he put on. He ever has been one for exaggeration and even something of a trickster in his time, although his comportment has shown a marked improvement.

But I was firmly on the side of Mrs. Molloy in this struggle. Twas handsome to see her husband so clean and clear of eye, with not the least taint of alcohol upon him. I hoped the

day might even come when he would join me in the
Temperance Pledge.

"Oh, can't ye think o' some terrible task ye could set me
to? In your high capacity of a major, to which ye've
climbed up so grandiose? Haven't I done ye the devil's own
good in the past, from the mouth o' the Kabul River, where
the blue waters meet the brown, to those queer parts in New
York, where the cold was bitter as Derry boys locked out o'
Heaven? Help me, man! Save me from the blight o' me
married joys! Can't ye think on a way to help me escape the
cruelty o' such great and endless happiness? A fine bit o'
work for which Jimmy Molloy'd be the very man and the
only one who could serve ye? For I'm cravin' a daysunt holiday from all me terrible pleasures, and I'm needin' to go
soon, afore that Annie nails me to a cross with all her char-
ities." He looked at me morosely, as a chastised hound
might do. "She's made me so happy I'm wishing I was back
in jail."

I thought the fellow would fall to his knees and weep.
"Could ye not take me with ye, wherever ye have to go? For
I'm beggin' and I'm pleadin' with ye. And wouldn't I folly
ye to the very ends of the earth and back again!"

"Now, look you," I began.

"Oh, don't go takin' that terrible tone with me, I'm beggin' ye, Abel Jones! For it's well I know what comes after,
when I hear that awful voice in me innocent ear." He turned
to an invisible audience, whose approval he meant to win.
"And didn't I know him when he was a sergeant as light on
his mercies as a herring's hopes o' making it through a
Friday in Kilkenny? I'm down on me knees to ye, Abel, me
darlin' man. Won't ye spend your Christian affections on a
poor sinner and rescue an old friend from the lion's den o'
his joys? It's fair killing me to be looked after so, all fed up
and scrubbed till I'm bleedin' to death in the washtub."

He come closer still, treating me to the smile that landed him in the Delhi jail and somehow managed to get him out again. Although the cholera helped. "Now, don't go askin' where or why, but I've got me own resources, and what honest publican don't have, then, and I've heard it's the Irish are botherin' ye oncet again. And who, I ask ye, is the man for sortin' out the Irish, if not your old and devoted and loving friend Jimmy Molloy, who's dyin' o' horrible happiness at present?"

He shook his head as only an Irishman can, as if the world were ending for want of your farthing. "I'm *beggin'* ye, for the sake of old times and our comradeship, and while I'm a humble man and not one to go drudgin' up the past for his own selfish benefit, who was it but Jimmy Molloy what follied ye into the very jaws o' death, when everyone else in the company was fearsome and frightened? Who was it but me that come when ye stood all alone and surrounded by bloodthirsty Afghanees, and our little Sergeant Jones shouting for all he's worth, 'Rally, the Old Combustibles! Rally to me, you bastards!' Oh, don't I remember it like it was Saturday morning? And who was it carried ye back to the surgeon and safety, and you all screamin' and streamin' with blood, and ragin' that I was to put ye down and save meself, and haven't I got me own dear little Sergeant Jones over one shoulder and a great turbaned nigger comes on with a sword as big as—"

"Jimmy!" I grasped him by the wrist to calm him down. *"Listen to me!* You're a married man now, see. With responsibilities. And a good wife who loves you dearly. You have to settle down and try to lead a proper life. Annie Fitzgerald—I mean 'Mrs. Molloy'—has been a very savior to you."

"Jaysus, Mary, and Joseph, that she has!" Molloy agreed

with a glum exuberance native to the Gael. "It's worse than the plague and the cholera, how awful I been saved by that woman." He did not try to escape my grasp, but surrendered to the touch, as if he were a hound that needed petting. "But what if a man an't born to live good and proper?"

He tried to smile, but come up with no more than a ghost of his lifelong humor. "Sure, and ye know me for the man I am, Abel, and I don't know why you're pretendin'. I'm not the sort for parlors and lace curtains. Ye said it yourself, a thousand times, how I'm worthless and no good. And only think o' the shame in which ye found me, and the wicked degry-dation, when I made off with the regimental silver and took me lusts to the 'oories, and I didn't even have the daysuntcy about meself to go over the wall to the next cantonment and steal from the black-hearted Highlanders, instead o' from me very own poor officers. Although they were a cruel pack and the buggers deserved it."

"That is all in the past," I assured him. "We are in America now, where every man may have a second chance. And you are all reformed and prosperous—why, Mrs. Schutzengel has given me to understand that you've added a small hotel to your public house, and purchased another out-let for libations, besides. I also hear that your dear wife keeps everything nice and orderly."

"Oh, that she does and she do. Don't ye know, she's got us lookin' to buy yet another public house to come after, for there's terrible fortunes to be made o' the war in Washington." I do believe a real tear graced his eye. "But an't it in the Bible itself, God bless us, how wealth is a wicked sin and not to be wished for? She's out to make me rich, that Annie is. And then where would I be, I'm askin' ye that? As it is, me life's a shameful happiness." He shud-dered still more fiercely than before. "Why, it's in the

Gospels, an't it? If I was to come up rich, I'd be damned for all eternity, and wouldn't that spoil everything I've got planned?"

He come up closer and closer, with those winning young looks that should long since have deserted him, for all his sinful ways and dissipation. I mean in the past, of course. "Tell me the truth, now, Abel, on the honor that lies in our many years' acquaintance: Ye don't believe we're all married forever in Heaven, do ye? We don't have to set up housekeeping on a cloud? Won't it be more like the army was, where oncet ye fall dead they strike your name from the rolls?"

Pitiful it was. But how could I help him? It is the queerest thing, how some men cannot settle down to the fortune the Good Lord grants them. I told myself that time would set Jimmy right, that he only needed to accustom himself to the quiet joys of domesticity. I knew his wife to be the best of young women and no shrew, and she loved him after so many had passed him by as irredeemable. In India, harlots welcomed him for his gay teasing and his antics, but they always took his payment in advance.

And I do believe that Molloy meant well when he married, and wished to make Annie happy and to behave. But, behind all his blarney and bluster, twas clear that morning that marriage had broken his heart. For there was not that quality in him that loves a regular life and a pleasant hearth. He was a wanderer. And though I could not say it to him outright, for it was my Christian duty to remind him of his vows and responsibilities, I knew him to be a good-hearted man, as kind as any on earth, and a better soul than many that inhabit the forms that fill the front pews of church and chapel. What are we to do with our brothers who cannot bear the love that good hearts offer them?

I sent him on his way, with false assurances that he need only accustom himself to his new manner of life, after which all would be well. How proud the lass had been, his Annie, when, upon my return from England the summer past, she had asked me to dinner at their modest home. She loved Molloy. And she loved the thought of the life she had planned for the two of them. Twas her and his misfortune.

But let that bide.

I assured my crestfallen friend that, should events in Pottsville require his assistance, I would telegraph for him without delay. But I could not invent a task out of thin air. That would have been dishonest. Nor, if I am to be truthful, did I wish any of my Washington acquaintances by me in Pottsville until I had found my way through certain personal embarrassments. And until that will had been read. I had my work for our government before me, and I would see it done. Murder had first call on my attention. But my private matters wanted watching, too.

I could not spare Jimmy any more of my morning, since I had to meet my train to go back north. Indeed, I had lacked the little time to say hello to any other friend, either Evans the Telegraph, who was dear to me as Wales itself, or Fine Jim, the newspaper lad, whose thoughts of becoming a drummer-boy alarmed me. For pretty young boys are not well-placed among grown men who lack all wifely companionship, and I will say no more on that sorry subject.

I watched Molloy go, with his shoulders slumped halfway to China. *Herr* Schwinghammer—a new boarder who worked nights in a printing establishment and could not get enough of Jimmy Molloy—accosted him as they passed along the street, asking where he'd been keeping himself all the while. But Jimmy only passed him by, dejected and unseeing, as if they were gliding ghosts from different centuries.

I WAS PUTTING THE LAST of my things in my kit for my departure, when a messenger boy brought a letter from Mr. Nicolay. The lad took my penny and ran off, so I realized the sender did not expect a reply. Still, I opened the missive immediately.

Twas a reminder. And a warning. Not to tell Secretary Seward anything I might learn about Russian involvement in the murder of General Stone.

I marched back into the kitchen to bid farewell to Mrs. Schutzengel, but found her uncommon glum amid her pots. Nor was she merely saddened by my leaving. Twas clear she was mulling old and future sorrows. Our journey of the evening before had conjured spirits she had not yet put down.

I gave the dear woman my best and took me off out the front door, for I barely had time to walk to the railway terminus. And I did *not* intend to squander my funds on a cab, even should one appear for my convenience. There was no threat of rain, and bodily exercise aids the soul and the digestion.

Halfway down the block my conscience stabbed me.

How often now had I turned to Jimmy Molloy for help when I needed it? And in his litany of remembrance and complaint, he had not mentioned a fraction of what he had done for me. Now, you will protest and say: "You did the Christian thing and what was right, returning him to the holy bonds of his marriage and his honest wife." But I will tell you, though you disagree: At times I fear I am too narrow a man, too quick in judgement and even a touch self-righteous. Only sometimes, of course, and not severely. But had I not just washed my hands of my old friend? Pilate, at least, could claim no standing acquaintance with Our Savior.

And I thought I saw a way that I might bring the illusion of our old adventures to Jimmy, while doing his Annie no harm, and possibly even help myself for my trouble.

I scrambled off toward Swampoodle, as fast as my leg would go. Twas not so far out of my way.

Now, I have told you of Swampoodle in the past, a slum that would shame the lowest Hindoo beggar. It is populated by the Irish, of course. Yet, the wealth of war was even telling in those intemperate streets. A year before I would have paused at entering the place by day, and had nearly received a beating there one night. Now, at least in the daylight hours, the place was mostly passable. Irish soldiers in Union blue brought Yankee dollars to those lanes of indignity, even as other Irishmen cursed the war. They were a people divided and, although the place was filthy and full of measles, even a Welshman could go there to see to his business nowadays. At least until dusk.

I found proper buildings under construction, and fewer morning drunkards sprawled in the alleys, with less of the leavings of night pots dumped in the walks.

When I come upon them, Jimmy and his Annie were hard at work in their little saloon, with her on her knees with a bucket and rags and Jimmy polishing up a new bar of mahogany and brass. Months before, there had been only planks and stools.

Jimmy looked over and Annie looked up, and their faces told a story. Jimmy was all cock-a-hoop with delight at seeing me prancing in, for he understood it meant I had been thinking on matters. Annie smiled at first, as she always did, but then her face took on a guarded look that was new to me. Once, she had pressed her Jimmy to serve my needs, but other needs had passed mine in importance.

Annie rose up slowly from the floor, drying her hands on

her apron. She was no beauty, but honest and decent and kind. She presented a welcoming smile.

"Major Jones," she said carefully. "Isn't this the happiest of surprises? Himself was just telling me how you went off on the cars, and here you are! Will you take a cup of tea, for the chill of the morning?"

I waved off the invitation. "Thank you, Mrs. Molloy. It is a gracious one you are. But I must hurry along. There is a train I must be on, see."

That reinforced her smile a bit.

I really lacked all time, so I plunged straight into things. Still, I spoke to her, though my words touched Jimmy. "It has occurred to me that your husband might be a help to my present efforts." Oh, her poor face fell at that. While Jimmy could hardly contain his child's delight. I continued, "And he may assist me in a manner that will return him to the warmth of his own home each and every night, if you will give your leave, Mrs. Molloy."

They swapped expressions, her own returning from the desert wastes to the sweet waters of relief, while Jimmy's mouth curled toward anger. His red mustaches took on a fanged look.

"And since when is it 'Mrs. Molloy this' and 'Mrs. Molloy that' between us, Major Jones?" she asked almost gaily. "I was always 'Annie,' before, and I hope I'm 'Annie' still."

I stepped a bit deeper into the saloon and stopped where a band of wet gleamed on the floor. The air was rich with the smells of soap and beer, of sweat, slop water and ashes.

"Here is the thing of it." I turned to face Jimmy. "I would ask you to inquire about a certain Daniel Boland, who has confessed to a murder then run away. Most like, he is in Canada, but the asking will not harm him, if he is. And I will tell you: I do not think him a killer, but may be wrong.

There is more of a story to matters than I can tell you this morning. But ask, if you will, after Daniel Patrick Boland and see—"

"Daniel *Patrick* Boland?" Molloy asked in a bewildered tone. He gave a lightning stroke to his red mustaches. "But everybody knows the poor sod's dead. Didn't the English hang the poor bucko for his deeds in the Forty-eight? Only Boland out of the whole sorry lot o' them took to the hills when their whole silly scheme fell to pieces. And only Boland fought like a man, while the rest o' them hid in the rafters or under their beds."

He shook his head at the fortunes of his race. "The rest o' the Rebels was gentlemen bred, so the English couldn't hang many o' that lot at all, but packed the lads off to their disciplines, down in the dreads of Botany Bay, or some such carnivorous place. Boland, the sod, was only a blackleg miner, is how they tell it. A hard one who give up his all for Ireland, and killed two constables and an English sergeant, besides. They hanged him in the Castle yard in Dublin. And a lovely commotion it was, so I'm told, with no end o' cheerin' and weepin'. Oh, he's famous and honored and happy in his grave, that one, for there's nobody loves a dead martyr like a living Irishman. But he's dead as Coogan's cat, is Danny Pat Boland."

"No, no," I said, although I was thinking the while, "I am speaking of a young fellow from Pennsylvania, who was alive just weeks ago. And still is, if I am not mistaken."

"Well," Jimmy mused, "Boland's a common enough name, an't it? And there'll be no harm in my asking around, I suppose." He glanced at Annie, testing the waters there, then turned his curiosity back to me. "I wonder if Boland's own son might not carry his name?"

The very thought had struck me as he spoke. Twas one of those moments when things begin to make sense. At last I might have found one piece to fit into the puzzle: Why those truculent sons of Erin were so determined to spirit young Boland off. If the lad was the son of a famous Irish rebel, they would move Heaven and earth to protect him. A priest might even be convinced to lie. For the Irish will do far more for heroes dead than ever they do for their champions while they live.

And I saw another likely thing. The son of a great Irish rebel would not go to Canada. Where the queen's writ ran and such a one would be watched. Or handed over to the U.S. authorities, and good riddance. The English government don't like ours, but they like the finest Irishman even less.

I had to take me off without delay. I imagined I heard train whistles and saw the pillowy steam clouds of departure.

"Jimmy," I said, "just *find* him. Find Boland. Wherever he's gone. Find him, man. You can do it. Daniel Patrick Boland. Find him for me."

I fear my voice betrayed an ill-mannered excitement, for Jimmy grinned like a crofter who had stumbled on a pot of fairy gold. He said, "Sure, and I smell the smoke, but from over here I can't see where you're on fire, man. Ye'll be dancing a jig for us next, and buying the round."

My face and voice returned to a proper sobriety.

"Find him for me, Jimmy."

He opened his mouth to assure me that he would traipse across the stars if need be, but I had no time to listen to his merriment. I had an undesired thing to say. And it broke Annie's heart.

"When you find out where he is, Jimmy, don't use the telegraph. Come to Pottsville and tell me in person, you understand?"

Oh, he beamed and nearly bellowed in the throes of his new-found liberty. At last, he had the license that he wanted.

I looked at poor Annie, who was fighting back her tears. I realized that we were opponents now, and that the poor child might even learn to hate me.

"Good morning to you, Mrs. Molloy," I told her, tipping my cap. And thus I ran away from what I had done.

thirteen

THE DEPARTURE OF MY TRAIN was delayed beyond my tardy arrival. A solicitous railway fellow guided me to an empty car—a rarity in those days—and I sat myself down and opened my German grammar. For time must not be squandered. Besides, I was in flight from other thoughts. Of murders. And of home.

A fine, florid fellow, dressed up to the nines, stepped into the car and sat down. Now, the gentleman had his pick of seats, but chose the one that faced me, which seemed queer. But then he was foreign, as a fellow saw at once, and rich to a bloating. The grander the fortune the American possesses, the darker the hues of his clothing. But the European celebrates his wealth in silks and colors, with jewels for studs and yellow gloves and walking sticks of ivory. My fellow passenger was a man in his prime, with whiskers as neat as a cat's tucked into his high collar, cheekbones that swelled out like upended cutlets, and oiled hair combed forward at the temples. I did not think him likely to be a Methodist.

Hardly a moment after he took his place, the train began to move.

I sought to reapply myself to the reasons why *Gefahren* and *Gefahr* were separate of meaning. But my fellow traveller stared at me until I looked up again.

When he had my attention, he cleared his throat, touched lightly at his cravat, and said, "Why, I find we are companions, sir!" His accent spoke of Grosvenor Square, though he was no more English than a Parsee. His little mouth formed a smile that stretched the flesh over his cheekbones and made his whiskers bristle. He leaned toward me, as if beginning a confidence. "How splendidly fortuitous! That is, if I have not mistaken the company by which I find myself distinguished?" He removed his glove and extended a large, white hand with a daintiness one expected of a missy. "Edouard de Stoekl."

"Major Abel Jones," I told him, although he seemed to know. Twas then I noted a burly fellow blocking the doorway down at the end of the carriage. Doubtless, another such like stood to my rear.

"Ah! Then I was correct! How very fortunate for me! I've wanted terribly to make your acquaintance, you know. One hears such disturbing things . . . and I wished an opportunity to speak privately with you, to promote a view of events I believe you may find more comforting than that described to you by a certain baroness . . . who is, to the general benefit, confined at present."

He was the minister fellow from Russia, Baron de Stoekl, and a greater combination of masculine chestiness and priss I never did meet before that day or after.

"Oh, but you needn't be dismayed that I know where you were last evening," he continued. "Really, Major Jones, I find myself *de*luged with such reports—I suffer applications from the most unlikely quarters! The enthusiasm with which the residents of Washington spy upon one another, then advertise what they have learned . . . why, I must say that your capital is a city that can*not* be entrusted with a secret."

"Unlike the capital of Russia?" I said. I fear I spoke with a nasty undertone, for I was miffed to think I had no privacy. And I had been trapped neatly upon that train, which made me feel a fool.

The baron merely chuckled. "Ah, but I see you've had report of our St. Petersburg, Major. Indeed, the Russian has an inclination to secrecy born of his inclement history. We who look westward for our inspiration have a great struggle ahead of us." When he leaned toward me again, I smelled a perfume, which I will admit was pleasing. Although I do not favor scent on a gentleman. "We live in the most beautiful city in the world, you know. Our canals are more beautiful than those of Venezia, and our palaces are without peer—designed by Italian and German architects, of course."

He glanced through the window, as if he might glimpse the capital of all the Russias beyond the glass. But all there was to see were trees thinned of their leaves and a guardpost flashing by, where bored soldiers watched the railway line and shivered.

The baron brought his eyes back to mine own. Hard little squinters, they were. "Dear Pieter . . . so lovely, so generous of proportion! It's simply delicious to walk there, along the embankment, on one of those endless June nights . . . to let oneself slip into a reverie, or chatter with a friend! Yet, so many of His Majesty's subjects fail to appreciate what we have, what they are given. They wallow in intrigues and mystical nonsense. It can lead to . . . unnecessary dangers."

He put on his diplomat's smile. "Perhaps you will visit us one day, Major Jones? How I should like to show you the beauties of our dear city! We Russians and Americans really are rather alike, you know. In so many ways. Huge countries. Enormous! With wealth yet untried. You have your frontiersmen, we our cossacks. We share concepts of magnitude no other civilized peoples would comprehend. Personally, I see our two countries as the pioneers of humanity—not merely husbandmen of crude wastes and deserts. Really, you *must* visit us. As my guest. When your fraternal struggle has been resolved."

I did not think it likely I would visit him. Or his country.

The Russian minister clapped his hands. The sound was as loud as a shot. For an instant, the fellow seemed to have become an oriental potentate, merciless of expression and impatient.

"Andrey!" he barked. *"Sichass! Bistra, bistra!"*

A fellow shouted, *"Sluzhu!"* and rushed up behind my back, coming on with such alacrity I turned my head to ensure I was not attacked. He wore a bottle-green uniform coat so fine I could not tell if he was an officer or a servant. With a folding table under one arm and a basket in his hand, he looked over his own shoulder, barking in turn at a smaller fellow, who wore a braided uniform of blue. The second lackey leapt forward with bottles and glasses.

Baron de Stoekl let them work, reserved again, still and prim and satisfied. The two fellows flipped up a table, spread out linens, laid china and silver, set glasses, and produced a meal of items every one of which looked odd, excepting the bread and butter. The smaller fellow in blue filled tumblers from a bottle of water, but when he moved to pour me wine—ruby-red it was—I left him in no doubt that I wanted none of it.

When he saw I would take no wine myself, the baron waved the bottle away from his own glass. A moment later, we sat as intimates again. Except for the guards at the ends of the carriage.

"I trust you will forgive me my indulgence?" the baron said. "I always take a second breakfast, a habit from my own country. Our weather demands a certain fortification." He smirked. Not at me, but at some stray thought. "Although the Russian soul, our *Russkaya Dusha*, rather prefers mortification, I think."

He lifted his water tumbler.

"To President Lincoln!" he declared. "To the undivided Union!"

I brought the full glass to my lips and, just before I drank, a wicked odor saved me. It was not water at all, but some sort of spirit.

The baron was well along in his swigging—indeed, his glass was half drained—when one of his eyes alerted to my reluctance.

He lowered his glass. "But you do not drink, Major Jones! Not even to your president? Am I *so* unwelcome to you?"

"I have taken the Pledge, sir, and do not partake of alcohol."

The look of astonishment on his face reminded me of the time in the maharanee's palace when Molloy and I come face to face with an elephant in a bedchamber.

"Pledge?" he asked, befuddled for the first time in our interview.

"The Temperance Pledge, sir. I will not despoil the flesh the Good Lord has granted me by partaking of liquors or spirits."

He stared at me. "*Nye mozhet bit . . . eto nye vozmozhno . . .*" he shook his head. So shocked he was that next he fell into German, exclaiming, "*Gott im Himmel, dass ist was neues unter der Sonne . . .*"

"Good it is for the health of body and soul," I explained, "and I do not doubt that Temperance will triumph in our lifetimes."

The fellow drained the rest of his glass, in search of his lost composure. Setting the tumbler down again, he barked, "*Andrey! Vodku prinosi! Botilku prinosi!*"

His demand was answered by a great scurrying and pouring, after which the bottle which I had mistaken as a container of water remained near the baron's hand. The lackey disappeared again, trailing worry and woe.

The baron dabbed a bead of moisture from his mustache and said, "But it seems I know still less of your American customs than I had believed! 'Temperance,' you say? I shouldn't think it would be a success in Russia." He took a draught from his brimming glass and closed his eyes while he swallowed. "Of course, my own family is German, you understand. We are not creatures of excess like the Slavs. Still, a man requires a certain warmth . . . a certain invigoration . . ." A sudden thought brightened his aspect. "And now you see that I haven't been spying on you at all! Surely, I would have known such a thing as this matter of Temperance, my dear major."

"Then who *was* spying on me?" I asked. I tried to look him in the eye, but fear my gaze strayed to the foodstuffs, which looked tempting. The substance of Mrs. Schutzengel's breakfast had begun to wear away.

"A minor figure, a craven soul," he assured me. "It hardly matters." He followed my eyes. "But, surely, you won't reduce me to the embarrassment of dining alone, Major Jones? *Do* try a dumpling . . ."

It is not polite to refuse an offer of hospitality, see. I ate along to keep the fellow company. And the truth is I was as curious as I was hungry now, for I recalled the multitudinous flavors of India, of which I once was fond. The natives et far better than we soldiers did and kept their bowels in better fit and order. Except when the cholera come round, of course.

And there had been a person in Lahore who cooked up lovely morsels for my pleasure.

"You must try *this*," the baron said, gesturing toward a mound of whatnot. Twas odd. He spoke with his mouth half full of cucumber slices, which is not proper doing in society. Yet, otherwise his manners were all prettiness. "It's done just so. Take up one of those little pancakes—still a bit warm, one hopes—spread a dab of cream over it, then spoon this on top. No, no! You must be generous with yourself. More, more, *more!*"

The foodstuff he pushed toward me was a pile of glistening beads, gray with a hint of amber. I followed his example and rolled up the pancake, then took a curious bite.

Now, I will tell you a thing: The Good Lord put many an edible gift upon this blessed earth, and I speak as a man who has experienced the very best Welsh kitchens, as well as the savory blandishments of India. But I never put anything into my mouth that tasted quite like that. I cannot describe it to you. Nutty it was, and salty, and buttery, and silvery, and all bursting on the tongue until it seemed to explode into my brain. I never have known so small a thing to carry so great a flavor as those beads. I liked the dish better than a beef-steak, which is saying something.

He read the query on my face and answered it. "*Ikra.* The eggs of the sturgeon. Something of a peasant food, but we do enjoy it with our vodka. It's becoming quite the indulgence in Paris, I'm told. And Lord Cardigan is reputed to have acquired a taste for it before Sebastopol." He smiled. "But you *do* enjoy it, I see. I shall have to send you a few pounds."

I fear I ate more than the baron himself. And I began to wonder whether Russia might not be worth a visit one time or another.

He drained his tumbler—for the third time, I think—and called for another bottle of the spirit. Again, the lackey ran to and fro, as if his life would be forfeit if he walked.

The baron touched his napkin to his lips, laid it beside his glass, shifted his contented bulk with a grunt, and said, "Please, please. *Do* continue eating. I'm terribly sorry I didn't have Andrey bring along more of that . . . but see here. I'm afraid I shall have to step down at Baltimore, so I beg you, Major Jones: Allow me to put my case."

I swallowed the last of the fish eggs and cream, which nearly broke my heart. I cannot tell you how lovely fish eggs taste.

I wondered if the eggs of a trout might do as well.

The baron leaned across the wreckage of our repast. "On my honor as a gentleman, I swear I shall tell you the truth, Major Jones. First, we did not kill your General Stone." He wrinkled his mouth in distaste and I noticed that his lips were pink to a rawness inside. "I will leave his name thus. Stone. It's less offensive to my ear that way. We did not kill him, although I might not have been able to make that claim, had some other hand not intervened. We did not know Stone had these anonymous enemies—though revolutionaries often do."

He lifted one shoulder then the other, as if to make his coat sit more easily. "You may have encountered a fellow in this Pottsville of yours. A certain Count Stavrogin. A distasteful man, who works for a distasteful arm of our government. I have no authority over his actions. He was sent to this country to apprehend Stone and return him to Russia, but I think Stavrogin would have killed the man, had the opportunity presented itself. He was utterly possessed by his pursuit of Stone. His search had crossed the world. It lasted over a decade."

He shifted in his seat again, as if the thought of this count fellow disturbed him. "Stavrogin had located Stone at last, in this Schuylkill County of yours. He made his connections quite artfully, if I know anything of the man, and prepared his way in advance. Not, one suspects, without applying certain gifts of money. Yet, he was destined for disappointment. Count Stavrogin arrived in your city the day after General Stone's murder."

The minister twisted his mouth into a satisfied little smile. "Doubtless, he felt a measure of chagrin. Stavrogin desired the pleasure of a confrontation, you see. After all those years of searching . . ." His wrinkled smile retreated into a look of bemusement. "But the count's a man of the world, after all. Once he came to his senses, he was gratified that Stone was dead, finished. Through the good graces of your government, we even acquired the body as proof of the affair's resolution for His Majesty and Prince Gortshakoff. Stavrogin's on shipboard with the coffin as we speak—and I only hope he doesn't do anything addled. His elder brother was killed in a certain bombing, you know. In an officers' casino in St. Petersburg."

Baron de Stoekl scrutinized my face before proceeding. "Whatever stories you may have heard of Stone, good or bad . . . they are irrelevant to my cause. He is dead, and we Russians had no hand in his murder. I promise you that. His Majesty will regard the matter as closed, and it need not trouble us further on an official level. Or, I think, on any other level."

He canted his head, still judging me. "Perhaps you wonder why this man should have mattered so to us? The answer isn't simple, I'm afraid. But I assure you that everyone wished him dead. *Par example,* Stavrogin hated Stone because of what Stone did, *and* because of who Stone was. A son of the tsar's trusted German nobility. As I am myself. The Russian aristocrats are a backward *assortiment.* Resentful voluptuaries, almost to a man. Brutes. We Germans compose the modernizing force. And, at last, we have gained the upper hand. The Slavs hate us for it."

He poured himself another drink, swallowed a great gulp, then continued. "Tsar Alexander is much in the mold of your President Lincoln. Oh, certainly not in outward forms. Not at all. But His Majesty has taken a firm grip of our Russia, and he is shaking it. For once, the great Russian myth of the 'good tsar' has been realized. Tsar Alexander is a man of lib-

eral temperament, of great humanity. We have inaugurated
trials by jury. For the first time in our history. His Majesty is
liberating the serfs, our peasants, just as you seek to liberate
your slaves. He wishes to bring modern practices to our government, to turn Russia westward, to expand the railways,
our industries . . ."

The baron's eyes had altered their tone from the cynic's
twinkle to the believer's fiery glow. "And all the while these
Russians . . . these *chornie aristokrati* . . . they resist him at
every turn, complaining that His Majesty is betraying the
soul of Russia, the noble spirit of the Slav, even the
Orthodox Church. The army would prefer to wallow in its
old abuses and drunkenness, while the landholding classes
would smother the infant of change, if only they could. All
of them, the fools, imagine that time can be made to stand
still. Or even to run backward. But Russia must adapt to
modern times! His Majesty's our only hope, you see. We either change . . . or *après nous, le déluge*."

He tapped the table for emphasis and the silver and china
chimed. "I meant what I said to you earlier: Russia and
America, these are the two lands of the future, the hope of
the world. Just as you have your great war, we face a great
struggle between those who would turn Russia westward toward European civilization . . . and those who would cling
to their Slavic fairy tales, to their ignorance and filth and
crushing poverty."

He formed a determined smile. "Count Stavrogin wished
revenge upon Stone because, to him, Stone represented revolution, the West, and the influence of us Germans upon His
Majesty—oh, do not look for sense or logic with the
Russian, Major Jones. You never shall find it. They crawl
through the mud and call it a mystical experience." He lowered his eyes, staring into a pool of bitter waters. "*I* wanted
Stone brought to justice . . . as did all of the tsar's loyal sub-

jects of German lineage . . . because Stone had been one of us and he betrayed us, endangering our position and our cause. Stone was a fool, you see. An absolute fool. He thought of himself as a grand revolutionary, but he played into the hands of the most reactionary elements in Russia. We had to finish with him to prove we did not consider him one of us any longer. Anyway, the man's methods were a nonsense. The future will not be hurried along with bombs and assassinations. Russia must be moved by reason, by science . . ."

"But he had become an American, see. And—"

The train whistle blew and the baron held up his hand. Rough houses hurried by, prelude to the prosperous glories of Baltimore.

"He's dead," the minister said flatly. "And it is a benefit to every sensible person in my country. As well as to the relations between our two countries." He fixed his eyes upon me with all the intensity he could muster. "As long as no one 'bears false witness.' We Russians did not kill your General Stone. We are as mystified as you are as to who did the deed, or why—indeed, I may have to discourage Prince Gortshakoff from rewarding the perpetrator, if ever he is identified." He shook his head. "I wish I could help you further, but cannot. I only beg you to believe what I have told you."

"And the woman in the madhouse? The baroness? Would you kill her, if you had the chance? Because she betrayed your high society?"

He smiled at my simplicity. "But my dear Major Jones! How should we ever find the opportunity to do her the least harm, when her own friends and comrades have determined that she shall never walk free again?" He shook his head. "That's why I have no patience with men such as Count Stavrogin, you see. I speak of him as one of the devils, but, in truth, I see him more as an idiot." He smiled his small, tormented smile again. "Crime doesn't really interest him, you see. He's enraptured by the punishment. They're all like that, Stavrogin and his associates. Every one a gambler. With Russia's future. And gamblers always lose, sooner or later. His bureau would go to any length to imprison revolutionaries, torture them, exile them, execute them. But that's all so unnecessary, so unhelpful! Given time, revolutionaries always destroy themselves. After all, they're gamblers, too."

The train began to brake and slide and screech. Clouds of steam passed the windows of our car. Between the billows, I saw soldiers in blue standing about. Guarding the yards. For Baltimore had begun the war with little sympathy for our Union's preservation.

The baron clapped his hands. In moments, the litter of our meal had disappeared. The instant the train stopped, the minister stood up.

"I *beg* you to believe me," he said. "Neither my government, nor any of its agents killed General Stone or played any role in the matter. You must look elsewhere for the guilty party."

He put on his proper manner again, all diplomacy and pleasantness and frills. "I still cannot believe my good fortune in our encounter." He wrinkled his mouth, spreading his whiskers on one side of his face, but not the other. "Curious, I think, how a random meeting such as ours may change the course of history. For the better, one trusts." He offered me that delicate little hand again, a thing unmatched to the manly corpulence of the rest of his person. "*Adieu*, Major Jones. Ah! But I should say, '*Auf Wiedersehen!*' I do hope you will visit me in St. Petersburg one day!"

And I will tell you how selfish and small the human heart can be: The fellow had come to talk of murders and great affairs of state, and my duty lay in diligence and sobriety of purpose. But as he left the carriage, followed by a flurry of

uniforms and hampers, I caught myself hoping that he
would keep his promise and send me a pound or two of
those fish eggs.

I BELIEVED HIM, SEE. And not only because he had given me
a treat or two and saved me the price of a lunch at the
Baltimore station. I will admit we Welsh are suspicious by
nature. It comes from dealing with the English for centuries.
But there are times when I judge I can trust a man. And I
rarely have been wrong. I had an uncanny sense that all he
had told me was true. Regarding the murder, I mean.

Perhaps it was the sort of thing that works down deep in
the mind. I had collected bits and pieces of the affair, which
my conscious thoughts had not yet put together. But somewhere within me perhaps I already knew what had happened, how the general's murder would be explained. I will
only tell you this: It was not fish eggs and curdled cream that
made me decide from that morning on that the Russians
were not the murderers. And I would be right. For the murder of General Stone had to do with a darker matter than
vengeance. God knows, there was no hint of justice in it.

I thought and thought as the train rolled on, over bridges
repaired or new, through low forests and marshes and then
along the Delaware, where smoke plumes from the factories
and mills heralded our approach to Philadelphia. I marked
the Cawber works, which I had visited in the course of the
Fowler affair, and wished I had the time to pause and visit
the fellow. I wanted his advice, see. About certain railroad
matters and colliery affairs. Nor do I speak of my private interests, but of the peculiar situation in our county that had
made such a delicate matter of the general's murder. I had
heard, of course, many a sorry rumor about Matt Cawber
since his fair wife's death, and doubtless some were true.
But he remained a man whose judgement I would trust in

business affairs. And I was inclined to trust him in other matters, as well.

I could not linger in Philadelphia, but only took the time to hurry from one terminal to another to catch the Pottsville train. Philadelphia, too, was burgeoning with the wealth of war and I was astonished at the price asked me by a vendor for a pair of boiled eggs. I gave him a proper tongue-lashing for his greed, but paid. And I will tell you: Although they kept my belly in line until I reached my hearth, those eggs of the hen could not approach the splendor of those fish eggs.

What kind of fellow would think of eating fish eggs?

My moods were not dependable that autumn. The nearer the locomotive come to our dear Pottsville, the gloomier my deliberations grew. Even duty could not hold my thoughts. Oh, I was determined to set matters straight and intended to find Mrs. Boland, to learn whether her madness was real or feigned. And I would have answers of that priest, Father Wilde, about his bloody linens. If necessary, I would confront the Irish, the lot of them, and this time I would not be put off with riddles and tricks of speech. But all of that fled my thoughts as steam and speed devoured the afternoon.

Usually, I like a railway journey. No matter how often I find myself on the cars, the ease with which the landscape flees the eye fills me with a pleasant melancholy, a sense of time's passage as sweet as it is bitter. But that day my thoughts only darkened with the miles.

I wished to think on duty, to plot and plan, but could not wrench my thoughts from my wife and son. I did not even dwell on the matter of the will, which would be read out soon enough. No, it was the seed of evil that concerned me, the wages of sin. Twas as if I had held it all in until my fears swelled to a bursting.

Why is the world made so? Why should my Mary Myfanwy have suffered because her uncle was in fact her father and did a thing so evil I rage to think on it? Her back is not bent, not really. There is only a mild curving, though it gives her discomfort. But what has she done to deserve even that, and why would the Good Lord make a child pay for the sins of its parents? I know that God's ways are ineffable, but I wish with all my heart I could see the justice in things. What if an even greater weakness had been implanted in my Mary? What if the years would tell on her unfairly? What if her faculties should fail her? What if I should be left alone? Healthy and hearty she always seemed, and clever as could be. But what if she hid weaknesses within her? I could not bear the thought of my darling's loss.

Damn him, why had Mr. Evans chosen me to suffer his confession? Why not tell his whore? Or shut his mouth until he could tell the Devil? Why tell me?

Oh, I remembered the attentiveness with which he always had played with our young John. All the while he had been watching for a sign of inherited weakness, either of the body or the mind. Think as hard as I might, I could see no such mark upon the boy, although he sometimes did seem awfully afraid of me. But then I was an absent father, little more than a rumor, taken by war to distant fields, returning briefly, with terrifying scars. I thought our John a normal boy, happy and robust. But well I know the fragility of our lives and our happiness.

What if the new child, sleeping under my dear wife's heart, should carry a monstrous taint from its moment of birth? Could we hope to escape a family curse with so few consequences?

I even remembered the kindness of my darling's late mother in a different light. The Reverend Mr. Griffiths had hated and despised me until he died. But his widow had done me the charity of forwarding one crucial letter to my beloved, whom I had thought forever lost to me. Now I won-

dered if the woman had thought her daughter would find no
better hope than Abel Jones, if she secretly had viewed her
only child as despicable, casting her toward me to be rid of
her. Had she believed I would be well served to wed the
daughter of incest?

Is there a crueler word upon this earth?

I know I am a selfish man and that my thoughts veer to
blasphemy. But when I thought of the effect of Mr. Evans's
dying words upon me, I felt like Job. No matter what he
had written in his will, for good or evil, generous or cruel,
that sinner's legacy to me was doubt and fear.

All I wanted of this earth was the goodness and health of
my family about me. I wished the war away and I hated the
thought that I must soon return to my part in it, although I
could not say such a disheartening thing to Mary. She needed to believe that I believe. Oh, she is right that I am sometimes blind to the meanness of the world. But she believes I
am better than I am, and stronger, too.

I rode toward Pottsville, lonely and forlorn. The railway followed the river through the hills. Towns flashed by in the early
dark, with lamplit windows hinting of other lives. I wondered
how much sorrow those people knew. I should have pondered
that murdered girl and the murder of our general. But I sat in
the dusk of the car with murdered hope.

"SHALL I BEGIN?" Mr. Hemmings asked. His office was lovely with books of law and wood polished up like brass, although the air was tainted with cigar smoke. I sat between
my Mary and, at a decent remove, Mrs. Walker. The latter
figure had possessed the sense of decorum to enter the offices of Mr. Hemmings's firm through a rear door. And
veiled. But now she sat there, got up in a widow's weeds and
straight-backed as a lady at her tea, with no more expression
upon her face than a statue made of marble. She was a fair

one, Dolly Walker, almost beauteous. I will give her that. Well fitted she was to lead honest men astray.

Myself, I was all awry that day. One moment, I found myself feeling sorry for the creature in her mourning. For what must life be like when all of our entrances are made through back doors and no one treats us with the least open respect? Then I would berate myself for my folly. The woman had made her life, such as it was, and now she sat positioned to rob my Mary of her rightful inheritance.

Mr. Hemmings made a sound deep in his throat, more a growl than a purr, and repeated, "*Shall* I begin, then?"

He was looking at me, although I was the party least concerned. But then I was the only man present, excepting himself. And men of Mr. Hemmings's generation did not look to the ladies for authority.

I remembered my resolutions and turned my face to my darling. She nodded. And gave my hand a squeeze. As if to encourage me. As if the will had more to do with me than it did with her.

To answer the demands of common courtesy, I aimed an inquiring look at Mrs. Walker.

She nodded in her turn. She had lifted her veil and it angered me unreasonably. For though my Mary is a great, unblemished beauty to me, the untutored eye would favor Mrs. Walker. With her haughty carriage. And her back as straight as the barrel of a musket.

"You may begin, Mr. Hemmings," I told the fellow. Black as a crow he was, and somber. As a barrister or solicitor always should be. A fellow who has read the law must encompass the gravity of an undertaker and the character of a gentleman of the cloth. Where would we be, if such folk made a spectacle?

Standing behind his desk, Mr. Hemmings settled his spectacles on his nose and broke the document's seal. Unfolding the papers, he turned—just so—to let the window light the testament's contents.

There was a great muchness of "know all ye present" and "soundness of mind," of "the Commonwealth of Pennsylvania" and "the County of Schuylkill," all read out in a voice that might have been reading verses from the Bible. I noted that the last revision of the will had been concluded but a month before, and I worried that Mrs. Walker's charms had gotten to the old man. I am ashamed to think on it now, but the sin of greed was upon me as I perched in that leather-backed chair. I could tell you that I was only on the look-out for my Mary's proper share, and that would be the truth, to a degree. But the selfishness within me had a purpose of its own, and not a noble one.

I sneaked a glance at Mrs. Walker, who sat there imperturbable. As if she hadn't the least care in the world.

My dear wife looked at me, not at Mr. Hemmings. She took my hand again.

Mr. Hemmings read out the minor bequests, which were alarmingly numerous. An elderly maidservant was pensioned generously, while the other members of Mr. Evans's household staff were remembered with nice amounts. No doubt, I told myself, to buy their continued discretion. But I could find no fault with his remembrances of miners crippled in his service, or of pit widows and their children. In each case, the size of the award was excessive by our Pottsville standards and I knew the other colliery lords would dislike the business. Nor could I stop myself from tallying the sums as Mr. Hemmings read on, for I am, first and foremost, a good clerk.

He left a smaller amount to his church than was customary for a man of his social station, but devoted one thousand dollars to the care of the county's indigent. And then there were bequests to distant relations in Wales, of whom I had not heard a whisper spoken.

I fear I was inching forward on my chair. For I heard his fortune whittled away, and still the giving went on.

Then, with a pallbearer's look drawn over his face, Mr. Hemmings paused, breathed deeply, and raised his eyes above his glasses to inspect the three of us. I think I must have squeezed my angel's hand unto a hurting. But her grasp did not desert me.

With the ghost of a sigh, the lawyer settled his eyes on Mrs. Walker. Then he read on. "To my kind and devoted friend, Mrs. Dorothea Walker, née Brooke, I leave the sum of fifty thousand dollars, free and clear. Further, to Mrs. Walker, I bequeathe the following properties in the Pottsville Borough: Her current house of residence on lot 55, Minersville Street, as well as my share of those houses erected on lots 67, 68 and 69, Minersville Street, in which properties we have enjoyed a like and mutual interest, as recorded by the firm of Hemmings and Briggs, and registered in the County of Schuylkill. Finally, to Mrs. Walker, the Florentine screen from the ladies' parlor in my Mahantango Street abode, and my silver-headed walking stick, bearing the inscription, 'To Chummy-Chums,' returned to her for the sake of my remembrance."

I do not remember clearly, for I was shocked to a numbness, but I may have gasped at the figure Mr. Hemmings had read out. For my tallying, based upon my knowledge of the colliery books I had kept before the war, told me the lion's share of his available wealth had now been apportioned. We might have ten or twenty thousand dollars for my Mary, but no more.

Now you will say: That is a very fortune, and how else would you come to such an amount, you greedy man? But I will tell you: Although you are right that I was greedy and presumptuous, I wonder how you would have felt sitting in my place?

I looked at Mrs. Walker, expecting to find her beaming in her triumph. Instead, her face was streaked with tears and she lifted a flowered handkerchief to her lips, then began to sob.

She was shaking her head, as if denying all.

Mr. Hemmings paused in his reading, patient as a lawyer fellow must be. But Mrs. Walker didn't see him, for her eyes were shut tightly now.

Of a sudden, the creature snapped opened her eyes and stared over at my darling.

"Mary," she said, "I'm sorry . . . I didn't know it would be so much . . . I didn't know . . ."

Now, my beloved is a lady, first and last. And she replied in a voice with no hint of jealousy or discourtesy.

"It was his to give," she said. "And he gave it where he loved, Dolly."

Mrs. Walker turned her face away from us. Oh, I would not be unjust. Perhaps she felt some deep emotion for the man. Perhaps we never sink so low that our heart is void of affection. Perhaps the murderer loves his wife and the robber adores his children.

But I was heartsick.

"Shall I proceed?" Mr. Hemmings asked. He got a nod from me, but twas a nod from an empty shell.

"To my dearly beloved niece, Mary Myfanwy Jones, née Griffiths, I leave the sum of two hundred thousand dollars, free and clear . . ."

I know I gasped at that. As did my darling. For we had no idea the old man had possessed such wealth in his private accounts. That is the quietness and fortitude of the Welsh for you. Mr. Evans ever had been strenuous at his labors, I will give him that.

". . . further, to Mary M. Jones, all remaining papers of investment, notes, bonds, and sums that shall remain after the bequests listed above and below have been paid. Also, to Mary M. Jones, my residence on Mahantango Street, with all its grounds and furnishings, except as stated above; my interest in the Marquand Building, lot 143, Centre Street, and my interest in the Thomas and Thomas Building, lot 44, Market Street, said properties deeded and recorded in Pottsville, Pennsylvania. Further, to Mary M. Jones, all my property holdings in Bala Cynwyd and Chester, Pennsylvania, and all lands deeded in my name in the borough or holding of Cape May, New Jersey, as well as improvements thereon. To Mary M. Jones, my personal holdings in the Pennsylvania Railroad and in Cawber Iron and Steel, free and unencumbered. Finally, to Mary M. Jones, the portrait in pencil and wash of her mother, the late Virginia Griffiths, née Evans, wrapped in velvet and kept in the top, right drawer of my dressing table."

My wife's hand and mine own had parted, for we had been plunged into worlds of disbelief. At a time such as that, a fellow does not know what he is about, see.

Mr. Hemmings read on. "To my beloved grandson, John Evan Jones, to be placed in trust until his majority, the sum of fifty thousand dollars. An additional sum of fifty thousand dollars to be held in unnamed trust against the birth of a second, healthy child to my niece, Mary M. Jones, after which said birth it shall be held in trust in that child's legal name until said child's majority is attained."

Mr. Hemmings gave me a queer sort of look, then added, "To Major Abel Jones, husband to Mary M. Jones, I bequeath the Evans family Bible."

The lawyer fellow avoided my eyes and rushed into the testament's closing paragraphs.

"All lands and properties owned or leased by Evans Coal and Iron, incorporated in the Counties of Schuylkill, Carbon, and Berks, and all works, improvements or struc-

tures thereon, as well as all movable assets, subscribed
rights of way, and funded permits, said assets valued by sur-
vey in July 1862, in the sum of one hundred sixty-seven
thousand, four hundred, thirty-two dollars and ninety-one
cents, I bequeathe jointly, in even shares, to Major Abel
Jones, husband to Mary M. Jones, in recognition of his diligence as a man and his loyalty as a husband and father, and
to my friend and companion, Mrs. Dorothea Walker. Major
Jones shall have the deciding vote on business affairs, and it
is expected that Mrs. Walker shall be a silent partner in the
management of Evans Coal and Iron."

Mr. Hemmings gave us quite a set of looks upon that revelation, and, if I must be honest, I am not certain whom he
pitied the more, myself or Mrs. Walker. For Mr. Hemmings
knew me for a man of firm convictions.

And then he read the last bit, which come as near to a
great surprise as the rest of the stipulations. "Joint executors
of this will shall be Major Abel Jones of Pottsville,
Pennsylvania, and Mr. Matthew Cawber, resident of
Philadelphia, Pennsylvania. All attested and signed by myself, Evan E. Evans, and witnessed by Harvey Hemmings,
Esq., on this 19th day of September 1862. May God forgive
me my sins and remember my virtues."

I think the air in that room was as heavy as a souper fog
in London. Oh, we could see each other clear enough. But
we all had a blundering feel about us, as if we could not get
up and walk without tumbling over the furniture or colliding
with one another. I fear it was a mood akin to drunkenness.
Although no spirits had been taken, of course.

After what he considered a proper interval, Mr.
Hemmings said, "If I may . . . given the peculiar division of
certain assets of the deceased . . . if I may ask your attention . . . our firm already has received an offer that we have
been asked to convey to you . . ."

We all looked at the fellow. As if he could take back all he had just given, as if he might declare he had made it all up.

"We have received an offer that would relieve you of the cares of managing these mine and colliery operations . . ." he looked sagely at me and my uniform ". . . an anonymous consort of gentlemen offers to purchase the holdings and assets of Evans Coal and Iron for the sum of two hundred twenty-five thous—"

"*No,*" Mrs. Walker snapped. Almost a shout it was. She was up on her feet, with a sunburned color in her handsome face. "*Evan* built it up. And Evan left it to us." She looked down at me. "We won't sell it."

Mr. Hemmings looked at me. And his somber face asked, "How will you manage a colliery and mine, while you are away at your wars." He looked to me for common sense, see.

"No," I said, and I must say I surprised myself. "No, Mr. Hemmings, we will not sell Evans Coal and Iron. And if they have already offered such an amount, then we know it is worth more. For the wicked prey on the grieving, that I will tell you. We are not selling the Evans properties, see."

"Not at any price," Mrs. Walker insisted. Although I would not have gone that far myself.

Mr. Hemmings gazed at each of us in turn, then looked us all over again. He plucked the spectacles from his nose, laid them down on the green mat on his desk, and said, "Of course, you realize that each of you will require the services of a trustworthy, established law firm in your business endeavors. Just as dear Mr. Evans required our services. If I may suggest a similarly advantageous arrangement . . ."

WE STEPPED INTO THE HALL, the lot of us tottering. We had been made rich, you understand. In time, it would emerge that my Mary and I held assets worth over half a million dollars, which placed us among the wealthiest folk in Pottsville.

Twas almost Philadelphia wealth, although I will tell you we never lost our heads over the matter. For Methodists embrace their good fortune with sober mien, as they do their disappointments and disasters. But half a million dollars, in money and papers and properties! Of course, that day there was only a glorious vagueness about the sum. But I will admit that my criticisms of Mr. Evans were muted, at least for the moment.

I resolved to pray for his immortal soul. Clearly, his sins had weighed awfully upon him, or he never would have confessed his doings to me. And repentance is the first step toward salvation, a matter Our Savior made clear and good John Wesley explicated for the benefit of Mankind. We must not be too harsh in our judgements, for there was good even in a crucified thief.

As we stood all muddled in that narrow hallway, with its smell of soap and ashes and mildewed files, Mrs. Walker took advantage of my lack of self-possession.

She held out her hand to me.

"Looks like we're partners, ducks. I 'ope we may be friends, if only quiet-like."

I took her hand in mine. Twas warm, though gloved in black kid. As a gentleman, I could do no less, you understand.

I had not even begun to think about the implications of our new relationship. Nor did I wish to ponder it just then. I only wanted a breath of cold, clean air, to verify that all was real and not some laudanum dream.

But Mrs. Walker had me prisoner and would not release my hand. Her face was fittingly earnest, though I misapprehended the reason until she spoke again.

"Major Jones . . ." she began, seeking for the proper words to reach me. I fear she thought me something of an ogre, for she had grown to view all men as pliant and I was not.

I was about to excuse myself, when the woman found her tongue.

". . . Major Jones, forgive me do, but I 'ave to seize upon this opportunity, for Mary says you been obstinate. I don't know where to turn, I don't, and I'm desperate, I am. Even Mr. Evans, God bless 'im, was no 'elp to me in the matter, and you're the last 'ope I 'ave, with your 'igh connections."

She clutched my hand as a young recruit clings to his musket while marching into a volley.

". . . Nobody cares, not a one of them," she said bitterly, "though gay enough the brood of them carried on when Kathleen gave them their 'appiness of an evening." Tears returned to her eyes, though different in temper from those shed in the office. There was anger now, even rage. "They won't 'ear a whisper about 'er fate, not a bloody one of them will. Not that Fatty Gowen or the magistrate, nor any man among them, they're all so afraid of their secrets pouring out." She could no longer control herself and she sobbed. "I fear the poor girl's been murdered these two months."

fourteen

"KATHLEEN BOLAND was a lovely little thing," Mrs. Walker told me. "Not twenty years old, she wasn't, but wild as a camp full of gypsies."

We sat in Mrs. Walker's private parlor, a room I found extraordinarily pink. It had that gimcrack lavishness that heathens sometimes get up to, all flimsy and false when you take a second look. I found it not lascivious, but sad.

I could not invite her home, of course, so her residence had remained our only choice. Understanding she was, for she led me in through the alley door, sparing me the embarrassment of the front entrance, where company might be encountered. Nonetheless, one missy in relaxed apparel emerged from the kitchen and hooked her arm through mine, declaring, "I'm game, if you are, Shorty," but Mrs. Walker gave the lass a reprimand that stung her to a blush.

"I 'ad to put some manners on Kathleen," my hostess told me from her nest of pillows. "When she came around knocking and asking for work, she was raring to take on two or three gents at a time, if the money was flowing. I would 'ave turned 'er away from my door for the shame of 'er, if she 'adn't been as pretty as you please. But I left 'er in no doubt, I did, that I always keep an establishment of the 'ighest tastes and quality. Our gentlemen visitors ain't allowed no more than a smile and a squeeze in the public rooms, for I won't 'ave Sodom and Gomorrah under *my* roof. I always tell my girls, I tell them, 'Ladies, just show the boys enough to give them a proper 'int of what they're in for. And close your door be'ind you when you're entertaining, for a gentleman is easily embarrassed.' "

She sighed over her professional travails. "I tell you, Major Jones, just as I told Kathleen that very first day when I seen 'er, all looking fresh and pert as the flowers in May . . . I said to 'er, 'One at a time and easy does it, and wash up proper after.' Dr. Carr keeps telling them, but it's a battle to get them to listen, and the careless ones pay the price." Mrs. Walker had chatted herself into a disheartened state. "It's rare to meet a proper young lady these days. Though Kathleen Boland could 'ave passed for a princess. Until she opened that shanty-Irish mouth of 'er's."

I sat there listening and not listening. I still had not gotten very far past the name. Kathl   Boland. Boland. Kathleen . . .

"What color hair did the lass have?" I asked. I fear I interrupted Mrs. Walker, which is rude. But she did not seem to mind.

"It didn't know if it wanted to be red or brown, it didn't. But she had an 'andsome crop of it."

"Might you describe it as 'cinnamon' in color?"

Mrs. Boland considered my proposition. "I suppose that's as good a way as any to describe it. She 'ad a great flash to 'er, Kathleen did. The other girls were as jealous as old maids at a cotillion. Shall I call for some tea, then, shall I?"

I declined her offer. I feared the very contagion of the place. "And she come from Heckschersville, Miss Boland did?"

Mrs. Walker betrayed her surprise. "And just 'ow did you

know that?" A doubtful look darkened her brow. "I don't re-call you ever coming around to—"

"No, Mrs. Walker. Nothing of the kind. It is only that a fellow in my position hears things."

"Well, you're 'earing more than I do. Since poor Kathleen disappeared that first week in September, mum's the word among the 'igh and mighty. Oh, they were all 'appy enough to take an interest in 'er while she was alive, the sort who wouldn't 'ave tipped their 'ats to 'er in the street. But now that she's gone, it's as if the girl never existed."

"So . . . Kathleen Boland was from Heckschersville and she—"

"And that's where she took 'erself off to, the morning I saw the last of 'er. 'I'm only away for the Monday and Tuesday,' says she, 'for I've things to put in order bye and bye.' " Mrs. Walker took on the sentimental look that is a ready companion to immorality. "She never showed 'er face among us again. I know something awful's 'appened to 'er. She's murdered, sure as there's secrets kept at the bank. Murdered as dead as a salted cod. For we found almost three 'undred dollars in 'er room, and she ain't been back for it. I'm still 'olding it for 'er, I am. I keep things honest and fair in my establishment, though the girls all wanted to spend it on a wake. They've got the Irish 'abits, even those that 'aven't a drop of Irish blood. 'And what if she ain't dead?' I told them, although I know she is. If I can't put that money back in 'er 'and, it's going in the poor-box."

My hostess tutted over life's misfortunes. "Saving up 'er money for 'er betterment, Kathleen was. Though I think she liked the life well enough . . . she would 'ave found some parts of it 'ard to give up, and pity the man who ever tried to bind 'er. She was ruined from the start, and she enjoyed it, our Kathleen. No 'arm intended to the poor child's memory."

"So, Kathleen Boland returned to Heckschersville. To put something in order. And you are convinced she was murdered?"

"Well, she ain't come back, now 'as she? With three 'undred dollars left in 'er room. And wasn't the poor thing terrified when she left us? 'I don't want to go, but I 'ave to,' that's what she said to me. She was frightened as the deuce, with her gabbing of witches."

"Witches?"

Of a sudden, Mrs. Walker smiled. I do believe the room brightened around us. It even appeared that she still possessed all her teeth. Nor were they fouled.

"You're going to 'elp me, then, are you? Oh, I says to Mrs. Jones, to your Mary, says I, 'E's a romper, that 'usband of yours, even if 'e likes to pretend 'e's a parson.' I knew you'd 'ave an 'eart for a poor, murdered girl."

"I will help you, if I can, Mrs. Walker. Indeed, I believe I may be able to get to the truth of things rather quickly now. But when you speak of witches . . . did Kathleen Boland believe—"

"Family problems, it was. With 'er brother. 'Danny' she called 'im. Danny Boland. She loved 'im up and down, the poor girl did, for 'e was all the family what was left to 'er. The brother 'ad a wife that was a trouble to 'im. And I don't mean a trouble of the usual sort."

"The 'usual sort'?"

"You know. The woman nagging, and the 'usband drinking and wasting all 'is earnings. Or roving about. Fighting to break their bones. There wasn't none of that sort of thing between them. Kathleen said 'er brother was the very model of an 'usband."

"And Mrs. Boland? Was she a 'very model' of a wife? Or was she . . . one of these witches you spoke of?"

Mrs. Walker rolled her eyes toward Heaven. " 'Witches'

might be one way of putting it. And a nice way, if you ask Dolly Walker. You know 'ow superstitious the Irish are, with their spells and curses and whatnot. But the woman was Bedlam mad, I could tell that much from 'earing Kathleen talk. And none too nice in 'er morals, thank you, and 'er a married woman," Mrs. Walker added, not without indignation.

I would learn in the years to come that Dolly Walker had an almost ferociously prim sense of how the world should be beyond her walls. Her views were not terribly unlike my own, in some regards. Although I do not mean to suggest a comparison. She once proposed to me that, if wives would carry themselves proper when they went about their business, her establishment would go bankrupt in a fortnight. Her profession taught her the virtues of fidelity, and she always valued kindness above all, although you would not trick her out of a penny. And, to be fair, she never asked for a penny that was not hers by right.

But let that bide.

"What else did Kathleen say about Mary Boland?"

Again, she regarded me with a level of curiosity that approached suspicion. "You know of 'er, too, then? Mary Boland?"

"I have heard some things said of her, though in another association."

"Well, witch or no witch, she sounds like the queen of all the sluts to me," Mrs. Walker declared. "And she don't go collecting for it, neither. At least not to 'ear Kathleen tell it. Kathleen was against that marriage from the start, for the woman 'ad a terrible reputation, even among her own kind. I can't say what Kathleen believed down in her 'eart of 'earts, but she swore to me this Mary was a fairy woman. A 'changeling,' she called 'er. The sort what draws men on, whether they're wishing to go or not. The Irish call it 'putting the come-'ither' on a body. But if you ask Dolly Walker, I just call it waving about what shouldn't be waved in public. Not by a lady."

Mrs. Walker grimaced, rendering her fair face unappealing, if only briefly. "Oh, 'come-'ithers' and spells be buggered. It ain't 'alf so fanciful as that. Look 'ere, Major Jones. Some girls 'ave it, some don't, and there's an end to it. And I've known many a foolish woman in a position like mine who took such a one as that Mary Boland into 'er establishment, thinking the men would come knocking down the doors to get at 'er. But that's just the trouble. They *do* come knocking down the doors, and shooting pistols and throwing knives, or pitching acid at the face what troubles them. Killing themselves in the yard, and a dozen kinds of foolishness besides. No, a lady in my position needs to know 'er girls, and she's a fool if she takes on the sort that don't know when to stop. Or what can't stop themselves or the gentlemen." She shook her head. "It's bad enough when a fellow can't control 'imself. But a body expects more discipline from a woman."

"So . . . even after her marriage . . . Mrs. Boland was . . . liberal with her favors?"

"She would've disgraced the very 'ore of Babylon," Mrs. Walker said, "if the 'alf of what Kathleen told me was true. And 'er a married woman, disgracing 'er own good fortune." She looked at me again. "Oh, Mrs. Jones is a lucky one, I can tell you that. For she kept 'er wits about 'er when she went to 'er picking. She knew it ain't the shiny apples what tastes. I wish I'd 'ad 'er sense in the days of my youth and my innocence . . ."

Twas curious, see. I felt compelled to console the woman by telling her not all marriages were perfect in their arrangements. That hearts stray, however much we

Christians may regret it. But she seemed to have convinced herself that marriage was the highest form of
good, despite the abundant evidence she must have seen
to the contrary. But who among us does not have illu-
sions? And I was not about to criticize the institution of
marriage to a woman of her calling. Besides, my thoughts
were teeming and tumbling, and straying far afield from
the dells of happiness.

Is it witchery, then, when a woman makes a man adore
her? Is that all it takes to lead from the bed to the gallows?
Or to the stake? I do not believe in spells. But I have had
some acquaintance with desire. In my case, it was full of
the madness of love. But I have seen love change to the
madness of hatred. Was Mary Boland a "witch" because
men wanted her? Or did men want her because such things
as witches exist among us? Even if their magic is of the
flesh?

I cannot say if there are spells and curses, but I have
known enchantment in my life.

Oh, I had a muchness to ponder.

"But was there a specific matter that led her homeward
just then?" I asked. "A particular incident? If she was Irish,
see, I cannot think it would have been a pleasant matter for
her to return to Heckschersville. Not after taking up her . . .
profession. For the Irish are great ones for the virtues of
their women."

"Bogtrotters, with patches on their arses and their elbows," Mrs. Walker said dismissively. "Kathleen wasn't
afraid of that bunch. She 'ad 'er mind made up to go and talk
'er brother back into 'is senses."

"About a specific event, though? And how did she plan to
go about it?"

"Oh, she didn't say so much as that, she didn't. Only that
she'd 'ave a great talk with their priest and remind 'im of 'is

duties. Forever mumbling about witches and spells, she was. She felt it was 'is place to keep such things in order. They're 'opeless in their superstitions, Major Jones, and they think a priest's as good as Jesus Christ. I told 'er not to go, I did. I told 'er she was well quit of 'im, and lucky at the cost she 'ad to pay."

"Quit of . . . of her brother, do you mean?"

She let out a great and unladylike "Ha!" Then she wrinkled her face as if detecting an odor. "It's that fancy-boy priest I was talking about. I told 'er she was better off for leaving the patch and getting shut of 'im." She looked at me as directly as a man might. "Just who do you think made a ruin of 'er in the first place, if not their blessed priest? That one ruined Kathleen worse than the baggage you pick off the streets, with the things 'e made 'er do. But she said she'd 'ave it out with 'im, once and for all. And if 'e wouldn't 'elp, she'd tell all the world what 'e done."

I DASHED FROM THE ROOM, absolving Mrs. Walker of the need to escort me out. After nearly colliding with a pair of alarmingly immodest young women—they chuckled at me, for reasons of their own—I regained the back door and launched myself out through it.

I knocked down the fellow who was just about to enter. Twas the parson of our chapel, the Reverend Mr. Grimes.

He went down on all his points, and I was stumbling dizzily. My cane had skated away when our skulls collided, and for a moment or two my balance was as disordered as my senses. But soon enough I digested my victim's identity and exploded with explanations and apologies. But the parson did not listen. He was more enlivened by the need to excuse his presence at that back door to me. I believe he said something about moral redemption and poor, misguided souls, but his face was as red as the silks of a Sindhi dancing girl.

I do not believe he heard one word I said. He blathered. Then, with a nasty smile that assured me "I-won't-tell-if-you-don't," the fellow turned his back on the house and scooted down the alley as if dogs were giving him chase.

Now, I will tell you: Such behavior does not become a Methodist. And certainly not the pastor of a chapel. Beyond that, I will leave you to your judgements.

Nor did the encounter seem as important as it might have appeared on any other day. My mind was reeling and rushing about, intoxicated by all I had learned from Mrs. Walker. I had at least half of the puzzle, see. I still could not say who murdered General Stone or why, but clear it was that the priest had murdered Kathleen Boland, the child he had seduced and then corrupted. When she returned and threatened him, he had killed her rather than risk her public censure.

That was, by far, a sorrier matter than Methodists sneaking into disorderly houses.

I decided to go to Heckschersville as soon as I could arrange it. Even if I arrived there after midnight. I meant to have it out with the priest. And he would not find me so easy to dispose of as a poor, ruined Irish girl.

I had another fear, as well. I believed the priest had murdered Mary Boland, too. I had not seen her after that morning when I caught the priest scrubbing blood out of his linens. With fresh blood on his shoulder. And I bore much of the blame, if the priest had killed her. For I was the one who had frightened him by telling him Mrs. Boland watched his house and that I had spoken with her. Twas clear she had known a great deal about the priest's doings. Likely she knew of the murder of Kathleen Boland.

I still could not explain why her husband had taken the blame upon himself for the general's murder and why he had fled from the woman he loved so dearly, no matter her sins. Had Danny Boland been in despair over the murder of his sister? Did he even know of her death? Why had he run shouting his guilt through the streets? Had he come unhinged, or had there been a plot? I could not say, but that priest knew many an answer.

Had the priest murdered the general, too? Because of something the general had learned? I was not being frivolous in my suspicions, for I will tell you a thing: With murderers, the murdering rarely stops. One crime draws on the next. But how could a man in holy office bring himself to do such evil works?

I recalled that old Donnelly, the leader of the Irish, had insisted that no man among them had killed the general. Did a priest count as a man to them, with his pledge to live his days out as a celibate? How did their minds work? And what had witches to do with the whole affair? Was superstition their tool, or just a nonsense?

The priest held the key, and I would have it from him. He would stand trial for the murder of Kathleen Boland. And likely for killing Mary Boland, too. I wondered what he had done with that one's body? Had he hidden her in his holy ground, as well? And what had become of the waste of Kathleen Boland, after they dug her up again?

The Irish were devoted to their priests. Yet, they showed a plain dislike of this one. Would they shield him from a charge of murder? The murder of one of their own? Did they hate and fear the rest of us so deeply?

I hurried me down the steep of the hill from Minersville Street, vaulting along on my cane. Twas a fine thing, that cane, a gift from a wicked man, and yet I kept it. I told myself it was because of the practical blade concealed in it. But the man himself kept a curious hold on me, and we were destined to meet again, in an unexpected place. But let that bide. I hurried across Market Street and up the little slope to Norwegian, where my family would be waiting. There would be no time for pondering the legacies we had received, nor even for the sober calm of mourning. I would have to change into my second-best uniform, to spare my better dress, and hurry along to find myself transportation to Heckschersville. I did not even think to pause for dinner, which is unlike me.

I had a piece of the solution, and I did not mean to let go until I had the rest.

I climbed the stoop and went into our house, not without a curious sense of loss. For we had been happy there, although we had only rented it. It had been our first true home. And now a mansion loomed on Mahantango Street, up among the grand folk.

I felt a shudder within me, as if I could not let my old life go.

But go I would. I knew that. As surely as I would take me off to that priest's house.

That was a day of surprises, I will tell you. Sitting in my parlor was Mr. Matthew Cawber, the great industrial fellow of Philadelphia. And Mr. Cawber was sitting in my chair. I had met him and come to respect him, but had not suspected his business ties to Mr. Evans until I heard the will read out that day. And now he was in my home, which was a humble place, compared to the mansions he dwelt in.

Mr. Cawber was not a particularly large man, yet he always seemed to crowd the room he occupied.

My darling was passing him coffee. She looked a handsome woman in her mourning rig. A lady who can wear black is said to be the very truest of all beauties. Queer to say, young John sat at Cawber's feet, staring up at the man in fascination, although he had yet to master his fear of me. Fanny watched him, too, from her chair by the coal stove.

And Mr. Cawber was a sight to see. He was the blackest white man that ever I have known. His whiskers, given a touch of gray by the tragic loss of his wife, climbed almost to the sockets of his eyes, and his hairs were menacing wires. He looked like that Vulcan fellow in the myths, which suited, I suppose, since he had made his fortune casting iron. His hair was black, his eyes were black, his dress was black, and the look upon his face was black as coal. He was the sort who glowered even at those persons well-disposed toward him.

He grunted when he saw me and did not rise. He never was a fellow for formality.

"Abel Jones," he said, as if reading a label set upon me. "This whip-smart wife of yours has more sense than twenty bankers and a nigger bootblack put together." He took his coffee from her and muttered his thanks. "That's a rotten scar you picked up on your cheek. You look like the devil."

I do not look like the devil.

"Good it is to see you, Mr. Cawber. Although I am surprised—"

"Right. I know what they say. 'Matt Cawber's gone mad, lost all his senses.' Let 'em talk. They'll find out. Here I am." He took a smacking sip of Mary's coffee.

"Yes, Mr. Cawber. But I don't—"

"Sit down," Mr. Cawber said, as if the house were his own. "And listen."

I sat me down. It is not that he wished to be rude. But he had a broken-knuckles way about his every gesture. As if he had been slugging all his life. And for much of that life, he had been.

"Jones, I knew what was in that will. Came up here before you could do anything foolish. Evans Coal and Iron. *You* can't manage it. Even if you take that idiotic soldier suit off, you're not an engineer. And mining's engineering, first and foremost. Unless you just mean to dig a pit and die in it." He grunted. "Too many fools around here already. All talking on and on about their 'Mammoth Vein.' Well, it's only mammoth if you can get to it. State engineers told them years ago. The seam drops off and goes a mile deep. Deeper. They wouldn't listen. Dug blind. Now three-quarters of them are wondering what to do and crawling down Broad Street begging for loans. Except for old Johns. Smart man, Johns. Evans was nearly as smart as Johns, but he always shied away from the bigger risks, whether they made sense or not. Still, Evans Coal and Iron is one of the few outfits that holds leases on lands that are worth going at with a pick and shovel. Those leases, and the land Evans bought outright, amount to pure gold, my friend." Mr. Cawber made a fist to warn the world. "The money men are either going to try to buy you out, or they'll run you out. So I'm going to take care of things for you. I'm going to take your worst worries off your hands."

"Mr. Cawber," I began, as my darling passed me my own cup of coffee, "Evans Coal and Iron is not for sale. Not even to you. Look you, we—"

"I didn't say a damn thing—pardon me, ladies—I didn't say a thing about buying anything. Now, did I?"

"No, but—"

"Why don't you just sit down on your hat and listen to me?" His black brows had gathered until his impatience appeared volcanic. "I don't plan to *buy* anything. You're going to *give* me a one-third share in Evans Coal. You and Mrs. Walker, between you. By the way, I hear that woman has a good business head on her shoulders." He snorted. With him, it was a form of punctuation. "You're going to give me a one-third share, and I'm going to do three things for you. First, I'm going to back you with the capital you need to dig deep, and to do it the right way. You couldn't afford it, even if you were to touch your wife's inheritance. Which you'd be a fool to do. Second, I'm going to protect you from the Reading. The railroad crowd are the ones who want to buy you out. They're setting out to construct an empire for themselves. If you won't sell, they'll blacklist you and refuse to carry your coal unless you pay fees so high you'll be bankrupt in three months. When you're really up against it, they'll tell you they don't have any cars available to carry your coal and they'll laugh while you count the empties rolling down the valley. But I can turn the tables on them. They'll be begging to haul our coal, at discounted rates. Third, I'm going to bring in the finest mining engineer on two continents and put him in charge of the practical side of things. And I'm going to pay Tom Caxton so well he'll just laugh if anybody tries to bribe him or hire him away. His salary's going to be my affair, and I'll take that charge myself. But we're going to pay fair wages, top to bottom, even if we have to take a loss now and then. I'll put in capital to start, but our long-term aim is going to be to build up capital. We're not going to put a penny into our own pockets for five years. We're just going to stack it up. To get us through the bad years, when they come. And they always come. That's when we're going to want to have the ready funds to buy up property ourselves. You can decide who keeps the books. I trust you when it comes to watching the cash box. But I'll approve or disapprove of any capital investment above one thousand—no, above five hundred dollars. Caxton will come directly to me about that kind of thing. At least until you come to your senses and get rid of that peacock soldier suit of yours."

He held out his hand. It bristled with hair, all the way down to the knuckles. Still more hair escaped his cuff.

"Deal?"

I looked at the fellow. I did not like to appear a weakling in front of my own family, you understand, nor do I like to be bullied. Not that I believed Mr. Cawber meant me ill. Much to the contrary. But he was the sort of fellow who would knock down any door he encountered before he bothered to try if it was unlocked. He recalled to my mind that Hindoo god who is a destroyer and creator all at once. I had to hesitate for the sake of my manhood, see.

Cawber glowered at my evident mulling. "Yes or no? Do we have a deal or not? I don't have time to waste."

"Mr. Cawber, I cannot speak for Mrs. Walker, and—"

"I'm not asking you to speak for Mrs. Walker. Mrs. Walker can speak for herself. Do you and I have a deal? Yes or no?"

He looked as if he would leap from his chair and begin to tear down the house if I failed to answer.

"Yes," I said, with a sidelong glance at Mary. She did not look as if she disapproved.

Cawber stood up. And I stood up to join him. We met before the stove and clasped our hands.

Young John smiled. Slapping his tiny palms together. "Ebbelzo!" he declared. Which was his way of saying, "Applesauce."

"Good," Cawber said. You half expected the fellow to breathe fire. "We're partners, then. I'll have my lawyers draw up the papers. Not that two-tongued fool who worked for your uncle. Oh, we'll keep that crowd on, just to keep an eye on them. But I'll have my Philadelphia boys take care of anything that matters."

He released my hand. But his eyes still pierced mine own.

"We're going to give those bastards in the Reading a run for their money." He turned, almost with a bow, to my Mary and to Fanny. "Beg your pardon, ladies. Business talk. Didn't mean to be rude." And he turned again to me. "Cawber Iron takes a good percentage of the coal the Reading hauls, and plenty of other fellows will listen to me when I tell them where to buy their anthracite. And I control the shipping docks they all need, at least until they smarten up and build their own. They try to break us, and we'll throw in with the Lehigh, to spite 'em." At the prospect of a fight, Mr. Cawber grinned. You could almost hear the bones crack in his cheeks. "We're battlers, you and me. Sounds like Dolly Walker's a scrapper, too. We're going to give those"—he glanced at Mary—"those *fel*lows a hammering they won't forget. And we're going to have us a high time doing it." He swung his attentions back to Mary. "We aren't going to bother a lady's capital, either."

He picked up his hat and stick. It did not appear that he had worn an overcoat, despite the cold.

"Oh, but Mr. Cawber," my Mary said, stepping forward in rather a rush, "won't you stay for your supper, then?" To my astonishment, I saw she was somewhat taken with the fellow. And Fanny's young face gleamed in admiration. Now, I respect Mr. Cawber for his honesty. But honesty has rarely appealed to ladies. I could not fathom what they all found appealing in him. To put it as gently as possible, he was gruff.

"Thanks, ma'am. Wouldn't intrude on your grief. Next time I call, I'll eat everything you put in front of me and ask for more. Right now, I've got a call to pay on Mrs. Walker." He slapped his hat onto his head without waiting to go out of doors, tipping it to my wife and to Fanny, which was hardly how things are done in a family parlor.

"Mr. Cawber—"

"It's 'Matt' from here on. And you're 'Abel.' None of that Society Hill twaddle. Understand?"

"Well, Matt, it is only that I wished to tell you that there is a quiet rear entrance to Mrs. Walker's establishment and—"

"I don't go in back doors," he said.

fifteen

$\mathcal{J}$ WAS NEAR ENOUGH TO MIDNIGHT as I climbed the hill to the priest's house. We had come the long way round, through Coal Castle, since that road was more certain in the darkness. I had asked Mr. Downs to let me dismount a mile shy of Heckschersville. For I wanted no attention paid to my visit.

I tapped along the streets of the patch with a hard frost setting in. The moon was bright and the earth wore a veil of silver. The wind was down. I heard men snore behind ramshackle walls. The heaviness of their days told on the Irish, wearying them to a slumber just short of death. No one saw me go, although a cat snarled at me from under a porch. Peculiar creatures, cats. I have read that they were worshipped by Egyptians.

Up I went, with the earth aglow, past the ragged walls of the boneyard. My memories of the place were hard companions. I kept a watch as I went, although they had no reason to expect me. My soldiering years have left me alert to the darkness. And midnight wore a strangeness on that hill. The priest's house was dark, but moonlight swept the cross above their church.

I touched at the trace of my Colt beneath my greatcoat. It is a thing I do when I grow wary.

I would tell you that I did not hear a sound, to give you a

sense of the stillness, but that would be untrue. Down in the valley the pumps were at their labors, drawing up the water from the mines. Throbbing, they sounded like engines under the earth. Like drums down deep.

Just before I come to the sorry splinters of steps that led to the priest's door, I stopped. It struck me that I might have a look around. To see if there were tubs of bloody washing, or anything else that might confirm his guilt.

I know how to walk in the darkness. The leaves were crisp and unswept, as if strewn there to warn him. But I took my time and put my heels down carefully. I could have crawled with greater speed, but haste killed many a soldier.

A muted light, hardly more than a hint, outlined a window toward the rear of the shanty. Twas the sort of glow that might filter through a shroud.

I eased toward it. And began to hear rhythmic, slapping sounds. And moans.

I met a stench that passed right through the walls.

The window's frame sat high, brushing the top of my chest. At first I thought I would not see a thing, for the drapery was opaque. Anxious I was, for a body was in a torment. That slapping sound told of someone being whipped. I knew the song of the lash from the punishment barracks, where the native troops were subject to its hymn. Little cries, of a gender indeterminate, spoke of a suffering deeper than the bone.

I pressed my face up close. And found a crack between the cloth and the wood.

The priest was on his knees, naked, before a candlelit crucifix. His back was to me, and his body was scourged to a horror. He put me in mind of the sepoys and sowars we flayed alive in the Mutiny. As I watched, he lashed himself over one shoulder, then the other, repeating the pattern and groaning. His face rose toward the Cross, toward Heaven, only to drop down again. There was as much blood in that room as there is in a surgery.

I understood those linens in the washtub.

But that was not the worst of it. That room was the fellow's bedroom, and I could see one corner of the bed. Upon that bed, I saw a woman's foot. It was mouldered and black, a part of a corpse long dead.

I staggered backward, making a dreadful ruckus. The sound of the lashes stopped and I heard movement. I slipped back into a shadow of trees and bushes, then kept me still. It is motion that gives us away in the hours of darkness, signs of life that betray us. Night forgives us the imitation of death.

The priest tore the drapery to one side, staring wildly into the darkness. The moonlight polished his features and his nakedness. His face mirrored Cain before the Throne of God.

Twas then I stepped into the light, where his eyes could find me.

THE PRIEST LAUGHED. That is what he did as he sat before me, in the stink and rot of his rooms. With a blanket wrapped around him, as if he were a beggar from the Bible. He laughed. But he did not laugh as you or I might do.

He wept, as well. He sat before me, laughing and weeping, gargling fragments of words that made no sense. It was wretched in that place. I am no delicate flower, but a soldier who has seen cruel things aplenty. Still, I kept gagging, over and over, until I feared I would not be able to master myself.

He sat in his parlor full of books. The painting of his sister hung askew, almost as if a child had been annoying it, clinging to the frame. I stood before him. I wished to touch nothing, nor to sit down. If he had lashed his body with a whip, I lashed him with words. I cannot quite explain the rage I felt. But I struck him, relentlessly, with language as sharp as any I ever have used. I dare not tell you all the things I said.

He laughed, and did not hear me, and looked through me as if I were not there. He had seen me well enough outside his window. But not now.

I slapped him, hard, upon the cheek, then struck him again. That was a foolish thing to do, illogical. My blows could not compete with the pain the fellow had inflicted on himself. Perhaps the violence was for my sake, not for his.

"You killed her, you filthy pig. You ruined a child and made a slut of her. And you killed her . . ."

His lip was bleeding. All of the man was bleeding. Blood traced down his naked calves, fleeing the folds of his blanket.

Without the least warning, he looked up at me, almost as clear and pleased with himself as he had been the last time we shared that room.

"You don't understand anything. Do you?" he said.

I tell you I wanted to strike the man again. But I did not. "I understand . . . that you are no more than a monster."

He laughed. As if he were afflicted with hysterics, like those creatures I had seen in the asylum.

"I didn't kill her," he told me. "Good Lord, how could you think that?" His mood had changed again, and his voice was no more than a whisper. He gazed into the shadows, not at me. "I couldn't . . . I would have slain God Himself, before I harmed her."

It was a terrible thing for a priest to say.

He cradled his head in his hands, furrowing that white hair of his with his fingers. "Can't you see *anything*?" Abruptly, he looked up and met my eyes. "Nothing at all?"

"I see a filthy man. Who keeps a corpse in his bed. A blasphemer." My voice had all the disgust a man can muster.

"And how would *you* go before your God? If you wouldn't even repent the thing you'd done? If you couldn't bear to repent it? If every drop of blood in your body and every breath you took cried out to have your sin back? If you loved your sin more than Heaven and earth joined together?"

I recalled the fragment that runs, ". . . something dreadful is in this place . . ." but did not speak it.

He waved his arms madly, sweeping his head from side to side. Struggling with demons, with pain. "Don't you see it? Don't you? All of this is about *love*, not about hatred. Everything happened because of love. *Real* love, flesh and blood love. Not some frightened obeisance to a statue. Or reverence for a spook we've made up to scare ourselves, to keep us in misery. Your murders were done out of love, because of love. It's God's joke on us, you see. That's what love is. God's joke." He lowered his head again. "I despise Him."

"Before you get to the judgement of God, you will face the judgement of men."

"Do you think that will be so terrible to me? Now? Don't you understand that I loved her more than I prized my immortal soul? *If* the soul is immortal . . ."

"It was not your place to love her."

He twisted his face into a parody of all that is human and good. "That's His joke, don't you see?"

"You speak of God, when you should speak of the Devil."

He denied me. "How do you tell the difference? I can't anymore."

Perhaps Hell reeks like those closed-up rooms, where the priest hid his beloved.

"That is another blasphemy," I said.

He shook his head. Somberly this time. "I cannot . . . I will not believe that love is ever a blasphemy."

"Your own books say—"

He waved his arms again, as if to strike me. "What good

are books? How long did it take me to learn that? Words. Nothing but words upon a page. And every word a lie. I wasted every day of my life until I met her. I'd burn every book on earth to have her beside me again. Alive." He found my eyes. "Really, don't you see the joke? To make me love her so, then to take her life over an idiocy, over a misunderstanding? To steal her away from me? After I chose her above salvation?"

His face contorted, as if he would wail his grief. But he only collapsed against the back of the sofa. The blanket must have scourged his wounds anew.

"She *was* my salvation . . ." he told me.

"You drove the child to a bawdy house."

Tears pulsed from his eyes. "You don't understand that, either. She did that to save me. To save my soul. She ran away from me, from us. She didn't think there was any good in her. She blamed herself. For the shame. That's what her faith did for her. That's what her Holy Church did. Filled her with guilt and blame. For the wanting . . . the desire that God put in her. Everything she had learned from her faith taught her that she had to destroy her joy, that joy was impermissible. And she tried. She didn't become a whore the way you mean. That was only her body. She did it to crucify herself, her heart. Her soul. That's what we taught her God wanted. It wasn't prostitution. It was penance."

"You're a coward to blame God."

He smirked. "I damn God."

"You've damned yourself. By the accords of your own faith."

"Then let me be damned. If she's in Hell, I want to go to Hell. To be with her. I want no part of His Heaven . . ."

"You are an evil man."

He smiled, almost like the cool fellow he once had been.

"I'm a man. I've learned that much. Perhaps that alone makes me evil."

"We must struggle against evil. Against temptation."

"Against love?"

"If you did not kill Kathleen Boland, who did?"

"I can't tell you that."

"Because you're lying."

"Because I gave my word."

I wanted to slap him again. Harder. "Your *word?* Your *word,* man? The word of a priest who turns girls into whores? The word of a priest who keeps his lover's corpse in his bed? Your *word?*"

"I gave my word. Hang me. It doesn't matter." He smiled bitterly. "Perhaps we'll be happy in Hell. Perhaps that's the only chance any of us has for happiness."

He was mad.

I could stand the stench no longer. Nor could I stand the wicked man before me. I should not have soiled my own soul by arguing with him. Perhaps I should have shot the fellow dead.

I longed for fresh, clean air as I never had before and have not since.

"I will come back tomorrow," I told him. "For you. And for her. Do not do anything foolish before I return. And do not try to run away from the law."

He mocked me with his laughter. "Run? From your pathetic law? I'm running from God, you ass. I'm not running from you."

I LEFT HIM THERE and took me outside. I had to pause at the foot of his steps, to gulp the night deep into me, to find some purity in a rotted world. I wanted air and bearable explanations. I had not even asked him of Mary Boland. For I was flummoxed. All my theories had collapsed. I no longer be-

lieved the priest had killed his beloved. I did not think his
character strong enough for that.

Perhaps you see the pattern of things already. But I could
not. I needed one great piece to make sense of the puzzle,
and I could not know how soon that piece would come to
me. I reeled, despite the support of my cane, almost drunk
with the stink that had entered my lungs. The icy air was not
enough to cleanse me, inside or out. I had the scent of her
rottenness in my nostrils, on my tongue. It had seeped into
my clothes. Into the heart of me.

I took my first steps down that hill in a welter of anger and
disappointment, of shame and wounded pride, confused by
the priest's sulfurous arguments. I grumbled threats toward
him, only to keep myself from too much thinking. A sorry
creature he was, blaming God and love for loathesome sins.

I stepped into the trees and vomited. I could not get her
corpse out of my mind, see. When I had gone into that
house, to force the priest into an admission, I entered his
bedchamber to confirm the corpse's identity. It was
Kathleen Boland, and no question. Kathleen of the cinnamon hair. Twas even longer now, for the hair continues to
grow on a corpse for ages. He had covered her in a white
gown, but the rot come seeping through. The bed appeared
as though he slept beside her.

I retched until my belly burned and my throat was raw to
a misery.

As I wiped my mouth, I saw Mary Boland before me.

She looked as beautiful as Guinevere must have done. Or
perhaps she was a fairy princess, indeed, with her hair too
black for description and the moonburned white of her skin
framing tyrant's eyes.

"Mrs. Boland," I said. Twas all the words I could manage
in my surprise.

And then I saw the witch. Or the old woman, I should say.

The leprous creature, her flesh corrupting the moonlight. She stood behind Mary Boland and off to the side. As if relying on the younger woman for protection. Or using her as an instrument.

"Nun kommt die Stunde des Todes," the old beast cackled.

Mary Boland drew a knife from her shawl. "You're keeping him from me!" she screamed. "You're keeping my Danny from me!"

As she shrieked out those words, she hurled herself at me. The violence of her assault was almost stunning. The fiercest Afghanee was nothing to her. I lacked the time to lift my cane to parry her. I barely managed to thrust my left hand between the blade and my chest.

The knife plunged into my palm, a shining, quicksilver thing. The tip erupted from the back of my hand with a splash of blood. My own gore struck my face. That knife might have been heated in Hellfire, for the pain was instant and scalding.

I stabbed my cane into her bosom so fiercely she let go of her weapon. The blade remained in my hand, pinning it to the air. Mary Boland clutched herself, recoiling. The old woman rushed toward me with her claws.

Quick as could be, I unlocked the sword inside my cane, flinging the sheathe to the side.

The old woman stopped an inch short of impaling herself. Mary Boland, who meant to attack again, crouched down as an animal will. Longing to spring.

I teased my blade at one, then at the other, warning them off. All the while, pain raged in my hand. I have been wounded a plenty of times, but remembered no such a sensation. Twas a great, scalding burn, like a muscle tormented by spasms. My fingers would not move. The big blade wobbled and dangled from my flesh. I wanted to tear at it and howl, as a dog will.

I pressed my skewered hand against my coat. Feeling the hot blood smear. My paw might as well have been held against a skillet.

"I will kill you. Both of you," I told them.

They began to circle me. Like beasts. Snarling. Cackling. The old woman's skin was diseased to a luminosity. The moonlight seemed to melt it from her bones. Mary Boland looked as beautiful as anything on this earth. And feral.

Perhaps there were such things in the night as witches.

Mary Boland had an animal's wiles. She sensed me. Something dreadful about me. About all of us. About Adam. She dropped her shawl from her shoulders and I heard cloth tear. In a moment, the woman had freed her breasts. The glow of the heavens showed her to me.

"Do ye want this?" she hissed. "Is that what you're after wanting? That's what ye all want, an't it?" She eased toward me, pressing up against the tip of my blade, and began to hike her skirt. "Come hither to me then. Come and take what ye want . . ." She lifted her skirt until she had exposed her long, white nakedness. And her darkness.

The old crone edged toward me all the while. While the younger woman sought to bewitch my eyes.

I did not press my blade into Mary Boland. Instead, I slowly drew it back. Unable to harm her. The two of them closed their distance, ever so slowly. I smelled their stink the way I smelled that corpse. Two distinct scents they had. As different as life and death.

I stepped rearward. Crushing frozen leaves. Terrified that I would trip and fall. With the blood running off my fingers, soaking my greatcoat and dripping down onto the earth.

"Keep you back," I said. "Or I will kill you."

"Ye don't want to kill me," Mary Boland said. Advancing an inch at a time. "That's not what ye want of me. Come now. Let me kiss the blood from where I've hurt you."

She held her skirt at her waist with one hand and stretched out the other toward me. Reaching for me. Beckoning.

"Keep away . . ."

So queer it was. I have killed many a man, God forgive me. Yet, at that moment, I could not put my blade through a creature who had just stabbed me. Or even through the old woman.

The crone began a nonsense incantation. It thickened the night. And seemed to shade the moon.

"Come on, my sweet," Mary Boland said. "Come take what ye want now . . ."

The hilt of the sword-cane was pressed into my own stomach. The long blade shivered. I felt that, in a moment, the woman would take it from me.

"Come to me," she whispered.

The women must have seen him in the moment before he struck. Or they heard a sound I did not. They both cringed back, as if I had thrust my blade at them after all. An instant later, he fell upon them, swinging a stick.

"Get off with you," he barked. "Get off, you filthy devils."

He slashed at them with his stick and I heard it crack over their shoulders, across their backs.

"Get away, now," he commanded.

The two women screeched and cursed at him. But they did not put up the least bodily resistance. They scuttled off, Mary Boland struggling to free the skirt she had dropped and caught on a nest of nettles. She got a fierce clubbing for her efforts and finally ran off to the sound of ripping cloth and leaves crisp underfoot.

And so they left me.

"For the love o' sweet Jesus," the man said. "Put up your bloody, damned knife. They're only a pair of crazy women."

"Witches," I gasped.

He laughed. Twas an iron sound. "They'd love ye for thinking it, wouldn't they? The hag . . . and that other one?"

It was John Kehoe. The fellow they called "Black Jack."
But his beard shone blue in the moonlight, as anthracite will
go blue in the flicker of a lamp.

Twas then he saw my hand.

As he watched me, I propped my blade against a tree and
pulled the knife out of my palm. Now, I am not a weak man.
And I have dug a bullet from my own leg, when the surgeon
died of the bloody trots himself and the column was fighting
for its life in the Pushtoon hills. But I nearly dropped as I felt
the blade slide out of me. My bowels quaked.

As soon as I had the knife free, the pain collapsed to an
ache. But blood there was in plenty. And I still could not
move my fingers enough to speak of it.

"You'll have to take yourself off and have that seen to,"
Kehoe told me. "Or you'll bleed to death and we'll have the
blame for another one."

THERE WAS NO DOCTOR IN THE VALLEY, of course. For miners
and laborers did not merit such attention. Kehoe wanted to
be shut of me, but I remembered Mick Tyrone's insistence
that wounds must be washed clean at the earliest chance. We
never fussed with that sort of thing in India, but Mick was
no fool and I made Kehoe lead me down to a pump.

He worked the handle, a long, creaking affair, and the
icy water poured over my wound. I tried to let it into the
crack where the blade went through, but there is a limit to
what a man can do to himself. A woman popped her head
out of a window to ask what the doings were, but Kehoe
told her to take herself back to her slumbers. I cut a great,
long strip from my shirt—which troubled me, for the garment was recently purchased—and Kehoe helped me bind
it about my paw.

"You'll need it seen to," he repeated.

We stared at each other. The moon was falling and the

silver light made the side of his face look hard and bright as plate.

"How did you know?" I asked him. "Were you following me?"

"If I was, I'd say ye were the luckier for it."

"Were you watching me? Or watching the priest? Or the women?"

"I was sleeping," Kehoe said. As if that would suffice for an explanation.

"And you heard something?"

He sighed. As men will when they see that they must answer. "No, boyo. I was sleeping and I had a dream, if ye have to know. A quare enough dream it was, and lucky ye are that I had it."

"This isn't a dream," I said.

"Oh, I can tell the difference, laddybuck. No, I dreamed a gypsy woman was shaking me by the arm. A brown-skinned bit she was, in some sort of heathen get up. Shaking me and telling me I must get up that instant. And getup I did. To nothing at all. Nothing but the cold beyond the blankets. But I stepped out of bed to have a visit with the night pot, and then I heard something that wasn't a dream at all. I heard footsteps where no footsteps should have been. And when I had me a look out Donnelly's window, there ye were. Walking up the street like a one-man parade. So I thought ye might want following. For I was half a pint sure ye were going up to the priest's house. And I didn't see that any good would come of it. Now . . . does that satisfy your great, Welsh curiosity?"

"No," I said. "Tell me. You must have waited while I was in with Father Wilde. You must have . . . God, man, don't you people know what's going on up there? You *must* know. It's unpardonable."

"We'll settle our own affairs."

"Will you? Before Mary Boland kills someone else? The

way she killed Kathleen Boland? Oh, I see it now. That I do. And I do not doubt that she killed the general, too, though I cannot yet see the why of it. But I will get to that in time." I wrinkled up my mouth. "You and your Mr. Donnelly, with his 'No man among us killed your general.' Playing me for a fool. Because it wasn't a man who did the killing, but a woman."

"Ye want to have that hand looked after," Kehoe said. He turned his back and began to walk away.

"I know Danny Boland didn't kill anyone," I called after him. "I understand, see. I can help him. If you help me."

Kehoe did not turn to me again.

"I know about his father," I tried. "I know why you all protected Danny Boland."

But Black Jack Kehoe was never a man to be swayed by another's words. He got to things in his own time, not before. A hard man, he was, and a capable hater, never shy of doing what he thought necessary. But he did not deserve the fate that Franklin Benjamin Gowen would prepare for him in a dozen years time.

"I'll be back," I nearly shouted. "With a warrant for Mary Boland's arrest."

By that time, he was little more than a shadow.

sixteen

"YEP, THERE'S A DOC IN MINERSVILLE, all right," Mr. Downs informed me as the wagon creaked along. "Doc Hooper. Say he's more inclined to cut things off than sew 'em back together, but I guess it saves him some trouble that way." His fingers wrestled within his nasal cavities. "Major, you are one man who just seems born to get himself hurt, if you ask me. Last feller I knew like you, he fell out of a tree he shouldn't of been in to start with. Broke his neck dead. I tried to tell him, 'Homer, you don't need to climb no tree to drink no whisky, it tastes just fine here on the ground.' But he wouldn't listen, now would he? Had to climb that tree. Poor, old Homer. Damned fool wasn't even Irish, though his widow was. Get on, mules, get on."

It was a long journey.

The ache in my hand was a trivial thing, though the bleeding did concern me. I felt a seep that wanted proper tending and my rag of a bandage was soaking. Mr. Downs speculated that he might soon witness the amputation of my hand, if not of my arm entire, and I half thought he might propose my beheading as well. I do not think the teamster had a mean character, but many's the man who delights in another's misfortune. The fallen angel makes our heaven sweeter.

Had I delighted in the priest's misfortune? That may sound queer, yet I could not help but wonder. I had been so merciless with him, furious unto a rage. Now his words returned to haunt my ears. All his prattling on about love. And God. I had wanted so badly to wound him, to prove that he was wrong, to make him see it. To make him admit that things were best my way.

Perhaps the priest was mad. Perhaps Father Wilde had a streak of evil. Perhaps I was right to chastise him. But my slapping and barking did not sit well with me afterward.

You see, I harbor deep doubts of mine own, though it shames me to speak of them. So many of God's projects leave me mystified. Not least regarding matters of the heart. Had Mrs. Walker loved Mr. Evans honestly? Had she been able to love him, truly and yearningly, despite her spendthrift attitude to virtue? Is love less a hothouse flower than a doughty weed triumphant? Are we in error to think that love needs virtue? Have we been given a will to love that cannot be extinguished? Does all our Christian diligence only blind us, leading us to mistake a gift as poison? Might love renew virtue?

What of Mary Magdalene's redemption? Are we so pleased by her moral reformation that we fail to remember her love for Jesus Christ? Was her changed behavior more important than her change of heart? Why was she stalwart below the cross, when all His disciples fled? Why did *she* go to the tomb? And why did Jesus show himself to her? I do not suggest impropriety, only that love is more than good deportment.

Is all love equal in weight on the scales of Heaven? How could that be, when so much love seems soiled? Or is the filth in our eyes, not in the loving? I cannot answer such questions, and wish they would leave me in peace.

The difficulty is that I had come to believe that Mrs. Walker *did* love Mr. Evans. As it appeared he had loved her. Yet, he had loved his sister, to an agony of the soul. Danny Boland loved his wife so hopelessly that he accepted his

own sister's murder at the hands of his beloved, then took
the blame for a general's death, willing to go to the gallows
to spare a madwoman. All because he loved her. And the
madwoman had attacked me because she believed that I was
keeping her from her love, though God alone knew why she
thought such a thing. She had killed her husband's sister,
when Kathleen Boland tried to break their marriage. Perhaps
the general had been killed because she feared he might recruit Danny Boland for Thomas Francis Meagher and his
Irish Brigade. I still felt parts of the story come short where
the general was concerned, yet the priest might have spoken
truly when he said it was all about love, all the murders, all
the sorrow and suffering.

The priest loved enough to sleep beside a corpse.

I wondered how much love there was in me.

I was ashamed, see. My hand gave less discomfort to me
than my memories of selfishness and greed. About the will,
I mean. I had been far from any love, except self-love, the
day it was read aloud. I sat there lusting for riches on which
I had no more claim than a beggar. Less claim than a beggar's, for the wretched have a right to Christian charity. I had
sworn to myself that the inheritance was due to my Mary, to
our John, to the child unborn. Yet, I sat there slavering like a
dog held from his dish. When the bequest to Mrs. Walker was
read, my heart curdled within me. As if the money had been
robbed from my purse. So mean I was I could not bear that a
man had left his property to his beloved.

I had not known that I could be that way. I never have
sought riches, except the riches of the heart and soul. I was
content enough with our material state before Mr. Evans's
death, and had enjoyed only temperate hopes for the future.
To me, there had been more joy in a loving smile than in a
fistful of silver or piles of banknotes. Travesty though it
seem to you, even battle pleased me more than money.

I could offer you a dozen and more excuses. I might blame the unsettling Mr. Evans had dealt me with his confession. And true it was that I worried now, most bitterly, about my Mary's health and our children's future. But the fact is simply that I had been greedy.

I deserved far less than the Lord and life had granted me.

I thought about a welter of things, in those haunted morning hours of cold, still dark. Twas as if that journey tore a veil from my eyes. I thought of the painful curve to my wife's spine—though it is not so evident as that—and suddenly understood her dislike of Fanny. The child was straight and strong and almost a woman. The Lord forbid, my darling feared the child would become a rival for my affections. For I will tell you a secret now: My dear wife does not believe herself a beauty. She thinks that she is ugly and ill formed. Not all my love has ever quite persuaded her of the loveliness of her person. Poor Fanny's heart is grateful as a hound's. But that quality of heart only worsened matters.

No matter how relentlessly we love, I fear we never reach the beloved's heart. Not to its fullest depth. We never know for certain what resides there. We are blessed by the coincidence of our affections, but coincidence is fragile. The unexpected word destroys our world. Mr. Shakespeare saw the frailty of love, as surely as he understood love's awesome power. Again and again, he reapplies the theme. That terrible Moor would rather believe a liar than his darling, the lord of fair Sicilia condemns his flawless queen. Yet, Macbeth loves his wife to the bloody end, despite her many deficiencies of character. Even Cleopatra, fickle and tawny, loved more deeply than she knew herself.

I know there are betrayals in this world, see. But I wonder if we are not better served by ignoring faithless acts by those we love, instead of living trustless and on guard.

I lack the mind and education to make sense of such matters. I console myself with prayer and the hope of forgiveness. I know I am a flawed and sorry man. I wear my morality like a suit of armor, instead of keeping mercy in my heart. Perhaps it is my long years as a soldier, but I yearn for rules, for order, and for clarity. I condemn others unfairly. I do it out of fear that chaos lurks. Sometimes, it seems to me I live in terror.

Often, I have passed for brave. Yet, I have a coward's heart. Bravery of the flesh is a minor matter. A drunkard or a fool can be a hero. But courage of the heart is rare and estimable. I wish I might trade one sort for the other.

Well, we must have faith and go through. There is no end of reasons to doubt the Lord's wisdom. We must pray past our errors. It is a terrible vanity to argue with God. We must pray and have faith, and go through.

We creaked into Minersville before dawn and woke the doctor. He grumped, but sewed me up. My hand had an alarming look with the journey's blood washed away. Twas black and blue, and stiff, with a raw-meat gash in the palm and flaps of flesh on the back where the blade had emerged. The doctor offered me a swig of brandy for the discomfort he meant to cause me. I declined, of course.

To the disappointment of Mr. Downs, Dr. Hooper saw no cause for amputation. He told me that, if I escaped infection, I might recover most of the use of the hand. The blade had passed between the bones as if perfectly aimed, but made a mess of the ligaments and such. He cautioned me not to disturb the pus when it formed.

Mr. Downs and I took coffee at the German hotel and gobbled down a breakfast. The food was abundant and fortifying, the joy of it marred only by my driver's boundless affection for his nose. We forget, see. I had spent my midnight in a house with a rotting corpse, then was attacked by a leprous crone for my troubles. Now I was repulsed by my tablemate's manners, as if I had been raised in a country manor.

Perhaps that is our secret, the gift the Good Lord grants us to help us through: We forget.

MR. GOWEN HAD NOT FORGOTTEN ME. But he did forget himself.

"Good Christ, Jones, you can't burst into a respectable law office looking like that," he instructed me. "You're unshaven. And you stink."

I had not bothered to seek him at the courthouse, but had gone straight to his chambers down along Centre Street, where I found him behind a china cup of coffee and stacks of papers tied with red or blue ribbons. When he stood up, he looked like a well-fed walrus in one of those picture books.

"I want you to write out a warrant for the arrest of Mary Boland, wife of Daniel Patrick Boland, of Heckschersville, on a charge of murder."

"What sort of nonsense are you up to now? I've warned you to leave the Irish in peace. Does Washington really want to stir up trouble?"

"Sit down and write the warrant, Mr. Gowen. Or I will see you arrested by the provost. And then you may write the warrant from a cell."

"Ah, yes. That infamous letter that you bear. What if I don't go along?"

"Then you will go to jail."

"And if my constituents choose to defend me? I might not be able to control them, you understand."

"That is an idle threat. Sit down and write. Do it now, Mr. Gowen."

He sat down. But he did not take up pen and paper at first. He glowered at me. "You're a fool," he said. "In more ways than one. And I'm warning you. There are no deputies or magistrates available to assist you this time. They're all occupied with other charges. You'll be entirely on your own, if you insist on having it out with the Irish." He flicked his fingers toward my bandaged paw. "Literally single-handed, it appears."

"Write."

He smirked, as men do when they are beaten but wish you to think they retain some superiority.

He angered me, so I did a nasty thing. Quite on the spur of the moment. I began to build a great lie, which is unworthy of a Christian. It emerged, though, that the lie would continue to benefit me for years. This world of ours is not a simple place.

"You did not ask me the name of the person Mrs. Boland is accused of murdering, Mr. Gowen."

He looked up at me, with the barest hint of suspicion on his brow. "General Stone, I assume."

"No, Mr. Gowen. That charge will come in due time, I believe. This warrant is for the murder of Kathleen Boland."

He was a strong, aggressive man. But he could not control the color of his face. It went from the pink of bluster to a pallor. In a slice shaved off a moment.

"I see you have heard the name before," I said.

"Never in my life. Who is she? A mother? Sister?"

"A sister. Whose choice of occupations was lamentable. She worked in a disorderly house. Where I am told many of our leading citizens traffic."

"I wouldn't know anything about that. Listen here, I'm a respectable, married man."

"I made no suggestions regarding your own person, Mr. Gowen. Calm you down, now. But since you are elected our district attorney, you will have to learn all about these sorts of things."

"So, you want a warrant . . . written out for the murder of a whore? Instead of a general?"

"I thought you were the one concerned with the law's impartiality, Mr. Gowen? And with the plight of your loyal Irish voters?"

"I think you're making this up." It was a foolish ploy for the fellow to try, but he wanted badly to regain the upper hand.

I was having none of it. "You know better than that, Mr. Gowen. And it seems to me you are writing very slowly."

"I take it there is a body? Proof of some sort?"

"Proof there will be in plenty," I assured him, "and more than some will like. But there is another thing . . . about this Kathleen Boland. Strange it is that no one seems to know of her, although I am told she enjoyed a great popularity during her stay here in Pottsville. And doubly strange it is because Miss Boland kept a diary of those who consorted with her . . ."

White as the polar snows the fellow went. I do not mean to suggest he engaged in such untoward commerce himself. I cannot say. And do not care. But he had knowledge of the sins of others.

". . . and the diary happened to come into my possession."

"That filthy bitch!" he cried. He made to leap from his chair in his anger, but his generous breadth of hip and stomach tugged him back down, in full accordance with Mr. Newton's law. "Dolly Walker's going to be run out of town over—"

"Ah, now that is interesting!" I observed. "You did not know of Kathleen Boland's existence, and yet you know of her association with Mrs. Walker . . ."

"You little bastard." Wasn't there raw hatred in his eyes? He was not a man who liked to be bested. And he would have his revenge, though it took him years. Even then, twas me who found him at the scene of his suicide later on, and not the other way round.

Now, you will say: "That was a shabby trick, to lie about a dead girl and her doings, to say she kept a record when she did not. And bringing suspicion on Dolly Walker, too, of whom you have already shown a great jealousy." But I will tell you: The legend of that diary book gave Mrs. Walker safety and credit of which she would never have dreamed. More than all her newfound wealth could have bought her. I will admit I had acted on selfish motives, without due circumspection. But it proved a stroke of fortune. We both were feared by powerful men thereafter, Mrs. Walker and myself, and had our way in little things and big. You will forgive me a supposition, but perhaps there is a form of natural justice: Those men would regret their sins of the flesh all their lives.

Although there never was a diary kept, I persuaded Mrs. Walker to trust me in the matter, when I met with her to report Kathleen Boland's fate. Dolly Walker thought me sly and canny, for she saw the matter more clearly than I did myself. "Serves the buggers right," she said, "for caring nothing for our Kathleen, after the way they all used 'er." In the years to come, I always knew if a gentleman from Mahantango Street or another fine address had visited Kathleen Boland by the way he showed me deference and took almost laughable care not to offend me.

"What's your price?" Mr. Gowen asked me.

"For what?" I asked innocently. "Do you want to buy Mr. Evans's collieries, too? It seems that every—"

"Don't you play the little Welsh fool with me. Don't you dare!"

"And what is it that you plan to do, Mr. Gowen? If I play the 'little Welsh fool'?"

"Just tell me your price for the diary. I'm certain there

will be interested parties." He attempted a smile. "Listen, Jones . . . for God's sake . . . you've been catapulted into the ranks of wealth and station in this town. You wouldn't risk destroying some of the leading men of Pottsville, would you? What would be the point of it? The leading citizens of your own home town?"

"Then you know for a fact that some of those leading men appear inside the diary book?" I asked him.

Oh, he was fair raging. When he grew angry, Mr. Gowen's powers of reason failed him. It was a worthwhile lesson to me. But other men would hang because of his temper. John Kehoe among them. That was long after the events of which I speak, of course.

"Just tell me what you want."

"I want you to calm yourself, Mr. Gowen, and to write out the warrant I have asked for."

"What do you want for the diary? Let's not waste any more time."

"The diary," I assured him, "is not for sale. I suspect the book may never see the light of day. It may be as if its pages never existed. After all, it would not be my decision alone, would it? To reveal its contents?"

"What do you mean? What are you saying?"

"The diary is safely on its way to Washington. Where other eyes will review its contents. Discreetly. I know they will take pains to keep it safe. Unless they should find an urgent need in some unfortunate circumstance . . ."

"That's blackmail!"

"No, Mr. Gowen. It is only blackmail if I ask you for something. And I ask for nothing. Excepting the warrant, which don't figure. Would you like to write it now?"

I INTENDED TO RETURN TO HECKSCHERSVILLE before we lost the daylight. I had instructed Mr. Downs to change out his mules, rest a bit, and meet me at my door at eleven o'clock. I was stabbed and weary and dirty as a Hindoo, but I had endured many a march without sleep or food or even a draught of water. I thought I might have just a scrub and a shave, then go back to my duties. I did not plan to visit my own, dear darling at her dressmaking establishment, for I had no time to spare even for her, though I meant to leave her a note. Oh, I was ready to solve all the crimes in the world, emboldened by my triumph over Gowen.

I had not reckoned with the failings of age. At thirty-four, I was not the robust young fusilier I once had been.

I took me home and splashed myself up from a bucket in the yard. Twas bracing in the cold, and I thought it would keep me going. I only went up to our bedroom to shave in the warm and say my morning prayers.

I merely lay down on the bed for a single moment, never intending to sleep. In my Indian days, a five-minute rest was as good to me as a night of heavy slumber.

When I awoke, heavy as guilt itself, the light had shifted to leave the room in shadow. Twas almost evening, rushing toward night.

I leapt from the bed. And I heard a familiar voice. A voice that had not yet been heard within my home.

I snapped up my braces and went for the stairs. But I found myself pausing to listen, although each moment was lost to my endeavors.

Twas Jimmy Molloy. He was sitting down in my parlor, telling stories. His audience at that time of day had to be young John and Fanny, for my Mary would still be working in her shop. I did not have to see or go downstairs. I knew each gesture Jimmy Molloy would employ. For he was born to tell his stories, as the Irish tend to be. In India, the garrison children loved him, though the officers' wives viewed his lowliness with disdain. He would even tell his stories to

the native brats. They understood not a word, but he made
them laugh with glee before he finished.

Now he was telling John and Fanny a tale from our shared
past, from one of those two times he saved my life. He imitated the colonel's voice remarkably, then got the worried
tones of our captain, too. Then he mimicked me.
Exaggerating, of course. I do not believe I ever sounded that
full of myself.

Yet, for all his talk of swords and severed heads and forlorn hopes, there was a goodness in his telling, a kindness
that nearly brought a tear to my eye. For in his story, *he* was
not the rescuer. I was. I carried him to safety, though the
truth was that Molloy had carried me. He made me out a
hero to those children. And what man would not delight in a
child's adulation?

I heard enough, then took me down the stairs.

"Well, now, Jimmy, that is not how I remember the business," I began. But I was forced to pause against the banis-
ter. For the children both looked up at me, John without his
usual dread—although he could not have understood the
story—and Fanny with more than her customary affection.
"I recall that you were the hero of that day," I resumed.

"Me?" he exclaimed, with all his Irish drama. "Now,
when was I ever a hero, Sergeant Jones . . . I mean, Abel? If
it weren't for ye and your valiant carryings-on, I would have
been skewered by Billy Afridi and eaten up for his breakfast!" He turned to the children again, for one last moment.
"Ah, but it's terrible, dreadful tales I could tell ye both, of
the great meandering heroics of himself, no less than your
father. Do ye know, the fellow was six inches taller then?"

"He's not really my father," Fanny whispered. Mary had
saddened her heart more than a bit.

"Well, that's not what his nibs has been after telling me,"
Jimmy said to her. "When your da there come back with ye

under his wing, all adopted and grafted onto his family tree, he says to me thereafter, he does, 'Jimmy, I plucked up the fairest flower in Scotland, and in merry, old England besides. And do ye know, she's agreed to be me very own daughter forever, for that one's a merciful lass with a golden heart . . . ' "

He made Fanny cry. She rose and fair leapt up the stairs to meet me. From two stairs down, she clutched me about the waist and could not bring herself to speak a word.

"There, there, Fan," I told her, petting that lovely thickness of hair she had, "he has only told you what is true, and I am the lucky one, see. My Mary and me, we are the lucky ones . . ."

Then I remembered myself. "Good Lord, Jimmy. You should have awakened me . . . somebody should . . . I called for a wagon . . ."

"Oh, he's out there picking winners, for all the world to see, and he's waiting most obedient all the day. Are ye off to fetching up murderers, then? Can I come?"

"And how would you know what I—"

"Well, there's a warrant lying here for all the world to read at their pleasure, an't there?"

"That is a government document, Jimmy, and—"

"Oh, leave off, would ye? I'm here to tell you I've found your Danny Boland, and the least ye could do was to let me ride along with ye on your campaigning."

"Jimmy, you are ever a welcome sight to see. But this matter has to do with your Irish brethren. They might mark you as a traitor, seeing you by me."

"Oh, if that's all what's nagging after ye, I've a fearful confession to make. I've had it up to me ears with being Irish. I'm think o' declaring meself a Turk. Or maybe a Spaniard. Or, God forbid, a Welshman. For there's a limit to how many crosses a man can bear in the name of Erin."

Fanny had loosened her hold a bit, alarmed by our conversation. Happily, John was oblivious.

"Now, Fan," I said to her, "I must go about my business for one more night. You are to tell Mrs. Jones that I am safe. And there is no need to mention the bandage about my hand, which is no matter. Tell her I am safe and that I love her, and that I will be back in the morning. And that everything is fine."

She tugged me down to whisper in my ear. Her tears had slowed, but had not stopped entirely.

"I was afeared," she told me. "I heard ye'd gone rich and thought I'd be a low baggage to ye. I did na know—"

"And who would sing to me of an evening, then? You're no more a baggage than the Queen of England. Now gather up John, for I think he wishes a feeding."

She did as she had been told—she always did—and disappeared into the kitchen. In a moment, I heard her filling the stove with coal, while John complained of the world.

"I'll get my coat," I told Jimmy.

"Ye'll let me come with ye, then?"

I am afraid I smiled at him indulgently. Although I really had meant to be severe.

"I cannot imagine a better friend beside me," I told him.

seventeen

CLOAKED AGAINST THE COLD, we sat in the back of the wagon and put our heads together. For I had things to share with Jimmy about our destination that would not do for the ears of Mr. Downs. Perched on his bench and deprived of our whispered secrets, the teamster urged his mules along and complained.

"Man can risk his life, and he's still treated like dirt, like he can't be trusted no ways," our driver told the stars above our heads. "Just treat him like he's dirt and he can't be trusted." He repeated those phrases over and over, like one of those Catholic women saying her beads.

I believe he steered the wagon into ruts and holes on purpose. My spine might as well have been riding a heathen oxcart.

"Jaysus, Mary and Joseph," Jimmy said to me, "ye mean to tell me he's got a girl's corpse in his bed, when for all his sins he mought as well have him a live one?"

I waved my bandage to warn him to lower his voice. "I believe he loved her, Jimmy. Beyond reason."

"Oh, there's reason enough to keep an eye on priests, I can tell ye that, for when I was an innocent altar boy in Dublin, a great, hairy—"

"Now tell me about Daniel Boland," I insisted. For painfully slow though our journey might be, the miles were slipping behind us. Minersville lay to the back of us now, with but a cold hour to go.

"Oh, he's hale and hearty, that one, Private Boland. They've signed him up for the Irish Brigade, all right. The 69th New York, and they're a rum lot, if ever I saw one coming. Firemen and such, and not a man to be trusted from amongst them. Though they must put a fright in the Rebels, for they put a great fear into me. Oh, Abel," he lamented, "there's days I come round to believing that me fellow Irishmen should not be trusted with firearms or liquor. At least not with both at once. If ye'd seen the wicked disorder of their camp . . ."

"So Boland has found refuge with General Meagher? One Irish revolutionary protecting a fellow Irish revolutionary's son? There is sense in the thing."

"Well, I'm not sure how much protecting there is to the business," Molloy said, "for there is a war going on, ye know, and they've jined him up to fight. And there's no soldier anywhere, not on this earth, who has a greater talent for dying in droves and packs than an Irish volunteer."

"You were an excellent soldier, Jimmy. When you were sober, of course."

He gave me a poke. "And sometimes when I was not, if I could squeeze an honest word out of ye."

"You were a fine soldier, and I have known many fine Irish soldiers, although I must condemn their—"

"Well, an't that the sorrow o' the doings? Don't we make lovely soldiers, though? And handsome corpses, too. But I had proper leadership back when I wore the scarlet . . . proper leadership, starting with yourself. But that Irish Brigade is just what it says, Irish from top to bottom. And I'll tell ye the truth, ye would not like its bottom."

"I saw them at Antietam," I told him. "They showed splendidly, you know. With Meagher of the Sword leading—"

" 'Meagher of the Bottle' would be more like it," Jimmy told me. "For he's fond o' the broth, that one, and a terrible friend to shenanigans. For all his fine manners and speechifying, he's more the wild chieftain than a general. If the Rebels don't kill him, he'll come to a sorry end."

The coal-haunted valley we traveled gathered the chill and kept it. We passed broken lines of shanties where bodies crowded for warmth. An empire of coughs those patches were, all coal dust and consumption. Webs of smoke rose moonward, as if to choke the stars. Twas a hard life in those days, and I will tell you: When suddenly you have come into a colliery and mine operation of your own, the bothered lungs and discouraged eyes become a part of your business. Perhaps I would not be a success as a man of property and capital, for now that I had been lifted up I felt a new pity for those who would stay below.

I had become responsible for them, see. Nor do I mean to speak in Christian platitudes, with which we comfort ourselves while doing nothing. I could not see them through their walls, but those ill-fed families were real to me as they never had been before. I knew the mines well enough to know that men would lose lives or limbs to make me richer. Twas almost as if I could see their faces before me, the men who would live on legless and useless, begging a bit of tobacco from sons put to work too young to swing a pick. Our America is the land of opportunity, and there is true. But opportunity is fickle, and unfair.

The wagon creaked, as if its joints had rheumatism. Jimmy wiped his nose on a rag from his pocket. My Colt prodded my hip beneath my greatcoat. And I thought, inevitably, of the Irish, unable to sort their hatred from their fears.

"The Irish follow Meagher, wherever he leads," I observed, returning to our discussion in a voice slowed by the cold. "Our Union is lucky to have him."

Twas odd to find myself defending Irish honor against an Irishman.

Jimmy rolled his eyes about, gathering up the moonlight. "And why shouldn't they follow him, then? He's brave enough, and I said not a word against himself and his valor. As ye used to say in India, whenever the lads would try to whip them a nigger for stealing or moving too slow, we all must make allowances. No, ye'd never get an Irishman to follow a sober general."

"But you did. You followed sober generals. And sober colonels. And sergeants."

"Now, an't that the silliest thing I've ever heard tell? Of course, they were sober, the most o' them. And I followed them true enough. But they weren't Irishmen, either. Who would follow a sober *Irish* general?"

"You know, the Duke of Wellington was—"

"And that reminds me, don't it now, that I had a great, worrisome question for ye. Something that I've been wishing and hoping to have your thoughts upon, Abel. What do ye think of this bucko Charles Darwin?"

I did not see why my mention of the Duke of Wellington should have put Jimmy in mind of Mr. Darwin, but he always had jumped about himself, whether leaping parapets in battle, or springing away from a soldier's chores in camp. He come to me originally from poor Sergeant Bates of the sappers, who died later on, delirious, on the march to Delhi Ridge. Bates had warned me that Jimmy Molloy was the laziest man alive, but when I gave my new fusilier a proper sergeant's greeting, Jimmy had only replied, "Jaysus, now, I didn't join the army to work, did I? If it's fighting ye want, I'm your man, Sergeant Jones, but they tried to put me to honest work in the sappers, and I mought have stayed home in Dublin if that was me purpose." And he had proved the bravest of the brave, a description I once heard used—doubtless inaccurately—of a French fellow.

"Jimmy, Mr. Darwin has unsettling theories, which could only disturb your—"

"Dr. Tyrone believes him, don't he? Black Protestant though he is?"

The wagon delivered a sudden and bone-shaking jolt.

"Dr. Tyrone believes in a number of peculiar matters that need not—"

"But don't Darwin say how we all come descending from monkeys?"

"Yes, but you must not—"

"Well, it don't seem fair to Jimmy Molloy, blaming them poor apes for the sins o' humanity. Do ye not remember that lovely little monkey ye had, the one I used to—"

"You fed him sweets," I said. "Which were not good for the little fellow's digestion."

Jimmy laughed. "But he liked a sweet. And he slept atop your own cot, not on mine, so I didn't see how the poor sod's digestion concerned me."

"Jimmy, Charles Darwin is an atheist. His propositions contradict the Bible."

"Oh, and do they now? Ye know, that's the very business that's troubling me. For I don't for the life o' me see the contradiction. I look at it this way: Don't ye remember how long the days seemed when we went marching through the wilds o' the Punjab? And how we'd sweat ourselves sick, though the calendar tried to tell the world it was winter? Or how long the nights would seem when a battle was all begun, but not yet finished, and the poor, wounded fellows was lying betwixt the lines and gasping their last breaths out o' themselves? So, maybe a day wasn't always exactly a day, do ye see what I'm after? Maybe those seven days God used to make us from mud pats and such were longer days than ours? Maybe one o' his days was a million years? For it does seem to Jimmy Molloy, and I don't mind telling ye, that making the heavens and earth in but seven of our days would be asking for a ramshackle job round the edges."

"Now, Jimmy," I began, "strange it is, but I will admit to pondering similar thoughts myself, in regard to the matter of time and the power of the Lord to alter it. But such thoughts are a snare to the unwary, and the divine wisdom is beyond our comprehension. We must accept that the Bible says—"

"Oh, we know what it says, though the priests would as soon we did not, for they love to have secrets in Latin and all sorts of punishments threatened and intimidated upon a person for all o' his innocent troubles. But maybe the whole thing was only made up to begin with? By God Himself, I mean. If the Bible is the Word of God, as they're always insisting it is, He must have had the devil's own time deducting out ways to explain all His doings to us. Like a general trying to explain his great plans to a private, to the dullest kiltie in the Highlanders. So maybe He spoke in parables, like Jaysus Himself had to do with those blockhead disciples, who never quite seemed to get what He was about, with their doubts and denials? Like father, like son, ye know. Maybe God was explaining things in a way the likes of us could get through our heads? Maybe he kept things simple in all His explainings, the way ye used to do with the Irish recruits who weren't as clever or quick or as handsome as I was? Maybe He just explained it all as best he could at the time and He's up there shaking His head that we took it so serious?"

"Mr. Darwin contradicts more than the Book of Genesis, Jimmy."

"But didn't God create Charles Darwin, too? Didn't ye say near those very same words yourself on some similar matter? Abel, I'm scratching me head and me other parts besides, but I don't see why it must be a choice between them. Maybe this Darwin's just figuring out what God really wanted to say back when men were too stupid to understand His meaning? Why, me own grandfather couldn't sign his own name, so ye can only imagine how foolish and backward the people must have been in those Bible days, all those hundreds of years ago." Jimmy sighed. "Don't ye begin to feel sorry for God, when ye think of it? Having to explain how He made the world to some poor, drooling gramps or an English baronet? Why, when I start thinking upon the Good Lord's disappointments with the pack of us, it's almost enough to turn me back to the Church . . ."

I never did have very much luck explaining religious matters to Jimmy Molloy.

THERE WAS NO JAUNTY PIANO playing within those tavern walls. Twas late, of course, but that was not the matter of it. Standing in the street with Jimmy beside me, I sensed a foulness of mood I could not explain. But real it was. As real as the Colt in my belt and the cane in my hand.

Jimmy sniffed the air. He was an old soldier, too.

"If we was back in India," he muttered, "I'd be thinking the natives were less than happy this evening."

"Well, let us go in and find out," I said. I fear my tone showed more resignation than fortitude. My body wanted still more rest than my afternoon nap had given it. And a good stabbing tells on a fellow. I worried that I lacked the spunk I needed.

There was hardly half the crowd I had found when last I paid a visit to Ryan's Hotel. And less than half the welcome, cold as the first had been. The miners looked up from their pipes and cards as if they had spotted the hangman from Dublin Castle.

But the men I wanted were there. Donnelly sat in his cor-

ner by the stove, below the dusty green banner that hung on
the wall. Kehoe was with him. And only Kehoe this evening.

I made my way between the tables, with Jimmy on my
heels.

Mr. Donnelly met my eyes, but did not pretend to greet me.

"Good evening to you, Mr. Donnelly," I said, "And to you
Mr. Kehoe. This is my friend, Mr. James Molloy, of
Washington."

Mr. Donnelly looked up into Jimmy's face. "Why Mr.
Molloy, when ye first stepped inside, I took ye for an informer.
But here at close quarters I see that you're only a fool."

The taunt was meant both to provoke and test, but Jimmy
only answered with a smile. Perhaps his months as a publican had taught him that jibes are better off ignored.

"And a pleasure it is to make your acquaintances, gentlemen," Jimmy said.

I saw there was no point in false politeness. "Mr.
Donnelly . . . may we sit down? I have serious matters to
discuss with you." I glanced at Kehoe, who remained impassive. "Very serious matters."

"Ye may sit, if sit ye must. But not that one. I'll have no
Irish traitors at this table."

I turned to Jimmy, who appeared not the least bit troubled.
He always was unflappable in a fray, a man who could load
his musket steadily while swords flashed round his head.

"I'll stand by the bar and wait for ye," he told me, "for
a man of business must pay attention to the ways of the
competition. Though I can tell you already the place needs
a wash."

And off he went, with the hard, late drinkers grumbling in
his wake.

I sat me down. Before I could begin, Mr. Donnelly had
something of his own to say.

"Major Jones, if I found myself in your circumstances this

night, I'd take my companion and ease out on the quiet. For the men ye see about ye are unhappy. And worse than unhappy. Far worse. For they know ye as a man with a fondness for corpses. And this very morning, before the dawn, the body of a little girl was stolen from out of her coffin, before her family could plug her in the ground. Dead of the croup she was, not six years old. The good people of our village have morbid suspicions."

"You know that I had nothing to do with such a thing."

He raised one eyebrow, then the other. "It does not signify, does it, what I may know or I don't? The truth of things is often the least of the matter. It's what folk believe is in the pot that makes the porridge taste."

"Mr. Donnelly, I know where Daniel Boland is."

"And do ye, now?"

"He's enrolled with the 69th New York, in the Irish Brigade. Under General Meagher."

"More fool him, if it's true. And Meagher's a fool for fighting for a Union that would rather squander Irish lives than niggers."

"We both know why he was sent to Meagher for shelter."

"Ye know what ye know, and I know what I know. They may be different things."

"I have in my pocket a warrant for the arrest of Mary Boland. For the murder of Kathleen Boland. I believe the woman killed General Stone, as well, though I will admit there is more to that than I have yet put together."

"And what do ye plan to do with your grand piece o' paper?"

"I want your help."

He chuckled. "Now, isn't that a high ambition on your part, Major Jones?"

"I want your help in bringing Mary Boland to justice. You know she's mad. She won't hang. She will be put where she can do no more harm. I want your help in finding her and bringing her in without injury to herself."

"Ah, I see you're a man who has a great faith in miracles. Are ye certain you're not a member of our Church?"

"Look you. I know Daniel Boland is innocent. I know he made a false confession to save his wife. Because he loved her so dearly, no matter the terrible things she had done. I want to help him."

"Then you can leave him alone."

"I can't. He must recant his confession. He has to justify himself in the eyes of the law."

"And testify against his own wife?"

"Then you admit that she killed Kathleen Boland. And—"

"I admit nothing. We're only having a pleasant conversation. Did ye notice how the weather has turned toward winter, Major Jones?"

"He would not need to testify against her. The law allows—"

"Whose law? *Whose* law, Major Jones? Your law, not mine."

"Help me, for the love of God. The woman might kill more innocent people." I held up my bandaged paw, as a frustrated child might have done. "She tried to stab me last night." I looked at Kehoe, who remained silent and grim-faced. Then I turned again to Mr. Donnelly. "But you know that, of course."

"Oh, I noticed the rags on your mitt. As for killing innocent people, would ye count yourself among them? Among the innocent, I mean?"

"If you would help me, it would be better for all," I said, almost in despair. With their help, all things might have been done more easily, without hard repercussions and further misunderstandings and accusations. But if they would not assist me, I was prepared to climb those hills with only Jimmy beside me, to comb through the countless ravines and over the crests until I found Mary Boland and put an end to her killing. I would not turn from my duty. If need be, I would fight to see it done.

Donnelly shot an odd little glance toward Kehoe. Black Jack got up at once and strode across the room to Jimmy Molloy.

"Your mother was a whore for every English drunkard in the Counties," Kehoe said for all the room to hear. "When she could find an English drunkard who would have her."

Jimmy, who had not been served any liquor, put on his famous fool-the-sergeant grin. "Oh, yer honor," he said, in an Irish accent pressed to an extreme, "me mother was niver a hoor in her life, for she never took less than a pound for the least of her doings. Nor was she County born, but Dublin bred. And we all know who the drunkards are in Dublin. Wicklow men, the lot of them."

"You're a filthy, low traitor. Damned to Hell."

"Now, Mr. Kehoe, if it's a fight you're after wanting," Jimmy said calmly, "can't ye say it outright, like a man?"

I began to rise, to intervene and spirit Jimmy away, but old Donnelly caught my wrist. When I looked at him, his face managed to tell me, "Wait," without another word spoken.

Jimmy smiled as wide as the Irish Sea. The truth is that he never minded a fight and was the champion pugilist of our regiment, reknowned from Peshawar to Pindi. And beyond. He laid down Hawkins the Hammer, the pride of the gunners, in less than sixty seconds in Lahore. Kehoe had the advantage of height and bulk, but he would need a great deal of skill and luck to best Jimmy Molloy.

The two of them peeled off their coats and waistcoats, while a rush of men and the aproned barkeep pulled back tables and chairs to form a ring. Even the ladies of the house—

two sisters alike in their plainness—filed out to rescue the crockery and see a bit of sport.

Donnelly and I stepped up to the gaggle of spectators, for they blocked the view from the table. The roughest of men made space for Donnelly immediately and, grudgingly, for me. Beginning to shout and bark, the men called, "Give him a puck where he needs it, Jack," or "Show him the door the hard way."

Kehoe and Jimmy took up their stances. Kehoe had a brawler's crouch, wary and watching. He wanted to slug, to spend as much strength as he could on his opening blows, to put an end to things. Jimmy, rolling on his feet, was another sight to see. His dukes were up and his back arched rearward like a bow. You would not see a better fighting posture in London or even Merthyr. Jimmy was out for sport.

Kehoe prowled, like a dog looking to bite. Though taller of person, his crouch made him the shorter for the moment. Jimmy turned smoothly to follow the other man's circling. Jimmy looked regal, Kehoe looked rough and hard.

Black Jack surprised himself by bumping a chair with his backside. A fighter who meant to hurt would have set upon him then, taking advantage of his instant of confusion. But Jimmy was wise. He knew that if he seemed to win through any unfair advantage, the room would turn against us, full of violence. Anyway, Jimmy was a curious sort. Ferocious in battle, he sought to kill, not wound. But as a pugilist he liked to box, almost to fence. In the ring, he fought to win, but not to hurt for his pleasure. Although he did a great deal of harm to any man whose face got in the way of those bullet-quick fists.

"Go on, Jack . . . put an end to the sissy-boy's prancing and dancing," a burly, bearded man called.

"Put some Mayo manners on him," another fellow suggested.

Suddenly, Kehoe believed he saw an opening. Because Jimmy let him think it.

Black Jack led with his big left fist, meaning to finish the business with his right. But neither fist landed on Jimmy. One-two-three, Jimmy smashed Kehoe's lips and cheekbone and nose.

Shocked, Kehoe reeled. Not backward, but forward. With blood splashed off his lower lip into his beard. Jimmy could have finished him at once, for the man had only his strength and no proper skills. But Jimmy, God bless him, was cleverer than I had imagined. He knew he must not win the match too swiftly. Shaming Kehoe would do no good at all. It had to look like a fight. For my sake, as much as Black Jack's.

It is a point worth remembering, see. Never humiliate a man, if you can gain what you need while sparing him shame.

Jimmy let Kehoe land a pair of blows. Against his chest, not his face. He sneaked in close then, one-two-three, the way he always liked to land his set, costing his opponent a chestful of air.

Raving the lot of them were after that, as if only Kehoe's fists had found their mark.

"Get him, Jack, get the prissed bastard . . . put his head back to his arse and see how it fits."

Kehoe swept in fiercely, determined to punch his way through Jimmy's defenses. But Jimmy hit him so hard it snapped his jaw back. Kehoe staggered and dropped against two miners. A lesser man would have hit the floor and stayed on it. But Kehoe did not even pause to gather himself. He forgot about slugging or boxing and lunged for Jimmy as if he meant to wrestle him. Jimmy side-stepped. He could have broken the fellow's jaw, as I had seen him do to a number of boxers—always to the colonel's chagrin, for a broken jaw put a soldier in the sick ward—but Jimmy chose to deliver a single blow to Black Jack's stomach.

Kehoe bent like a clasp knife folding up, but somehow he grabbed Jimmy by the waist. A moment later, they were both on the floor, rolling over. The crowd surged in, but Donnelly warned them back. So they all contented themselves with encouraging curses, flailing their fists through the air to demonstrate what they would do were they in Kehoe's place.

Jimmy and Kehoe rolled cheek against cheek, until they were stopped by the bar. Kehoe, to his credit, did not bite or do other unclean things, but, for a brace of seconds, Jimmy looked to me to be in a bad way, pinned against the wood by the larger man's weight. But Jimmy had not survived Seekh and Pushtoon and mutinous sepoy without resources. An instant later, he broke away clean, jumping back to his feet. Quick as a trickster at the autumn fair. Kehoe, too, climbed up on his pins, but his doings were much clumsier. And his breathing come heavier.

Jimmy let him get up. Then he landed a blow that caught Black Jack so perfectly on the chin that the bigger man went down like a gun carriage tipped from a rampart.

He struck the floor hard.

"Jaysus, that one's a slaughtering, tough bugger," Jimmy proclaimed, falsely. He was leaving the fellow a compliment, where another man would have gloated. Oh, Jimmy had learned a great deal in his wandering years, between the Delhi jail and the streets of Washington.

The miners were unruly. Things could have gone awry. But Donnelly kept them in line.

"A fair fight," he declared, "and worth the price of the watching. Mrs. Ryan, John Kehoe wants a bit of water in his face, will ye see to it?" He reached out his hand to Jimmy. "Mr. Molloy, I shake your hand in respect of your sporting skills, but not for anything else. Tis handsome ye are at your fisticuffs, that I will grant ye."

Jimmy shook his hand, though not for long. Of a sudden, he seemed most anxious to leave the saloon. "Abel, come on," he told me. "We've used up our welcome here and I think we'll be going."

I saw no point in delaying myself. For Donnelly had his own game and would not be hurried in making his next move. Twas clear enough. And I did not want the Irish to talk themselves into a vengeful temper. I recalled the mention of the little girl's corpse, stolen away from her family in the darkness. God only knew what purpose lay therein.

Outside, I turned us back to the road and the wagon we had left in the teamster's care. But Jimmy caught my arm.

"Abel," he said, voice held down to a whisper. "Now, which way would be that boneyard ye were on about?"

"Up there. Behind us. In the other direction." I looked at him. My eyes had not yet re-learned the dark. Full in the moonlight, his face was merely a paleness. "Why?"

"Well, the fight was all put up, as ye could see. Nor did I hit him so hard at the end as it looked. Though, Jaysus, he fell down beautiful, didn't he? When he had me clinched up against the bar, he whispered in my ear, he says, 'Wait for me by the graveyard, and now put me down with a good one.' Then he let me up, and I put him down. Really, I didn't hit him so hard. Jaysus, I hope I didn't do him too heavy a damage."

There had been one unfortunate occasion upon which Jimmy's opponent, a Geordie blacksmith put up by the lancers, had stayed out for three days.

WE WAITED IN A SWALE by the boneyard wall. I saw no light up in the priest's house, although twas not so late as it had been during my visit the night before. When I saw what no man should have seen.

Twas cold.

"Do ye ever feel a loneliness for India?" Jimmy asked unexpectedly.

"No," I lied.

"Sure, and I thought ye'd be the type of man what serves out his term and takes a job tending the telegraph or such, just to stay out there in the dust with his sweetheart. Raising up brats what ain't white nor brown but both."

It was not a subject I thought fit for discussion. "I would not mind some of the heat, if I could borrow a bit of it this night. There was nothing else for me there."

"But if your Ameera hadn't of died on ye, mightn't ye not have stayed on, don't ye think?"

"You forget, Jimmy. I was sent home. A disappointment to the regiment."

"Oh, I heard all about the matter, even down in Delhi Hole. But I always said to me fellow unfortunates that ye only went to bits because she died on ye. Her and the little lad. The Mutiny come too soon after, that was all. It broke me own heart to see you all dull and desponded, after ye learned she was dead and burned in a stack. Oh, the only reason I come to regret the business with the regimental silver is that I wasn't around no more to keep ye properly occupied. I've always said to meself, I did, 'Jimmy, ye let poor Sergeant Jones down, just when he needed ye most.' But after Delhi was taken and won, I only thought it was time for a brief celebration. And they never should leave such valuables lying about."

"You had enough loot to get drunk on. A hundred times over. We all did."

Jimmy sighed. "Well, who knows why a fellow does what a fellow does? Looking back, it didn't come out so bad, now did it?"

"No, Jimmy. We are both well married, and life is—"

"Oh, would ye not use such terrible language in me own presence? Here we are, having a grandiose time, just like we used to do, and wouldn't ye know but he brings up the subject of marriage."

"It is a wonderful institution."

"The truth is, Abel, I've always had me conflicts with institutions. For they always want to change a man, and they all say it's for his betterment. But what if a fellow is happy the way he is?"

"But you love your wife, your Annie."

"Oh, love her I do. And no question. But I love her the more as I'm standing here than I do when she's standing there." His voice grew earnest. "I love her, that's sure. But I can't bear the life that goes with it. It's dragging me down, Abel."

We were spared further discussion of such matters by the sight of a figure climbing up the hill. I let the intruder approach, then called to him softly.

Twas Kehoe well enough. As he come up to Jimmy, he rubbed his jaw and said, "You're a mean little bastard. I've got blood all over meself."

"Mr. Kehoe," I said, "do you intend to help us, then?"

He paused a moment, letting me wonder. Then he nodded. "I'll help ye. And I'll watch ye all the while I'm doing it. For there'll be no harm done to Mary Boland, not to one hair on her head."

"I have no wish to harm her. But . . . will she come peaceably?"

"I can't speak for the woman. But here's Mr. Donnelly's condition. I'm to guide ye to where she's likely to be, but when we get there, I'm to have the first persuading of her."

"And if she will not listen to you? If she won't come peaceably?"

He snorted. "Then we'll see. Won't we, though?"

"And where will we find her?"

"Gammon Hill. With the old Dutch woman. Unless they're both roving."

"And the old woman? What is her role in this?"

Kehoe shook his head in the luminous shadows. "She's got Mary Boland convinced she's a witch. That they're both witches. It's a dirty nonsense. Mary was always running off to her. She said they were casting spells together. It drove poor Danny half mad."

"And when she killed his sister? Did Danny feel half mad then?"

"God, man. What do ye think he felt?"

"But he did not give up his wife?"

Again, he shook his head. Black beard moving against the blackness of his chest. "Danny couldn't. He was a fool for the wicked sight of her. Damn the lot of them. And the lot of ye, with your war and your interference. I don't know, man. Perhaps Mary Boland *is* some kind of a witch. Maybe she put poor Danny under a spell. He couldn't give her up, and there was no talking to him."

"And she killed Kathleen Boland because she thought Kathleen would take Danny away from her."

Kehoe nodded. He did not need to speak.

"And General Stone? Did she kill him because she thought *he* would take Danny Boland away from her?"

Kehoe said a thing so foul I dare not report it to you. Then he continued, "Whoever put that idea into her head should be damned to Hell for all eternity. Christ and the saints, man, if ye know anything about him and about Boland or about the pack of us, ye know we would have defended your man with our lives. General though he was. He did a great turn for Ireland, more than once. Saving men on the run from the English gallows. He did not leave here with a single recruit for your mercenary army, that was a matter of argument between grown men. But he left here safe and sound."

"Until Mary Boland put a knife into his chest."

Again, Kehoe used language that scorched the night. "She should have been locked up a year ago. Two years. But Danny wouldn't hear of it. God, man, she was mad when he married her. Everybody knew it. They warned him. But he would not hear a word said against her. Not one word. He would have fought ten men, each twice his size, if they so much as whispered his Mary was odd."

"And you have no idea who told Mary Boland that General Stone had come to take her husband away."

"If I did, I'd kill the man."

"And you all made a promise to Danny Boland, didn't you? To get him to go off and save himself, after his false confession? You made a promise not to turn Mary Boland in to the authorities."

"He didn't want to see her in a madhouse. Great Jesus, man. Do ye not know what those places are like, then?"

Yes. I knew.

"Why help me now?"

"Oh, why, indeed? It isn't my choice, that much I'll tell ye. But it's clear enough that Mary can't run free any longer. God bless poor Danny. If we have more murders, then what do ye think will happen? To us? If she had put that knife into your own chest last night? What would have been visited upon us in your loving memory?" He snickered. Nastily. Bitterly. "We'd have your damned troops all over us, worse than the English themselves. And ye'd carry men off in chains for your war for the niggers. Tell me, man, since ye happen to be such a clever one. What choice do we have? No choice but to help ye, bastard that ye are."

"You saved my life last night. And I am grateful for that."

"I didn't save your life. I saved *us*. From the revenge that would have come after. Your life isn't worth a dog's piss to me. And now have ye had your answers enough? It's a long walk to Gammon Hill, and not a friendly one. It's a rare man who'll even go near the place by day."

"Because of the witch?"

"Because of the old woman," he said. "She's no more a witch than you are."

"But people believe . . ."

"Let them. They're no worse off than the fools who believe in your war."

"All right, then. Go we shall. But first, we'll ask Father Wilde if he will go with us."

"*No!*" Kehoe said. "No, ye will not bring the priest."

"And why not?"

"I'll have nothing to do with the filth of him. He deserves the madhouse worse than Mary Boland."

"He hasn't killed."

Kehoe had shifted just enough to bring his face into the moonlight. Twas as hard-set and bitter as any face could be.

"He's done worse than kill." Slowly, lips testing each word, he said, "And ye know it yourself."

"Does everyone know?"

"They know enough."

"And nothing has been done?"

"A letter has been written. The diocese will look after him. We'll tend to our own kind."

"Well, tend to him you may. I suggest starting by getting Kathleen Boland's corpse into the ground. Unless you want disease running through your valley. For now, Mr. Kehoe, I will tell you once and once only. I intend to ask the priest to come with us. He has some connection to Mary Boland, for she has been watching his house these many nights. I think he may have some power over her."

Kehoe began to reply, then stopped himself. Even then, the Irish had secrets I was not allowed to know.

"Ask the filthy man if he'll go with ye, then," he told me, in place of what he had meant to say at first. "But Wilde's a coward. I do not think ye'll persuade him. All ye'll have for your troubles is another great noseful of stink."

"And you? Are you coming with us? Or not?"

"I'll wait here. Until you're done with your priest. I'll not go any closer to that house."

I aimed my steps up the path beside the graveyard, tapping along with Jimmy at my side.

"Jaysus, they're a troubleful bunch," he told me quietly. "That Kehoe's from the civilized parts, but the rest of the lot are from Mayo and Sligo. And Donegal, more's the pity. We always said in Dublin that the men from Donegal are wild barbarians. It's the trees, don't ye know."

"The trees?"

"There's hardly a tree in Donegal."

"And what have trees to do with matters?"

"Lord, Abel, would ye not think for a moment? What kind of men do ye breed up without trees? In your own experience? Musselmens, Pushtoons, and Turks and all such like. Donegal's naught but a desert what's been misplaced. To tell ye the truth, I don't believe they're Irish. I'm surprised they even let Donegal men into the Church, for I've never known one who wasn't a heathen at heart . . ."

We stood at the steps that led to the priest's front door.

"Jimmy," I said, "you might as well wait here for me. You have smelled your share of death in your day and do not need a snoutful for your troubles."

"Well, if ye don't mind me whiling, I believe I'll pursue a cheroot." He reached into his pocket.

I rapped on the door. Twas dark within, but I knew the priest could hear me. I called his name. After knocking four times, I walked a ring around the house's exterior. This time, there was no light within that bedroom. But I could smell the monstrous stench within. I made my way back to the front door, where Jimmy stood puffing away. I knew I had been loud enough to wake the priest. Either he refused to answer my summons, or he was abroad himself.

I tried the door. It was unlocked.

As soon as it opened, an enormous reeking hit me. Twas almost a physical blow.

The thing of it was that I did not smell death alone. I smelled dying, too. A particular form of dying that I knew a great deal too well. It was a compound of odors no man will ever forget once he has smelled it.

I clapped the door shut and recoiled, near tripping down the steps.

"Jimmy, get back, get away," I cried. "It's cholera."

eighteen

THE PRIEST LAY QUIVERING ON THE FLOOR, smeared with his own wastes. His flesh was discolored and anxious for death, but his fevered eyes resisted. It is a terrible thing to see, the way the spirit clings to life, as if it knows of terrors we do not. Bright with vomit, his lips yearned to form words. Perhaps he sought to pray.

I did not believe he knew that I was present. I had steeled myself to go into that house, armed with lucifer matches borrowed from Jimmy. I lit the first lamp I found, careful of the bandages on my hand. And I saw him lying beside a tumbled chair in his parlor, trousers pushed down in a hopeless attempt not to soil himself. That had been his last capable action, shoving down his trousers toward his knees and struggling with his underclothing. Thereafter, the priest had not moved from the spot where he fell, except to wriggle and twitch as the cramps swept through him.

I had forced myself to go into that house, not out of Christian charity, but because I hoped he might confess to me. To light my darkness with something near the truth of matters. But hard it was to force myself inside. Cholera terrifies me, far more than any other disease, or enemy blades or ball. It has taken so much, so wickedly much, from my life. But a man must do his duty, no matter his fears.

I felt that I was walking into a snake pit.

So strange it was. Twas not the cholera season. But I had known cases, and not a few, when the cholera lurked beyond the summer's heat and struck the unsuspecting in their happiness. Just before Christmas, in '54, it killed Jenny Merton, the prettiest lass in the civil lines, and broke every heart in the garrison. Then it spirited off the adjutant's twins in the January drabs. Mick Tyrone believes it comes from bad water, while the old surgeons think there is something in the air. Perhaps the priest acquired the disease from keeping a corpse in his bed. That sounded likely to me. Or perhaps it was a judgement sent down upon him. Because he had lied about the cholera "death" of Danny Boland. Perhaps there is more justice than we know. And a harder justice than we might well wish.

Twas clear that the Irish had blackmailed the fellow into telling his cholera lies to the authorities. By threatening to expose his dalliance with Kathleen Boland. I saw that now. I even thought I saw into his torment. Yet, he had broken faith in so many ways I could not count them all.

I sometimes wonder if God is like a parent. He will forgive, but first you must have your punishment.

I wished to vomit myself, as I watched him lying there. The bouquet of stinks was so thick it greased the skin. For a time, I could not move another step.

In one of those lucid moments that enliven our march toward death, the priest sensed the light and another living presence. He grunted and pawed the air. Then his backside released another wave of wetness, and his legs kicked at his torments. The man was reduced to sputtering and slime.

I put the lamp down on a table out of reach of his jerking legs. And I took off my greatcoat, folding it over a chair not yet stained with sickness. The room was cold, the hearth long out. I moved myself toward the priest, one step at a time, forcing myself forward. When I was young and sturdier of heart, I had cradled the heads of dying soldiers as they spewed up the watery pudding the cholera cooks in our guts. But later events had shattered all my iron, leaving me soft and weak. Now, I dreaded the thought of touching a sick man.

He tried to grasp an invisible handhold in the air above him, as if to pull himself up. It was not a moment before he splashed back in his slops. He groaned as if his insides had been torn.

I cowered. I am no more a Christian man than one of Darwin's apes.

His eyes burned. Nor do I mean that as a figure of speech. They were hot things, reddened, as if cooking from within.

He puled a few driblets from the side of his mouth. Rice water and blood.

"Bury . . ." he said.

Another of those waves of cramps possessed him. Weak though he was, he twisted and bent, chewed upon by the Furies in his belly. He spewed blood out his bottom. And I stood there.

". . . her . . ." he said, the moment he stopped his twisting and flopping about.

I marched myself forward, one small step at a time. Until I reached him. I tried to spy a clean spot on the carpet, a dry little space where I might rest my knee. But the priest had splashed a halo of filth around himself.

I knelt down beside his chest. Twas hardly an instant before I felt the moisture of disease seep through my trouser leg.

His eyes were closed, his breathing rapid but shallow. He tried to make a word, but failed again. For all the liquid lost to him, he managed to weep a pair of tears, one from each of his eyes.

Quick as an animal strikes, he grasped my forearm. With one hand, then with both. Clutching me madly, as if I might

anchor him in our sea of life. Smearing my sleeve and my
bandage.

"Bury me . . . with her."

I tried to pry his fingers from my arm. But twas literally a death grip he had upon me. I pinched up the flesh of
his thigh with my free hand, for that is how you judge the
progress of the case. The skin remained puckered in a
ridge and did not resettle itself. There was too much water
out of him.

By morning, he would be dead and blue of skin. And
black of rot by evening.

"Bury me with her!" he cried. Those bright, scorched
eyes found mine.

"Yes," I told him. "Yes. Certainly. Yes." Although I had
little idea what I was saying. Nor did I mean to promise anything. The truth is that I wanted him to let go of me. He had
slopped his vomit all over my uniform. And my bandage
was wretched with filth. I envisioned contagion crawling
into my wound.

One of his hands released me. The priest fell back, shivering. His other paw slipped down to my bandaged hand,
taking it as a child will, although my fingers could not re-
spond to his grip.

Another pulse of spasms ravaged his body. He let go of
me at once and I had to throw myself backward, away from
him, to avoid being sprayed all over with puke and blood.

I only wanted to be clean. I am not made of the stuff of
saints or martyrs. I felt less for that man than a Christian
should have done.

He settled again, groaning. Applying his hands to his
belly to soothe it, he instantly tore them away, as if he had
just lowered them into flames.

I knelt, at a distance, watching him. I did not even think
to pray myself. I barely thought at all.

"God forgive me," he begged the ceiling. "God forgive me . . ."

My sense of purpose, even my sense of time, seemed to have quit me.

"Go on with ye now," a soft voice said. Twas Jimmy. "Go on, Abel. Do what ye have to do. I'll stay here with that one."

"Jimmy . . ."

"Go on. I'll keep the watch on him."

"You . . . should not have come in . . . the infection . . ."

And then he sounded more like the Jimmy I knew. "Oh, if the cholera wouldn't take me when I was deep in the Delhi jail, or when I was carting the bodies for me liberty, I'm not going to let it spoil me joys in America. Go on with ye now, I'll see to him."

"It is no laughing matter. You should not have come in here."

"I can't leave a priest to die alone," Jimmy said, voice gone serious now. "No matter what he's done. It an't within me."

"You . . . were never religious."

"Oh, I never was a grand one for their snoring in the pews. But there's some things won't let go of a man, once he's taught them."

Yes. There were some things that would not let go of a man.

"You'll be all right with that Kehoe," Jimmy added. "He's got two proper fists on him, and more than a little sense. Jaysus, it stinks like Molly Grogan's drawers in here. Did I ever tell ye me own mother hoped to see me take holy orders?"

When I left Jimmy, he was rooting about for rags. To cleanse the dying priest and give him comfort.

I STOOD AT THE EDGE OF THE WOOD, stripped to the waist and still wet. The night air bit. There is one good use for whisky, according to Mick Tyrone. I unstoppered the bottle, clumsily, and poured the spirit over my wounded hand and wrist. The bandage was long gone, stripped away and burned along with my tunic. Doubtless, the pile still smoldered behind the priest's house.

I held out my hand.

"Go ahead," I told Kehoe.

He doubted my wisdom, but struck a match and brought it close to my paw. A blue flame shot over my flesh. I will admit it was uncomfortable.

I did not act the child, though. I clenched my teeth and shook off the last of the flame, which had burned away near instantly. My paw would be doubly a bother now, and for a goodly time. But discomfort was better than cholera.

"If you please, Mr. Kehoe," I said. "Wrap it up now. Gently does it, thank you."

For such a rough-made fellow, he had a gentle touch. I wondered if he had a wife, a family. But that night was hardly a time for intimate queries.

He had shown only the briefest alarm when I told him of the cholera in the priest's house. At first, he thought I was joking with him, given the lies that had been told about the fate of Danny Boland. When I warned him more sharply not to come close until I had stripped off my clothing and washed myself, Kehoe stiffened, but thereafter he was ready enough to do all that was necessary. He went down to the patch, at my request, to fetch a bottle of spirits and substitute clothing.

In Kehoe's absence, I had gone back to the pump behind the priest's house. I stripped me down and splashed myself until I could stand it no longer. I felt as if I might freeze upon the spot.

Kehoe met me again down by the boneyard and did not laugh at my queer state of undress. I must have looked a madcap in the moonlight, outfitted with undergarments and boots, my cane and a Colt revolver. I stripped off the rest of my rags, set them alight, and pulled on enough bits of Irish frieze to lift me out of shame. Then I had Kehoe burn the taint from my hand before I continued dressing. He had tried to fetch items small in size, but haste had ruled his decisions. I had to turn back the sleeves and roll up the cuffs, which proved a trial for my tormented hand. I fear my friend Mr. Barnaby would have remarked that I did not "cut a dash."

I did have some concern about the garments Kehoe furnished me, for I am not fond of lice, and lice are fond of the Irish. But it was no time for a man to pick and choose.

"We'll need to get along now. There's a ways to walk ahead of us," Kehoe said. Odd it was. Now he seemed the more anxious of us to finish the business and bring in Mary Boland. "Are ye suitable? With that mitt of yours?"

"Yes, Mr. Kehoe. I am 'suitable.' Let us go, then."

He was a stalwart fellow, with strength in his legs and feet bred in a rough country. But he was not a talkative sort. His scent was of secrets.

We clambered over the litter of rocks that decorates the southerly slopes in our coal fields. I walked behind, while Kehoe followed the moonlight. He set such a pace that I had to push along with my cane to keep up with his longer legs. By the time we reached the top of the ridge we both were wheezing and warmed. I was even asweat, which is cleansing and good for the health.

"The strutting don't pain ye?" Kehoe asked. He sounded as if his lungs wished a longer pause. "With that gimp of a leg you're dragging?"

"My leg is little bother," I assured him. "When you are ready . . ."

We set out again, walking the bends and saddles of the ridge. In Schuylkill County, the mountains rise in endless

lines, as if nature has set out her ranks for a grand parade.
The hint of a path wound up and down, with changes of elevation just great enough to annoy a man. Kehoe stopped
short at the head of a ravine, where a man might have fallen
to his injury. The path turned sharply—unnaturally—to skirt
a derelict scene of shanties and the skeleton of an old colliery. Twas a small affair, on the scale of a past generation,
with its mine played out and abandoned.

We had to go along carefully thereafter, for the waste
banks will take a man into them, whenever they feel the
mood. There are types of silt that will swallow a fellow like
quicksand, and more fool the mother who lets her child play
on such. Where the earth has been stripped and piled, the
coal lands are like a desert, with great black dunes and many
a hidden danger. In an old works of that sort, we did not have
to worry much about mineshafts dropping straight, for the
old miners quarried the face of the rock, then drove tunnels
at a slant. Twas the airholes, concealed by the night or overgrown with vines, that would swallow a man and break his
neck to keep him. Or leave him alone and dying at the bottom of the drop, not to be found until some later happen-
stance. The earth had her ways of taking her revenge,
wherever men robbed her coal.

I followed John Kehoe precisely. For I still could not
know how much I finally might trust him. And I had no wish
to end my life in a coal hole.

The moon had begun to decline. Its pale light struck at a
slant now, casting giant shadows in the scrub, silvering the
trunks of the birches and tipping their leafless limbs with
buds of fire. The world smelled of autumn rot and iron cold.

Kehoe paused by a cart that had been stripped of its
wheels and left unexplained in the woods. As if it had been
abducted, robbed and murdered. The big fellow was puffing.
I will admit I was vain enough to take pride in his shortness

of breath, for I was fit as a fiddle, if a bit worn. All those years of marching had their benefits, see.

It is a curious thing. No matter how fierce the circumstance, men take delight in finding themselves superior in any way to their fellows. It is a sort of animal game we play.

"Not the half of an hour now," he assured me. Resting himself against the frame of the cart, he lifted his hat and wiped the back of a hand across his forehead.

"Hidden away it is," I said.

"Decent people won't let that old hag near them."

Playing tender with my hand, which was in high complaint, I said, "I hear they go to her for spells and potions."

"And fools they are for it."

"Then you are not a superstitious man, Mr. Kehoe?"

He spit. "Tis superstition keeps the Irish down. A man would think the Church would hold devils enough for them. The Irish need proper work and proper wages. Not make-believe witches. Or priests who tell them to bend to the yoke and wait for Heaven's reward."

I did not pursue that matter. For well enough I know that a man may criticize his own faith boisterously, but will fight another man to the death for slighting it.

It struck me that the earth had gone utterly silent. We had reached those hours of morning when sentries fall asleep and earn their death warrants. Around us, the trees that had grown from the gutted earth displayed branches that looked like claws, as if they had not sprouted naturally, but had scratched themselves free of a grave.

"Perhaps we should go on?" I said. For the moon threatened to set. And I did not want to enter that old woman's realm without its light.

"You're a tough little bird," Kehoe mused. "A man wouldn't think it."

Off we set again, with our shoes tapping over the hardened earth where the winds had swept off the leaves. Then, in the hollows, we made a helpless racket, crisping through the piles gathered in the lees. Twas a nasty thought, but those leaves seemed to me like scabs upon the earth. Except for our breathing and footfalls, there was no other sound. As if the earth had paused to listen and watch.

Kehoe brought us to another halt. When he spoke, he whispered.

"I've had your promise of ye," he said. "No harm's to come to Mary. I'm to speak with her. Should the lass go troublesome, I'll be the one to put manners on her."

"You have my promise, Mr. Kehoe. But come with us she must."

"Just keep a close watch on the old one," he warned me. "I know what Mary Boland's about, but I can't say how the hag will take on at the sight of us."

Twas not a pleasant night. Running from cholera to a leprous crone who mistook herself for a witch.

As I too often do when ill at ease, I touched my Colt. Twas belted outside of my threadbare coat and ready.

"Mr. Kehoe," I said in a hushed voice. "Do you have a way to defend yourself?"

"I'll pick up a stick as we're going."

"Look you. I have but one working hand. Take my cane. There is a blade inside. You undo this latch and—"

"I'll take up a stick," he said firmly. "And I'll see no swords or guns tried on Mary Boland."

To underscore his point, he chose a stick on the spot, discarded it as unsuitable, then settled on another.

We pressed on.

"Tis but a meager stretch now," he whispered. "So quiet with ye."

It seemed to me the air had grown much colder. Likely that was pure imagination. But little fits of shivering over-

took me. We entered a mountaintop glen and found ourselves within a puzzle of crags. The trees about us were few
and crippled and spare. Some were bent over as if to make a
fist. The last of the moonlight polished the stones to a white-
ness. I felt cast into a wasteland as barren as the soul of
Judas Iscariot.

Kehoe slowed his pace. Superstitious he may not have
been, but neither was he a fool. Caution was in order. Just at
the mouth of a hidden ravine, he stretched a hand back toward me.

Turning his bearded face for the quickest of moments, he
whispered, "Her shanty's behind the rocks. So take your
warning."

He was taut as the wires on a new piano. I could sense it
without touching him.

We went along at little more than a creep. Until the path
turned and revealed a patch of light.

"There," Kehoe said.

I sensed more than saw the outlines of the shack. Twas not
a pistol-shot distant.

I come up close to my guide. And smelled fear. Perhaps I
smelled as much of fear myself. Twas a Godforsaken place,
on a cheerless night.

"I will go first now," I whispered. Wondering all the while
if his stick might not come down as a club upon my own
head. I had no choice but to trust him, see.

"Go along, if ye will. But no harm to Mary Boland."

"I have no wish to do the woman harm."

"It's not your wishes I'm worrying over," he said. "You're
twitching like a cat."

"Well, then," I told him, "you will have to be steady for
the two of us." But the truth is he had more of the jumps
than me.

Healthy souls belonged elsewhere.

Slipping past him, I placed my feet as silently as I could. I was as alert as if going into battle. Watching all the while. In case the women had sensed us. For there are things that will not be explained.

As I closed on the shanty, I first smelled human droppings. The old crone had not bothered to dig herself a convenience and simply availed herself of her surroundings. And I saw that the shack was a haphazard thing built into the hillside and framed by mighty rocks. It seemed an attempt to extend a cave above ground.

Light filtered from an entrance of sorts, where draperies or skins did for a door. There was a glow from a window, as well, muted by oiled cloth or greased-over burlap.

I smelled cooking. Stewing. And rancidness.

Gripping my cane as tightly as ever I gripped a musket, I worked my way close to the dwelling. Wary of traps or alarms set upon the ground. Wary of everything.

I heard laughter. And dreadful voices. Women's voices. But hardly of this earth.

The last blade of moonlight cut across the hut, as if to sever the thatch of the roof from the planks and mud of the walls.

I crouched down low for a moment, focusing on the jagged light escaping the interior. I did not want to rush inside and find myself blinded in the crucial moment, so I tried to prepare my eyes. I would have liked to advise Kehoe to do the same, but I feared revealing our presence with even a whisper.

And I prayed a bit.

Standing up, with a firm grip on my cane, I marched for the door. And in I plunged, through a curtain of ill-cured pelts.

I hope that I shall never again see such a sight as that. The shanty was a warren of filth and carcasses. Mary Boland and the old witch were cooking. A black pot hung in the hearth. The fire thrilled its light through the room. To show what the women had done.

They had carved the joints and much of the flesh from their most recent quarry, which hung down from the ceiling, drained of blood. Hardly more than the torso and head remained.

It was the body of a little girl.

"Dear Jesus," Kehoe said behind me. His voice was vivid with fear.

The women watched us calmly, almost gaily. Mary Boland smiled and the old one grinned. As if we had been expected and were welcome.

"Have ye come up for your supper?" Mary Boland asked us, as impudent as ever. There were stains down her chin and neck, as if from blood. And still she managed, God forgive me the saying of it, to look a fiercesome beauty.

"No," I said, mustering all my reserves, "we have come for you, Mrs. Boland. We have to take you with us, see. You are under arrest."

Of course, the old woman wanted arresting, too, for her morbid desecrations, but I saw that we must do things step by step. If we were to do them at all.

Mary Boland cocked her head like a lass bantering over the laundry.

"I warned ye that I'd say the old words over ye."

"Mary . . ." Kehoe began, voice choked and shocked and struggling, "ye must come down with us now. For your Danny's sake. It's Danny wants ye to come down. Come on, lass. We'll go on together."

Mary Boland's brow compressed in doubt.

"I don't believe ye. They've taken Danny off. Him there. The dirty Taffy. Him and the rest of them."

Yet, I sensed that she had begun to quarrel with herself.

"He's back, your Danny," Kehoe said. His tones were gaining strength. "I swear to ye, he's come back. But he's weary and sick, and he could not come himself to ye. He's calling ye, Mary. He wants ye to come down to him."

"Let him come hither to me," she snapped.

"He's ill, Mary. He's sick and in danger, your Danny. Come on, girl . . ."

Her expression was that of an animal unsure of the voice that lures it.

An impulse made me glance at the old woman. But I was too late.

"*Du bekommst mein Liebchen nit*," she shrieked. *You will not get my darling.*

She reached into the hearth with her bare hand. With a dazzling sweep, she culled a torch from the fire and thrust it into Mary Boland's hair. Just where her tresses met the wool of her shawl.

Mary Boland lit up as if doused in pitch. For a freeze of seconds, she stood there, bound to the spot. Motionless, but for the flames exploding from her hair and racing over her shoulders.

I saw her face, white and astonished, wrapped in a bonnet of fire.

Then she screamed. Tearing at herself. Running into the wall. As if she might break through to a pool of water. Stumbling into the table, spilling its litter of bones and bowls and slops. Striking the dangling carcass with her face.

Kehoe tore the Colt from my belt and shot her.

Howling in some devil's tongue, the old woman rushed toward me. I rammed my stick into her bosom, pushing her off. But she did not go down or retreat. A dog with rabies comes at a man that way. Her face was that of a breathing corpse, something dead but risen. Yet, her good eye was as vital as a living eye could be.

One-handed and awkward, I barely had time to fling off the sheath of my sword-cane before she attacked me again. She ran straight into the blade. As if she did not see it. Or did not care.

Perhaps the old woman loved Mary Boland, too? As helplessly as Danny Boland did?

She charged halfway up the sword before it slowed her. Struggling against the steel to get her claws on me.

The room was ablaze behind her. Mary Boland had fallen against the wall and made it her pyre.

I smelled the old woman's breath and felt the spray from her lips. She wrenched her feet forward, helping the blade glide through her, approaching the hilt. Desperate to reach me.

"Deine Seele gehört mir!" she croaked. Blood oozed from her mouth. Only, it was not blood as you know it. It was black.

I released my grip on the blade and stumbled rearward.

The old woman nearly fell forward when I let go, but she righted herself with a growl. The tip of the sword stuck out of her back, with the hilt approaching her stomach. But she did not grasp the handle, as dying men do. All her remaining vigor was meant for me. Her fingernails, long and brown, desired my flesh.

My back slammed up against a wall. With her claws inches from my face.

Kehoe shot her. The first bullet did not put her down, but only spun her about. The second shot conjured a look of wonder to her face. Only the third round, fired from three feet away, dropped her to the floor.

Black Jack Kehoe fired again, splashing blood from her throat. After that, he kept on pulling the trigger, even though all of the chambers had been emptied. Pointing the revolver at her, he clicked away with the urgency of madness.

The roof had begun to burn above our heads. With the fire sneaking behind us, toward the door. But Kehoe stood in a trance. Staring at the creature who was still undead, writhing on the floor and spewing blackness.

Her eyes no longer saw us. God knows what they saw. She gargled heathen words and chuckled blood.

A finger of fire reached the wraps on her ankles. Snarling and open-eyed, the old woman did not react to the flames as they overtook her. The fire climbed her legs, then raced up her back. But her face showed no mark of pain. Only of hatred and wonder.

Perhaps her soul was already immersed in far more terrible fires.

I took back my Colt and pulled Kehoe from the shanty. No sooner were we outside than he was sick. I dragged him along, despite his retching and reluctance to come away until he was finished. We both reached safety just as the roof fell in.

Flames rushed after us, roaring and angry, as if they wished revenge for the old woman's death. But we had gotten free and the fire sulked back. Then something especial burst in the heart of the ruins. A pillar of fire shot into the moonless sky.

Instead of faltering, the flames redoubled their power, as if they had reached a hidden reserve of fuel. They lit the hilltop barrens above the glen. That must have been a bonfire seen for miles. If any eyes were watching.

That is how I lost the cane given to me by the Earl of Thretford himself. That is how the murderess of General Carl Stone and Kathleen Boland perished. And that is how Black Jack Kehoe learned to hate me. He always blamed me for Mary Boland's death, for causing him to let down Danny Boland. For putting him in the position where shooting the woman was the kindest thing he could do. It did not matter what horrors he had seen in that shanty, or what he had learned of the woman he meant to protect. It only mattered that he had failed, and he never could bear failure.

Kehoe hated me from that night on.

I never hated him, see. I even tried to save his life years later, as Gowen schemed to hang him. My efforts were in vain, of course, with our courts reduced to tools of wealth, dealing vigilante justice to men so desperate they defied the Reading Company's private army. No, Kehoe was not the evil man the annals would have you believe. He did foolish things, and some bad ones. But everything he did he did for the sons and daughters of Erin. He had his rigorous honor, in the Irish grain. He grew hard and bitter as time progressed and every promise made to the miners was broken. His judgement was sometimes poor and he trusted the wrong men, not least that unscrupulous Pinkerton man, MacParlan. But he was never the cold-blooded killer of popular legend. Indeed, his fault was that he failed to kill MacParlan when he should have.

But let that bide.

We went down the hill together that night, unwilling to speak a word.

nineteen

JIMMY AND I WENT INTO QUARANTINE in a watchman's shack below the Thomaston works. It was an ordeal for both of us at first.

I was rambunctious with wanting to make my report, which was set to comfort everyone. The Russians bore no blame that I could see, for their agent had come too late. Nor had the Irish miners been at fault, for all the commotion had come of the deeds of a madwoman, and the Irish had only tried to protect their own. There was no threat to diplomacy or politics, and I wanted my masters to know it to ease their minds. But I was stuck in a shanty with no recourse but to wait from day to day for signs of cholera.

Jimmy always found confinement a burden, for he is a lively man, enamored of motion. He cannot even sit for very long.

Yet, men adapt to the needs of their situations. Soon enough we calmed into a sort of soldierly housekeeping, sitting about the coal stove as the season withered and telling stories of comrades lost in time. Jimmy made me laugh, which is a gift.

November's early days of gold dissolved into weeks of drizzle. We talked again of our marching years, when the monsoon rains did not so much fall as attack. Interludes sneaked into our afternoons when we did not speak at all, but only mused to ourselves. We might have been an old married couple, given the way we kept company.

My own dear wife drove up a number of times, when the weather permitted, for now she had a carriage of her own. Oh, she looked a very queen, my Mary did. She could not come closer than fifty feet, but I read the heartsick worry on her face. That, too, is the stuff of marriage. When you are properly blessed with a loving partner, you become so closely bound together, so joined to one another, that no threat upon this earth is so great as the prospect of losing your husband or your wife. I worried over her health and she over mine, if for sharply different reasons. She gave me our John's love and, after a pause, told me that Fanny had moped herself near to a sickness with concern for me. Something there was in my Mary's tone that said she had begun to accept the lass. Glad of it I was. It may have been as simple a thing as coming into funds. Hereafter, there would be enough for all. Or, perhaps, my Mary had leapt that greatest hurdle placed before our hearts and saw she could do no better than trust my love.

My darling wrote to Mrs. Molloy for Jimmy, and a letter arrived in little more than a week. Annie Molloy could not leave the family businesses—all her employees were Irish, after all—but she sent a letter so full of love that it left poor Jimmy morose. Business was blooming, her heart was full, and she had just discovered herself to be with child.

"You'll be a splendid father," I assured Jimmy. But I fear I saw horizons in his eyes.

My Mary also telegraphed my carefully chosen words to Mr. Nicolay:

JN. NO FOREIGN INVOLVEMENT. NO IRISH BLAME. SIMPLE CRIME. MURDERER DEAD. WILL REPORT IN PERSON AFTER QUARANTINE. AJ.

I expected that might be enough to assuage the fears of all
the parties concerned, at least temporarily. I worried that Mr.
Seward might nurse a grudge against me for not reporting
first to him, as he had asked. But he proved a wiser, greater
man than that. The results of my work contented him, as he
himself told me later. He only wished to keep those Russians
out of things. And I am unashamed to admit that my doings
gained me praise from Mr. Lincoln, who was pleased to be
able to tell those German fellows that a madwoman killed
their general and he had proof of it. My only fear was of
Mrs. Schutzengel's likely disappointment, for she wanted to
blame the Russians with all her heart. But even she only
sulked a bit, when I told her what I could. Then she made me
a German pie from poppyseeds and molasses.

Mr. Downs had the duty of bringing us foodstuffs—
although my Mary delivered treats, as well—and, given the
teamster's habits, I was not convinced that all sanitary mea-
sures were suitably enforced. But we survived.

That hand of mine was a bother, but I found a bit more
strength in it every day. I seem to be a collection of damaged
parts.

My Mary brought me a Bible, too, for in my haste I had
failed to replace my pocket Testament, and Scripture is a
comfort that a man should enjoy each day. At first, I kept my
studies to myself, but Jimmy asked if I would read aloud, to
pass the time. Of course, I was glad to do it, for when those
words ring out the world improves. Queer it was, though.
Jimmy had been brought up in his church, more or less—I
thought of that poor Pip, who was brought up "by hand" in
Mr. Dickens's book—but he did not know the stories in the
Bible, at least not those that are given to us between the days
of Moses and those of Christ. He sat there by the stove,
smoking a pipe and listening to each verse in fascination.

Some of the stories left him scowling and skeptical. Of

Daniel in his den, Jimmy said, "Sure, Abel, ye know enough about lions and tigers to know the beast would have et him as soon as the mood come on." And he insisted that Jonah would have drowned in the belly of that whale, or come to a nasty grief in the whale's digestion. "Don't ye remember," he asked me, "when we cut the baby out o' the snake that time in Cooteewallah and there weren't much left but bones?" He was, however, much impressed with Judith, describing her as a "right handful, that one," for the manner in which she had despatched Holofernes. And fonder he was of the tale of Susannah at her bath than I thought proper. He liked the battles, too. Told of Joseph and his brothers, Jimmy said he had heard of a similar case in Wexford, back in his mother's day. A family sold off one of their own to a press-gang. Of Solomon's immortal song, Jimmy remarked, "That's handsome jabber, that is. I'll have to remember those words when Annie goes sulking."

His final judgement on those tales was that nothing much had changed, that people were people. He did not seem to be edified in the least.

Mr. Donnelly come strolling by, when the weather broke for a brace of cold, blue days. He called a halloo from the roadway, standing there with an impish grin on his mug.

"Ah, an't it lovely to see ye primed in your health," he said, "and no trace of the black cholera anywhere near ye."

"Not so far," I allowed, though reluctantly. Cholera was the single thing I would not hear discussed. Nor would I think on it.

"Sure, and that's a blessing," he went on. "And there an't been another case of it come amongst us, either, so I'm thinking we're free of our troubles, the saints be praised." His grin faded until his expression matched the chill of the afternoon. "Would *ye* say we're free of our troubles, Major Jones?"

"I would say . . ." I called across the field of wintering weeds, ". . . that you are free of the troubles that concerned me. And of those which concerned the government in this matter. I wish you might keep yourselves free of future troubles, as well."

He smiled again, but differently. "Wishes are tender things, are they not? And wounded by the world, in all its cruelty . . ." He waved away our discussion with his walking stick. "It's a lucky man ye are, Major Jones. And not such a bad one, perhaps, though others mought argue it. Well, I was only having meself a stroll. I'll be off, then."

"Mr. Donnelly?"

He paused.

"Did you do as I asked? Did you bury them together? The priest and the girl?"

He shook his head, invoking a smile still colder than before. "That would have been against the laws of the Holy Mother Church." His eyes turned stony hard. "And it an't for the likes of us to interfere. Good health to ye, Major. If ever ye pass our way again, look in on us."

He ambled off, whistling to fool the world, as the Irish do.

In our last week of confinement, nature showed her temper once again. Rain dripped through the cracks in the roof and the coal stove threw more smoke than it offered heat. We wrapped ourselves in blankets and waited for dawn, as we had done in the passes above Peshawar, when our regiment went hunting Afghan bandits. Oh, lucky we are that America is far away from that lot, for the Afghanee is a genius of discord.

On the holiday of Thanksgiving, the morning broke as clear as a young girl's eyes. That pleased me. For I am fond of our holiday of thanks. I understand it began in the wilds of New England and has wandered southward over the years, although it still is muchly a Northern affair.

I thought to myself that Mr. Lincoln should make Thanksgiving a holiday for all our nation, and I resolved to suggest it to him, if ever I had the chance. For lovely it would be to set aside one day of the year for our families, to give the Good Lord thanks for our endless blessings. Look you. If it were made a holiday by decree, instead of merely by custom, as it is now, we might introduce a law demanding universal Temperance once a year. And that might be a noble beginning, leading one day to the banning of liquor outright.

Too many men grasp a holiday—even Christmas itself—to drink themselves to the Devil. The year before, I had witnessed our army's antics, with immodesty in the Washington hotels. They made of Thanksgiving no more than a drunken frolic. The newspapers, which you have read yourself, attempted to exploit the day for their commerce, advertising champagne and oysters and such. No, Thanksgiving deserved a formal elevation and a return to its antique purpose, without the corruption imposed by modern fancies.

But let that bide.

My Mary brought us a basket filled abundantly. Although she could not join us in our shanty, her spirit was present as Jimmy and I shared our feast. There was turkey and ham and boiled beef and sausages. With a battalion of garnishes, washed down by innocent cider.

After our dinner, as we sat with the buttons loosened on our trousers, a matter crept up to nag me. Without thinking, I launched into a complaint.

"Jimmy, I have told you," I said, "up and down and twice over, about the murders. But there is one small matter that devils me still, for I cannot see the bones of it."

"What are ye going on about now? It seems to me that you're well shut o' the lot of them. And good riddance, says Jimmy Molloy."

I nodded, agreeing. "Yes, but look you. I still do not see who it was that told Mary Boland that General Stone was set to take off her husband. What was the sense of it? The man had given up on recruiting in Heckschersville. He was going away when she murdered him. Why whisper that lie in her ear and incite a murder? I cannot see which party had the benefit. The Irish had no cause to wish him dead. Why bring trouble down upon themselves?"

Jimmy made a series of faces that explored the entire Irish repertoire of amazement. He pulled his jaw, and rolled his eyes, and swept back his hair, and shook his head, and muttered and sputtered and clicked his tongue, then smiled to show me the remnants of his dinner.

"Jaysus, Mary and Joseph!" he cried. "Are ye telling me that ye can't see something so simple?" He shook his head with all the drama that lurks between Dingle and Derry. And he sighed enormously. "Abel, me darling man, ye were ever a terrible fool for a man so crafty. Is that the way they make the Welsh, or are ye just short of your pint? Why, it's clear as an empty glass who wanted him dead. Clear as an empty glass, and just as sorry!"

"I have no idea what you're talking about."

He pulled another face, then leaned toward me, settling his elbows just above his knees. Twas a posture I remembered from our barracks days.

"Now, if ye'd only think, ye'd reach your conclusion. What was General Stone after doing, I ask ye?"

"Attempting to recruit troops for the Union. But he failed and—"

"He failed in Heckschersville," Jimmy said, exasperated. "But that don't mean he might not have succeeded where next he got up to persuading and preaching and promising."

"I don't see what you—"

"Don't ye, man?" He waved his head and shoulders at my

folly, smacking his knee with the palm of his hand and smacking his lips thereafter. "Now, if General Stone, God rest his soul—even though the bugger was a general—if he had succeeded in his recruitment efforts around your great and grandiose Schuylkill County, what with his letter from Meagher himself and all his radical speechifying, what would have been the results of that, I ask you? Will ye only tell me that?"

"Well . . . more Irish might have joined the army." That seemed obvious enough. But I still did not see his point.

"And if more Irish joined the army, Abel, what is it ye'd have less of here at home?"

"Jimmy, if you mean to have a laugh at my ex—"

"Just answer me now, if ye want to solve your riddle. For the answer's dancing in front of your very eyes, man. If more of the Irish joined the army, what would ye have less of here in this plague-ridden county of yours?"

"Well . . . I suppose . . . we'd have less drunkenness."

Jimmy shook his head at my lack of sense. "You're cramming the matter all full o' complications, bloody-minded Welshman that ye are. Now listen to the question, would ye only do that, if it please your royal majesty? If the Irish were to take themselves off to the army, what would ye have less of here at home?"

"Less Irishmen?"

He clapped his hands and affected a near swoon. "Now he's after the fox and ahead of the hounds! If ye had less Irishmen here in your kingdom of coal, what kind of Irishmen might ye have less of, pray tell?"

"Well, most of them are miners or colliery laborers, of course. A few are respectable trades—"

"And if ye lacked miners and didn't have labor in excess, if there was barely enough to go scratching your coal from the ground, instead of a hundred poor bogtrotters begging

for every cruel job that comes open, what would happen to
wages, if ye don't mind telling me?"

My God. I saw it. Jimmy was right. The answer *had* been
in front of my face all the while. It was ugly as sin in a
chapel. The coal men, the colliery lords, had commissioned
one of their agents to tell Mary Boland—a known or suspected murderess—that General Stone was about to take her
husband away. In the hope—the expectation—that she
would kill him. Because they feared Stone might succeed
with the Irish and raise up regiments of miners and colliery
lads. Because the present glut of workers kept wages down
and profits as high as possible. Because patriotism stopped
at the door of the bank. The priest had declared it was all
about love. But this was only about the love of money.

Perhaps the same lips had whispered to the murderess that
I kept her husband from her, and that was why she took her
knife to me?

But who could have known enough about Mary Boland's
doings to recommend her as the perfect instrument? Given
the care the Irish took to conceal their community's secrets?
Unless there was an informer and traitor among them, I did
not see who might have known of her madness. Who could
have approached her, for that matter? Unless we speak of the
Irish themselves, who might she have been willing to believe? Certainly not a stranger. Who could have gone among
the Irish without arousing suspicion? And who in that valley
answered to the powerful?

I saw the man before me. As clearly as you do.

ON THE DAY that Jimmy and I were deemed free of infection,
I did not take me home to Pottsville at once. I had a final call
to pay in the valley.

"Now, I just don't know why you'd want to go back
there," Mr. Downs said. "Ain't you had enough of them

damned Irish?" He paused to insure his nose was thoroughly scoured. "Don't mind my saying, I think you Welshman
are all crazy. Comes from all that hymn-howling. And you a
rich man now, I hear tell. Get on, mules."

"Take me to the colliery office, please," I told him. "It will
not be a lengthy matter, and we will all be home in time for
supper."

Grumbling, he steered his wagon back toward
Heckschersville.

When we pulled into the yards, the workers took pains to
ignore us, although a few gave Jimmy dirty looks. For
Jimmy was Irish as boiled potatoes, and the Irish do not like
to see one of their own consort with their enemies. And the
Irish see enemies everywhere. Perhaps that is their gravest
superstition. I wished them no harm and even might claim
that I had done them good, yet they could not help but view
me with hostility. Twas not only the matter of the uniform
that I had put on to celebrate my release. The Irish nurse old
grudges, stewed in blood, forbidding them to like the Welsh
or English. I might have been the reincarnation of Mr.
Cromwell himself, for all the welcome I had.

I got me down from the wagon and told Mr. Downs and
Jimmy Molloy to wait. Looking around at the vale of blackness surrounding the shaft and the colliery, with an ear
cocked to the racket of the works, Jimmy declared, "Jaysus,
I'd rather be a soldier half-dead than a miner."

In I went and along I went, ignoring the protestations of
the clerks. I threw open the door to Mr. Oliver's office and
found him hunched over a ledger. The window behind his
shoulders had been repaired.

I drew out my Colt and put a bullet through the glass.

The window exploded outward this time. Mr. Oliver
dropped to the floor, where I left him for a moment while I
assured the clerks that I had only been saying hello.

"Mind your business now," I told them, "or I will have a talk with Mr. Donnelly."

Then I stepped into Mr. Oliver's room and shut the door.

"Get you up now, Mr. Oliver. For we must have a talk."

"Don't shoot me!" he mewled from behind the desk. "For the love of Christ, don't shoot me!"

"I do not intend to shoot you," I assured him. "But I do intend to resolve a simple matter."

He clambered up, clumsy and frightened. Craven he was. And greedy, perhaps. But certainly not brave.

"Sit you down," I pointed at his chair with my revolver.

He sat down. "You've got no business here," he said, with fragile truculence. "You're on company property."

"And were *you* on company property," I asked him, "when you told Mary Boland that General Stone had enlisted her husband and meant to return to take Daniel Boland away?"

He was as guilty as Cain. His face all but shouted it.

"That's crazy," he said, without the least conviction. "That's the craziest thing I heard."

"Who put you up to it? Gowen? The lot of them?"

"You're a madman. You're crazy. I've never been within a hundred feet of Mary Boland. I only ever saw her across the yard."

"That is a lie, Mr. Oliver. You have told me differently yourself."

He was frightened and confused, which was precisely the condition I wished to have him in.

"I don't know what you're talking about. I never told you anything."

"Don't you remember? You told me what a splendid-looking woman she was."

"A body could see that from here. I didn't need to get close."

"But you also told me that you found her stinking. Now,

I don't believe you could smell her from here, Mr. Oliver. Although I will admit she wanted a wash."

"You're trying to trick me."

"No, Mr. Oliver. You have tricked yourself. You whispered in Mary Boland's ear, knowing that your words would cost the general his life. I believe you set her to murder me, as well. But let that bide. You are an accomplice to murder. That is enough. And now we are speaking of your life and no one else's."

"You can't prove one damned thing."

I smiled. "Mr. Oliver, I do not intend to prove it, see. Although an accomplice to murder deserves the gallows. What I intend to do is to tell your little secret to the Irish. And you can square the matter with Mr. Donnelly."

White he went as the snows of distant Russia.

"Don't," he said. The word passed awkwardly from his mouth, as if his lips were frozen. "Don't do that. Don't . . ."

"Sorry I am, Mr. Oliver, but—"

"They'll kill me. They'll murder me."

"—justice must take its course, one way or the other."

"I have a wife and children . . ."

"As Mary Boland had a husband."

"She was crazy as a loon. She'd already killed Boland's slut of a sister."

"Yes," I said, "that fact was crucial to your calculations, was it not? You knew she was mad, you knew she had killed, and you knew why she had done it. You knew that she thought her husband was worth a killing, if anyone ever tried to take him away."

He looked at me with a combination of wariness and terror.

"You and the men above you," I went on, "you knew the Irish already had much to hide on behalf of the Bolands. You knew they would fight to shield Mary Boland, for her husband's sake. Even if she had murdered President Lincoln. You did not count on Daniel Boland declaring himself a murderer in an attempt to spare his wife, that you did not. That is why you did not wish to go to the magistrate, when he wished to pretend to guilt. But the Irish settled even that matter for you and schemed to hide Boland away. You were using the Irish like puppets, while the lot of you worked against them. To keep them hungry and hard at work for your pennies."

"I swear to God . . . I swear I'll do anything you want. As long as you don't tell Donnelly . . ."

"Well, I must be off now," I told him. "Things to do in plenty. I think you may wish to go careful around the Irish, from now on."

"*Please*, man, I swear to God . . ."

"Was it Gowen?"

He hesitated.

"Good day, Mr. Oliver." I took me across the threshold of his room.

"*Yes!*" he cried. "Him. All of them. All of them together. I was only doing what I had to do. For the love of God, man . . ."

I walked away, with the clerks in the outer office forming a gauntlet of curiosity.

I heard Mr. Oliver rushing around from the back of his desk to follow me.

"Don't!" he cried down the hallway. "Don't do it, for the love of God."

I did not deign to give him a backward glance, but left him there, devoured by his fear. I did not tell his secret to Mr. Donnelly, or to any of the Irish, since that would have been murder. But I was content to let Mr. Oliver spend his days in fear, never knowing, looking over his shoulder and jumping at every noise.

The truth was that I could not prove a thing, though all seemed so obvious now. Had I tried to take Mr. Oliver into custody, to have him as a witness against the big men, he would not have survived his first night in our jail. Oh, I saw a great deal now. My Mary Myfanwy was right. I had not known Pottsville. But I knew it better now. A little better.

The bitter thing was that the rich and powerful men were safe. I would give a full report to Mr. Nicolay. But I knew that our government would not welcome scandal in the midst of a war, nor would they fancy trials that relied on logic, without irrefutable evidence. But it gnawed at me. For I believe that justice must be served.

Mr. Gowen visited me, before I left for Washington. He found me in conversation with Mr. Caxton, the engineer of whom Mr. Cawber had spoken—and a young man who seemed as sure of his business as he was sure to please the ladies and girls. Mr. Caxton was just explaining the cleverness of Mr. Evans's leases, when Mr. Evans's servant announced Mr. Gowen.

I suppose I should not say "Mr. Evans's" when I speak of this or that. For these things belonged to my wife and to my family now, although my Mary took to her change of station more readily than I could do, moving us into the grand house on Mahantango Street while I was reminiscing with Jimmy Molloy and waiting to see if the cholera had a taste for me.

Anyway, Mr. Gowen come in. Clear enough it was that he was displeased at the sight of Mr. Caxton's charts and maps and person.

"Jones, may I speak to you in private?" he asked.

"This is Mr. Caxton, who—"

"Yes, yes, I know. I need to speak to you alone."

I nodded to Mr. Caxton, who was the sort of fellow who

grasped things quickly. He went out, shutting the door of Mr. Evans's study behind him.

"Three hundred thousand dollars for the Evans properties," Gowen said. "Fifty thousand for the whore's diary. That's their final offer."

"Whose final offer?"

"Take it or leave it."

"I will leave it, then. The properties are not for sale. And I have told you that the diary book is in Washington."

"You're a fool."

"I do not doubt it, Mr. Gowen. But fool or no, the properties are not for sale."

"Don't you think you should ask your wife before you refuse me?" he sneered. "Or Dolly Walker?"

"Why don't you ask them yourself? You will find them made of stouter wood than me."

"Then you're all fools. The days of the small operator are over. You'll be broken quicker than a china plate." He patted his pockets, as if searching for that watch of his. "Matt Cawber won't save you, either. He's yesterday's man."

"And you, Mr. Gowen? I take it you are a man fit for the future?"

"What do you think?"

"I think that I would like you to leave my home."

"*Your* home?" His eyes looked about dismissively. "You're like a monkey got up in a swallowtail coat and an opera hat."

"And then there is the matter of General Stone's murder, Mr. Gowen. And of your complicity in it."

He laughed, though the laugh was a hollow one. "Oh, Oliver told me about that little scene you played for him. You know there's nothing to it, Jones. If you had proof of anything, you wouldn't have gone after him quite that way." He smirked. "Would you have?"

That was true enough. But we both knew what we knew. And we knew that the other knew it.

And we knew that we were irreconcilable enemies.

I rang for the manservant, which gave me a childish pleasure, and told him, "Mr. Gowen was just leaving."

JIMMY MOLLOY had preceded me to Washington by a day, but I did not lack for company on my journey. Mr. Bannon, the newspaper fellow, sat beside me all the way to Philadelphia. He congratulated me on solving the murder case, although he still pretended to have no knowledge of Kathleen Boland or her Pottsville activities. With a grand harrumph, he declared that the Irish had been taught a thorough lesson, although I did not quite see it.

Now, I am a civil fellow and ever ready to learn from conversation with a cleverer man than myself, but the truth is I had been looking forward to a bit of private time upon the railway. I fear I must make a confession, see. You have heard me complain about the iniquity of the novel, which is, after all, no more than a book full of lies. But I have also admitted to indulging myself with that tale from Mr. Dickens, which brought a tear to my eye before its end. Poor Pip. I really thought he deserved a greater happiness, and that girl was nothing but trouble, from start to finish. But Mr. Dickens behaved as Mr. Shakespeare would have done and made things true to life. My confession is that I had procured myself a copy of *The Pickwick Papers*, which had been recommended to me by Mr. Barnaby. And I found it a great delight, all chock-a-block with characters who rise up from the pages to make friends. I had hoped to read more about Mr. Pickwick's travels and travails, but Mr. Bannon commanded my attention.

Now, you will say: "You told us that the novel was an instrument of the Devil." But I will tell you: A man must live

and learn, and I was wrong. And that is what comes of con-
demning a thing of which a man has no knowledge. I find
the novel a wholesome thing, and edifying. So there.

As we rolled toward the metropolis of Reading,
Pennsylvania, Mr. Bannon described a fantastic array of
crimes and sins, assigning each to the Democratic Party, for
he remained displeased with the recent election. He let
loose for fifteen minutes on Mr. Gowen, but I learned nothing new. Then he explained why the Irish would never be fit
to become Americans. Thereafter, he mocked Irish fears of
abolition.

"Their dread is a mockery of reason," Mr. Bannon explained to me. "Once freed—once his breeding is no longer
supervised—the Negro is bound to die out among the superior races. He never will come north in significant numbers.
His tropic constitution could not bear the cold at a civilized
latitude. I expect that the moment he finds himself free,
every last Negro will line up to go to Mexico, or to South
America. To warmer climes, where he can indulge his pen-
chant for indolence, his lack of natural ambition. I suspect
he shall find a happier welcome among the Latin races.
After all, the Spaniard isn't particular about such matters,
from what I hear. No, Jones, you just wait ten years and
there won't be a Negro left in these United States . . ."

Well, he was an educated man and I could not then say
whether he was right or wrong. But well enough I knew that,
before the Negro might go anywhere, there remained a war
to be fought for his liberation. And I was to see even more
of it than I had seen already. For after I rendered my full report, which was nicely received by all, one final task remained to me.

Even though he was innocent, Daniel Boland had to return to Pottsville, for the sake of the legal formalities. He
had made a confession and needed to recant before Judge

Parry, to make things right and tidy. Although I had not yet laid eyes on Private Boland, I intended to stand by him, for I judged that he had suffered enough for his folly.

Jimmy Molloy had found young Boland in the 69th New York, in the Irish Brigade, in the Army of the Potomac. When I set out to bring him in, that army had gathered to smite the Rebels at Fredericksburg.

twenty

WE WERE WELL INTO THE EVENING DARK when Jimmy and I crossed the pontoon bridge into Fredericksburg. The first thing we saw, by a bonfire's light, was a sergeant wearing a lady's private garments over his uniform. He danced about, waving a bottle, while soldiers enjoying the warmth of the flames cheered him on.

Twas not the way a sergeant should behave.

I would have given the fellow a proper talking to, but his own officers stood about unconcerned. Some even seemed to think his jig amusing. Then I heard the sound of breaking glass. Windows shattered from a second story, as rifle butts thrust out and retreated again. A family's possessions come flying after, dresses and draperies, night pots and pictures and shoes. The soldiers in the street below ducked out of the way and laughed. Chairs and a cabinet crashed down next, followed by a mattress. The lot went on the bonfire.

That was but the beginning of the night we shamed ourselves.

The battle had not yet been joined, save for some hours of skirmishing, but a great attack was planned for the morning and nobody kept it a secret. We had stopped to pay a call on General Burnside's staff, to have our passes countersigned, and found matters disordered, with a useless commotion of officers plunging about. The headquarters had been put up in a landowner's house, along a ridge on the safe side of the river. It felt a bit removed from the fight for my tastes. If a general cannot control his battle after it has begun, his plan had best be a fine one, that I will tell you.

The Army of the Potomac was a curious thing in those days. The staff men had nearly mastered the art of feeding and clothing an army, of marching on time and even of massing their forces. But they could not plan a battle to save their souls. The generals, one then another, waited too long to strike, demanding certainty before they moved, dallying over maps until General Lee gave each fellow his whipping in his turn. As General McClellan and all his successors proved, a well-drilled army meant little unless its leaders were fond of a scrap. Calculation is well and good, but too much caution makes a man a coward, and perfect plans on paper are naught to boldness of heart.

The best that I could say of us was that we had learned to lose without disaster. Nor could the men be faulted, in my opinion. We had veterans now, troops every bit as soldierly as our enemies. When handsomely led, they fought like blue-backed devils, only to lose the day when their generals failed them. Our boys took their lickings, then went another round. The Rebels must have grown annoyed, for time and again they beat us fair in battle, but could not make us quit. The Rebels might defeat us, see, but lacked the means to destroy us, and the war in the East had come down to a bloody stand-off. And bloody it was, with a wastage of life that would have shamed a heathen potentate.

But let that bide.

We did not speak with the general, although I spotted him through an archway. Burnside looked asleep on his feet, bedeviled and worn down, which is not an encouraging state on the eve of a battle. Amid the coursing of staff men, he seemed the party least concerned in the business of his army.

I noted General Hooker, too, who come strutting in with an aide and made no secret of his discontent. I overheard him instruct a colonel, "It's going to be a goddamned mess, and you can tell him I said so." Then off he huffed. A dashing fellow Hooker was, though somehow more of a sergeant than a general. He was fit to fight with his hands, but not with his head.

The moment our passes were countersigned, we left to go down to the bridges, working our way through a muddle of regiments waiting to cross the river, past wagons skidding and slopping through the mud under a barrage of curses, ambushed by obscene volleys of speech fired off by gunners unlimbering fieldpieces in the cold and dark, on uneven ground. Even there, upon that confused hillside, sutlers managed to cry their wares and men who should have been in uniform themselves wandered from one clot of soldiers to the next, collecting last letters home, which they promised to post for a small consideration.

The soldiers we passed ran the gamut, as soldiers will when battle looms ahead: nervous or exuberant, resigned or simply weary, sick with premonitions or foolish in their confidence, chastened by knowledge or comforted by their ignorance. Some ate rations they should have saved, while others squatted, white-rumped, in the trees, sick in body or, possibly, sick of soul. They smelled of wool soaked through and not quite dried, of cartridges newly issued, of sweat and urine and weather. Mules and horses churned the earth, threatening to trample incautious boys in greatcoats too large for their shoulders. And all of them, all the lads waiting to suffer, to die, or to live by a miracle, reflected the light of a burning town in their eyes, on their brass and leathers and steel.

Flames rose from a warehouse across the river, from commercial buildings here and an old barn there. As if the regiments gone across had lit great torches to light the way for the columns of men trailing after. We heard shots, too, but any man who had soldiered before could tell there was no real fighting.

At least the regiments short of the bridges maintained a semblance of discipline. Their roughness was that of tired men, impatient at the lack of sensible orders, but no more than that. The pontoons marked the division between an army that still deserved the name and an army gone over to riot.

As the provost passed us onto the bridge ahead of a forming brigade, we met a dogcart returning, drawn by a pair of captains instead of a pony. Its bed was piled with loot. The firelight revealed a painting of cherubs, who looked unpleasant, mischievous and fat. A massive frame rimmed the artist's Heaven, propped up by a traveler's trunk stuffed too full to close. A chair with a needlework back perched high and empty, a throne for a fallen king of Mr. Shakespeare's. Velvet draperies swirled over a spittoon, and a fine sweep of brocade trailed after the vehicle. A major closed the little procession, with a bottle of port or sherry in each of his hands.

Reflected flames stretched over the river, splashing the thieves with light that changed them to devils. The provost sergeant made not the slightest effort to stop them. I sensed that these were not the first rogues to pass his post that evening.

Twas then we saw that sergeant got up in a lady's intimate garments. It was a double shock to me, for in India only the officers dressed like girls.

Jimmy tugged me along the streets, for I was incensed by the spectacle and felt I should intervene. We might have been back at the siege and sack of Delhi, after we burst through the Kashmir gate and gave the niggers what for.

The only difference was the lack of corpses. These boys in blue destroyed and stole, drank and made great fools of themselves. But in Delhi we killed, and we called the killing good.

Still, I could not quite believe that our officers countenanced viciousness and plundering. This was not Delhi or Lucknow, or—God forbid—Cawnpore. The citizens of Fredericksburg were white of skin and recently our fellows. We hoped to regain their allegiance for our Union, to win them over to Mr. Lincoln and liberty. But this was a rape of possessions, if not of persons.

Such actions make of war a bitter thing. The truth is that men can bear to kill each other. Some even learn to enjoy it, as Jimmy and I knew well. But when you ravage homes and drive out families, the hearts of your enemies harden and mercy fades.

The town seemed largely emptied of civilians, which I suppose was a blessing. Doubtless, they had fled before our crossing, for I had been told that General Burnside dithered, in perfect emulation of McClellan, throwing away his impetus and advantage, allowing the Rebels to fortify themselves on a ridge behind the town. I could not see their lines in the dark, but the situation did not sound very encouraging. Perhaps the soldiers gone wild around me had seen the Rebel entrenchments and their guns. Perhaps they knew full well what the morning must bring.

Drunken men there were in plenty, and the fondness for dressing up in ladies' things seemed to have swept through the army. A got-up band played at a corner, while soldiers danced all fancy with one another. Some of the boys wore paint on cheek and lip. And everywhere we found broken glass, crunching underfoot, jagged in ravaged window frames, catching firelight from a block away.

A white-haired gent who had lacked the wit to flee

begged a corporal not to loot his household. The old man tottered, tear-stricken, while the soldier staggered forward, bearing a grandfather's clock upon his back. God only knew what the corporal believed he might do with it, for he could not carry it with him into battle. At best, he would possess it for a night. The old man attacked the thief with withered fists. With a profane cry, the corporal let the clock crash to the ground. We heard a brevity of chimes and the groan of works undone. The old man sat down on the stoop of his house and wept, although that did not stop another pack of soldiers from pushing past to see what they might find.

The only houses partly intact were those taken over by officers and staffs. Guards stood before those doors, watching in envy as their comrades frolicked.

The army had dissolved. Had the Rebels attacked that night, they could have had the lot of them as prisoners.

Oh, there was fighting enough. But that had to do with fists, with blue sleeves striking blue, as soldiers battled over loot they would cast aside on the morrow or simply settled grudges nursed too long.

One group of fellows, whose regiment must have crossed early, had gotten up a theatrical performance, costumed in finery scavenged from the town. A wisp of a lieutenant, of the sort Americans mark as a college man, declaimed the words of Rosalind distressed. He spoke so fair that majors lowered their bottles and captains grew stern-faced as they fought back tears.

A few doors on, debauchery resumed. The better officers and sergeants did attempt to rein their soldiers in, but when discipline breaks it is like a dam collapsing. Alcohol was the fiendish spur to much of our disarray. The day when Temperance triumphs in our land will mark a glorious date of celebration, after which all behaviors will be bettered, spirits cleansed, and men and women kinder to each other. We will fight less, and think better of our fellows.

A soldier sang a bawdy song that would have shamed the Magdalene before her reformation. He gave us a chorus, right in our faces, fumed with whisky and spite.

The damnable thing, if you will excuse my language, is that these were not the men of the Irish Brigade, but normal fellows just like you or me.

A pair of cannon fired in the distance. It sounded like guns ranged from the Rebel lines. Not long after, we heard screams and shouts, for the enemy had taken aim by the light of the fires. Yet, no one in the streets paused in their revelry.

"Serves the Reb hoors right," a private declared as he put his foot through a portrait of a woman in old-fashioned dress. His comrades pitched crystal glassware against a wall, while a sergeant made his water on a pile of satin gowns. Soldiers passed with hams stuck on their bayonets. Deep in their cups, a circle of Germans sang, *"Am brunnen, vor dem Tore . . ."*

In the street next on some lads had rolled a piano into the walks. They drank champagne wine from the bottle, singing Mr. Foster's songs, which verge on the ribald. A pair of fellows in cocky hats brought a bleeding boy past on a litter, but no one paid his wounds the least attention.

I will not tell you the town resembled Hell. Twas nothing so grand as that. It only made me sick at heart, for an army must pretend to purpose and dignity. When order breaks, we see the truth about ourselves, that soldiers in the best cause are still butchers.

We must believe in higher truths. Even when those higher truths are lies. Otherwise, no good man can stay a soldier. Unless he turns his back upon the good.

Let that bide, too.

We collided with the Irish Brigade. Lads were posted with fixed bayonets to protect the pleasant street the mickies had claimed for themselves. Shamed though I am to admit it, the Irish fellows showed no worse than the other troops we had passed, no drunker and no wilder. Truth be told, they almost looked like regulars, if a bit flushed and unsteady.

"Take yourselves off," a private told us, displaying his bayonet, "or I'll put me darling here where the sun don't shine."

"We are looking for General Meagher," I told him. I began to draw out my pass, but a sergeant gave me a hard push from the side.

"Ye can go do your thieving elsewheres," the sergeant said, all belligerence. The respect he owed my rank was dead and gone, killed by the evening's disgraces.

He gave me another shove and Jimmy tensed.

Quick as I could, I shook my head to tell Jimmy not to swing. For Jimmy was ever ready with fists when a friend of his was threatened.

"Sergeant," I said, in my firmest tone, "we have come to see General Meagher. We have been sent here by President Lincoln, see. We have our passes, signed and countersigned, and you should be—"

"Did ye hear the likes o' that, Seamus Mahoney?" the sergeant laughed. "This banty cock's from Lincoln himself, he says."

He pushed me again.

That was enough. In a moment, the sergeant lay on the ground, with the tip of my new cane pressed against his throat. Jimmy held the rifle from the sentry. The private himself lay flat in the road, pondering a starry reach of sky. A great lot of Irish come at us then, ready for a glorious bit of sport, but I swapped the cane into my left hand—I still could not close the fingers quite to a fist—and drew out my Colt, with the hammer back and ready.

The sergeant was a bully, a bar-room champion, whose mouth was markedly larger than his spirit. Though twice my size, he let me pull him up by the collar until he stood on his feet again. I rested my pistol's muzzle behind his ear and asked him nicely to lead me to General Meagher.

We went down that street at the head of an Irish mob, accompanied by grumbling, guns and torches. Jimmy walked backward, musket leveled, while I kept my Colt pointed into the sergeant's brains. By the time we reached a handsome house with flags set before the door and flaming sconces, we had gathered at least a hundred soldiers behind us. They were not well disposed toward Jimmy and me.

"Jaysus," Jimmy hissed in my ear, "I hope their buggering general an't passed out."

Meagher himself stepped out of the door to look into the hoopla. The mob stood roaring and growling in high complaint. When they saw him, wreathed by flames and banners, their cries redoubled, heathen warriors clamoring for their chieftain.

I recognized him from his portraits in the illustrated weeklies and from my distant glimpse of the man at Antietam. He was a handsome fellow, indeed, just beginning to succumb to his mortal appetites. A green sash girdled a waist no longer youthful, but his face shone sculpted and lordly. An Irish cavalier he looked, with his fine mustaches and elegant, soldierly bearing.

The general paused two steps above us all, framed by a lovely doorway yet unsavaged. He swayed a bit as he took in the scene. After their tantrum of acclamation, the soldiers quieted down. As their ancestors might have done for Tara's king. When the street had grown sufficiently still to echo the calling and cursing a block away, the general opened his mouth to pronounce his judgement.

He burped. Magnificently.

Steadying himself, Meagher considered the temper of his countrymen.

"Jesus Christ and the holy saints of Ireland," he said, making an extravagant sign of the cross, "the Rebels must have Irishmen among 'em, for they cook up the finest whisky this side of Athlone." He puffed out his chest and preened his waxed mustaches, staring into the faces behind me as if he meant to share a secret with each and every one of them. "Why, I'll tell you what we'll do, lads. In the morning, why don't we go for a stroll in a southerly direction and take a few more barrels of it from 'em? I've heard they've got kegs of it stacked to the rafters in Richmond!"

The men hurrahed him, and clear it was that he feasted on the sound of their approval.

"Steady now, lads, steady," he cautioned. "We'll content ourselves with a dram or two this evening, for tomorrow both armies shall look upon us to have their instruction in valor . . . nay, not only the armies, but all the world must turn its gaze toward us . . . to take a lesson in courage, from the sons of Napper Tandy and Edward Fitzgerald . . . the avengers of Wolfe Tone and Robert Emmet. For no man should mistake the heart and soul of this war . . . I say let *no* man mistake it . . . the enemy who once wore red, now wears a coat of gray. *He* it is who would impose an aristocracy . . . an aristocracy of landed wealth and human servitude . . . upon this fair Jerusalem, these free United States, this land of succor . . ." He straightened his back, grown solemn of expression, and posed with arm outstretched. "Let any man who ever has spoken ill of the Irish nation . . . let every one of Ireland's enemies and each of her false friends . . . take his comeuppance from your conduct tomorrow, my lads!"

He glanced back toward the flags set by his door. "I'm sorry to say our brigade's new flag has not come down from

New York—but what of that, lads, what of that, I ask you? *Our* brigade don't need a flag to follow . . . the sons of Ireland have only to follow their hearts." He swayed again, but fixed himself by settling a hand on a railing. "Where are my brave boys of the 69th? Where are my brave boys? Will you lead us along with your own green harp tomorrow? Shall we follow the flag with the green harp set upon it?" Oh, they cheered him then. "Shall we all fall in on the flag of the 69th?" he asked again. He had the speaker's art down to a mastery, allowing time for the crowd to urge him on.

He grinned. "We'll show 'em the meaning of valor, that we will, lads. And if some of us don't return from the fields of glory, well, the rest will drink a toast to the fallen with Richmond's finest whisky!" He held up both arms. "*Erin go Brach*, Ireland free and Ireland forever!"

They raised their rifles and waved their caps, swung bottles and bits of loot. They might have been lifting broadswords and pikes into the midnight sky. Jimmy and I were forgotten now, as those fellows cheered their general, shouting for Young Ireland, or recalling the lads of the '98 and the boys of Vinegar Hill. "Remember Fontenoy!" a red-whiskered captain cried, although not even his grandfather had been alive when that great battle was fought. They do not let go, the Irish, they do not let go.

At last, Meagher calmed them, waving his arms to tame their wild hearts. "Off with you now," he told them, "and mind you sleep enough to make a fight of it. For we'll have no laggards among us, come the morning."

As the crowd began to break apart, he looked down at me and the sergeant, whose brains I had been threatening with my Colt. "Holy Mary, Sergeant O'Toole," he said, "would you let that poor devil go that you've got in your grip there?"

The sergeant gave a clown's salute and slipped away with his comrades.

Meagher began to descend the steps, then thought better of his condition. He steadied himself on the railing again. "Jimmy Molloy!" he said with a pussycat's smile. "Come back to your kith and kin, have you? Did you bring yourself back to join up at last, or just come for another palaver?"

WE SAT ABOUT A TABLE in a handsome room all full of books and pictures. A half-dozen bottles of whisky and brandy wooed a pitcher of water. But the strange thing was that General Meagher was not unsteady at all. His tipsiness had been an affected thing, put on to appeal to his angry soldiers. I saw at once he was canny as Whittington's cat.

Against a backdrop of acolytes, who were deep in discussion of New York City politics, Meagher listened as I explained my purpose. When I had done, he preened his mustaches, nodded his head, and looked me in the eye.

"It's a sorry, bloody business," he said, with nary a trace of drink in his speech or manner. "Danny Boland's da was the only proper fighting man of the lot of us in those days. And I'm sorry to see the boy come into misfortune. Fusser Donnelly wrote to me, you know—you'd know him as 'Thomas,' I think—and I broke the news to the wretched lad myself. Now, how do you tell a man that the woman he loved above life itself was burned to death in a horror? I couldn't for the life of me tell you the words I said, but the poor devil understood me. Oh, Danny Boland's a broken-hearted man."

He inched forward in his chair, bending toward me. "So you want to take him back to your Pottsville courthouse? To put him to rights with the law and see things settled?" He cracked the flat of his hand upon his knee. "Fine. I'm for it."

General Meagher turned to an aide, "Clancy, would you go out and get young Boland by the collar? Bring him in to us, would you?"

Returning his eyes to me, he continued, "I'll be glad to have him out of here, to tell you the truth of it. For the fight tomorrow's going to be a cock-up. We should have been on them days—if not weeks—ago, but Burnside couldn't screw up his courage or begin to make up his mind. If we reach the Confederate lines tomorrow, I'll say my thanks to Jesus Christ and luck." He paused to take a drink. Of aromatic brandy, not of whisky. "Best to get Boland out of here. He'd throw himself away, that's sure. He's thinking how he'd like to die, no doubt. The lad needs time to mourn her, then he'll find his consolation elsewhere. Every broken heart comes right in the end."

He glanced toward a dark-haired, deep-eyed major. "Isn't that right, O'Hanlon? Isn't Sally Tomorrow every bit as lovely as Sheila Yesterday?" Without awaiting a reply, he returned his attentions to me. "Take young Boland out of here tonight. He's the last of his line, and it's too good a line to lose for a young man's folly." Of a sudden, he smiled. His teeth were imperfect, yet his grin lit up the room. Meagher had the gift so rare among men of inspiring even those who disapproved of him. "But I'm not the host I should be, am I? I'd shame a Belfast butcher with my heartlessness. Have you two gentlemen had your supper this evening? We've splendid hams the boys found in the cellar."

We did not get to the hams before Boland come in. At first sight, I thought him a hard boy, for, small though he was, he had some bulk and the square jaw of a brawler. But when he stepped closer, I saw that his strength was illusory. Muscles could not mask a gentle character. He had a poet's eye and woman's lips.

"Private Boland," Meagher said, in a hale, officious voice, "this is Major Abel Jones. He has arrived from Washington, along with Mr. Molloy—whom I believe you'll recall from a previous visit? They've come to escort you back to that

Pottsville of yours, to clear your name and set you right with the law." He wheeled toward me. The sash at his waist fluttered handsomely. "Isn't that right, Major Jones? Private Boland has nothing to fear from the law?"

"That is correct," I said, addressing the pair of them. Then I narrowed my interest. "Look you, Private Boland . . . we know that you have done no crime, and that you meant no ill. But you must come home and tell that to the judge, for the law must record your statement and speak you free. You must retract your confession. I will back you myself, son, and you have my word there will be no betrayals."

"You shall leave tonight," General Meagher told him, as if it were a trivial consideration. "You'll be back among us a week hence, I expect. Perhaps sooner."

"No," Boland said.

His voice was not loud, but it revealed a stubbornness that robbed the well-meant smiles from my face and the general's.

"Respecting your rank and position, sir," Boland told his commander, "I won't go. Not tonight. I won't be seen as yellow-tailed."

"Nothing of the kind, nothing of the kind!" Meagher assured him. "I don't expect we'll have more than a minor scrap tomorrow . . ."

But Boland knew better. The general's charm fell short.

"Me da was no coward, and I'll be none," the private told us. "Begging your pardon, I'd rather fight beside me own, than go skulking off with the Welshman who killed my wife."

The lad knew more than I had hoped, and much more than was good for him.

"Show proper respect," the general said sharply, "to Major Jones. Or you'll spend tomorrow under arrest, and we'll see how you like that. Nor do I understand such an absurd accusation. I've had communication with—"

"I'm sorry for the choice of words," Boland said. "But I'd rather go into arrest than run away."

He turned to me, then. With hatred burning deep down in his eyes. God only knows what his people had seen fit to tell him.

"If the law would have me go, then, can't it wait a day? No Boland ever ran from a fight, and I won't be the first. Sir," he added, as an afterthought.

Meagher looked at me. Pretending to let me decide. But I saw that he had changed his mind with the fickleness of the Irish and would not force Boland to go. Not before the battle. For when the talk is of courage and fighting, or being thought a coward, the Irish discard their soundest resolutions. And without the general's support, I could not separate Boland from his comrades.

When I did not speak, Jimmy made an attempt to introduce common sense.

"If it's fighting ye want," he told Boland, "I think ye may have it in plenty, and more besides. For tomorrow won't be the end o' the war, that's a promise, and ye'll have your chance to die a dozen times over, if that's what you're after. Go back and clear yourself with the law, man. Then ye can fight free and clean for the Union. Or for Ireland. Or just for the sport, if that's the sort of man ye are."

Boland eyed him coldly. "If ye have such a great knowledge of fighting and war, Mr. Molloy, why aren't ye in a uniform yourself?"

I nearly cut into Boland then, to tell him that Jimmy Molloy was the bravest man he ever would meet and that he should be ashamed. For I saw his words had taken Jimmy aback. And I did not like what I saw on Jimmy's face. He was a discontented man, see, unhappy in his marriage, a rover at heart. And war is too great a bait for such fish to resist.

Meagher interposed. He had turned from backing me to supporting Boland, and that was the end of it.

"Perhaps," the general said, polite but wearied, "you might grant us a grace of one day, Major Jones?" Immediately, he turned to Daniel Boland. "How's that then, lad? If Major Jones waits until the battle's behind us, will you go along with him willingly? And behave as a gentleman should?"

It may be that Boland saw he could ask no more. Or perhaps his thoughts were darker and more fateful. But he answered, "Yes, sir. Thereafter I'll go, with no complaint against anyone. After the battle, I'll go."

Meagher nodded, not without some sadness. He did not wait for my agreement, but told the lad, "Off with you, then. And get yourself to sleep. You'll do us no good tomorrow, if you're tired and lagging behind."

Boland saluted imperfectly, turned his back, and left. As if he were the general among us. That is how the lot of them were, see. Independent of mind and prone to division. The Irish could talk themselves into a feud over matters beneath a Welshman's or Englishman's notice. Perhaps it spoke best of Meagher's genius that he managed to bind them together as well as he did.

I felt worn out myself. With the exhaustion that comes over a man when he sees that he has failed. I had begun the business to uncover the facts of a general's murder. But I had already left more death behind me than the murderess herself. Perhaps Donnelly and Kehoe—even Gowen—had been right. The best that might have been done for the Irish was simply to leave them alone.

I had sought to do my duty. But even duty may leave a bitter taste.

General Meagher sought to enliven me, and he did persuade me to take a bit of ham, which was smoked to a suc-

culence honoring the pig. He offered me a corner in an upstairs room, where I might sleep warm and keep myself
from the frost for the rest of the night. I did not make even
a courteous protestation, but took myself off to sleep, guided by a tipsy aide who found all the world amusing, including me.

As I climbed the stairs that discouraging night, I left
Jimmy below with his countrymen, answering queries from
General Meagher as to Irish prospects in Washington's city
government.

IT WAS BUTCHERY, not a battle.

With the morning mists heavy upon us, Jimmy and I took
leave of General Meagher, whose demeanor had grown
sober in every respect. He knew what lay ahead. Although
he sought to be jovial with us, his levity did not convince.
Meagher wore a uniform of green, not blue, and now his
sash was gold. Striking he was in his finery, but his counte-
nance was that of a man bound over. We left him amid an assembly of grim-faced officers.

We found a perch in the upper floor of a house near the
edge of town, where we might watch the fight as it unfold-
ed. After making certain that the building—looted, ravaged,
soiled—harbored no sharpshooters who might excite our
enemy's attentions, we took command of a lookout, knocking the last shards of glass from shattered panes. We knew
our business, God forgive us the cruelties of our service, and
sat a bit back from the window, in the room's shadows,
where we might see without being seen from without.

At first, there was little enough to view, for the winter fog
adored the river valley and would not leave its bed. But we
heard the army readying itself. Disembodied voices barked
commands, the bootfalls of companies, regiments and full
brigades clapped over the earth. Their drums remained

silent, in a clumsy pretense at stealth, and the regimental bands, whose members soon would trade their horns for stretchers, were not allowed to disturb the Rebels' breakfast.

The efforts at secrecy, half-hearted, were of no use. The Confederates knew our army had come. They had watched it gather for days and even weeks. If they did not know the certain hour of attack, it mattered little. The only manner in which we might have surprised our enemies would have been to leave them unmolested.

The town grew still more reverberant with the sounds of our preparations. Too many men crowded too little space and the noise of jouncing canteens alone was enough to alert the enemy. Sergeants snapped out heathen oaths as stray boys sought their comrades. Iron clanged on tin, steel rang on iron. And a low hum, a noise not akin to music, but to animals crammed in a pen, rose from soldiers packed into streets and alleys, awaiting orders to unfold their ranks in the fields beyond the town.

I heard a horse's hooves, but saw no horse.

Just below our perch, men marched along. Judging there was no danger yet, we moved close to the window and looked down. Twas no parade, but a labored movement from somewhere in the rear, herding another thousand blue-clad boys to where the brigades would align to await the drumbeat that sounded them forward to battle. We saw only flashes of faces, even when we briefly leaned out of the windowframe. The tops of caps bobbed along the street, their insignia dulled by wear and the weather. The soldiers wore leather packs strapped over their greatcoats, but those would be set down before the attack. White hands gripped wooden rifle stocks, the tip of a mustache disappeared in a cloud of frozen breath, and a face turned up to find us—as if one lad of them all sensed we were watching. They clattered along and whispered, somber, nerve-ridden, excited and resigned.

Their flags remained furled in gray cloth sheaths, waiting for the sun and the sight of the enemy.

It took a long while for the mists to burn away, and then the sky cleared in patches. We heard a cannonade begin off to the left, followed by the popping of distant rifle shots. The battle had been joined on other fields. In the town there was only this marching to and fro, orders cried in impatient voices, and the galloping of individual horses, carrying messengers on their backs who must rush their puzzle pieces to the generals.

Sudden as lightning, a battery opened up, much closer now, but still to the left of our vantage point. That was the provocation that brought us the battle. Union guns fired behind us, bombarding the Rebel lines from across the river, where the ranges allowed. They must have stood above the mists, with a clear view of the enemy.

The fire slackened again, allowing the heated fight downriver to swell and fill the silence.

The attack had not properly begun, yet wounded men already stumbled back through the streets or come borne along on stretchers. One bloody-faced fellow, beard all gore, tottered along with a look of flawless astonishment. He staggered past a clot of lads on the march. They revealed their rawness by stopping to look at the mess of him, until an officer rushed up and gave them the devil.

The air brightened, infiltrated by sunlight, and the veil of mist burned away.

I saw Death.

The Confederates lined the ridge behind the town. I never had seen such a splendid defensive position. At the foot of the ridge, their infantry waited behind stone walls and earthworks, protected by sunken roads and all the barriers ingenuity, spades and muscles might provide. Behind them, rising up the slope, artillery pieces occupied beds dug level, with earth piled about to protect both guns and gunners. Above those stages of soldiers and smoothbore cannon, their rifled guns frowned just below the crest, where groups of officers stood about, gawking at maps and pointing, while horsemen cantered along with reports and orders. They had been given time to prepare a reception for our boys, and they had not wasted a moment. The Rebels' tiered positions allowed them to strike us with concentrated artillery without a risk of harm to their own infantry. The foot soldiers themselves appeared to be ranked deep enough to fire volley upon volley in rotation.

It was lunacy to attack those positions. No army in the world could have carried their lines.

But there would be an attack, and no mistaking it. Perhaps General Burnside felt he had no choice, given the clamor for blood in Congress, where political men who would never fight themselves nor risk the lives of their sons demanded war to the death, no matter the cost. And the editors of too many of our newspapers had grown ferocious in their criticism of Mr. Lincoln's conduct of the war, refusing to see from the safety of their offices that victories cannot be gained by wishes alone. I sometimes think those newspaper fellows killed more of our men with their ink than the Confederates did with their bullets.

Perhaps Burnside hoped for a miracle. Maybe he was played-out and resigned. I cannot say. But any sergeant worth his salt might have told the general he was not engaging in battle, but simply sentencing thousands of men to death.

Our brigades stood ready. With their loot discarded and packs set upon the ground in long brown ranks, lines of men in greatcoats waited just beyond the last houses, where fences gave way to fields. Only scattered outbuildings spoiled the beauty of their formations. A few regiments,

whose commanders were confident they would reach the
enemy, stood with bayonets fixed, though most remained
prepared to exchange volleys. Officers turned their horses
over to orderlies, patting the animals once or twice, then positioned themselves near their colors.

Down the river valley, the fighting was hot. But here, before the town, only a few stray cannon shots reminded the
waiting men of the morning's purpose. But those harassing
fires did damage enough. Some balls shattered a company's
front, leaving clots of dead and writhing wounded. But the
lines closed up again, while medical sorts rushed forward to
clear the casualties. We had grown skilled at looking after
our wounded, though still unable to spare them needless
wounds.

The attack began with shouted commands, then drums. A
band played in the distance, ineffectual and small against the
spectacle of thousands of men stepping off. The first regiments rippled forward, with officers stretching out their
swords to keep the men aligned, while sergeants pressed the
slow men to keep pace. Some regiments appeared quick of
foot and willing, while others plodded solemnly, waiting for
the Rebel guns to open up *en masse*.

Even before the gunners yank their lanyards, before the
crackling of rifle volleys begins, a battle is noisy. A hundred
commands are shouted at once, thousands of boots tramp the
earth, and the soldiers' kit clangs and chimes and jounces.
Nor had the rest of the army paused to witness the attack. In
the street below our lookout, more regiments moved up,
crowding into the fields to take the place of the men who had
gone before them.

Some of our boys went forward that morning with shoulders bent, as if struggling against a headwind. But the
breeze, chill though it was, blew at their backs. Mayhaps it
was a normal response to the storm of death they expected.

Folly, twas all folly. We had built a massive army. But General Burnside had driven it into a narrow, fatal place, where our strength could not be brought to bear decisively. As so often our army had done, we would fight in bits and pieces, handing the Rebels advantages beyond those they had earned.

Even allowing for the restrictions of the terrain, our opening attack was of insufficient strength. The brigades that went forward did not even fill up the fields, but diverged as they marched, opening gaps between themselves and letting the Rebels concentrate their fires. Could Burnside see his doings from his position across the river? We sent those men to be sacrificed, not to win.

Our ranks of blue had not crossed a third of those broken fields when the Rebels opened with guns.

A combination of ball and explosive shells tore into our lads. I never saw such a sudden loss of life. Where a solid shot ripped through the ranks, it painted red streaks in the air, splashes of blood from disintegrated bodies. Men and boys flew skyward as if they were circus performers. A few did turn to flee or threw themselves to the ground. But the miracle was that the rest of the soldiers went forward, marching onward, many a line with rifles still dressed on their shoulders.

Flags fell down, then rose back up. Men closed the gaps where comrades had fallen away, contracting their lines toward a shifting center and thinning the rear ranks. In the intervals between company formations, and in the greater plots between echeloned regiments, the winter fields were pocked with corpses and wounded men—twitching, cowering, crawling. And still you heard the shouts, gone hoarser now, amid the roar of the guns. The moving lines lost their suppleness and order, just beginning to waver, as men misjudged the pace of unseen comrades. All staring straight

ahead they went, into death, with the fixity that is a human
utmost. Rare was the officer who bothered to dress his company's ranks any longer.

Regiments broke into an aggrieved trot, impatient to close
with the enemy and end their helplessness.

Twas a spectacle, I give you that. But one to shame a
Christian.

Halfway across the field, there was a ditch, cut at a diag-
onal to the town, with a stream or a race running through it.
The first men clambered into the depression. It broke the last
traces of order in the regiments that entered it, even those
that had shown well under the guns.

In most spots along the line of the attack—or attacks, I
should say, for the effort had fragmented badly—the Rebel
infantry held their fire until our men passed the ditch and
tried to re-form in the meadow. When the Johnnies opened
up at last, entire ranks dropped in place. Feathers of gore
preened from their skulls, blood fanned from legs and backs.
Their greatcoats kept most of the corpses neater than you
will see them in a summer battle, but the mess would be
grisly enough for those in the grip of it.

Regiments buckled, but smaller groups pressed on. As far
as they could. Under the orders of their surviving officers,
some of those still alive and whole got back into ranks to
level their own volleys at the Rebels. But the Confederates
were protected by their defenses, while our men stood in the
open. And bravery does not count against a bullet.

The attack began to dissolve. Nearing the Confederate
lines, an uneven swale dipped into the earth, a depression so
mild the eye did not mark it until you saw our boys lose
height as they entered it. Twas as far as any man got in that
first attack.

Man by man, then company after shattered company, our
lads went to ground and stayed there. Clinging to the faint

protection the dip in the earth provided. Other soldiers milled about back in the ditch, while the weakest of will skulked off the field, despite the threat of punishment for cowardice. The wounded crawled where they could.

Perhaps the Rebels had been angered by the misbehavior of our troops in Fredericksburg, for they had eyes and ears and must have known. Anyway, it was the first time that I marked them shooting wounded men as the poor devils dragged themselves off.

If Burnside meant to make a show, to please the scribblers and senators, that should have been enough. Those first attacks were finished, before a single regiment—or a single Union soldier—reached the enemy lines. Torrents of fire coursed from our enemy's guns, as if the air itself had been ignited. No man could stand before that storm and live.

It should have been enough to show any general with a pair of eyes that the odds was hopeless. Yet, more of our brigades had begun to advance. Only to be shot to bits by the rows of enemy cannon and to fade away before the volleys of ten thousand Rebel rifles.

The madness continued for hours. All piecemeal it was, feeding handsome regiments and brigades into a grinder. It no longer struck me as brave, but only wanton. Somewhere a regimental band mocked all the misery, playing jaunty tunes to urge men on.

Out on the field, there were stretches of ground where you might have jumped from one body to another, dead and living both, to make a game of never touching the earth. I could see only a portion of that swale, but it was almost solid blue now, with the survivors who could make no further progress toward the enemy seeking safety behind their brothers' corpses. Some men even rolled and shoved the bodies of the fallen into barricades for the living. Wherever they did so, the dead would begin to move again, slightly and sullenly, as countless rounds punched into them.

Men burrowed into the wreckage of cloth and flesh. The closer you looked to the forward edge of those bodies, the thicker the piles and the grislier the scene. They were packed in like young snakes in a nest, tormented and writhing. Hundreds of other able-bodied soldiers refused to leave the ditch that divided the field.

And then I heard another band play, just when I thought our attacks might have been halted. These musicians played with a blitheness careless of the day. Twas an Irish reel, all quickness and jollity.

I saw them unfold from the alleys and lanes, ordered up at last. They dressed their ranks in good order, not a pistol shot from our perch. Our house had not gone unscathed by shell, and Jimmy and I were dusted over with plaster, but we lacked the sense to tear ourselves from the spectacle. I think I may claim that both of our hearts quickened. For this was the matter of the day to us.

Meagher did not dismount, but rode along their lines. His men cheered him, as if he were leading them off to a picknick, with free beer and prizes for all. Indeed, they did not have the concentration of flags before them that had led all the other brigades. But I saw one field of green unfurl, at which the lads in the ranks stood straighter and prouder. Every man wore a green sprig in his cap.

Even in the battle's lull, the valley remained in a tumult. The guns had only slackened, the way a glutton at table slows, although he will not cease eating. Odd rifle shots competed with screams and shouts. I saw Meagher speaking to his men, gesturing with his sword as he restrained his high-spirited horse. But I could not catch his words.

Twas only one brigade. And its strength had already been sapped by the summer's battles. Antietam had bled it badly. But those lads showed proud and fine as the Guards on parade.

They stepped off to the beat of a half-dozen drums, with their bandsmen silent now. The breeze tugged that green flag toward the enemy, as if even nature wished to lead them on. That very same wind, light and cold, swept off a great deal of the smoke, leaving the field of battle unusually clear. A still day would have shrouded the valley, but now the smoke only hung in pockets or drifted above the firing lines of our enemies. It was almost as if General Meagher had been a prophet: All the world could see the Irish advance.

Those lads had pluck. My heart nearly broke to see them go, yet I tell you I felt like cheering. As some of their comrades did along our lines. The Irish marched as if they were the invincible heroes of old, taking pains to dress their ranks, even keeping step as best they could. Oh, those lads had taken their general's words to heart. They meant to show us all what they were made of.

And the Irish always like a good scrap, of course.

When the enemy's cannon, confident of range, opened upon the Irish, they did not react as the other brigades had done. They closed up well enough. But instead of gritting their teeth, they shouted defiance, a thousand men and more, threatening revenge as they quickened their pace.

The guns ripped lanes right through them, dissolving men, detaching limbs, tossing bodies heavenward as bad-tempered girls fling dolls. The blue ranks entered a band of smoke. When they re-emerged, their numbers were markedly fewer. And still an angry core of them were shouting, threatening, cursing and damning their enemies. I could not see Meagher any longer, nor any man on horseback. The officers who did not lie dead were leading their men on foot.

They reached the ditch where the mill-race ran and fair leapt down into it, shoving stragglers aside and scrambling up the other bank, as if in a contest. I thought they might make a wild charge from the spot. Instead, God bless them, they rallied to their standard and their officers, forming up in perfect order again.

Impatient, the Confederate riflemen opened fire, knocking down the Irish by the dozen. But Meagher's lads only closed their ranks and stepped off once again. I saw bayonets now. The Irish intended to reach the enemy, even if they had to do it alone.

Their attack had been virtually unsupported, with other brigades advancing on faulty lines and out of sequence. But the Irish did not look back or to their sides. Already shot to pieces, they plunged into the chaos of the swale. For the first time, their ranks broke, corrupted by the carpet of survivors and corpses, foiled by our instinctive reluctance to step upon the dead or even the living. They seemed on the verge of coming apart completely, simply because they had trouble placing their feet. I thought they might go to ground with their comrades, joining the roiling blue mass in that shallow dip.

Above the din of the day, I heard a roar. Of human rage. And I saw the remaining Irishmen, struggling to keep their order, break into a trot, then into a run. Undaunted even then they were, unwilling to give up after coming so far. They rushed the Rebel lines, a handful of men against thousands.

For a pair of moments, if no longer, I believed the Irish might reach that wall of stone and earth and gray and flashing rifles. Their lines were gone, their flag was either down or shrouded in smoke, but the last of the Irish Brigade charged forward like wild Afghanees or rabid hounds.

It looked as if a handful would get in among the Rebels with their bayonets. But I was looking at dozens of men, not hundreds nor a thousand. A massed volley from the base of the ridge collapsed their charge in an instant. Farther back, a few stray clots of men still stood and fired their rifles into the gray ranks before them. But those men, too, recoiled, crumpled, fell or dropped to the ground to load then thought better of rising again.

Not half an hour before, they had been a brigade as fine as any on earth. Now nothing remained but a thickening of the blue cloth dressing the earth.

"The sad, sorry bastards" was all that Jimmy said. Even he could not find a joke that day.

In later years, the survivors of the terrible Battle of Fredericksburg argued, as aging veterans will, as to which regiment come closest to the Rebel lines. None reached it, of course, though more than five thousand men fell in the attempt. The old men argued and nattered and, sometimes, lied. But I was there, and I will tell you: Those bold sons of Erin lay nearest to the enemy, the bravest almost close enough to touch the men who slew them.

Now, you will think me weak, but the truth is that I wept. Not for long, see. But long enough it was for Jimmy to turn away so his gaze would not embarrass me. Or perhaps his own eyes were teary. I never thought quite so badly of an Irishman after that day.

But let that bide.

The slaughter went on, well into the shades of the evening. Stubbornness, folly, madness, ignorance, vanity, and incompetence, that is what our high commanders gave us. General Burnside did his best to throw away an army. The only good I can say of him is that, when the defeat demanded a scapegoat, he took the blame upon himself like a man. But that is not enough, see. He humbled himself, but first he killed men in the thousands, to no purpose. Remorse will not bring any father or son or husband back to life.

It was going to be a glum Christmas in the North. And all for naught.

The sacrifice of regiments and brigades only stopped by the light of burning ruins. For the hundreds of men who had crept or crawled back into the sheltering streets, thousands still lay upon the field, thousands dead and thousands wounded, all lying in the frigid cold, and still more men lying among them unscathed, but unable to withdraw with the Rebels shooting at any hint of movement that showed against the backdrop of the town. More buildings burned now, though this time the fires had been lit by Confederate gunnery.

Jimmy and I abandoned our vantage point, only to find the stairs had been shot away by a Rebel cannonball. We had to drop down to the floor below, which was a bother to my leg, but little matter compared to the day's other miseries. We had to go a bit slowly through the streets, though, for my blasted leg was unwilling to behave.

We had to go carefully, too. For Rebel sharpshooters made a game of seeking targets amid the dancing light, and, now and then, a Confederate gun would send a ball down one of the vertical streets, to sweep it clean.

The lanes were a shambles of wounded men and shocked survivors. Sullen and drained, they sat against walls or in doorways, or sprawled on ruined lawns. Few seemed concerned enough to hunt their regiments, while elsewhere little knots of men were all that remained of brigades. You would think that men would be glad to have survived, that they would find some joy in it and think themselves lucky. But that is not the way the soldier feels things. There was only loss, and shame, and guilt, and a relief so fragile it was not yet quite believed.

Many feared the fight would resume in the morning. Rumors plagued the living and mocked the dead.

Even in the streets where houses burned and crackled, or where sergeants called the roll of broken companies, you heard the screams of the wounded off in the night. In the ravaged heart of the town, ambulances rolled along in columns, efficient in this second year of war. But the vehicles were still too few in number, for no one had expected such a bloodbath.

We found the house where the Irish brigade had quartered its staff the night before. Meagher was there, uniform scorched and muddy, his fair face stunned. A much-diminished knot of officers had gathered about him. They were drinking quietly.

"My brigade," Meagher said to no one. "My lovely brigade. All gone."

THE SOLDIERS WHO had not regained the town lay out all night, exposed to a frost that fell hard. Many a wounded man who might have lived froze upon those fields. In that crowded swale, men robbed canteens from corpses, only to find the water frozen through. The living sneaked against one another for warmth, regardless of identities, ranks, or old animosities. In the ditch that cut the field, the water thickened to ice tinged pink with blood. Merciless, the Rebels watched for any sign of life.

And the lads still alive come morning, who had not scuttled back to safety in the dark, remained upon the field all through the next day, freezing, thirsty, terrified, hungry, dying. Twas only during the second night after the battle that the Rebels eased their vigilance and the other survivors crawled back.

On that second night, the cries of the wounded were far less of a bother. So many had died in the absence of a truce, lying under that winter sky until they could no longer cling to life. Later, of course, there was a brief cease-fire, to bury the dead.

Jimmy and I were weary men, for we had done our best in the night after the battle to help bring in the nearest of the wounded. My leg would not allow me to manage a stretcher,

but I did my best to crawl out to the boys with Jimmy and we
lugged in several dozen of them between us. Enough to leave
us covered with blood and stinking. I hope some of them lived.

The hardest wounded men with whom you must cope are
the boys who beg you not to move them, to let them lie there
and not add to their pain. Some ask you to kill them. You must
bring all those in, too, for that is our Christian duty. But it is a
hard thing. Especially when a broken boy uses his last bit of
strength to make a fist, threatening to kill you if you do not let
him be. You bring them in legless and robbed of arms, with
their manhood shot away or their faces shorn off. The conscious ones think of their sweethearts and dread their lives. You
bring them in begging and screaming, or deeply unconscious.
And you pray to God that you have done a good service.

That second night, we went again to seek General
Meagher, but only saw him from a distance, for the fellow
was holding a grand reception for visiting politicians. I believe they brought him his flags, after all. There were
speeches and oaths and food and drink, and the Good Lord
knows how they managed it. His brigade was ruined, true
enough, with less than half the names answered at the
muster. Yet, Meagher would not quit—not yet—nor would
his Irishmen. The lot of them acted as if they were a grand
brigade again, though barely the strength of a regiment. The
Irish pluck hope from the lip of the grave. The men were
certain their ranks would fill back up, although our army's
regulations would finally do what the Rebels had not ac-
complished. But that is another tale.

An officer who recognized us invited us into the party,
where the general was holding forth with heady grandilo-
quence. Amid the smoldering ruins of the town, with the
wounded still lying about and the army a savaged thing,
General Meagher was describing the liberation of Ireland, to
be effected by our Irish veterans, once we had taken

Richmond and trounced the Rebels. The prospect seemed little better than a fairy tale that night, and the fellow's flights of fancy left me sour. But perhaps that is the very heart of the matter: The Irish have endured so much they must resort to fantasies and find their refuge in dreams.

We would have been welcome at a back table, but neither Jimmy nor I had the stomach for it. We thanked the fellow who greeted us, but begged off.

Twas the final time I saw General Meagher, who would leave the war in bitterness not long after, angry that he was not allowed to rebuild his brigade. He applied himself to politics then, not always for the better. He never was disloyal, but his heart was broken by our government's callousness. And by Fredericksburg. He died but a short time after the war, still young, out in the West and in a sorry circumstance. When last I glimpsed him, he was laughing at his own joke as he raised a cup.

Jimmy and I walked along toward the pontoons, without further companionship. For the name of Daniel Boland had not found an answer when the roll was called. Nor did he appear later on, among the lists of the wounded and convalescing. I cannot even say where his body lies, for the Rebels held the ground. We buried our men at their sufferance and in haste.

We walked through the shame of ravished streets, past men who had fought honorably and less so, past the bivouacs of fresh regiments put over to stave off a possible Confederate attack, and along by the squalid remains of units shot to pieces and waiting for orders, or for officers, or simply for the vigor to lift themselves from the spot. We walked in dreary light, almost in darkness, between campfires built at streetcorners and the hurricane lanterns at sentry posts. And then I heard singing.

We were passing through a rough encampment of Irishmen—not those of the Irish Brigade, but some of the

tens of thousands of others who served our Union. And from
the next crossing we heard a well-sung hymn. Welshmen the
singers were, I could not mistake it. They were singing an
anthem of Charles Wesley's, reverent and warm, in a harmony of two parts, then of three.

I expected the Irish to make a fuss, to call cats and shout
and complain. But the strangest thing happened. Those
Irishmen, though their souls belonged to Rome, began
singing along with the Welshmen. Perhaps it was a result of
months in encampments, but many knew the words to the
hymn and near all knew the tune. In another minute, the
street resounded with song.

I stood transfixed until the singing ended. Then Jimmy
tugged me along. For we had a long journey before us.

Before we passed on to the next crowd of soldiers, the
Irishmen took up a song of their own, "Mollie of the
Downs." It is a lovely air, all loss and pining.

The Welshmen just ahead joined in, as the Irish had done
on the hymn.

Twas thus we made our way along to the bridges, with the
music of many voices in our ears. I stumbled once, my leg
still an annoyance, and Jimmy caught me by the arm. He
kept his arm laced through mine own thereafter. We felt the
cold off the river, chilling our faces. But the singing at our
backs was lovely warm.

Just shy of the provost's station, we had to wait for a battery to pass, all whinnies and curses and rumbling and
clanging and creaks. As we waited for the guns to cross the
river, I listened to the last of the fading harmonies.

"Well," I said to Jimmy, "we are all Americans now."

The adventures of Abel Jones will continue in:
Way Down Babylon

History
and
Thanks

As with each novel in this series, I owe thanks to numerous people who assisted me with my research or otherwise encouraged me. Chief Dale Repp of the Pottsville Police Department, whose hospitality is as deep as his friendship is enduring, acted repeatedly as my host and "events coordinator" during my investigations into the remarkable past of Schuylkill County, Pennsylvania. His splendid wife, Cathy, never allowed me to leave the Repp home until I had been fed well enough to win a blue ribbon at the farm show.

My mother keeps the newspaper clippings coming, in case I miss anything back home, and my old school pals, Rhon Bower and Bruce Evans—Welshies the two of them—have been consistent, gracious supporters of Abel Jones. Katherine McIntire Peters, my wife (and a candidate for Protestant sainthood) is not only my savage first-line editor, but my literary conscience and moral compass. She is far more important to me than any book.

Thomas P. Lowry, M.D., the author of several fascinating books on Civil War subjects, was as helpful as ever. The most generous researchers I ever have encountered, Tom and his wife, Bev, provided me with their court-martial records on the Irish Brigade, as well as with other priceless sources. They are kind, lovely people, whose pioneering research work remains underappreciated.

The staff of the Historical Society of Schuylkill County proved wonderfully helpful, even on short notice, and did all a researcher could ask. The society's director, Dr. Peter Yasenchak, serves his community very well, indeed, and special thanks go to the county's "walking encyclopedia," Leo Ward, the society's president and the author of the valuable paper "Unrest: Civil War Draft Resistance." Tom Dempsey also offered important insights, and both Jean Dellock and Karen Gibson went out of their way to assist me. All of the staff of the Historical Society are justifiably proud of their home and heritage. Now housed in a fine old building on Pottsville's Centre Street, the society has a great deal to offer the scholar, casual historian and tourist alike (then cross the street to Beauregard's for the best lunch in the coal regions).

I must stress, however, that the views implicit and explicit in *Bold Sons of Erin* are strictly my own and should not be blamed on the staff of the Historical Society or on anyone else who assisted me. Doubtless, some would argue with my take on history—I call it as I see it, and that's that. As a Schuylkill County native during my formative years (when the natives were restless, indeed), I drank deep of the historical currents that have never ceased flowing between those hills and coal banks. Later experience as a soldier and an intelligence officer gave me useful tools to approach historical records with a healthy skepticism, but the interpretation of history in a region so fraught with struggle as the anthracite coal fields of Pennsylvania remains a matter more contentious than politics. It is, literally, in the blood.

When Faulkner commented to the effect that, in the South, the past wasn't even past, he might have been speaking of Schuylkill County. Indeed, in the sense of living with the omnipresence of history, the county seems to me the most "Southern" territory in the states that fought for the Union in our Civil War. The past is certainly present in the abandoned mines and colliery-spoiled hills, in the waste banks half-disguised with birches now and in the architectural remnants of King Coal's glory days. But these are merely things. The past lives on vitally in the ethnic communities of the coal towns and in the combativeness so many residents still feel over events that happened well over a century ago.

The legacies of early capitalism, of nascent unions and great strikes, of buccaneer coal barons, powerful railways and fortunes made and lost on the backs of miners in the world's richest veins of anthracite . . . as vivid as all that remains to those of us who were born with coal dust in our blood, the great, inextinguishable debate is over the Molly Maguires. Did they even exist? I do not doubt it. Were they murderers? Some of them were, beyond dispute. Did they deserve to hang? Some did, but others appear to have been railroaded—an especially appropriate term, given the career of their chief antagonist, Franklin B. Gowen. What about John Kehoe, the alleged ringleader of the Mollies, hanged by one governor, then pardoned a century later by another? It appears that he was guilty of doing all he could to better the lot of his Irish brethren, but his hanging looks to have been more a matter of convenience than of justice. And what of Gowen himself, the "ruler of the Reading," as one adoring biographer dubbed him? I think my views are revealed clearly enough in the pages of this novel.

There is, of course, much more. Among other subjects, this novel deals with the formative days of the Mollies, when the Irish were divided between those who supported

the Union war effort, hoping to win acceptance with their
blood, and those who wanted only to work and earn a living
wage and who did not see a stake for themselves in that
great conflict. I hope, one day, to write more about the
Mollies, in the violent years after the war. Yet, I know that
nothing I might write could please all parties.

As with all true partisans, the people who keep the past
alive in Schuylkill County expect one to take sides, either
vilifying the Molly Maguires, or viewing them as innocent
freedom fighters—or simply as stage-managed victims. I
believe the truth lies in between, as the truth so often does.
But moderation is no more popular among the historically
minded than it is among the avidly religious. I hope only
that those who are not shackled too snugly to the past may
find in this novel a few insights into a history largely forgotten outside of the anthracite fields.

It is a remarkable history. Although the plot of this novel
is a fiction, it is based, as closely as possible, on historical
events. In the autumn of 1862 (and thereafter), the Irish miners of Schuylkill County simmered in near rebellion. They
did, indeed, stop a troop train and remove several hundred
recruits. They destroyed draft records and employed violence
against registrars. The authorities were cowed, when not pan-
icked. And the troubles blooming from Cass Township and
centered on the mining patch of Heckschersville really did
reach the ears of President Lincoln, who responded with the
Solomonic message to Harrisburg reported in these pages.

If you go to Heckschersville today, following a county
road through scarred coal lands, you will be welcomed first
by an Irish flag painted on the side of a rock. The old company houses, neatly maintained, display no shortage of
shamrocks and other symbols of the heritage of their inhab-
itants. The people combine the pride of the Irish with the
tenacity of mining families, even though the mines have

long been closed. The village is a quiet, unassuming place of diminished population now, and it is hard to believe that American labor history was made in its dusty streets, its mines, its colliery. But the ghosts are there, waiting for anyone with a sixth sense for history. I hope the people of Heckschersville, whose ancestors struggled for what they believed to be just, will not judge this book too harshly. They have much of which to be proud.

There are, as always in a work of fiction, some fabrications. One must be highlighted: I make it a rule never to use a real man of the cloth as a character in my novels. The priest, Father Wilde, is a purely fictional character, invented to feed the engine of the book's plot and to embody specific issues of the period. In reality, the Reverend John Scanlon was the pastor of St. Kiaran's (as it then was spelled) throughout the Civil War. He served the Catholic population of Heckschersville without blemish for a decade, until the status of the parish was elevated in 1868. There is no historical scandal attached to St. Kiaran's church.

For those who would like to learn more about the historical foundation of this novel, the following books seem to me the best with which to begin:

On the Molly Maguires, the reader cannot do better than Kevin Kenny's superb, balanced *Making Sense of the Molly Maguires*. Of the many other works dealing with the Mollies, the late Arthur H. Lewis's *Lament for the Molly Maguires* remains an old favorite of mine. For the true history buff, Allan Pinkerton's dishonest and bigoted *The Mollie Maguires and the Detectives* is a hoot. Grace Palladino's more recent *Another Civil War* draws its prejudices from the political left, but is well researched; it may be read for the facts presented, though the reader must suspect a number of its conclusions.

The development of anthracite mining in the nineteenth

century is masterfully presented in *St. Clair*, by Antony F. C. Wallace. Examining the industry through the development of a single town in Schuylkill County, Pennsylvania, the author does a peerless job of re-creating a lost world. This is one of the finest works of scholarship I ever have encountered.

Irish folklore, history and sheer "Irishness" have given rise to a publishing industry all their own and there is no shortage of texts available, from the mawkish to the magnificent. I have been especially impressed by one recent book. *The Cooper's Wife Is Missing*, by Joan Hoff and Marian Yeates, is harrowing, but illuminating reading. Anyone who takes exception to my portrayal of the persistence of old superstitions (beliefs with which I still contended as a child in the 1950s) should sit down with this book. Describing a gruesome murder "justified" on supernatural grounds in late-nineteenth-century Ireland, the book certainly makes the case that the old ways die hard (not only among the Irish, by any means).

Any writer who dares to describe a Civil War battle on the page must take the *War of the Rebellion, Official Records of the Union and Confederate Armies* as his primary source, turning thereafter to regimental histories, diaries and memoirs. Again, I believe that my own military career has enabled me to read those documents with a sharpened eye for self-justification, ambition and masked reality. The language changes, but not the character—or characters—of the soldier. Yet, every battle of that war also has inspired multiple modern works seeking to interpret events for those who lack the time or the inclination to plough through original sources. Regarding the Union debacle at Fredericksburg, I have been particularly impressed by George C. Rable's *Fredericksburg! Fredericksburg!* which is not only finely researched and well reasoned, but handsomely written, as well.

Finally, heartfelt thanks to all the readers who have followed Abel Jones on his adventures thus far. Without an audience, a writer is merely a noise unto himself.

—Owen Parry

Masterworks of historical suspense by critically acclaimed author

OWEN PARRY

FADED COAT OF BLUE
0-380-79739-9/$6.99 US/$9.99 Can

A recent immigrant to America at the time of the Civil War, Abel Jones finds himself mysteriously chosen as a confidential agent to General George McLellan.

SHADOWS OF GLORY
0-380-82087-0/$6.99 US/$9.99 Can

In a snow-swept Northern town, Union officer Abel Jones struggles to solve the murders of Federal agents who were tortured to death.

CALL EACH RIVER JORDAN
0-06-000922-5/$7.50 US/$9.99 Can

Union Major Abel Jones survives the battle of Shiloh only to face the riddle of a different kind of massacre . . . forty murdered slaves.

HONOR'S KINGDOM
0-06-051079-X/$7.99 US/$10.99 Can

Major Abel Jones returns to London and Glasgow, the lands he once left in hope of a better life, on a mission essential to the Union cause.

And available in hardcover
BOLD SONS OF ERIN
0-06-051390-X/$24.95 US/$38.95 Can

Available wherever books are sold or please call 1-800-331-3761 to order.

AuthorTracker
www.AuthorTracker.com

OP 0404

LET *NEW YORK TIMES* BESTSELLING AUTHOR

DENNIS LEHANE

TAKE YOU TO THE EDGE OF DARKNESS

Sacred
0-380-72629-7
$7.99/$10.99 Can.

Mystic River
0-380-73185-1
$7.99/10.99 Can.

Darkness, Take My Hand
0-380-72628-9
$7.99/$10.99 Can.

Prayers for Rain
0-380-73036-7
$7.99/$10.99 Can.

A Drink Before the War
0-380-72623-8
$7.99/$10.99 Can.

Gone, Baby, Gone
0-380-73035-9
$7.99/$10.99 Can.

Shutter Island
0-380-73186-X
$7.99/$10.99 Can

Available wherever books are sold or call 1-800-331-3761 to order.

🕮 **HarperAudio**
An Imprint of HarperCollinsPublishers
www.harpercollins.com

📻 **AuthorTracker**
www.AuthorTracker.com   DL 0204

 **HarperTorch** *An Imprint of HarperCollinsPublishers* www.harpercollins.com

NEW YORK TIMES BESTSELLING AUTHOR

BERNARD CORNWELL

"PERHAPS THE GREATEST WRITER OF
HISTORICAL ADVENTURE NOVELS TODAY."
Washington Post

The Grail Quest series

THE ARCHER'S TALE
0-06-050525-7/$7.99 US

A brutal raid on the quiet coastal English village
of Hookton in 1342 leaves but one survivor: a
young archer named Thomas. This terrible dawn
sets him on a path toward his ultimate quest: the
search for the Holy Grail.

VAGABOND
0-06-053268-8/$7.99 US

Five years have passed since Thomas began his
quest for justice. Now, as England's army fights in
France, her Scottish foes plan a bloody invasion
that will embroil the young archer.

And available in hardcover

HERETIC
0-06-053049-9/$24.95 US/$38.95 Can

In the flames of unceasing war, Thomas' heart, will, and courage
will be supremely tested in the conclusion of an epic quest for
vengeance and the greatest prize in history: the Holy Grail.

www.bernardcornwell.net

Available wherever books are sold
or please call 1-800-331-3761 to order.

www.AuthorTracker.com

BC 0404

Listen to
Master Storyteller

BERNARD CORNWELL

The Archer's Tale
0-694-52609-6/$25.95/$38.95 Can.
6 hours/4 cassettes
Performed by Tim Pigott-Smith

Vagabond
0-06-051080-3/$25.95/NCR
6 hours/4 cassettes
Performed by Tim Pigott-Smith

Gallows Thief
0-06-009301-3/$25.95/$38.95 Can.
6 hours/4 cassettes
Performed by James Frain

Heretic
0-06-056613-2/$25.95/$39.95 Can.
6 hours/4 cassettes
Performed by Tim Pigott-Smith

Sharpe's Escape (Unabridged)
0-06-059172-2/$39.95/$59.95 Can.
15 hours/9 cassettes
Performed by Patrick Tull

Available wherever books are sold
or call 1-800-331-3761 to order.

HarperAudio
www.harperaudio.com

BCA 0404